A PRINCE
WITHOUT A
KINGDOM

A PRINCE WITHOUT A KINGDOM

Timothée de Fombelle

translated by Sarah Ardizzone

CANDLEWICK PRESS

Text and cover design copyright © 2011 by Gallimard Jeunesse
English translation copyright © 2014 by Sarah Ardizzone

Picture of the *Hindenburg* © Corbis

First U.S. edition 2015

Library of Congress Catalog Card Number 2014957056
ISBN 978-0-7636-7950-7

15 16 17 18 19 20 BVG 10 9 8 7 6 5 4 3 2 1

Printed in Berryville,VA, U.S.A.

This book was typeset in Perpetua.

Candlewick Press
99 Dover Street
Somerville, Massachusetts 02144

visit us at www.candlewick.com

But my heart is like a precious piano — double-locked, and the key lost.

— Anton Chekhov

CAST OF CHARACTERS

Italics denote real historical figures

BORIS PETROVITCH ANTONOV murderous Soviet agent tasked with killing Vango

EMILIE ATLAS girl who secretly prowls the rooftops of Paris; resistance name Marie; a.k.a. "the Cat"

LIEUTENANT AUGUSTIN AVIGNON Boulard's ambitious second-in-command

ETHEL B. H. Scottish heiress and orphan; in love with Vango; lives with her brother, Paul, at Everland Castle

PAUL B. H. Ethel's older brother; Scottish heir and orphan; RAF pilot who fights in the Spanish Civil War and for the French Resistance

DOCTOR BASILIO doctor on the island of Salina; hopes to see Mademoiselle again

NINA BIENVENUE cabaret singer who achieved fame at La Lune Rousse in Montmartre, Paris

SUPERINTENDENT AUGUSTE BOULARD eminent police detective at the Quai des Orfèvres (Criminal Investigations, Police HQ, Paris)

MADAME MARIE-ANTOINETTE BOULARD Boulard's mother

CAESAR mysterious resistance leader for the Paradise Network

GIOVANNI CAFARELLO murderous pirate who left Salina for New York with a stolen fortune; a.k.a. Gio

DORGELES Voloy Viktor's right-hand man, and a thug

MADAME BLANCHE DUSSAC concierge for the Paris apartment block where Boulard lives; friend of Marie-Antoinette Boulard

COMMANDER/DOKTOR HUGO ECKENER commander of the *Graf Zeppelin;* friend of Vango; member of Project Violette

MOTHER ELISABETH leader of the Abbey of La Blanche on the island of Noirmoutier, off the coast of western France

DOCTOR ESQUIROL Max Grund's personal doctor; member of Project Violette

CASIMIR FERMINI proprietor of La Belle Étoile restaurant in Paris

MAX GRUND chief representative of the Gestapo in German-occupied Paris

HEINRICH KUBIS headwaiter of the *Graf Zeppelin*

CAPTAIN ERNST LEHMANN captain of the *Graf Zeppelin;* Hugo Eckener's second-in-command

MADEMOISELLE Vango's childhood nurse; a.k.a. *Tioten'ka;* a.k.a. "the Bird-seller"

WERNER MANN German World War I fighter pilot; member of Project Violette

BROTHER MARCO cook at the invisible monastery on the island of Arkudah

MARY housekeeper at Everland Castle; guardian of Ethel and Paul

INSPECTOR BAPTISTE MOUCHET assistant to the superintendent at the Quai des Orfèvres (Criminal Investigations, Police HQ, Paris)

NICHOLAS son of Peter, the gardener at Everland Castle; Ethel's ally

ANDREI IVANOVITCH OULANOV violin player from Moscow studying in Paris; blackmailed into spying for Boris Petrovitch Antonov

IVAN IVANOVITCH OULANOV father of Andrei; lives in Moscow

KONSTANTIN & ZOYA IVANOVITCH OULANOV younger siblings of Andrei; they live in Moscow

JOSEPH JACQUES PUPPET former soldier turned boxer from the Ivory Coast; now a barber based in Monaco; member of Project Violette; a.k.a. J. J. Puppet

SIMON the bell ringer at Notre Dame Cathedral in Paris

JOSEPH STALIN despotic ruler of the Soviet Union

SVETLANA STALIN eight-year-old daughter of Stalin; a.k.a. Setanka; a.k.a. Setanotchka

STELLA a girl from Chakva

GIUSEPPINA TROISI Pippo Troisi's abandoned wife; a.k.a. Pina

PIPPO TROISI once a farmer from the island of Salina; now an "asylum seeker from marriage" at the invisible monastery on the island of Arkudah

VANGO washed up on the island of Salina as a child; now a young man searching for his identity; a.k.a. Evangelisto; a.k.a. "the Bird"

BARTOLOMEO VIAGGI pirate from the island of Salina; killed by Giovanni Cafarello

LAURA VIAGGI daughter of the late Bartolomeo Viaggi; from the island of Salina

VOLOY VIKTOR nefarious arms dealer; also goes by many other names, including Madame Victoria

VLAD THE VULTURE Soviet agent; rival of Boris Petrovitch Antonov

WEEPING WILLOW mysterious, sickly figure who is hidden away in a valley in the Caucasus Mountains

PADRE ZEFIRO leader of the invisible monastery of Arkudah; mentor of Vango; member of Project Violette

1918. At the age of three, Vango is washed up on a beach in the Aeolian Islands in Sicily, with Mademoiselle, his nurse, who claims to know nothing about their past. He grows up on the island of Salina, sheltered from the world, among the birds and climbing the cliffs.

At the age of ten, he discovers the invisible monastery, which Padre Zefiro founded in order to protect a few dozen monks from the mafias that were after them. Vango is accepted by the community, and lives between his island and the monastery. But, four years later, when he announces to Zefiro that he wants to become a monk, the padre sends him away to find out about the world before making a final commitment.

So Vango spends the year of 1929 as a crew member of the *Graf Zeppelin* airship, by the side of Commander Hugo Eckener. On board he meets an orphan called Ethel, who is traveling with her brother. But Vango is being pursued by unknown forces who want him dead, and three weeks after meeting Ethel, he is forced to leave her.

A few years later, just as he is about to become a priest at the foot of Notre Dame Cathedral in Paris, Vango is accused of a crime he hasn't committed. The senseless witch hunt continues, and Superintendent Boulard and his men join the ranks of those already pursuing him. From now on, Vango leads the life of a fugitive across Europe, as he tries to discover why such hatred follows him.

Padre Zefiro has now left his monastery and is fighting against the arms dealer Voloy Viktor in order to keep the promise he made to three friends, twenty years earlier, in the trenches of Verdun.

In the middle of this whirlwind, Vango finally learns about his dramatic arrival in Sicily as a child: offshore from the islands, his parents were killed in their boat by three men, led by one Cafarello. Vango and his nurse escaped. Cafarello betrayed his co-pirates, sunk the boat, and disappeared with the lion's share of the mysterious treasure that was on board.

Vango sets off again into the unknown to find Cafarello and uncover the great secret of his life.

PART ONE

NEW YORK,
MAY–DECEMBER 1936

AN ENCOUNTER IN THE SKY:
VANGO AND ETHEL

Lakehurst, New Jersey, September 1, 1929

The rectangle of crumpled corn was their hideout.

They were lying next to each other, draped in the gold of the crop. All around them, fields stretched as far as the eye could see, proud and tall beneath the sun. The airship on the ground was just visible, a few kilometers off, like a shimmer of silver in the grass.

She was twelve perhaps, and he fourteen. She had run after him through the corn, which had closed up again behind them.

"Go away!" he had called out.

She had followed, without the faintest idea of where he was heading. Now they were huddled on the ground, face-to-face, and she was crying.

"Are we hiding? Why do we have to hide?"

Vango put two fingers to Ethel's lips.

"Shhh. . . . He's here. He's following me."

Not even the ears of grain rustled. Complete silence, except for a sustained summer note, a deep note you might call the sound of the sun. Vango had a crazed look in his eyes.

"Tell me what's going on," Ethel whispered.

The parched earth soaked up the traces of her tears.

"There's nobody here. I don't recognize you anymore, Vango. What is the matter?"

Ethel had only known Vango for three weeks, but it seemed to her as if their meeting was the beginning of everything and that in her entire life she had never really known anybody else. Three weeks had been like a small eternity together. Hadn't they traveled all the way around the world?

They had even forgotten about the other passengers on board the Graf Zeppelin, the crowds that gathered at each stop-off, the newspapers reporting on the great airship's adventure, the magnesium flashes from the cameras falling over them like a shower of white rain.

In their hearts, it had been just the two of them flying: from New York to Germany, and then nonstop to Japan. After five days let loose in Tokyo, they had crossed the Pacific in three days, flown over the bay of San Francisco at sunset as part of a flotilla of small aircraft, been given a standing ovation in Los Angeles and Chicago, and finally landed at Lakehurst, near New York.

Enough for at least one lifetime. Or perhaps for two lives joining together?

"Please," she whispered, "tell me what you're frightened of. Then I can help you."

Once again he put his hand over Ethel's mouth. He had just heard a clicking sound, like a weapon being loaded.

"He's here."

"Who?"

Ethel rolled over onto her back.

Vango wasn't the same person anymore.

Three weeks earlier, they had been strangers. They had met in the skies above New York, on the first night of their voyage. Ethel wished she could be back there, reliving it all, second by second, beginning with the first words, "Don't you ever speak?"

She had said nothing, of course, which had been her response to every question for the past five years. She was leaning against the window, holding a glass of water. They were one hundred meters above the tallest skyscrapers. The vertical night sparkled below them. She wasn't interested in the person who was talking to her.

"I was watching you with your brother," he had remarked. "You never say anything. But he's very good at looking after you."

He had turned his head to discover a pair of green eyes staring at him.

All the other passengers were asleep. She had left her cabin in search of a glass of water and had found this boy, sitting in the semi-darkness, in the small kitchen of the airship. He was peeling potatoes. She supposed he was working as a kitchen hand.

And then, as she headed for the door to return to her cabin, she had heard him say, "If you like, I'm here. If you can't sleep, my name's Vango."

These peculiar words had stopped Ethel in her tracks. She had repeated them to herself, before wondering, And if I can sleep, will he still be called Vango?

Against her better judgment, she had glanced at him. She saw that he was peeling his potatoes as if they were precious stones, with eight perfect facets. Above all, she saw that he bore no resemblance to anything or anyone she had ever met before. She had walked out of the room. The Zeppelin was already some distance from the coast. Manhattan was just a shiny memory in the sky.

When Ethel returned to the kitchen shortly afterward, Vango had admitted, "Like you, I've said very few words in my life. It's your silence that's making me so chatty."

It was her smile that betrayed her. She had sat down on a crate, as if she hadn't seen him. He was singing something in a language she didn't recognize.

Vango could no longer recall what he had said to pass the time. But he hadn't stopped talking until morning. Perhaps he had begun with the potato he was holding between his fingers. Boiled, sautéed, roasted, grated, stewed: the humble potato always astounded him. Sometimes, he would even cook it in a ball of clay, which he would smash afterward with a stone, as if it were an egg. From the potato, he would no doubt have gone on to talk about eggs, then chickens, then everything that lives in the farmyard, or that lends its scent to the vegetable garden or the spice shop, or that falls from the fruit trees with the sound of autumn. He had talked about chestnuts exploding, and the sizzle of mushrooms in the frying pan. She was listening. He had got her to smell the jar of vanilla pods, and he had heard the first sound to pass her lips as her face approached the jar to sniff it: like the sigh of a child turning over in her sleep.

They had even looked at each other for a second in silence. She seemed surprised.

Vango had continued. Later, he noticed the small bundle of vanilla pods bringing tears to the girl's eyes; even the acrid smell of yeast on the chopping board seemed to make memories rise up for her. He watched her beginning to thaw.

The next day, as they passed the thirty-fifth meridian, Ethel had uttered her first word, "Whale."

And sure enough, below them was a drifting white island, which not even the pilots of the Zeppelin had spotted. A white island that turned gray when it rose up out of the foam.

After that word came the word "toast," then the word "Vango," and then other words too: sounds that filled the eyes and mouth. This lasted for nearly two weeks. Ethel could feel life returning, the way a blind person recovers their sight. Her brother, Paul, sitting at the table with the other guests, had watched her getting better before his eyes. He hadn't heard the deep timbre of her voice since the death of their parents.

But just before leaving Japan, on the twenty-first of August, she had seen something crack in Vango's gaze. What had happened that evening of their world tour?

Ethel suddenly remembered that all dreams have to come to an end.

Now, here they were, lying in their den of corn and sunshine. They should have felt so close, the two of them, on this particular morning, now that they were far away from the others at last. But instead she noticed the way Vango's hand was trembling as she valiantly brought hers close to it.

"The balloon's about to depart. You must go," whispered Vango.

"But what about you?"

"I'll catch up."

"I'm staying here with you."

"Go."

She stood up. Vango tugged her back down again.

"Stay low and walk as far as the last row of corn, over there. Then run to the Zeppelin."

Something fell to the ground, behind Vango.

"What's that?" Ethel wanted to know.

Vango picked it up and tucked it inside his belt, in the small of his back. It was a revolver.

"You're losing your mind," said Ethel.

Vango wished that were the case. He wished that he had made everything up. That the invisible enemy who had tried to kill him three times in one week had never existed, and that Ethel's hair could sweep away the shadows lying in ambush all around him.

Ethel let go of his hands.

"You made me a promise," she added, after taking a few steps. "Will you remember?"

He nodded, his eyes no longer able to focus.

She vanished into the corn.

After she had been walking for ten minutes, with her matted hair stuck to her cheeks and eyes, Ethel heard two gunshots being fired in the distance behind her. She turned around. The pool of gold lay still, as if at low tide. Ethel could no longer tell where she had set out from, or where the sound had come from.

The blaring of the airship's horn was summoning her. Ethel turned full circle, unable to decide what to do; then, remembering Vango's pleading look, she continued walking toward the Zeppelin.

Commander Eckener's booming voice was making the kitchen window vibrate.

"Where's my Piccolo? What have you done with him?"

Otto Manz, the chef, shrugged, causing all his chins to disappear into his collar.

"He was here at midnight making a sauce for me. Try this!"

Otto held out a steaming wooden spoon, which Hugo Eckener pushed aside.

"I'm not here to discuss your sauces! I'm asking you where Vango is."

The kitchen was at the front of the airship. The canvas giant tugged at its mooring ropes, preparing to leave America. In its hull, ten of Christopher Columbus's sailing ships could have been lined up end to end.

A pilot officer appeared at the door.

"We're also missing two passengers."

"Who?" bellowed Eckener.

"My little sister, Ethel," announced a twenty-year-old man who had entered behind the officer.

"This isn't a summer camp! This is the first round-the-world trip by air! And we're running an hour late. Where are these kids?"

"Over there!" exclaimed the cook, looking out the window.

Ethel had just cleared a path through the crowd surrounding the balloon. Her brother, Paul, rushed toward the window. She was alone.

"Get her on board!" ordered the commander.

They reached out to haul her up; the steps had already been taken in. Paul greeted her on the threshold.

"Where were you?"

Ethel thrust her fists into her pockets. She was staring at her brother. She sensed that she was teetering on a narrow causeway. She could either dive back into the silence she had inhabited before Vango, or she could set out alone on a new journey.

Paul sensed his sister's vertigo, and he watched her with trepidation, as if she were a cat on a glass roof.

"I went for a walk," said Ethel.

Eckener appeared next to them.

"What about Vango?"

"I don't know," answered Ethel. "I'm not Vango's keeper. Isn't he here?"

"No, he's not here!" boomed the commander. "Nor will he ever be again. We're leaving."

"You're not going to set off without Vango?" remonstrated the cook.

"He's fired. That's it. We're off. . . ."

Eckener's voice faltered. Ethel looked away. The orders rebounded all the way to the flight deck. Otto Manz collapsed against the partition.

"Vango? You can't be serious!"

"Don't I look serious?" roared Eckener, his eyebrows sticking up.

"At least try this sauce for me," pleaded the cook, still with the wooden spoon in his hand.

But before the taste of truffles could reverse destiny, Eckener had disappeared.

Suddenly, the voice of Kubis, the headwaiter, could be heard calling out, "There he is!"

Ethel bounded into the corridor and made for the dining room; pushing aside the travelers who were gathered at the window, she scanned the airfield that was filled with soldiers and onlookers.

"There he is!" declared Kubis again, from the neighboring window.

And sure enough, Ethel could see, beyond the crowd, a man, running and waving his arms.

"It's Mr. Antonov!"

Boris Petrovitch Antonov had also been missing from the roll call.

"He's wounded."

The Russian had wrapped a scarf around his knee and he was limping.

This time, the white wooden staircase was put back in place for him to embark. The latecomer explained that he had tripped on a foxhole while stepping back to take a photo.

His eyes were fixed on Ethel.

Boris Antonov had small wire-framed glasses and a waxen complexion. He was traveling with Doctor Kakline, a Russian scientist and Moscow's official representative for escorting the Zeppelin over the Soviet Union. Two weeks earlier, Eckener had decided to bypass the north of Moscow, where tens of thousands of people waited to no avail. Doctor Kakline had demonstrated his Siberian temper, but it took more than that to make Hugo Eckener change his mind.

Kakline was now busy dealing with Antonov. But he didn't even glance at the bloodstained bandage on his compatriot's knee. Instead, he was grilling him with a barrage of hushed questions. Kakline seemed to be satisfied with the outcome of Antonov's adventure. "Da, da, da," he kept saying, pinching Antonov's cheeks as if he were a good soldier.

The passengers felt the surge of takeoff. This was always the most emotional moment, as the flying ship pulled away from the shouts of the crowd and slowly rose to silent heights in the air.

Old Eckener was in his wooden chair on the starboard side, near the flight deck windows. His blue eyes were tinged with sadness. He was thinking about Vango, the fourteen-year-old boy who had just spent nearly a year on board the Graf Zeppelin. From very early on, he had imagined a mysterious destiny for the person he called Piccolo. But he couldn't help becoming attached to him. From the outset, he had dreaded the day when Vango would disappear.

Eckener was gazing down at the corn. The balloon had already risen two hundred meters. The hive of activity in the hangars at Lakehurst had been left behind, and only the crop fields were in view now. But when he saw, down below, in the soft mist and expanse of yellow, a boy running through the ears of corn, Eckener rediscovered his smile. He stowed that sight in his memory, along with all the others: the Sahara hurling itself into the ocean from the cliff tops, the grid formation of the gardens at Hokkaido in Japan, the full moon over the dark forests of Siberia. Each moment was a miracle. It was as if the harvesting had been forgotten about, in order to make it possible for a young man to cut a furrow through the corn as he ran beneath the balloon.

Ethel was in her cabin. Her hands against the glass, she leaned into the window without ever taking her eyes off that tiny dot moving across the field below her. The crazy racing of the blue dot was slowly losing ground against the shadow of the balloon. Her heart pounding, Ethel leaned even farther so as not to let him out of her sight.

"Vango," she whispered.

At exactly the same moment, behind the partition wall, Doctor Kakline dropped his champagne glass.

The crystal shattered against the corner of a table, making Comrade Antonov stand up.

"Are you quite sure about that?" muttered Kakline, pushing the window slightly ajar.

"Why?" inquired Boris Antonov.

"I'm the one asking the questions here," insisted Kakline, as he glared at the floor.

"I . . . I didn't have time to go right up to the body," stammered Boris. "But—"

"What d'you mean?"

"But I saw him fall."

"You didn't check?"

"The zeppelin was about to take off without me. . . ."

The blue dot disappeared. Kakline gritted his teeth.

"You idiot."

Exhausted, his legs having taken a thrashing from his race across the field, Vango stopped. He bent over and clasped his knees, unable to catch his breath. The purring of the engines was becoming fainter now. Slowly, Vango stood up. His eyes were fixed on the horizon until complete silence was restored.

THE CORPSE IN THE BLUE COMET

Lakehurst, New Jersey, seven years later, May 1936

Rusty warehouses had been erected where the cornfields used to be, but Vango still recognized the black earth between his fingers. He crouched down at exactly the spot where he had watched Ethel disappear all those years ago.

It was here that his life on the run had begun.

Seven years later, he still didn't know what his enemies looked like.

Day hadn't broken yet. Vango had arrived in New York by boat the evening before, on a third-class ticket. He had made for Lakehurst, where the *Hindenburg,* the new flying monster from the house of Zeppelin, was due to land for the first time.

Vango wanted to have a word with Hugo Eckener.

There are some people whose schedules are advertised in block capitals at newspaper kiosks. To find out where they are, all you have to do is listen to the newspaper sellers in the street calling out, "Eckener in New York with his *Hindenburg!* Buy the *Post!*"

On their way back from Sicily, Vango and Ethel had traveled to France before boarding a boat to cross the Channel at Le Havre.

When they docked at Southampton, she had made her way back to Scotland. And Vango had set off for America.

Ethel couldn't understand why he was deserting her on the dockside, when they had already been lost to each other for such a long time. He couldn't even tell her what he planned to do. This time, he hadn't made any promises. She was shivering in the cold. He had stood there, saying nothing, with the rain streaming through his hair. Ethel had walked away. The ship's horn announced the end of the stopover.

No good-byes. Always the same scene being played out. He would never forget that look in Ethel's eyes, beneath her hood: a sort of threat. She hadn't made any promises either.

Night was clinging on in the west. The airship wouldn't arrive until after midday. The air still felt cool, and in the distance, the landing field was empty. Vango lay down under a few lingering stars.

Through the window of a corrugated iron shack, a man dressed in black was spying on him.

Silent seagulls circled above Vango. On the bridge of the transatlantic liner *Normandy,* approaching the coast, small squadrons of gulls had been watching over him, as they would have followed a plowman or a trawling fisherman. Now they had found him again, despite the gloom, in the midst of these hangars far from the sea. Five or six gulls pretending to be nocturnal birds. Vango fell asleep, hypnotized by the flapping of white wings.

The man in black, clad in a bandit's coat, waited a while before emerging from his hideout. He approached the boy and leaned over his sleeping face. Concerned, the birds kept a close eye on things. The man glanced up at the circle they made in the night sky, then untied Vango's shoes. He put them in his poacher's pockets and headed off.

When daylight woke him, Vango sensed thunder in the offing, and through his half-open eyes, he glimpsed a stormy sky. But on heaving himself up with his elbows, he discovered that his shoes had disappeared. He searched the grass around him. Checking his belt, he could feel the cloth roll he was looking for, containing the precious stones. So his old shoes were the only things that had been stolen. Nothing else.

He tipped his head back to get the measure of the storm. A rumbling sound was coming from the gray sky, streaked with glints of mercury. But this particular sky was powered by four enormous engines and carried more than a hundred passengers: it was the *Hindenburg* airship arriving from Europe.

Vango stood up, feeling dazzled. When he had traveled on board the *Graf Zeppelin* with Ethel, back in 1929, he could never have imagined that one day Commander Eckener would succeed in making an infinitely bigger and heavier airship rise up into the skies, complete with a smoking room, a revolving door, and even an aluminum baby grand piano covered in yellow leather. But Eckener's dreams could make mountains fly.

Vango started to sprint barefoot toward the landing field.

The crowd was packed in tightly around the barriers. Ranks of curious people kept arriving. As he passed among them, Vango missed the sense of genuine exultation he had noticed on previous occasions. Something seemed to have tarnished the crazy, childish joy he had always witnessed toward the *Zeppelin*. There was a surprising silence all around him, making the orders being given to the airmen — who were preparing to grab hold of the balloon's mooring ropes — ring out even more loudly.

Vango knew what had changed.

A few weeks earlier, there had been a lot of talk about the propaganda dropped over Germany from the new *Hindenburg* balloon. Every province was showered with leaflets depicting Hitler, while loudspeakers blared Nazi songs: this terrifying spectacle had sullied the airship's image, even in America. And now, despite the spray from the crossing, the circle around the swastika on the zeppelin's flank glistened the color of blood.

The balloon had come to a stop. The footbridge was brought out from its underbelly. Vango recognized Captain Lehmann, posted at the entrance to greet those about to disembark the airship. When they appeared at the top of the steps, the passengers cast victorious eyes over the crowd. There wasn't a single crease in their white shirts, or a hair out of place, and their shoes glistened. Still, they looked different from the rest of humanity, as if they had returned from another world.

Such was the magic spell cast by this flying machine.

Vango decided to let the passengers disperse before approaching Hugo Eckener.

A blond woman was making her way down the steps. She was flanked by two young men, who looked like hotel bellboys, carrying her suitcases and furs. Vango stared at her. At a thousand dollars a ticket, it was rare to travel onboard the zeppelin with staff. Usually, they would follow separately in the hold of a cargo ship, accompanying the parrot cage and the twelve suitcases of clothes.

Another passenger quickly stole the blonde's top billing, attracting the photographers' attention. His name was on everyone's lips. He was a famous singer returning from a European tour. His lips were fixed in a publicity-shot smile. Vango was carried along by the crowd without even realizing it. Caught up in the whirlwind of journalists and curious bystanders, he felt himself almost being lifted off the ground. There was a police cordon to protect the star, but the scrum trampled the cordon and threatened to turn violent.

Vango bobbed along like a cork in this human tide. In the middle of the fighting that had broken out, a face rose up and immediately disappeared again.

Stunned, Vango just had time to recognize it. He tried to elbow his way against the current. The face was perfectly etched in his memory.

The man had trimmed his mustache into fangs, while sideburns hid part of his cheeks, and he wore a brown trilby pulled low over his eyes. But it was him.

Zefiro.

Vango had spotted his friend Padre Zefiro, abbot of the invisible monastery on the island of Arkudah, who, some months earlier, had mysteriously abandoned his monks without giving any indication of his whereabouts.

"Padre!" whispered Vango.

He received two blows to the head and slid to the ground.

Over to the west, in Indiana, an engineer called John W. Chamberlain, emancipator of housewives, had just finished building the first fully automatic washing machine, which relied on a force known as the centrifuge. And it was this same centrifugal force that sent Vango spinning slowly in an outward direction until he rolled on the grass, whiter than a sheet.

On opening his eyes, he spotted a coat disappearing behind a car. Vango recognized the trilby and went after it.

Zefiro . . . He couldn't let him disappear again.

Chevrolet buses were filling up with passengers as Vango drew nearer. He saw Zefiro chasing a handsome purple open-top car before jumping on board one of the buses. Vango climbed into the next one. The convoy was slowed by the flow of pedestrians. Horns tooted, and the yellow buses lurched over the bumpy grass before rediscovering the delights of pavement.

The man sitting next to Vango on the bus eyed his neighbor's shoeless feet suspiciously. He kept his hands tightly pressed against his pockets, for fear of having his fob watch stolen. The last thing the passenger could have imagined was that Vango, the barefoot beggar, had sewn into his belt a pouch of rubies valuable enough to buy up all the shoe factories on the East Coast.

The journey didn't take long. At quarter past seven that morning, the yellow Chevrolets pulled up in front of Lakehurst station. A few passengers got out. Spotting the trilby and the coat among them, Vango set off on their trail. The purple car was parked under the station clock.

Zefiro quickened his step and examined the car. It was empty. He entered the ticket hall, inspected the waiting room, and headed out onto the platform. Whistles shrilled across the station. The Blue Comet was on platform one. It pulled out, shrouded in steam.

It was a magnificent blue train—as handsome as a toy, with pale yellow lacquered windows. Vango made it onto the platform just in time to see the padre board the moving train. Pushing aside the stationmaster who was blocking his way, Vango began to sprint barefoot. Two other railway workers crossed the tracks in a bid to stop him.

"You shouldn't attempt to board a moving train, sir!"

The last carriage was a long way ahead of him, and layers of smoke prevented him from seeing where the platform ended. Vango put on a final spurt and jumped onto the back buffer of the locomotive. Just in time. The platform had disappeared beneath his feet.

At that very instant, the gleaming purple car exploded under the clock. The explosion was so powerful that it shattered all the windows in the station.

Vango clung to the train, leaving behind him the racket of shouts and whistle blows. All he could see was black smoke rising up beyond the platforms.

Vango didn't understand what was going on. Ever since he was fourteen, there had always been dangers and dramas trailing in his wake. The world exploded when he passed by. Ashes were all he left behind.

Recently, on the ocean liner to America, he had spent three hours in the rain one night, on the deserted bridge, his arms outstretched to the sky, hoping to wash away this curse. Two old ladies had scooped him up the next morning. They were Danish traveling companions, and they scolded him before lending him their cabin for the whole day so he could warm up.

"You silly boy! How irresponsible of you!"

They made him drink tea until he was full to bursting and they rubbed mustard poultices into his back.

"Were you out of your mind?"

Being on the receiving end of someone else's anger had never done Vango so much good.

The Blue Comet was a luxurious train offering a high-speed connection to New York. After its hour of glory, the Great Depression of 1929 had restricted its timetable. But this morning, all the seats were taken. Vango made his way through the carriages, one after another. He was wearing a gray velvet cap and had taken off his jacket, which he carried over one arm. There was nothing remarkable about him, provided you didn't look at his feet.

Nobody on board had noticed the explosion. The passengers were reading quietly or else dozing, propped against the windows.

Vango was looking for Padre Zefiro. The last time he had seen him, on the main concourse at Gare d'Austerlitz in Paris, the padre hadn't even recognized him. From that day on, there had been no further sightings of Zefiro: he was reported missing, believed dead.

Close by, in the front carriage, a lady was lounging on a first-class seat. She had exclusive use of the two end compartments and had stationed an armed guard in the corridor. Even the ticket inspector had received a wad of dollars to guarantee that she wouldn't be disturbed. She wore an angora stole over one shoulder, and from time to time, she rubbed her ear sensuously against it.

It was the blonde with the bellboys. She had left them in the adjacent compartment, along with the men in suits who acted as her bodyguards. On the seat opposite her, two other burly fellows in matching uniforms were waiting, hats on knees.

"I'm away for two weeks," she complained, "and no progress has been made?"

Neither of the men responded.

"Answer me, Dorgeles!"

No reply came from the man called Dorgeles, but his enormous neighbor opened his mouth.

The blonde made a violent *sssssshhh!* noise. This in turn made the stole on her shoulder ripple, and out of it leaped two blue eyes. It was a cat. The woman slowly lowered her head again, so that it would go back to sleep.

Dorgeles knew what the person hidden beneath this feminine disguise was capable of. He knew how urgent it was to placate the man behind the makeup: Voloy Viktor.

"We'll find him for you, Madame Victoria. We know he's after you. He'll come to us."

The blonde waved her hand, as if Dorgeles's voice still risked waking the cat.

"I can't sleep for a single second," she hissed. "I know that Zefiro is following me. I can smell him."

"Trust us. We're here to protect you."

"Can you smell it, Dorgeles? The stench of sulfur?"

She was hallucinating.

"You've got to trust us. You're putting yourself in danger by changing the timetable so often."

"Surely you can smell it, Dorgeles?"

It had never been part of the plan for Voloy Viktor to travel on board the zeppelin. Nor on this train, for that matter. Suspicious to the point of being obsessive, he had suddenly demanded that his big purple car pull up in front of the station in order for him to catch the Blue Comet.

"I could smell him," whined Madame Victoria. "I could smell him behind me. He's always there. Zefiro is after my skin."

"There was nothing to worry about in the car. He even missed you at the Plaza Hotel, back in May."

The blonde pointed a blue-painted nail at Dorgeles.

"You're the one who missed *him* at the Plaza! YOU!"

The cat snarled. Dorgeles stared at the floor. He was recalling the evening in New York when he had been trussed up and bundled into the trunk of his own car before he'd had a chance to figure out what was happening.

Next to him in the train compartment, big Bob Almond, from Chicago, who hadn't been recruited for the quality of his conversation, was starting to butcher his hat.

"You can rejoin the others," Dorgeles told him.

Bob stood up and banged his head on the ceiling. Then he made a small polite bow, hitting his neck against the luggage rack as he drew himself up to his full height.

When he had finally made it out of the compartment, Madame Victoria rolled her eyes.

"I wouldn't even hire him to scrape the muck off my hunting boots. How do you select your primates?"

They were both silent for a few minutes. Madame Victoria leaned against the window. Her eyes flitted over the countryside. How could anyone have recognized, in this swooning lady, the madness of Voloy Viktor, arms dealer and murderer?

"I have some news that will interest you," Dorgeles said softly, in a bid to regain lost ground.

Madame Victoria didn't respond.

"Some news as of yesterday evening," Dorgeles went on. "Did you know that Zefiro's sidekick, the one we photographed him with, has been identified . . . ?"

"His name is Vango Romano." Madame Victoria sighed wearily as she rummaged in her makeup bag. "Don't you have anything new to tell me, Dorgeles?"

"He arrived in New York last night, by boat."

This time, there was a flicker of curiosity on Madame Victoria's face. She looked at herself in a little mirror edged with mother-of-pearl.

"How do you know that?"

"I've got one of my men stationed in customs at the port."

Madame Victoria snapped the mirror shut. She produced a square of leather from her blouse and took out two photos, which she held up against each other.

"Now at last you're saying something interesting. I've always thought we'd get to the old one via the young one."

Dorgeles didn't even allow himself a satisfied smile.

He was only too familiar with his boss's mood swings.

"Show this photo to each of our men."

Dorgeles nodded and settled comfortably into the back of his seat.

"Now!" roared Madame Victoria. "Show them now! I want that little . . ."

Dorgeles grabbed the photo, stood up, and left the compartment.

* * *

Vango had only one carriage left to check. One last chance to find Zefiro. Suddenly, the shadow of the ticket inspector loomed before him. Vango pushed open the door to his right and disappeared inside before he was spotted. He found himself in the first-class lavatory. A curtain had been drawn across the window. It was almost pitch-black. Vango turned the lock. With his ear pressed to the door, he waited for the inspector to head off.

When he tried to take a step backward, he nearly trod on something bulky and limp on the floor. He bent down in the gloom and put his hand out. Using his fist to stifle his cry, he pinned himself against the wall, tugging the curtain clean off its rail.

There, curled up in front of him, between the basin and the toilet, was a lifeless body, almost naked, lying facedown.

2

STORMY WEATHER ON THE TRACKS

"Padre?"

Vango lifted the head by its hair and turned it toward the light.

For a split second, he had thought it was Zefiro. His sense of relief was almost shameful. Slowly, he bent over the body. The man was wearing underpants and an undershirt. His ribs rose and fell: he was still breathing. Vango knelt down next to him. There were no clues as to who he was. The man merely seemed to be asleep, his right hand closed around something. Vango leaned over him a bit more. In his clenched fingers, the man was holding what looked like a small pair of metal pliers.

Is that some kind of tooth extractor? wondered Vango.

He picked up the object to see if there were any bloodstains on it. Nothing. The fewer clues there are, the more the imagination runs riot. Vango started fantasizing about a patient's revenge against his dentist, and other macabre scenarios. Above all, he was conscious that he didn't want to be accused of another crime that he hadn't committed. He splashed some cold water on his face, undid the lock, and took a deep breath.

Vango pushed the door open.

Right there, waiting to come in, loomed the figure of Bob

Almond, Madame Victoria's henchman. Vango turned very pale, and his eyes bulged.

Bob was squirming in front of him. Not even his huge body was exempt from the calls of nature.

"I need to go in," he said.

Vango didn't budge, having shut the door firmly behind him. Bob stooped down to his level.

"Sick?" he asked, staring at the boy's pallid face.

"That's right," said Vango. "I'm feeling sick."

Bob sniffed, as if he wanted proof.

"Very sick," repeated Vango.

Bob Almond took a step backward to avert disaster. Vango seized the opportunity to lock himself inside the first-class lavatory again.

"Come back in five minutes, please," he called out from the other side of the door, between explicit retching noises.

He heard Bob walking away down the corridor.

Vango was at the back of his tiny hideout, shivering with fear. But he didn't really start feeling sick until, down by his feet, in that clammy air, the body of the tooth snatcher started moving.

When Bob Almond went to sit back down in the compartment, along with his three colleagues and the two bellboys, he was shocked at how patient he had been. He stared into space and thought about what he'd just done. Next time, as sure as his name was Bob, he would make that guy deal with his problems on the tracks.

"Dorgeles came by," mentioned one of his colleagues. "He wanted to know where you were."

Bob didn't answer.

"The boss says we've got to find *that*."

Bob didn't even glance at the square of shiny paper being held out to him. He was too busy staving off the call of nature. He got out his watch to calculate when he could try his luck again with the first-class lavatory.

"He's the new target," the other man continued.

Without paying it much attention, Bob took the photo of Vango Romano.

"I'm warning you—Madame Victoria wants him alive," his neighbor specified.

"Don't ask too much of Bob," joked one of the men, who appeared to be dozing under his hat. Everyone guffawed.

During this brief exchange of words, Bob Almond had begun to stare at the photo. The picture did the rounds of his left brain three or four times before it vaguely began to remind him of someone.

Then it came to him in a flash. He stood up, banging his head on the ceiling again.

"Crapola!"

A travel bag came crashing down from the rack.

Bob rushed out of the compartment, ran down the corridor, and arrived in front of the lavatory door. One kick of his boot was all it took to wrench the door off its hinges.

In the gloom, he could make out the whites of two petrified eyes. Bob smiled. He had him.

The men arrived one after another to witness Bob Almond looming ahead of them, dragging some wretched creature along by the hair.

"Here he is," declared Bob, who was bursting with pride. "Get Dorgeles! I've found his man."

But the person Bob was holding by the hair didn't look anything like the photo of Vango. This victim wore only a faded undershirt and underpants, and his teeth chattered while words dribbled down his chin.

Seeing the bewildered expression on his friends' faces, Bob Almond raised his catch to eye level.

"Crapola!" he bellowed.

He threw the man to the ground and returned to search the lavatory.

"Where is he? I swear, I saw him."

Just then, Dorgeles appeared.

"We've got to search the other carriages. He's on board!" boomed Bob.

"Who?"

"Him!"

Bob flashed the photo.

"Check the whole train!" Dorgeles instructed coldly. "And find the inspector for me. I want to talk to the inspector."

The men all made a dash for the second carriage.

Meanwhile, the victim was still writhing on the floor in his underpants.

Vango was walking between the rows of passengers. He didn't want anyone to notice him, but kept checking nervously behind him all the same. When he saw the inspector's uniform, ten paces away, he threw caution to the wind and tore down the aisle. The train tilted as it took a wide bend, and people were shouting all around him. He dashed from one carriage to the next, leaping over the screeching rails, pushing aside anyone who got in his way. A girl landed on the knees of an elderly rabbi, and a man with a pair of pigeons sat on their cage, crushing the bars and freeing the birds.

In a flurry of feathers, the inspector passed through the aviary, shielding himself with his arms. He tripped on a suitcase but managed to get up again. He appeared to be limping now, and held his cap in his hand. Never had so much energy been expended by a railway worker to catch a fare dodger.

The tornado had barely blown through before another followed, and this one was much more ferocious. Madame Victoria's men destroyed the debris left by those who had gone before them. Nobody could make any sense of the chaos.

Vango had now reached the last carriage. The inspector, who was just behind him, was losing ground to the gangsters, but he kept on going, dragging his injured ankle behind him.

Dorgeles remained in the first-class carriage, at the other end of the train. He kept his hand firmly on his gun. He was the only person left, along with the two porters, to guarantee Madame Victoria's protection.

"I bribed the inspector to seal off the carriage! Where is that moron?"

He tossed two guns to the young bellboys, so that they could mount guard with him.

Vango had arrived at the end of the train. In front of him, three doors opened directly onto the tracks. Dead end. There was nothing else for it. He knew he would be blamed for attacking the dentist. He was used to such accusations. The train was approaching New York, as it traveled along an embankment between vegetable patches and gray sheds. The poplar trees quivered when the Blue Comet sped past.

A cry. He didn't even have time to turn around. He saw the shadow of the inspector suddenly rise up, grab hold of him, and stagger with him toward one of the doors. Vango tried to break free while, with one jab of his shoulder, the inspector forced open the door. Vango let out a scream. The din was terrifying. The tracks flashed past like lightning. They were both about to fall.

Three men had just appeared behind them. The biggest held a Colt in his left hand.

"Don't move!"

The inspector didn't waver for a second. He gripped Vango even more tightly and leaped with him into thin air.

The three gangsters saw them roll and disappear behind a mound of earth.

Bob Almond fired seven shots from his Colt blindly into the bushes, shouting "Crapola!" several times as a point of principle. Then he trod on a railway worker's helmet emblazoned with blue stars.

A few carriages away, Dorgeles was still shouting himself hoarse.

"Where's the inspector? WHERE IS THE INSPECTOR?"

He stopped. A weak voice was answering him. Dorgeles looked down.

"Here I am. . . . I'm the inspector!"

Down on the ground, the man in his underwear held out his hand. He was writhing like a worm on the corridor floor.

Vango opened his eyes. He was lying in the middle of flowering strawberry plants. His roll down from the high tracks had left a large rectangle of flattened vegetation. He must have blacked out for several minutes. The sun was beating down hard.

He heard a man behind him.

"I'd do well to smash your face in, little one."

The little one turned his head.

There, with barely a crease in his tight inspector's uniform, sat the dark and handsome Padre Zefiro. He was perched on an upturned bucket and tucking into a tomato that was still green. Next to him, on the ground, lay a small bundle.

"Because of you, I missed my chance!"

He spat out the tomato skin.

"Seventeen years spent following him! A lifetime!"

Zefiro had never sounded so frosty.

"A whole life! And the lives of dozens of others, over there, in the invisible monastery, all in mortal danger because of you. Bravo, little one."

Vango didn't move or say a word. He was frightened of making things worse, of turning other people into victims simply by saying the wrong thing. Of starting a tidal wave by raising his little finger.

"Did I ask you to meddle in my affairs?" asked Zefiro. "He was finally in my grasp!"

"Who?" asked Vango weakly.

"Voloy Viktor."

Vango felt desolate.

"I . . . I'm sorry. But you shouldn't have meddled in my affairs either."

"They're the ones who were going to meddle with you,

Vango. They're after you as well! They want to pin you to their wall."

"Me?"

As usual, Vango could no longer tell whether he was the victim or the guilty party.

They sat there together, listening to the silence.

"Padre . . ."

Zefiro didn't answer.

"Padre . . . you saved my life."

"And I'm already sorry I did. It was a foolish act of compassion."

Vango hung his head. The padre was watching him out of the corner of his eye.

"They want you because of me," admitted Zefiro, after letting a few seconds go by. "Because they saw you with me in Paris. So it's my fault too."

Vango stood up. His body had been given a drubbing by the tumble he had just taken.

"Was the man in the first-class lavatory another of Voloy Viktor's dirty tricks?" he asked.

"No. I needed a disguise to get to Viktor. You do whatever it takes." Zefiro shrugged. "But I'd forgotten to pick up the ticket puncher. I was heading back to find it when I saw you."

"Padre . . . did you batter the ticket inspector?"

"He was corrupt. Viktor had bribed him. I'm not looking for excuses. I take full responsibility for everything I've done. I tried to booby-trap two of Viktor's homes last month. And this morning I fitted a time bomb inside his car. . . ."

Vango thought back to the explosion and the black cloud when the train had pulled out of the station.

"As long as Viktor is alive," Zefiro explained, "my fellow monks are in danger on their island. He will track down our monastery to the bitter end."

The padre held a grasshopper between his fingers as he acknowledged his friend's confusion.

"You're not sure if you still recognize me, Vango. But there is only one Padre Zefiro. The same man who built the Monastery of Arkudah with his bare hands, who sings God's glory before a tomato plant, who raises a clutch of monks in the middle of the sea, and who is determined to track down Voloy Viktor. They're all the same man, Vango. And I'm doing this in order to remain that man."

He contemplated the grasshopper in the palm of his hand.

"And now," he said, "I'm faced with the same question that's been there since day one. What am I going to do with you?"

Vango closed his eyes. He was thinking of the hanging monastery at the top of the island.

"Back there, they're all wondering what you're up to. They think you've gone mad."

Zefiro let the grasshopper escape before picking up his bundle and standing up.

"I have to destroy Viktor before I can return home."

It was Vango's turn to stand up.

"Where are we going?"

Padre Zefiro was already striding ahead. Then they both stopped and looked down at Vango's bare feet.

"Is there a problem?"

"They stole my shoes."

"Stole?"

"Yes, while I was asleep."

"You can't trust anyone these days."

Zefiro started walking again, past the vegetable gardens with their flowers.

"You're in luck!" he called out. And, from some way ahead, he tossed his bag to Vango.

"What's this?"

Vango opened the small bundle. There, wrapped in some clothes, was a pair of shoes. Vango couldn't wait to put them on.

"Thank you, Padre!"

"I hope they fit."

"I mean, what kind of person goes around stealing shoes?" muttered Vango to himself.

"Possibly someone who wanted to shake you off their trail," answered Zefiro under his breath. "Someone who didn't want you demolishing everything they've achieved."

Vango stopped in his tracks. He looked up and then down again, to examine the shoes properly, before staring at Zefiro in the midst of the cosmos flowers. Yes, the shoes fitted Vango. They fitted him like a glove, because they were *his* shoes.

Zefiro was laughing.

"Padre . . ." whispered Vango.

He couldn't quite believe it. Saboteur, terrorist, attacker of railway workers, shoe thief: it was a lot for one man of the cloth.

3

TWO TRAMPS IN THE SKY

New York

They headed for the big city, with Zefiro limping and Vango climbing along low walls. There was plenty to catch up on, and a lot to say to each other. They looked like two wandering pilgrims as they raised the dust on the road, eating the first fruits from gardens along the way and resting in trees.

Time sped by. The houses became packed more tightly together. The buildings grew taller as they sprouted more stories. The patches of green were harder to find. The factories gave off a throbbing noise. The cars forced the pedestrians to walk in ditches. In the distance was a blue line of skyscrapers.

Vango confided freely in the padre. He explained why he had come to America: to find the man who had murdered his parents, back there, in his islands. Giovanni Cafarello. The same man who had stolen more than his share of the mysterious treasure by killing one of his fellow pirates: Bartolomco Viaggi.

It was the first time Zefiro had heard this tale of pirates, murder, and treasure. The kind of story one tells children. He made Vango repeat the criminal's name: Cafarello. When Vango said it, a steel blade seemed to appear on his tongue.

"I'll find him," Vango declared, "and he'll tell me everything."

Zefiro understood his friend. Vango wasn't after gold or precious stones, or even the sweet taste of revenge. The only jewel he really wanted was the one that Giovanni Cafarello possessed: the secret of the boat, of the man and the woman he had sent down to the bottom of the sea. Cafarello would know who Vango's parents were, and from what star this child had fallen before being washed up on the black pebbles of Sicily.

Deep down, this was the only treasure that Vango was after: the secret of his life.

They stopped, from time to time, to shake the cherry trees. They filled their pockets while Vango told Zefiro about his last visit to the invisible monastery, about how disoriented the monks had been, and of their fear of losing their abbot forever.

"Brother Marco doesn't know if he's strong enough to replace you."

Zefiro seemed to be listening absentmindedly, but in fact he was constantly praying not to collapse. The invisible monastery was his life's work, and he had fought hard for it. Yet now here he was: a bandit, an irresponsible father, a warrior.

Sometimes he would duck behind a hedge, as if looking for wild berries, but once out of Vango's sight he would double up in pain and grief. He had abandoned his flock. Then he would start repeating the simplest words over and over again, prayers from his childhood, until he was able to appear again farther up the road, his face betraying nothing.

Later on, along the way, Vango described what it was like being an outlaw.

They never left him alone. Never. Night and day, they were there, everywhere.

"Will they stop one day, Padre?"

They had even tried to trample on his memories, by attacking the house where he had grown up, his island, descending on it like a squally wind and carrying off his nurse, sweet Mademoiselle.. Where was she now? Where were her hands working their magic with flames and wooden spoons? Vango had never stopped asking this question, despite being on the run, despite all the people after him in London. Yes, even in the streets of London, he told Zefiro, even in the forests of the Highlands, he could hear the dogs behind him.

"Dogs, that's right; I swear I heard them barking."

"Be careful," Zefiro warned him. "Your fear is preventing you from thinking straight."

Vango came to an abrupt halt.

"You think you're being followed—" Zefiro went on.

"What?" demanded Vango, grabbing hold of the padre's coat and shaking the black fabric in his fist. "You as well? Are you calling me mad?"

They were by a brick wall, set back from the road. Vango's eyes blazed as Zefiro deftly caught him by the jaw and pinned him against a telegraph pole. Then the padre raised him slowly off the ground so that Vango was on tip-toes, about to lose his footing, and in danger of being hanged.

"Calm down, little one," whispered Zefiro, suddenly letting go of his prey.

Vango collapsed on the pavement. Zefiro rubbed his shoulder a little, as if bitten by a midge.

"I said that your fear was preventing you from thinking straight. Now, are you going to listen to me?"

Vango sniffed and agreed to do as he was told.

Stroking his mustache, Zefiro took a step backward.

"Who says they're the same people following you around our islands, in London, and in the forests of Scotland? I've already explained to you that Voloy Viktor's men are now among those hunting you down. And the French police are after you as well. You're convinced that there's some dark force, one single enemy: in which case, why not head like a lemming for the cliff edge? But, if you stop and think about it, you might be able to do something."

Zefiro bent down and held out his hand to help Vango get up again. The young man allowed himself to be hauled up.

"Anyway, what about her? Why don't you tell me about *her* instead?"

Vango was startled.

Her?

He froze. He had never even mentioned her name. How did Zefiro know about her? He felt as if his secret were spreading all around him. He held his breath so as not to let it out.

"We're nearly there," said Zefiro.

He smiled to himself and let Vango catch up with him on the road.

He had asked the question on the off chance, without being sure. But his curiosity rarely let him down. There was always something to reel in when he cast out this particular hook. *What about her?* Even the most virtuous of his monks turned pale at the question. And Zefiro always felt moved by eyes suddenly turning misty, like marsh water, as a result of the line he had cast.

Her. For each of them, and even for Zefiro, those three letters represented someone specific, occasionally very far away, a dream, a shadow, or a regret.

Apart from the rustle of their clothes, the two men were silent until they reached the city center.

That same evening, two tramps set up camp above Manhattan, in the scaffolding of a tower. The low-lying clouds sometimes descended to their level. A grid of planks surrounded the unfinished skyscraper. Construction had been abandoned following an accident involving one of the workers. Zefiro took advantage of the building lying empty.

It was here that they made their nest, three hundred meters above Fifth Avenue. It began to rain. Vango lit a fire in a cast-iron tank from the work site, but Zefiro remained outside in the wet May air, standing on the end of a girder, watching the city.

"There he is," he declared.

"Where?"

Zefiro pointed to the top of another tower opposite. The Empire State Building was gleaming beneath the floodlights, but most of its windows remained dark. Just one row of picture windows was lit up.

"He lives there."

Vango drew closer.

"Two months ago," Zefiro went on, "I was confident that

it was a done deed. I arrived up there, convinced I'd thought of everything. Voloy Viktor was in his suite on the top floor, but then something happened."

"What?"

"I saw someone. . . ."

Vango was waiting.

"I saw someone, and after that I wasn't sure about anything anymore."

"Who was it?"

"You don't know him. The elevator stopped a floor too soon, on the eighty-fourth floor. The door opened. I was armed to the teeth. A man was standing there, waiting. When I saw him, I realized I wouldn't get Viktor that day."

"Tell me his name."

Zefiro wavered.

"He works with Superintendent Boulard, in Paris. . . . His name is Augustin Avignon. I realized that he too was going to visit Voloy Viktor, or that he'd just come from visiting him."

Vango recognized the name. Ethel had mentioned Avignon.

Zefiro gathered his thoughts for a few minutes before continuing.

"The elevator door closed between us. Avignon stayed there, petrified, on the landing. He recognized me; I'm sure of that. I blocked the elevator twenty centimeters before reaching Viktor's floor. He was holding a meeting in the reception room opposite the elevator door. I could hear his voice. But the door never opened. I went back down the eighty-five floors and tidied up my heavy artillery. A kid on the street was acting as my lookout. He hung around in the days that followed.

According to him, Voloy Viktor's protection was increased tenfold the next day."

"So . . ."

"Avignon must have spoken to Viktor. He's on their side. The right hand of Superintendent Boulard is a traitor. I'd had a premonition of this for some time."

"Does Boulard know?"

"Boulard? I couldn't set off back to Paris. I wrote to him, explaining everything. I can only hope that my message reached him."

Zefiro was watching the illuminated building. The curtain of rain could be seen in the floodlights.

"If I'd run the risk of dying that evening, Avignon would have carried on causing destruction. Now I know how Viktor managed to escape from us so many times. Avignon was never far away."

"Did you try anything else?"

"No. Three days later, Voloy Viktor left New York. I've been waiting for him to return, until this morning."

The rain was falling more heavily now.

"I had another plan to catch Viktor. And it might have worked. But it would have been dreadfully expensive. . . ."

Zefiro started laughing. The gulls were back, flying close to the scaffolding.

"I've always believed I needed very little to live on, Vango, but this time I've got nothing left at all. I couldn't even go back home if I wanted to."

The monk took a copper coin out of his pocket, big as a shirt button, and put it on the back of his hand.

"I haven't got enough to feed the birds."

He tossed the coin high in front of him. The seagulls swooped down and disappeared into the night with it.

"Come over to the fire, Padre."

Zefiro turned around sharply, as if waking up. On seeing the void below him, he started. Slowly, he crouched down on the beam and made his way back toward Vango.

"Voloy Viktor. In the end, he's all I can think about," said Zefiro. "What will become of me when my enemy is no longer here?"

He glanced down at the street, three hundred meters below them.

"What about you, Vango?"

The young man took the older man by the hand and helped him reach the floor again. Zefiro sighed as he looked at Vango.

"Our anger is propping us both up. What are we going to do afterward?"

Vango didn't know what to say. It was a fair point: how would life look afterward?

They drew close to the fire. Gigantic iron letters were waiting to be fixed onto the facade. Vango made his bed under the arch of the letter *A*. Zefiro lay down under two upside down *L*s that formed a roof over him.

One day, these letters would spell out a name above the city. Every tower in Manhattan was a monument to the glory of a different man. Some years earlier, an ordinary mechanic from Kansas, by the name of Walter Chrysler, had built a tower that was nearly three hundred meters tall, in order to remind the world that he had reached the pinnacle of success in less than twenty years. A forest of stone and brick was rising up in New York, born out of such legends.

A light wind blew through the wooden scaffolding. Zefiro had been asleep for some time. The embers were reflected in his steel shelter. The fire in the brazier had almost gone out. Night masked the padre's face.

On hands and knees, someone crept up on the monk. But before the person could lunge forward, something sharp slid across his throat.

"Don't move," hissed Zefiro, opening his eyes. Sitting up, he saw that his assailant was none other than Vango.

The padre was still holding the piece of sharpened zinc against his friend's neck.

"Don't creep up on me like that in the dark. What do you want?"

"Your plan for Viktor, is it really going to cost all that much?"

"Yes, little one, so go back to sleep."

"How much?"

"Leave me in peace."

Vango unclenched one fist.

"Would this be enough?"

In the flat of his hand lay four rubies, as big as chickpeas.

THE TROUBLE WITH DEER

At the same time, across the Atlantic, Everland, Scotland

Day was breaking. There was a spotless golden doe with bewitching eyes in the kitchen. She was lapping milk from a large salad bowl, the white droplets clinging to her eyelashes. She didn't notice the castle staff coming and going as the morning spectacle was played out.

Andrei was watching her enviously as he sat on a chair in the corner of the kitchen. Mary had made him take off his shoes before quarantining him among the copper pots and pans. He had gone away for six months only to appear again, without warning, at dawn. He knew he wouldn't receive a warm welcome.

"I want to work again. I want to speak with Master Paul."

But Ethel's brother hadn't been at home for several weeks.

So Mary the housekeeper had made Andrei sit down before giving him a good scolding and taking his jacket from him to wash it.

"I'm going to clean this right away," she had insisted, "because you certainly won't be staying. I'll see later on whether anyone is prepared to talk to you. But even if they are, Andrew, I wouldn't like to be in your shoes."

Lily the doe had come to drink close by, and Mary had asked Andrei to keep an eye on her.

"She mustn't go upstairs. They get up to such nonsense in this house. At Christmas, there was a horse tied to the piano on the second floor."

Andrei didn't take his eyes off Lily. He wasn't simply envious of the milk she sent splashing with each lick of her tongue. He envied her freedom, a good simple life, innocence, and the kindness that surrounded her.

Andrei, on the other hand, could sense the jaws of a trap about to slam shut on him. He was thinking of his family in Moscow, who would pay with their lives for what he was doing: his little brother, his sister, his mother, and Ivan Ivanovitch, his father, who had so badly wanted him to follow in his footsteps and become a mechanic. And he was thinking of the terrible Vlad the Vulture, and how his eyes were like two blades pressing into the back of his neck. Andrei was there to find Vango and hand him over to Vlad.

Mary had disappeared into the depths of the castle. Andrei watched Lily knock over the bowl with her muzzle and finish lapping up the milk from the flagstones. She politely wiped herself clean using her hoof in place of a linen napkin, then raised her head and made for the kitchen door.

"Lily!"

Andrei wasn't sure if he was allowed to get up.

"Lily, come here!"

Apparently, the deer didn't understand his Russian accent. She disappeared behind the door.

Andrei ran after her. Together, they crossed two small sitting rooms and a study lined with books. The cool May air wafted in through the open windows. There were triangles of sunlight on the bare wooden floors. The carpets had been draped over the windowsills. Every morning, Everland Castle yawned and stretched from head to toe.

Little Lily was capering around in this kingdom. She was sliding over the oak thresholds, polished to within an inch of their lives. Andrei had fallen behind while putting his shoes back on. He was walking on tiptoes now and calling out to her in hushed tones, constantly turning around for fear of being caught by Mary.

His first assignment on his return to Everland was to guard this deer. And he would do whatever it took.

Andrei slowed down when he saw Lily stop near a pedestal table with a small box on it.

"There you are!" he said. "Come here!"

She looked at him with all the freedom and innocence he had been admiring a few minutes earlier.

"Come here, Lily, Lilishka."

Three meters away from her, he found himself smiling stupidly and holding out his hand. But Lily raised the lid of the box with a nudge of her head and delicately removed three cigars, which she began to chew. Andrei bit his lip. The lid slid shut. Clearly, Lily had her habits. A bowl of milk and three Havana cigars for breakfast. The good life.

Suddenly, she sped off again and came out into the hall.

By the time Andrei arrived, he could see in a flash that the morning constitutional wasn't over yet. The doe was standing in front of the flight of stairs leading up to the second floor. It was a grand staircase with a thick carpet cascading down it in an irresistible red. With the final cigar poking out from her mouth, Lily gave Andrei a satisfied look before starting to climb the stairs. She seemed to be on familiar terrain, reaching the landing in just a few bounds.

Andrei hesitated before following suit. Wouldn't he be better off going back into the kitchen to find Mary, asking for her help and sobbing into her skirts? Lily must have sensed this sudden indecision, and put an end to such ideas by grazing on the golden tassels hanging off the curtains, causing Andrei to gasp in horror. He went after her again.

Lily had ventured onto the main landing. She slowed down a little in front of each window, to bask in the warmth of the sun. Her golden fur rippled on her flanks. She raised her head and half-closed her eyes. She looked cozy enough to go to sleep then and there. But each time, a mysterious call made her set off again. At the end of the landing, after sniffing the air one last time, she pushed open a door and disappeared.

Andrei remained behind the half-open door. He knew that this escapade was madness. But in the worst moments of folly, there always comes a point where turning back is more risky than carrying on.

So Andrei carried on.

He pushed open the door without even thinking, and went one step too far.

The scene that met his eyes in the large bedroom could have been depicted in a classical painting. The deer was curled up on the carpet, in a circle of sunlight, at the foot of a blue-silk window seat. And on that window seat were two young people, a girl and a boy, their shoulders touching, staring at the animal whose sudden appearance must have taken them by surprise.

47

But Andrei startled them. The boy pulled hastily away from the young woman, gathered up the papers that were lying all around them, and stood back. He was blushing terribly. The girl stared calmly at the newcomer in icy disbelief.

"I'm sorry," muttered Andrei. "I'm sorry. I'm sorry."

His lips kept on moving, as if repeating the same words until they were worn out.

Ethel didn't even get up. She was wearing suspenders that were slightly undone over a white shirt teamed with an old pair of tweed trousers, and she was barefoot. There was a blue silk band around her wrist.

Andrei looked at the boy, who seemed to be trying to hide the papers he had just picked up. He was the son of Peter, one of the gardeners at Everland. Nicholas was slightly younger than Andrei, and a lot younger than Ethel, who was nearly twenty.

But what astonished Andrei even more than this scene was what was going on inside him. Behind the fear, Andrei could feel a sort of anger, an all-consuming, invisible anger, something he hadn't experienced for a long time. For once, he wasn't just trembling because he was afraid; he was trembling with thirst and hunger and rage. He was jealous. And, in a split second, Ethel became more mysterious than ever, and beautiful enough to die for.

He was frozen to the spot.

Ethel seemed disinclined to turn on the charm for him. She looked weary. Her eyes didn't focus but slid across him, as if Andrei didn't really exist.

"What are you doing here?"

"I was looking for the deer," he ventured in his hesitant English.

He pointed to Lily.

"I'm disturbing you," he added.

"Why do you say that?"

"I thought you . . ."

"What makes you think you're disturbing anyone?"

He gestured toward the window seat, and then at Nicholas.

When his eyes met those of the gardener's son, he felt the urge to fight. Andrei had never enjoyed fighting. On his tenth birthday, to encourage him to give up his violin, his parents had sent him to learn the Russian martial art of sambo in a Moscow gym. But he had spent ten months on the bench, listening to the words of Master Ochtchepkov.

He took a deep breath.

"Where have you come from?" Ethel wanted to know.

"The corridor."

"Before that?"

"The staircase."

"Before that?"

"The kitchen."

She gave up and glanced at young Nicholas next to her. Ethel smiled, while the gardener's son looked distraught. Unlike him, she didn't feel embarrassed in the slightest. She didn't care what other people thought. No, Andrei alarmed her for more serious reasons.

"You think that you can just walk into my bedroom one morning . . ."

"I want to work."

"And what about when I had ten horses in the loose boxes this winter, with all their straw to be transported; you didn't want to work then?"

"I was with my parents."

He's lying, she thought instantly. But she could also tell that the word "parents" rang true: there was the same pain in his voice that there would have been in hers.

"I'd like to speak with Master Paul."

"Me too," she answered back. "I'd like that very much."

She stood up, and Lily the doe got up at the same time.

"But Master Paul isn't here." She sighed. "Go downstairs. Wait for me there."

Andrei left the bedroom. The way back felt very different, and not just because the doe was following him this time.

Nothing panned out the way he had been expecting.

Andrei didn't see Ethel again for a while, but he was given back his old bedroom next to the stables, where there was only one horse left. Mary made Andrei eat his lunch at eleven o'clock at the big staff table, before everyone else, like a naughty boy. In the afternoon, he saw Nicholas heading off in the direction of the lake. An hour later, he was asked to saddle the horse and tether it near the tower. At sunset, a slender figure could be seen galloping toward the lake. Andrei recognized Ethel. For a long time, he watched her disappearing into the distance.

Toward eleven o'clock that evening, he heard the sound of hooves on cobbles. He got up and went outside. He had left a light on in front of the stables, beneath which Ethel was unfastening her horse's girth. She saw him and looked away, with a peculiar smile on her face. When Andrei tried to help her, she was so lost in her thoughts that she nearly collided with him.

Again, Andrei felt that troubling sense of anger gaining hold of him. What was she thinking about? Or whom? And where had she just come from?

He left her to her own devices and went back inside the stables.

"For as long as Paul's away, you can stay here. I'll let you know when I need you. Paul will decide your fate once he gets back," declared Ethel, who had just entered the building.

Andrei nodded.

She went over to him and tilted his chin a little, so as to pin the Russian with her gaze.

"I'm keeping a close eye on you. I've never understood why you're here."

It was then, as he looked up, that he saw something on the band tied around her wrist: in the middle of the blue silk that shone in the light was the letter *V* and a saffron-colored star.

He knew that she had seen Vango again.

Paris, rue Jacob, at the same time

"It's him."

When Madame Boulard heard the knocking at the door, she put her knitting down on her lap.

"It's your Professor Rasputin."

The arrival of this visitor always set her on edge. Why couldn't he use the nice new doorbell that she'd had fitted?

"Don't call him Rasputin," said Auguste Boulard. "And

anyway, you can go to bed now, Mother. We'll be working in the dining room."

Superintendent Boulard went into the hall and opened the door.

"My dear fellow, you're right on time. As always."

It was the stroke of midnight. Vlad the Vulture was standing before the detective on the threshold.

The old parquet groaned as they made their way into the dining room. Superintendent Boulard went to draw the curtain across the glazed door separating them from the sitting room. Through one of the panes, he gave his mother, who had stayed in her armchair, a forced smile. The curtain closed.

Marie-Antoinette Boulard immediately put her knitting to one side. She was about to turn eighty-seven, and nobody was going to make her swallow tall stories.

These Russian lessons had worried her from day one. It had all begun back in March with the sudden arrival of Vlad. He had entered the apartment without warning, holding a metal bar in one hand, while the superintendent was enjoying his bath. Boulard had eventually gotten out of his soapy water and, after a stunned silence, had politely led Vlad into the dining room for a chat. He had emerged an hour later in the company of his visitor, who was, as he explained to his mother, his Russian teacher.

"Russian?"

"Yes, Russian."

"But . . . why Russian?"

"Because . . ."

Boulard attempted a Slavic dance step.

"Russian is interesting," declared the superintendent, who was still wrapped in his damp towel.

"And this gentleman is really a Russian teacher?"

"Vlad?"

"Yes."

"The best."

Vlad looked more like a butcher from the taiga. In his big hairy beard, Madame Boulard could see a resemblance to the photos of the terrible monk Rasputin, tales of whom had made the rounds twenty-five years earlier.

And now, for the fourth time in two months, Rasputin was here, in the next-door room. She could hear the sound of muffled voices. Madame Boulard tiptoed over to the door and pressed her ear to it.

What she could hear sounded like gibberish for the most part, but she thought she could make out the word "revolution." Just then, there was a scuffling noise in the hall-way. She rushed over to the door.

"Who is it?"

"It's me."

The door opened to reveal Blanche Dussac, the concierge of the building.

"Well?"

"Rasputin's here."

"I saw him go past my office," said the concierge. "Do you need any help?"

Madame Dussac revealed that she was hiding a carving fork in her nightie.

"Not yet. Don't intervene yet. I'll tell you when."

"Are there any new leads?"

Blanche Dussac was tantalized by this gripping story. She had climbed up the ranks from confidante to Madame Boulard's right-hand woman.

"He was talking about a revolution."

"Jesus wept! It's political."

"My son doesn't get involved in politics."

"Marie-Antoinette, do you really know your son?"

This was the first time the concierge had called Madame Boulard by her first name.

"I couldn't say, these days," admitted the superintendent's mother with a little sob.

"Where there are Russians involved, it's always political."

"Heavens above!"

"We need to warn the police."

"But my son *is* the police."

"Yes. Good point. Right."

"Let's wait. Next time, I'll hide in the dining room sideboard. Go back to your apartment now, Madame Dussac. I'll pop by to see you tomorrow."

An emotional Blanche Dussac gave the superintendent's mother a hug.

"Be brave. And take this. No, really, I insist, just to be on the safe side. You never know. But I need it back before Sunday; I've got my niece coming for lunch."

The intrepid Blanche Dussac headed back downstairs, leaving the carving fork in her friend's hands.

There were noises coming from the adjoining room. Madame Boulard rushed back to her armchair and picked up her knitting again. Vlad the Vulture and the superintendent appeared briefly, and then the front door slammed shut.

It was half past midnight. Madame Boulard could hear her son in the kitchen boiling the water for his hot-water bottle. He came back into the sitting room.

"Why aren't you in bed, Mother?"

"I don't feel sleepy."

Boulard noticed that she hadn't gotten very far with her knitting in the past half hour: she was still on exactly the same stripe of that woolen hat.

What had she been doing during their interview?

He screwed up his eyes. The superintendent was even suspicious of his own mother. In fact, he was feeling so confused that he thought he had just seen a pretty blond girl on the gutter in front of the window. He wiped his hand across his face. And why not pink elephants, too? He was worn out.

"I'm going to bed, Mother."

Before he disappeared, Madame Boulard challenged her son. "Auguste! How do you say 'good evening' in Russian?"

He didn't answer.

ON THE RIDGE OF A GLACIER

On the rooftops of Paris

The pretty blonde was the Cat.

She made her way around the tiled edge of the roof before jumping over a small courtyard and crossing a sort of zinc terrace that, in the dark, looked like it was twinkling with quartzes. Leaning over the other side, she saw Vlad turning onto the rue de l'Échaudé.

The Cat avoided a series of skylights with the lights on. She flanked one of those gardens in captivity, hemmed in by apartment blocks. She often thought about the animals that lived there as her neighbors, unaware that the rest of the world, with its grasslands and forests, even existed. The Cat spotted Vlad again at the bottom of the street, which looked like a canyon from her vantage point. She crossed the rue Visconti via the electric cables, conscious that from this point the route was impassable. So she let Vlad move out of sight while she dropped down onto the rue des Beaux-Arts.

The Cat ventured along the pavement, but the Vulture had disappeared. She ran as far as the Seine before retracing her steps. Vlad wasn't fast enough to have disappeared in a matter of seconds. And no car could have driven him away. So he must have gone inside somewhere.

Just then, the Cat noticed a metal shutter half pulled down

over a shop front. It belonged to a small café that wasn't quite closed yet: students and vultures were still being served. One glance revealed that Vlad was at the bar. Drink was the only thing that had the upper hand on Vlad. The tyrant became a slave when he could smell a glass of clear alcohol from a long way off.

The Cat found an old carriage entrance where she could sit in the shadow. For the first time, she had been able to hear everything that was said between Superintendent Boulard and the Vulture. Usually, the dining room window was shut. The Cat would be stuck on the gutter without understanding anything. When the frustration got to be too much, she would go to watch Boulard's mother starring in a drama of her own making, as she played the spy in her bathrobe, egged on by the concierge.

This time, Paris was basking in the balmy May air, and the window had been left open. The Cat hadn't missed a word. The conversation had proved very different from what she had been expecting.

She had always assumed that Boulard paid Vlad to carry out the dirty assignments he couldn't entrust to his regular police officers. This theory explained everything: the Vulture's visits to Boulard at home, the fact that they were both equally motivated to find Vango. . . .

In the Cat's eyes, Boulard was the mastermind. Even handsome Andrei was under his thumb. They were all relentlessly on the hunt for Vango, the murderer of Father Jean at the Carmelite seminary one April night in 1934.

But the truth, which the Cat had heard this evening, was much less straightforward. Boulard had lost control of the situation. The Vulture had him in his claws and was playing with him. Quite simply, he was using Superintendent Boulard and the French police in order to find Vango. He was helping himself to this world-renowned support for free.

The Cat had taken several minutes to grasp the terms of the blackmail. What kind of pressure could have gotten the better of the incorruptible Superintendent Boulard?

At one moment, in the dining room mirror, as she leaned in a bit, the Cat had seen the Vulture grabbing hold of a cake cutter and hurling it across the room. It had stuck in the heart of the pretty peasant girl painted on a small canvas.

"Mother!" Boulard had gasped.

And it was indeed possible to recognize his mother, seventy years younger, in front of an Aveyron inn. Her portrait had been painted by one Uncle Albert, who had moved to Paris to become an artist in the 1870s, and with whom the young Auguste Boulard had lodged when he had arrived in the capital to study law.

It was the only painting they had left by Uncle Albert. It was called *Nénette at Aubrac*. With Vlad watching, Boulard had rushed over to unhook the lacerated painting and hide it under the sideboard. The mark left behind by the frame was like a ghost on the wall.

The Vulture's action explained everything. The terms of the blackmail were set as Madame Boulard's life. If the son didn't cooperate, the Vulture would exact his revenge on the mother.

The Cat hadn't found out much more. Boulard seemed weary of the situation. He had tried explaining to the Vulture that his lines of investigation hadn't amounted to anything. He had reissued the description of a wanted person to every town in France. He had even alerted embassies abroad. The chief of police had expressed surprise at the investigation being reopened two years on. Boulard had needed to convince his superiors that another recent murder might also be attributable to Vango.

"I'm short staffed," he had explained to Vlad the Vulture. "My loyal deputy is suffering from a few health problems at the moment. He's been out sick rather a lot these past few months. Be patient."

Patient? Vlad didn't know the meaning of the word. He had about as much patience as a lit fuse at the end of a bundle of dynamite. Under her archway on the rue de Seine, in front of the little café where three art students from the Beaux-Arts were waving their theatrical farewells, the Cat, as she often did, turned her thoughts to Andrei.

Months earlier she had witnessed the meeting in the snow between Vlad the Vulture and Andrei, in the knowledge that Vlad had come to kill the young student. Hidden above them, the Cat had come close to calling out and throwing herself off her perch in order to save Andrei. But from the outset the meeting had taken a different direction.

Andrei had spoken very quickly. He claimed that he had a lead, that he was finally going to see some results, that nobody should touch a hair on the heads of his brother or his little sister back in Moscow. The thick snow blotted out the echo of Andrei's voice as he repeated the two children's names: Kostia and Zoya.

The Cat could picture Andrei so clearly, his violin case

pressed against his body, swearing he would find Vango as quickly as possible. By some miracle, the Vulture had been convinced.

And she remembered how, perched up on her rooftop, she had chosen to follow Vlad rather than Andrei a few seconds later, because that was where the threat lay: the man with a bloody knife hidden in his pocket, not the boy with the pleading eyes. And yet she wished she could have followed Andrei, to have become his shadow and never left him. On the sweet trail of the person she loved, who had no idea that she even existed.

But since that day, she hadn't set eyes on him again.

The sound of the students' voices petered out, and the Vulture left the café. The way he zigzagged across the Pont des Arts reassured the Cat. There was no chance of him disappearing into the night. She followed him as far as his hotel, behind La Samaritaine department store. He woke up the receptionist by kicking the front desk, then grabbed his keys and disappeared into the stairwell.

He was deep in his cups and wouldn't move before midday. One strike of a match and the Vulture would have gone up in flames like a Christmas pudding.

It took the Cat only five minutes to reach the Louvre. She slipped through the iron railings of the Jardin des Tuileries and sought the cover of the linden trees, which, at night, could have been mistaken for a fairy-tale forest. The park warden and his lamp were visible in the distance as he did his rounds with a dog on a leash. But the animal didn't pick up on the scent of the Cat in the middle of all those sweet springtime smells. One more flower wasn't going to make a dog bark.

* * *

She arrived back home at two o'clock in the morning and entered through the front door so as not to wake her two pigeons, who were asleep on the gutter.

"Emilie."

She stopped on the third step of the staircase. The chandelier was suddenly switched on. Her father was standing above her on the second floor. He was in evening attire, involving layers of vest and jacket, as well as a gray cape edged with silk. He let go of the light switch and walked over to the balustrade. With his top hat and gloves in his left hand, he waved at the Cat.

"Emilie . . ."

She held on to the banisters and kept climbing slowly. Her father sat down on the top step. He put his hat down on the carpet. Was a white rabbit about to appear out of it?

"Could you come and sit down here for a minute?"

His voice sounded weak.

The Cat sighed and crouched where she was, a few steps lower down. For several months now, her father had been a changed man. He had come to a stop.

For years, she had only ever seen him standing still in the large painting in the drawing room, with his slim mustache and the lion skin at his feet. And even in that painting, he held a watch attached to a gold chain in one hand, and was staring intently at it.

For years, he had only blown through her life like the wind. He would leave her visiting cards on the dresser in the entrance hall with a command scribbled on them. *Sleep. Eat. Obey.* The year when she had been sick, he had sent two words to the sanatorium where she was convalescing: *Get better!*

To begin with, she stored his visiting cards safely away in a box. They were always exactly the same: *Ferdinand Atlas,* with five or six different addresses around the world, so that no one would ever find him. And those scrawled commands: *Work. Stop. Love your mother.*

And then one day, without warning, when life had begun to take a different turn for him, he had started speaking in whole sentences, and even saying Emilie's name, saying it over and over again, when it no longer meant anything to the Cat.

Because for her, it was too late.

He could smile at her, he could reach for her hand in her pocket, he could smoke her out with kisses on her forehead, with the whiff of tobacco in his scarves, he could talk to her in never-ending phrases, he could show his open wounds, and even prostrate himself at her feet like a lion skin. But none of it would do any good.

Right now, she was the one, on the staircase, who seemed to be looking at her watch, impatient for all this to be over.

"I'd like to take you somewhere with your mother," he said. "I want to leave with the two of you. I've finished. I've done what I wanted to do. We need to leave quickly and find a refuge. Your mother won't accept that our time is over."

The Cat had heard all this before.

"Your mother wants to stay here. She doesn't want to start over again."

When his daughter didn't reply, Ferdinand Atlas asked her, "What about you?"

The Cat got up and climbed the remaining stairs. She gave

her father a wide berth, like a ship avoiding the reefs beneath the calm surface of the sea.

Ferdinand Atlas remained sitting on the top step. He felt a hand on his shoulder. His daughter gave him a peck on the cheek. He closed his eyes.

In her bedroom, the Cat half-opened the curtains to look at her pigeons. They were sleeping, resting against each other. She threw her clothes into a pile at the foot of a chair, put a record on the phonograph, and wrapped the horn in a towel to muffle the sound. She hesitated for a moment and looked out her window again, before finally lying down in her own bed. Her bed! She had been doing this rather a lot recently. It made her feel old, after years of sleeping only in a hammock on the roof.

The record was a piece of violin music.

Andrei had never said where he had gone, or where the lead was that he was following. She was afraid that he would find Vango before she did. But she was also afraid that he might never find him. Because if Andrei didn't complete his mission, Vlad wouldn't give him a second chance. What was Andrei's family like, back in Moscow? His little brother, Kostia; his sister, Zoya . . .

A few days later in Moscow, May 1936

"Are you hungry?"

It was a fine day. Mademoiselle led both children by the hand, up the steps to the Central Post Office. Konstantin and Zoya were wearing their school uniform smocks with no overcoats.

"We'll go to the park afterward. This will only take a minute. Look——"

Mademoiselle kept glancing anxiously all around her. And talking to the children without drawing breath: "Look how many steps there are! Kostia, pull your trousers up. I used to come here in the old days. You weren't even born then. I just want to see how much it's changed."

She had hidden the letter inside Zoya's pocket. Mademoiselle felt ashamed of taking advantage of this little girl to carry her secrets. She thought of seven-year-old drummer boys sent onto the battlefield to cross the enemy lines.

Mademoiselle had been living with the Oulanov family for a year and a half now. Her abductors had taken her from Sicily to Moscow, with no explanation.

As she walked into the Central Post Office, with its great row of booths, she stopped and held her breath. She was remembering the last time she had come here, to visit this hall the size of a railway station. That memory was over twenty years old now. But it had been the turning point of her life, the event that had led her to Vango.

Back then, she used to teach French and English to children in a family in Saint Petersburg. There were six children. The job had lasted only a few months. She was young, and she had been summarily dismissed: accused of trying to seduce the master of the house.

One evening, she had cooked him a meal when the rest of the family, including the governesses and cooks, had already gone to the country house for the summer.

The family's town house on the banks of the Neva River was deserted.

The wife had returned unexpectedly and seen the table laid for one, a small portable stove, and, in a cooking pot, a bewitching recipe that was as dusky as it was intoxicating.

"What is *that,* Mademoiselle?"

"It's for Monsieur. He comes back late at night. He never eats."

"What is *that?*" the wife had repeated.

"I thought . . ."

But the wife's shouting became louder and louder.

"What is *that?*"

An extraordinary smell wafted from the half-open lid. The sauce was simmering. The meat was rising to the surface of this magic potion. Sometimes, when a passing breeze blew the flame, the bubbling made the sound of a kiss. A white cloud floated over the edge of the pot.

A few centuries earlier, Mademoiselle would have been burned at the stake for cooking such a meal. But on this occasion she was put out on the street with her suitcases. And her beef bourguignon was thrown onto the cyclamen at the bottom of the garden.

She had first caught a train to Moscow, where, in 1915, she had found herself in transit in this same post office with a letter announcing her hasty return to an aged aunt who represented the only family she had left in France. The boy at the booth had sold her the stamps and pointed to the mailbox on the other side of the hall. She had hidden behind her handkerchief to hide how upset she was.

It was at that moment that he had come over. He had appeared as if by magic. He was wearing a red Cossack scarf and a woolen jacket.

"Are you French?"

Mademoiselle didn't dare reply. She hadn't yet let go of the letter for her aged aunt: the envelope was halfway through the slot.

"I heard you speaking Russian."

"Yes."

"And can you speak other languages as well?"

"Yes."

"Which ones?"

"A few."

The man was about the same age as she was. Mademoiselle tried to stand tall and proud to distract from her eyes, which were puffy from crying. But slowly she withdrew her envelope.

"Would you like to work?" he said.

She took another step backward and checked that her hat was firmly fixed on her head.

"Why?"

Her cautiousness was an effort. This man only inspired confidence.

"It would be to look after a child."

"In Moscow?"

"No, somewhere else. I don't know where. He's not born yet."

The man's eyes were shining.

She raised her chin proudly.

At first, she had feared this might be an indecent proposal. But his smile reassured her once again.

"Mademoiselle, please, if you would care to come with me . . ."

"Don't you want to ask any other questions of the person you're hiring?"

"No."

She pretended to deliberate. But she knew that her employer in Paris, from before Saint Petersburg, had died the year before. Nobody was expecting her. It was 1915, and France had been at war for months now.

"Please," said the man.

Without realizing it, she had already put the letter for her aged aunt back into her bag. He picked up her suitcases, and she caught the train with him to Odessa, where they boarded a boat sailing for Constantinople. They disembarked at night. Mademoiselle couldn't understand what was happening to her. Two sailors were waiting for them with a lamp. The war was raging on distant coasts. A long boat carried them from the port toward another boat lying at anchor farther out.

Suddenly, the man made the oarsmen stop and listen.

Mademoiselle had heard something too. Behind the sound of the dripping oars, above the hubbub of the old city of Stamboul, the cry of a newborn baby could be heard coming from the lit-up boat.

They looked at each other.

That was Vango's first cry.

Now that she had entered the same busy post office twenty-one years later, with Kostia and Zoya clinging to her skirts, Mademoiselle kept expecting the man in the Cossack scarf to appear behind her at any moment.

But times had changed, and the world was no longer the

same. The secrets in the letter she was trying to post weren't intended for an aged aunt.

Once more, she headed toward the large mailboxes that had been expecting her for more than two decades.

"A stamp for Italy," she murmured to the post office worker.

She had changed trams three times with the children, to make sure she wasn't being followed. The little girl's feet were starting to hurt. Mademoiselle kept spinning around to check whether anyone was watching her.

By leaning forward from time to time, she could see the edge of the envelope at the bottom of Zoya's pocket. Would this letter come to rest, one day, on the table of the good Doctor Basilio, between the fig trees and the black rock of the Aeolian Islands?

There was a note for Basilio inside, and another envelope, smaller but thicker, addressed to Vango.

If he's looking for me, if you see him, Doctor, if he passes by his island again, give him these five pages, which I enclose. It's very important. It contains everything I would have liked to tell him. And what about you, Basilio? How are you getting on? As for me, I'm well. I've been given some children to look after. They're wonderful. Without them, I'd have grown weary of living. And there you have it. Spring is in the air here. I don't know if I'll see you again, Basilio, but I think about you. Being far away from our home makes me feel rather differently about things.

There wasn't much else in the letter to the doctor, but

already, for the first time in eighteen years, she had referred to the island as *their* home.

"I want to go home, *Tioten'ka.*"

The little girl was looking at her.

"Yes, my sweetheart, we'll go home."

At last, they were in front of the mailbox with its brass mouth.

She reached over to Zoya's school smock.

"I popped something in there; stand still a moment."

Sliding two fingers inside the little girl's pocket, Mademoiselle grabbed hold of the envelope.

She felt a hand lock on to her arm.

"Don't do it, Mademoiselle."

She turned around.

"They're watching you. They're behind the glass in the booths, or else in the gallery, up there. Don't do it. Or they'll send you to Siberia."

Time stopped for a moment. A man was standing in front of her: the father of Zoya, Kostia, and Andrei.

"Please, Mademoiselle. If I'd allowed you to go through with it, I would have been condemning both of us."

She let go of the letter in Zoya's pocket. The children threw themselves at the man's legs.

"Daddy!"

The man hugged them tightly, while still talking to Mademoiselle.

"As long as they're sure I'm watching over you, they'll let you live with us. Don't try anything else in this vein. My older son, Andrei, is abroad. They're playing us off against each other. I was asked to keep you in my home. I've got no idea what you've done, but our lives, and the life of my son, have been linked for nearly two years now."

Mademoiselle knew that she slept in Andrei's bedroom, beneath his childhood drawings. She had seen a photo of him, tucked inside the accounts book. She knew that his family was worried about him. But she had never made any connection between her own fate and that of the serious-looking boy in the white-framed photo, his cheek against his violin.

"Come on."

The children held their father's hands.

Mademoiselle followed them.

They emerged into the bright May sunshine, at the top of the steps, and clung to one another as they made their way down, slowly, like mountain climbers linked by a rope on the ridge of a glacier.

LAST WORDS ON DEATH ROW

New York, summer 1936

History books don't account for what happened during the summer of 1936 on one of the most important construction sites in Manhattan. But building work on a tower was interrupted for several months. It all started in the spring, when one of the workers fell from the top. There was nothing unusual about this—dozens of similar accidents occurred every year—but it turned out that the victim was a Mohawk, forced to work on the construction site against his will. Out of solidarity, the other men laid down their tools for several days.

The morning they were due to return to work, the men had discovered mysterious inscriptions on the walls as well as up the service stairs. Incomprehensible graffiti had been painted in red letters, as tall as a fully grown man. It was a sinister sight.

ERAT AUTEM TERRA . . .

University linguists were summoned to the premises by the police. An elderly Latin specialist set to work.

He was able to decipher passages from the Bible. First of all, there were nine verses about the Tower of Babel, taken from Genesis. They spoke of mankind's desire to build a tower that would reach to the heavens. And of how God had managed to stop them. There was also a line in Greek taken from Revelation, in which an angel sounded his trumpet, "And there followed hail and fire mingled with blood, and they were cast down upon the earth."

In the wake of the Mohawk's death, the workers were frightened by all these signs. On the top floor, in the middle of one of the rooms, they had found the name RAFAELLO spelled out using eight of the nine letters intended for the illuminated sign above the tower.

Some of the men had recognized the name of the archangel Raphael, one of the soldiers of God: perhaps he was the angel referred to in the line from Revelation painted in bloodred letters. The workers revolted again.

Access to the work site was forbidden, pending further orders. Above all, the architects wanted to avoid anyone ransacking the building. So the workers were kept at a distance.

One morning, the owner of the tower paid a visit.

He took the freight elevator up to the top floors, with his female assistant and the architects following at his heels. Everybody called him the Irishman. In less than a quarter of a century, he had established a sprawling bank with business interests on both sides of the Atlantic. The rumor was that he had even ended up buying the small hotel where he had arrived as a young migrant.

Now, aged fifty, here he was walking along the scaffolding of his own tower. His many rings glinted as he held on to the girders. There were still at least another three months to go before the great tower would be finished. Staring out through a window frame with no glass in it, the Irishman ate a banana.

Opposite, rising up as if to taunt him, was the Empire State Building, which he had vowed in all the newspapers that his new tower would outstrip. The Irishman gave his banana skin to his assistant. He started laughing loudly when the architect promised to bring all the problems to a speedy resolution. He walked over to him and pretended to push the architect over the edge.

As he was about to leave, the Irishman noticed a pile of damp ashes in a corner.

"Do you have fires here?"

"Never," replied the foreman.

The Irishman bent down to dip his finger in the damp charcoal.

"So what's this?"

He drew a black cross on the foreman's forehead.

"Finish the tower on time."

Then he headed back down again.

His visit did nothing to change the workers' minds.

The first stage of Zefiro's plan could be heralded as a success. His theatrical flourishes had produced the desired results.

That August, Zefiro and Vango were able to set up their equipment at the top of the tower. They had positioned a high-precision telescope on a tripod, pointing at Voloy Viktor's windows. They were equipped with three typewriters, new clothes, and a makeshift office at altitude that was well stocked with rubber stamps, seals, and paper of all kinds. They had sold a ruby to pay for everything.

Tom Jackson, a young beggar from Thirty-Fourth Street, had been recruited for ground missions.

From their observatory, they followed every event in Viktor's daily routine. They noted the comings and goings in minute detail. Their aerial view of the different rooms of the eighty-fifth floor enabled them to keep a log of the times at which the guards were replaced, the regular visitors to the fortified tower, and the frequency of their visits.

Every evening, for example, most of the curtains were drawn, and the last visitor was always an elegant man whom Zefiro referred to as the lawyer. He appeared to address everyone as if he were master of the household. He would settle in the study. The closed curtains prevented them from seeing Voloy Viktor, who must have been dictating his last correspondences of the day to him from his bed. Then the lawyer would leave. But he was the first to return the following morning, at dawn, in time for Madame Victoria getting up. He would not be seen for the rest of the day.

At the end of the month, the first letter left Zefiro's scaffolding and crossed the road, care of Tom Jackson, who was unrecognizable in his attire as a young gentleman. The secret operation had begun.

So as not to be recognized, Tom kept his left hand (on which were tattooed the words "God Bless You") hidden in his pocket: the tattoo contributed to his notoriety across a patch of five streets and three avenues. He crossed the lobby of the Plaza Hotel as if he were thoroughly at home. He had never set foot on the marble floor before, but had spent his life staring at it through the glass.

Tom Jackson was the only person on Zefiro's payroll. Aged nine, he earned fifty cents per week plus a clothing allowance: a fortune.

Tom drank a glass of seltzer water at the bar, then moved off again, discreetly dropping the letter close to the reception desk. The security guards hadn't recognized him.

A Plaza employee picked up the letter and handed it over to the receptionist. Stamped with a European postmark, it was addressed to the occupant of the suite on the eighty-fifth floor. That same evening, it was presented to Dorgeles, who in turn gave it to Madame Victoria.

From their observatory, Zefiro and Vango watched the reaction to their letter. A meeting was instantly convened. That night, a dozen men in dark suits gathered in the main reception room of Voloy Viktor's suite. These men got out of their cars, posted vigilantes in the streets, and disappeared behind the Plaza's doors to reappear a few minutes later, three hundred meters up in the guest apartments. Zefiro had spotted several of them before in Viktor's entourage.

None of them looked like gangsters. Zefiro recognized a tailor from Brooklyn, a senator, and some businessmen. They were wreathed in cigar smoke.

"Let the show begin!" said Zefiro, with one eye glued to the telescope.

It would take months, but this time he was going to destroy Voloy Viktor. He was convinced of it.

Vango was getting ready to go out.

"See you later, Padre."

"Where are you going?"

The padre didn't like it when Vango ran away like this.

"Don't forget they're watching out for you in town."

"Look at me! Who would recognize me now?"

And sure enough, in the midst of all the rubble, by the

light of the oil lamps, Vango was transformed.

Dressed in a brown suit, his hair slicked back and hat in hand, he swiveled on one foot and grinned. He'd had a pair of small tinted glasses made for him: they were all the rage on Wall Street that summer. Vango didn't even recognize himself.

Ten minutes later, he was heading down Fifth Avenue toward Madison Square.

For the past few weeks, he had spent his nights in the Italian districts of New York. Vango had started with the cafés in the Bronx, combing one after another. Now he had moved on to southern Manhattan, where he had found a few restaurants that rose up like Sicilian islands in the middle of America.

On this particular night, he walked through the door of La Rocca. One of those islands in Little Italy that smelled of capers and bird's-eye chili, La Rocca was tucked behind brightly lit windows on the corner of Grand Street. It was Vango's first visit.

Toward midnight, the restaurant turned into a dive bar. The card players took over, and the lights were dimmed. But there wasn't the usual hushed concentration you might expect to find in a gaming room. The chef did the rounds of the tables serving parcels of delicious pastry, stuffed with pungent sausage meat, that oozed cheese when he sliced them on the board. The restaurant was noisy, and the backyard was filling up with empty bottles.

Vango settled over by the bar. He put his hat down beside him. There were only men in the room, apart from a young woman who stayed behind the stronghold of her bar.

She was permanently on the move, going from the serving hatch to the storeroom door. One moment she was on tiptoes trying to reach the bottles, the next she had disappeared, crouched down by the ramparts. It was as if she were performing a dance.

Vango thought of Ethel, whose eyes also landed on things deeply but fleetingly, like tiny daggers that were immediately withdrawn.

Recalling Ethel's gaze made him brush his fingers against the note in his pocket, which he had received from her a few days earlier. Three cold lines telling him to bide his time, not to return to Scotland without warning her, and making it clear that she was busy. Little daggers.

Vango didn't need to beckon the waitress. She shouted something he couldn't understand.

"What d'you want?" she repeated, moving in closer.

"I'm waiting for someone."

She had called him Lupacchiotto, which means little wolf. And Vango did look like one of the young wolves that roamed New York, hoping to seize their chance.

He was sitting near the sink. He knew that she would be back, sooner or later, to rinse the piled-up glasses. For now, she was filling five glasses from a bottle with no label. It was once again legal for bars to sell alcohol, after the bootleggers had thrived on fifteen years of Prohibition.

The waitress put one of the glasses in front of Vango. He hadn't ordered anything, but she slid it toward him. The manager came for the tray that was loaded up with the four other glasses. There were cheers on the other side for a win at *briscola* or poker.

"I'm looking for someone called Giovanni," Vango announced.

The waitress, who had started washing the glasses, glanced up to take a good look at him.

"Giovanni? Half my suitors are called Giovanni. So is my father, and my grandfather too."

"Giovanni Cafarello."

With her forearm, she pushed away a lock of hair from her eyes and stared at him.

"Cafarello?"

"Yes."

"Cafarello . . ."

She stopped and dried her hands. Her black eye makeup gave her a slightly older appearance, but she couldn't be more than eighteen. She shook her head slowly.

"Is that who you're waiting for? Cafarello?"

Vango felt his fingers tightening around his glass. He had asked about this man a thousand times. It wasn't the first time in two months that this name had gotten a reaction out of somebody. But this evening, there seemed to be an extra glimmer of hope.

"Yes, I thought I might find him here. I'd like to speak with him."

"Why?"

"I've got something for him."

She signaled to the owner, Otello, who came over.

"What's going on, Alma?"

The noise was swelling in the restaurant. Alma had to speak into her boss's ear.

"D'you remember Cafarello? This one's looking for him."

The man turned his gaze on Vango.

"Cafarello? Why?"

"I've got something to give him."

"What?"

"From his father, who stayed in the home country."

"Money?"

Vango didn't answer. The proprietor wiped a copper tap with a cloth.

"Haven't seen him for at least a year. Ask Di Marzo."

"Who's Di Marzo?" Vango wanted to know.

"The fat one sitting over there, at the back."

Vango left his glass at the bar and went over to Di Marzo, who seemed to be wedged between tables strewn with glasses, like a boat trapped in ice.

"Signor Di Marzo?"

In the man's enormous hands, his cards looked tiny.

"I'm looking for Giovanni Cafarello."

"Who?"

"Cafarello."

Di Marzo started laughing, and this made the ice crack around him. He leaned toward his neighbor, a small man with slicked-back hair.

"He's looking for Giovanni Cafarello."

The other man rolled his eyes and smiled.

"Cafarello . . ."

Vango politely pressed his point.

"Signor Di Marzo, I've heard that you can tell me where to find Giovanni Cafarello."

"Sing Sing," declared Di Marzo, slamming his cards down on the table.

Vango pricked up his ears.

"Sing Sing?"

"Sing Sing," the big man repeated.

Next to him, the small man with the brilliantine in his hair explained, "He's been at Sing Sing for months."

"But not for much longer," added Di Marzo.

They laughed again.

"Sing Sing," Vango echoed, feeling dazed. "Thank you, *signore.*"

With a knot in his stomach, he made his way back toward the bar.

"Have you found him, Lupo?" the waitress called out.

"Maybe. Sing Sing. . . . What does that mean?"

She nearly knocked over the pyramid of glasses on the draining board.

"It means he won't be eating here tonight."

"Why not?"

"You've got to travel up the Hudson. Two hours by boat. It's easier to get there than it is to come back."

"Because of the current?"

"No. It's the penitentiary for the north of New York. The prison for men on death row."

She no longer held his gaze. He suddenly seemed very far away.

Vango was trying to picture his parents' boat. The sound of footsteps on the bridge. The first shots fired at the sailors . . . a night of terror. He was thinking about Cafarello, the next day killing Bartolomeo Viaggi in cold blood, to steal his share of the plunder. Viaggi had a wife and three little girls in Salina. Had he sensed that he was out of his depth given what had taken place? Had he perhaps even felt remorse? In any event, Cafarello had killed him. Vango knew that only one of Viaggi's three daughters was still alive. Poor girl. He recalled Mazzetta's death as well, and pondered all these people's engulfed secrets. So many ravaged lives.

Finally, his mind turned to Cafarello in his cell at Sing Sing. The haunting racket of loud knocking on doors. Shouting in the corridors.

Several minutes went by.

"Lupacchiotto!"

Vango looked up.

"Leave the bandits alone," the waitress was telling him, with both hands on the counter. "Little wolves shouldn't go hunting in the thick of it. Go back home; forget about Cafarello and Sing Sing."

Vango stood up. He took a large bill from his pocket and slid it clumsily under the waitress's fingers. He knew that she was right about everything.

"Keep it!" she said, pushing the money away.

She turned her back on him. Alma had had enough of the banknotes that circulated from night until morning, leaving her fingers as black as her eyes. She wanted something else: hands that touched without any transaction taking place.

"Alma! Did he pay, the little one?" the proprietor asked behind her.

"Who?"

She turned toward the door.

"The one that just left."

"Yes," she said. "He paid."

Vango found himself at the port at three o'clock in the morning. The first boat would leave two hours later. The dockside was deserted. He knocked on the window of one of the huts there.

A man pushed the door ajar. They exchanged a few words. He seemed hesitant at first, but when Vango emptied his pockets, the ferryman grabbed his cap and stepped outside.

They went over to the boat. Vango helped the ferryman push it out from the dock and then jumped on board just in time. The engine took a while to start up. Vango was huddled in the stern, eyes closed.

How was this going to play out?

All he knew was that when he got to Sing Sing, he would request a meeting with Cafarello in the visiting room. *I've come on his father's behalf,* he would say. At Salina, in the Aeolian Islands, people talked about Cafarello abandoning his father in cowardly fashion, leaving him behind in his small house between two volcanoes while the son set out for America with the treasure. But who turns away his father's messenger when he's behind bars?

Vango didn't have a plan. What would he do when Giovanni Cafarello appeared behind the grille? He had no idea. But he was sure that on returning to the New York dockside in the evening, he would possess the knowledge he was after: the great mystery of his life.

The only thing he promised himself was that he would know.

At that very moment, in the small hours of the twenty-eighth of August 1936, in a corridor of Sing Sing prison, a man was waiting, flanked by four guards. They had woken him in the middle of the night.

"It's today; it's now."

He had stood up. The chaplain had spoken into his ear for a few minutes. The man had rested his head on the priest's shoulder. He wasn't even able to cry.

The voice of Lewis Lawes, the prison warden, had cut short that final humane moment.

"Giovanni Valente Cafarello, it is time."

He was in the corridor now. Even if he started shouting, the other prisoners might not wake up. It was all part of the ordinary prison routine at Sing Sing. Never, in the history of America, had there been so many death sentences as this decade. A few months earlier, four criminals had been executed in a single night at Sing Sing.

The warden led the condemned man and his guards into the room at the end of the corridor.

It didn't take long.

Fifteen minutes later, it was all over.

Lewis Lawes returned to his office and collapsed into his leather armchair. Despite running this prison for fifteen years, he was still openly opposed to the death penalty. He was always careful to note the final words of each condemned man in a white notebook. What he had heard in the early hours of that morning was something he had never heard before at the point of execution.

And yet it was what Cafarello had always maintained.

Spoken from the electric chair, however, these words had a new impact. Lewis Lawes grabbed the small white notebook from the shelf behind him.

He leafed through his most recent notes. There were prayers, cries of hatred or love, pleadings. Some condemned prisoners had begged for forgiveness. Others had proclaimed their innocence. And some had called out for their mothers with all the strength they could muster.

On the last page, he noted the name of Giovanni Cafarello in capital letters, and just below it he wrote:

AT A QUARTER PAST THREE THIS MORNING,
IN THE PRISON OF OSSINING IN THE STATE OF NEW YORK,
THE CONDEMNED MAN UTTERED THESE WORDS:
I AM NOT GIOVANNI CAFARELLO.

Lewis Lawes closed his notebook again. Outside the window, day was breaking over the Hudson River. There was the sound of a boat approaching.

SILVER GHOST

Everland, Scotland, August 29, 1936

Ethel kept rummaging through the underwear in her chest of drawers. The silk slipped through her fingers while she continued to cast her eye around her bedroom. Her nails came to rest on a groove in the wood. The bottom of the drawer lifted up to reveal a small packet of letters, which she pressed to her stomach. She turned around, pushing the drawer shut with her back.

Ethel stared at the envelopes in her hands. There were five of them tied together. She unfastened the packet, opened one of the letters, and went straight to the last line, where the letter *V* was written. Absentmindedly, Ethel moved word by word up the rivulet of blue ink, before looking up to survey her bedroom. The wooden floor creaked beneath her feet. Why did she have the feeling that she wasn't alone? For several weeks now, she had been convinced that someone was coming into her bedroom. She had spoken about this with Mary, who had assured her that she was mistaken.

Mary was even prepared to stake her honor on it. She had raised her arms and sworn blind that she was the only person to go in there and that no one could get past her beady eye.

But Ethel was sure about it. From morning to evening, the papers and books moved. And when she had walked in through the door a few moments earlier, the drawer was half open.

Ethel closed the envelope again. The fire was spluttering, unless it was the rain at the window. These brief messages, one or two pages long, weighed almost nothing in her hands. Next, she strode solemnly over to the fireplace, tossed Vango's five letters into the flames, and watched them burn. Sitting back on her heels, she nudged a triangle of paper that was trying to escape the furnace. It flared up all of a sudden. Then there was nothing left.

Ethel stood up. She had kept her coat on, and her expression was both serious and relieved. The wooden floor creaked again as she went over to the window and leaned against it. The engine of her beloved car was purring down below.

Nicholas was sitting on the hood, waiting. He wore a cape to keep off the rain. For the first time in her life, Ethel had given someone else permission to drive her Napier-Railton. Nicholas was allowed to go into town to do her shopping. He could be seen at the steering wheel of the racing car, speeding through the countryside. Sometimes, both of them were squeezed into the only seat as they set off in the direction of the lake.

Nicholas spotted Ethel at the window. He gave her a nod, but she didn't respond. Turning back to face the fire, she saw that the flames had died down now.

Shortly afterward, Ethel joined Nicholas in the car. The gravel flew out from under the wheels as they drove away from the main driveway of Everland Castle. Mary ran after them, to no avail. She was shouting. She wanted to know which bedroom to prepare for the Princess of Albrac, who was expected the following day.

A princess!

Mary was delighted about the visit. Ethel never invited anyone to Everland. There was just the Cameron boy, who paid a neighborly call from time to time without telling his parents. Now that he understood there was no point in holding out hope, he sometimes had tea with Ethel instead. She would smile as she listened to him talking about the girls who were presented to him. The most recent one was very rich, but so shy that he had only seen her hair and perhaps a hint of a nose between two locks.

Apart from these Sunday visits, the castle remained deserted. Paul was never there: he was off fighting somewhere in Spain. Mary was nostalgic for the days when, on autumn evenings, she had twelve chambermaids under her orders heating up forty beds with warming pans. Back in those days, Ethel's mother had fires lit all around the castle. One day, she had hosted Lord Delamere, who had arrived with two elephant tusks as a gift.

But a princess was even better.

Upstairs, in the silent bedroom, a ghost was becoming restless. The corner of the gray-and-pink eiderdown that covered Ethel's bed began to twitch. A body emerged from underneath the bed. It was Andrei. He lay on the carpet for a moment before pulling himself up on his elbows. His face was covered in sweat. He went over to the fireplace, grabbed a log, and stirred the embers. Then he made for the chest of drawers. He opened the relevant drawer, lifted up the strip of wood at the back, and found the hiding place. He went back to the fire, then back again to the chest, where he inspected every nook and cranny.

Ethel's arrival had caught him by surprise, just as he was about to search the drawer. From his hideout under the bed, he had seen her remove the little bundle of envelopes and throw it on the fire.

Had he just missed out on his first opportunity to track down Vango? He couldn't be sure. What about Nicholas? Were they his letters that she had burned with such indifference? He hoped that was it, yes: the letters of the gardener's son gone up in smoke. This idea made Andrei feel better about things. But he didn't really believe it. Did that good-for-nothing Nicholas even know how to write? Did he have a talent for anything other than worming his way into ladies' hearts, driving their cars, and setting up secret trysts in barns?

No, the letters were bound to be from Vango Romano. Andrei had been trying to locate them for ages. Where had they been posted from? If he'd been able to find them in time, their discovery would have been enough to appease Vlad the Vulture. Andrei and his family would have been saved.

The worst was that Ethel had probably burned them at Nicholas's request. Angrily, Andrei thrust his hands into the bottom drawer, hoping to find something there.

"Don't move."

He tried to stand up.

"Don't move!"

The voice was as chilling as the barrel of the hunting gun that someone had just slid inside his ear.

"Now, lie down flat on the floor. Slowly."

Andrei bent down and pressed his other ear against the wooden floor.

"Arms out wide, please."

His head to one side, Andrei made a cross shape with his arms.

He stayed like that for a few seconds before daring to look up at the person threatening him.

It was Mary, the housekeeper, who had entered without making a sound.

Andrei wasn't the least bit reassured when he recognized the face of his assailant. He should have guessed: this woman was capable of anything. Some days earlier, in the back kitchen, he had seen her slitting a pig's throat while breathlessly recounting the love story between King Edward VIII and Wallis Simpson.

"What are you looking for, Andrew?"

The vibration of Mary's finger on the trigger traveled down the length of the gun and reverberated inside Andrei's skull. She was going to kill him, and would have no scruples about doing so.

"What are you looking for?"

"Nothing."

Not satisfied with this answer, Mary let out a long sigh.

"How does it make me look, when I give Miss Ethel my word that no one else will go into her bedroom? How does it make me look, eh?"

Andrei wanted to move his head, but she thrust the barrel in a bit deeper.

"How does it make me look, Andrew?"

"Not good."

"That's right. Not good. Not good at all."

She glanced at the clock.

"Another four minutes and the Lawrence brothers will

be knocking on the door. They're coming to mend the floorboards."

She pressed hard enough with the gun for the floorboard beneath his head to creak.

"Can you hear that?"

"Y-yes," stammered Andrei.

She started again.

"I've understood," he gasped.

"You can hear it, can you?"

"Yes."

"So let's wait nice and patiently. And they can escort you off the premises."

A minute went by. Andrei was about to give up when he had an idea. He knew Mary, which gave him a head start. Master Ochtchepkov, who had tried to teach him the art of fighting in Moscow, used to say that half the battle was knowing your enemy. He closed his eyes.

"What did you want to steal, Andrew?" Mary grilled him.

Andrei opened his hand.

"That."

A haze of white cotton spread around his fingers.

On letting go of the drawer when the gun had pushed him down, Andrei had accidentally kept a bit of fabric in his hand.

"That?"

Mary bent over a little. She recognized the white brassiere that Ethel wore in bed on summer nights. A very long time ago, it had been part of her mother's wedding trousseau.

"That?"

"Yes," sobbed Andrei.

The pressure from the gun eased off slightly. Mary sensed the beginning of the only kind of story that could make her lose her head.

"Don't tell me . . ." She gasped.

A love story! She could smell a love story.

"Andrew!"

"I'll never do it again, Miss Mary. Never."

Tears appeared in Andrei's eyes.

"Please don't breathe a word of it to her," he begged. "Just tell her that I wanted to steal some money."

Mary stared intently at the young man's face.

Does he love her, or am I going mad?

"I don't want her to find out. I'm ashamed. She won't even look at me. A thief! Tell Ethel I'm a thief. I'd rather end up in prison."

Mary was losing her footing. This was glorious. She felt as if she were in the fifth episode of "Mists of Glory," when the shepherd discovers the queen swimming in the lake.

She had stumbled on the story in the kitchen one day, printed in the newspaper she was using to wrap the cheese. And she had started buying the latest installment each week, down in the village. From then on, Mary couldn't get a whiff of old sheep's cheese without thinking of the shepherd, hidden in the hollow tree, bemoaning his fate: "Why did I have to be born a shepherd?"

And in her most uncensored dreams, Mary looked like the queen, swimming breaststroke in the lake. In those same dreams, Superintendent Boulard played the shepherd.

"Kill me," said Andrei.

Mary came to her senses again.

This time, the boy had gone too far. He shouldn't take her for a complete fool.

"Tell your stories to Miss Ethel, you dirty common thief. If you're in love with Miss Ethel, then I'm in love with the viceroy of India! I don't believe your lies for a second."

There was a knock at the door. The Lawrence brothers were there.

"Wait . . ." Andrei whispered to Mary.

More knocking.

"Listen to me . . ." he pleaded.

Mary wavered, affording Andrei the time to say, "Lift up my right trouser leg."

Mary was taken aback. The situation was becoming positively indecent, but her curiosity won out. This was definitely worthy of a plotline in "Mists of Glory."

"Stay on that side of the door!" she called out to the joiners. "I'll let you in when I've finished tidying. This is a lady's bedroom, gentlemen."

Keeping the gun pressed to Andrei's face, she hitched up the fabric of his right trouser leg with her foot. If anybody had walked into the room right then, they would have seen a housekeeper of a certain age with her gun trained on a young man who was lying flat on the floor while she caressed his calf with her heel.

"Good God!"

There on the hock of Andrei's knee, carved into his skin, she had just seen the five letters that spelled Ethel's name. Yes, he loved her!

Feeling as if she had been thrust into the spotlight of the talkies, Mary started to blush. She was horrified at being cast in the worst role of all: the shrew punishing the spurned lover. But all was not was lost. In the audience's eyes, she could still be the person to forgive the blunders of a first love.

She could see them now, whole auditoriums rising to their feet and getting out their handkerchiefs.

When the Lawrence brothers walked in they found Mary with a gentle glow to her cheeks and, behind her, Andrei, with three hastily rolled up bedroom carpets under his arms.

"I'm taking this opportunity to get the carpets beaten," Mary declared. "Hurry up. I don't want the floorboards creaking anymore. There's another bedroom to work on as well. The Princess of Albrac is coming tomorrow. I don't want her to think she's staying in a haunted house!"

Then she turned toward Andrei.

"For goodness' sake, get a move on and go downstairs with that lot!"

It had stopped raining.

For the next hour, the castle rang out with the sound of hammers on floorboards and, outside, the thud of carpets being beaten with sticks in the damp grass. With each blow, Andrei disappeared in a cloud of dust.

Ethel returned alone very late that night. She parked her car in front of the second stable that was used as a garage, and jumped out. Her Napier-Railton had no side door, so clambering out was rather like emerging from a cockpit. Ethel took off her leather helmet and goggles, leaving them on the seat.

The castle was plunged in darkness. Just one window on the ground floor was still lit up. Ethel's thoughts turned to her brother. Whenever she came back at night, she always hoped to see his window glowing under the roof.

She'd had no news of Paul for several months now. He had returned to Spain in August, after learning of the deaths of four of his friends in the Castilian regiment in a massacre at Badajoz, close to the Portuguese border.

Ethel had read in the newspapers about the international brigades springing up to support the Spanish republicans against the nationalist coup. For weeks now, young adventurers from all over the world had been enlisting in Madrid. Ethel feared for Paul's life. She wanted him back, but this prospect also worried her. She knew he wouldn't approve of what she was doing.

Andrei heard Ethel pull up. He stayed lying flat on his bunk. The headlights were switched off. In the dark, he thought he could hear the sound of footsteps heading away over the gravel. He wrapped himself in his blanket so that all he could hear were the vibrations of the bats.

Suddenly, the lights came on around him. There stood Ethel. She was staring at Andrei as he shielded his eyes with his hand.

"Were you asleep?"

He noticed that her woolen headband was as white as her complexion.

"Follow me."

Andrei didn't dare move. He assumed that Mary had told her everything.

"Come on!"

This time, he got up.

He was standing opposite her now, and he had never been so close.

She looked at him for a moment before striding off toward the back of the garage.

"Hurry up!"

Andrei followed her. She wore a raincoat that dated from at least the war. The filaments in the lightbulbs were crackling on the ceiling. Bats flitted among the beams.

"Are you still tinkering about with the car?"

Andrei didn't understand. He felt cold.

Ethel tugged at the tarpaulin covering the white Rolls.

"I swear, I haven't laid another finger on it," protested Andrei. "I did as you said."

For a long time now, Andrei had been under strict orders not to repair the car.

Ethel nodded.

"Tomorrow evening, I want the engine to be running perfectly."

The boy's face lit up.

"Tomorrow morning," Andrei corrected her.

He was standing like a tin soldier, his arms by his sides.

"Tomorrow morning, if you like. But I won't be here very early. I'm leaving tonight. You can let Nick know when it's ready."

"Nick?"

"Nicholas."

"Who's that?"

"Peter's son."

"Why Nicholas?"

"Because it's for him."

Ethel noticed Andrei's expression changing.

"Is something wrong?"

"I—I don't understand," stammered Andrei after at least twenty seconds had elapsed.

Ethel took a step toward him.

"Is this car being used by anybody?" she asked.

"No."

"So I can do what I like with it. If I want to drown it in the loch, if I want to give it to my horse, if I want to plant chrysanthemums in the mudguards . . ."

"But you told me——"

"I've changed my mind."

"What about Master Paul?"

"He's playing at being part of the revolution in Spain. He's not going to come back just for a ride in the Rolls. You have to choose in life."

She walked lightly away. Andrei couldn't bear to think that he was going to have to repair this car for Nicholas.

"What about your parents?" he called out.

Ethel turned to face him.

"Yes?"

"Miss Mary told me that your father loved this car."

"Have I ever discussed *your* parents?" she replied, lowering her gaze. "Don't talk about things of which you have no knowledge."

She remembered a trip with her father when she was five years old. At the top of a hill, on their way back from Glasgow, he had let the engine cut out, and the white car had sped down the hill in complete silence. Ethel had been standing on the backseat, behind him. The wind had flapped and whistled through her dress, making it move like a ghost.

The following year, on seeing an airplane flying over the

castle, Ethel's father had stroked the car's bodywork and remarked, "Look at this poor car: it's worse than a plow compared with that bird!"

But in his eyes, the Silver Ghost had remained the most beautiful of plows.

"Let Nicholas know when the engine's working," Ethel told Andrei flatly. "And you can start by giving me some petrol; I'm leaving right away."

Andrei put a can behind the seat of the little Napier-Railton.

"I don't want to wake Mary. If she needs to know where I am, I'm heading north, to Ullapool. I'm going to collect someone off the boat, an old friend of my parents: the Princess of Albrac. I'll be back tomorrow."

When Ethel started up the car, the racket it made in the dead of night must not only have woken Mary and everyone else in Everland Castle, but also Lily the doe, who was sleeping far away in the bracken.

Andrei worked through the night. In the morning, he collapsed onto the straw. The Rolls had just started up first go.

When he awoke two hours later, the car was no longer there. He let out a cry, ran as far as the castle steps, couldn't find anyone, and headed for the kitchens. Scott saw him storm in, beside himself with anger.

"Where's the car?" Andrei roared.

The cook looked astonished. He wiped his hands on his trousers. He was preparing for the arrival of the Princess of Albrac that same evening.

"Weren't you here this morning? Peter's son, Nicholas, has repaired it. Everybody came out to see."

"Where's he gone?"

"I don't know."

Andrei slammed his hand down on the table, knocked over a bench, and stormed out through the service door. He walked down a path hedged with boxwood. Peter was in the rose garden, hacking out the rotten wood and deadheading the roses before the first blizzards of September did their worst.

Andrei grabbed him from behind.

"Where's your son?"

Moments later, Andrei had mounted a horse; attached to his belt was a wrench that weighed more than two pounds. He jumped over two gates before joining the path through the beech trees that led down to the lake. In the muddy ruts, he recognized the tracks made by the Silver Ghost. He coaxed his horse into a gallop again.

Reaching a rock where the path forked, he wavered. Ethel's car must have taken one of these turnings in the night, but it was the spacing of the Rolls's wheels that he recognized. Andrei took the left fork. His horse was becoming as nervous as he was. In under ten minutes, he was close enough to the lake to have a decent view of its shores strewn with rocks and gorse. He had never come this far before.

The path seemed to lead to a boathouse built close to the water's edge. Andrei brought his horse to a halt when they were still a way off, in order to survey the premises.

So it was here that Nicholas had his trysts with Ethel: a hut on the shores of a lake. Andrei thought about those interminable days when they disappeared off together. Well, it wouldn't happen anymore. He gripped the heavy wrench in his fist.

He noticed a few silver birch trees just behind the boat-house. They had already lost their leaves. And, behind the white curtain of their trunks, he could see the car. Andrei dismounted and patted the horse's rump, so the animal understood to head home. It set off, turning back several times to check if it shouldn't stay on a while, but it ended up trotting back in the direction of Everland.

Andrei hid the wrench behind his back and circled the building, keeping his distance. He flanked the hedge, without ever taking his eyes off the main door. A metallic noise could be heard from time to time, together with the sound of someone singing to himself. Nicholas was in there—no doubt about it.

Andrei approached the white Rolls.

It took him a long time to make any sense of what met his eyes. The car's hood was open wide and the contents had been ripped out. All that was left was a gaping hole, through which Andrei could see the grass. Gasoline oozed over the metal bodywork, which had been butchered by an ax. The white paint of the Rolls was smeared with greasy black stains. And yet none of this was the result of an accident: the engine had been deliberately extracted, like the heart from a corpse in an anatomy lesson.

A PRINCESS IN EXILE

Andrei ran his finger over a piece of ripped-out tubing.

There was nothing left. Where had all the components of the engine gone? Henry Royce himself, pipe in mouth, would have fine-tuned them with a nail file in his Manchester workshops.

Andrei wasn't trying to hide anymore. Fuming with rage, he launched his attack on the boathouse.

Just then, Nicholas opened the door.

"Andrei?"

His Russian adversary kept walking toward him across the grass.

"Stay where you are," Nicholas told him calmly. "You're not allowed in here."

Andrei gripped the enormous wrench between his fingers.

"Wait."

But Andrei had already raised an arm and brought down the first blow.

Nicholas fell against the door. The wrench had just missed his head, landing in the hollow of his shoulder instead.

"Stop!"

Andrei started kicking him.

"I'm going to kill you."

From where he lay on the ground, Nicholas realized that his powers of persuasion wouldn't be enough. He threw himself at Andrei's legs and gripped them so tightly that the Russian lost his balance. They rolled over in the mud. Nicholas was much heavier than his enemy. He quickly gained the upper hand.

Andrei was putting everything into the fight. Nicholas managed to turn him around and apply his knees to the small of Andrei's back. Then he grabbed hold of his opponent's wrists, disarmed him, and twisted both his arms behind his back, thrusting his face into the ground.

"Stop, or I'll break every bone in your body."

Andrei gave a final surge of resistance before surrendering.

Nicholas waited a little. Then he stood, picking up the wrench, which he hurled as far as he could. It landed in the gray waters of Loch Ness.

He turned back to face Andrei, who was slowly catching his breath and muttering in Russian.

"You almost killed me," said Nicholas, stretching as he stood over his opponent. Then he pulled open the door and walked into the boathouse. Andrei groaned and rolled over in the mud.

"You might as well come and take a look, since you're here," said Nicholas, popping his head around the door.

But Andrei remained on the ground for some time. Only his eyes moved. He had never liked fighting. Eventually, he hauled himself up by his elbows and then his hands, in an attempt to stand up. He wiped the mud from his face with his sleeve and limped after Nicholas.

As he entered the hut, Andrei gripped the door frame. He

put his hand to his mouth and gasped something almost inaudible in Russian. Nicholas was backlit, with the light streaming in behind him through a window that gave onto Loch Ness.

"Here it is," he declared.

There, in the middle of the large room, surrounded by a scaffolding of ladders, planks, and ropes, was a small airplane.

"I was the one who found it," explained Nicholas. "It was in smithereens, buried in the hill over there."

He gestured vaguely at the corner of the hut, but was in fact indicating the landscape beyond it.

"Miss Ethel's had me working on it for four months now. We'd nearly finished our project when you caught us out. Nobody else knows what we're doing."

"Buried?" murmured Andrei.

"Yes, beneath the hill."

He gestured again.

"Master Paul made the gardeners bury it in the middle of the night. I was still a kid. I remember seeing my father when he returned; it took him ten years to tell me where it was."

Andrei was staring at the small two-seater biplane. Above and below the fuselage were its superposed wings, which seemed to be held in place by magic. Some parts of the plane were already painted white, but where the engine and propeller should have been, there was just a hole.

If Andrei understood correctly, this little plane was the only thing connecting Ethel and Peter's son. The rest had been just his imagination.

"Master Paul mustn't get wind of this," said Nicholas. "He doesn't even know that it's always been Miss Ethel's dream to find it, so that she could make it fly again. He doesn't want anyone touching it."

"Why?"

Nicholas put his hand on the flank of the plane, and the scaffolding creaked.

"Their parents died in this plane."

Andrei felt his legs nearly give way. He went to sit down on a pile of wooden planks. How could something so light and handsome kill anyone?

"When I found it, the engine had disappeared," Nicholas went on. "I don't know where it went. They stopped building this kind of plane twenty years ago. I needed a seventy-horsepower engine. I'm sorry. . . ."

Andrei was thinking of the gutted Rolls waiting under the trees. Its engine lay here on the ground, in front of this white bird.

They didn't notice Ethel until she appeared, soundlessly, beneath the plane.

"Miss Ethel . . ." Nicholas began.

She didn't answer.

"Miss—"

"Peter and Scott told me."

Andrei was staring at a spot on the floor. His face was still smeared with mud.

"I thought—" The Russian began to explain himself.

"I'd rather you kept quiet. Please leave."

Andrei got up and walked over to the door, but Ethel called him back.

"Where are you going?"

"To the stables."

"Why?"

Andrei turned around.

"To work."

"No," said Ethel flatly. "You haven't understood: you're leaving."

Nicholas was watching Andrei.

"There are trains from Inverness," Ethel went on, "boats from Fort William, and there might be work in Edinburgh. Who knows? Leave. That's all I have to say."

The chasm that was opening up in Andrei wasn't discernible on his face. Instead, there was something resembling a smile on his lips.

The smile of people who are lost, reflected Nicholas, of people who put off believing what they've just been told. The smile of those standing before a collapsing house.

Nicholas thought Andrei was going to fall. He wanted to help prop him up.

"Don't move," Ethel ordered.

Nicholas stopped. He didn't take his eyes off Andrei. He had already seen his father, Peter, smile like that once. It had been on the day when someone had come into their home to tell them that Lord and Lady B. H., Ethel's parents, were dead.

Peter had always worked at Everland. He was born at Everland, just as his parents and grandparents had been before him. His son, Nick, had grown up there. And then one day somebody appeared, with a face as long as a bailiff's, to announce that a tiny plane, a Blériot Experimental II, from the Royal Aircraft Factory, had crashed in Egypt. The lifeless bodies had been found next to each other on the sand. The man explained that the estate would be sold, that Paul and Ethel would be sent to a house in London, that it was all over.

That was when Nicholas had seen the smile of disbelief on his father's lips.

He took another step toward Andrei.

"Don't move, Nick. Let him go."

Ethel had harbored doubts about Andrei from the first day. It was because of her suspicions that she had just burned all of Vango's letters.

She couldn't forgive Andrei for that.

"Leave," she repeated.

In Andrei's eyes, the last specks of dust could be seen settling on the collapsed house. They took a long while, and then he left.

On the road from Inverness that runs along the northern shores of Loch Ness, a horse and carriage were rattling along at top speed. Nobody could have imagined that the Princess of Albrac and her retinue were on board. The coachman himself had been surprised to encounter the kindly little old lady who had just stepped off the boat, clutching her handbag and holding out a large glass-jeweled ring for him to kiss. She was traveling with a young companion who appeared to be a close acquaintance of Ethel's, because she fell into her arms on the dockside. The princess had been seasick throughout the crossing, with the result that her complexion, which was usually like the lilacs in Parisian gardens, had turned porridge colored.

The companion, on the other hand, looked rather more fresh faced after the journey. Her job was to accompany the princess for the boat crossing, and she was expecting to catch the same boat back. But she let herself be talked into spending a night at Everland Castle.

Ethel drove away from the port in her racing car, leaving the two female travelers to continue at their own pace in the carriage.

After a final bend, just above the lake, the princess made the horses stop for the fifth time. She rushed over to the grass, where she was violently sick.

"We're nearly there," the coachman said, trying to comfort her.

"Excellent. Everything's simply marvelous; I won't be a second," croaked the princess.

"If you'd rather finish the journey on foot, I've just spotted someone from the castle coming to meet us. He could lend you an arm."

"No, thank you; you're very kind. It's over now."

The Princess of Albrac climbed back up into the vehicle, encumbered by her stiff, heavy dress. She lay down on the seat, using her handbag, which was stuffed with balls of yarn, as her pillow.

As soon as they had set out from Ullapool, her pretty companion had climbed onto the roof of the carriage, where she lay down and stared up at the gray sky. Likewise, she had spent the sea crossing on the tarpaulin of a lifeboat, which was tethered to the bridge.

She was agile and didn't like to feel trapped.

Hence her nickname, the Cat.

The carriage continued on its way again, before slowing

down when it passed a young man, walking in the opposite direction, with a violin case on his back.

"Is Miss Ethel there yet?" the coachman called out.

Head down, Andrei didn't reply.

It was all over for him.

Lying on the roof, the Cat was watching two black clouds crossing each other's paths without ever touching. If Andrei had answered, she would have turned around to take a look at him. She would have recognized his voice. But she was listening to the *clip-clop* of hooves, and to the gentle breeze blowing over the luggage. She had traveled so little that even the air in her lungs felt foreign to her.

Andrei was incapable of uttering a word. He felt like a man on death row. He was already picturing his family on board a train headed for the gulags in Siberia. As he passed by, he glanced inside the carriage. The curtain wasn't drawn. He saw an old lady lying down, and she smiled at him. Was this the Princess of Albrac?

The coachman cracked his whip, and the sudden spurt of speed startled the Cat. She got up on her knees and stared at the road disappearing behind her. Dreamily scrunching up her eyes, she watched the figure of the young man heading off into the distance. The Cat batted away the idea that had just crossed her mind. No. It was too silly. Why here? Why him? But she didn't take her eyes off the boy until he had vanished into the white haze of the road.

"My dear . . ." came a voice from below her.

The Cat bent over to push open the window and pop her head inside.

"Are you feeling better, Your Highness?"

"Much better," replied the little old lady, drawing on her reserves of energy. Her complexion had gone from the color of porridge to that of fresh butter.

"I've been meaning to ask you, my dear, when it comes to petticoats, how many do princesses have to wear? Because I'm awfully hot."

"You can take off as many layers as you like."

"Was I good?" whispered the princess, as if she had just come off stage.

"Very good. You were terrific."

The Princess of Albrac gave a modest smile.

In real life, her name was Marie-Antoinette Boulard.

It had all begun four weeks earlier in Paris.

One morning, before leaving for work at the Quai des Orfèvres, the superintendent had informed his mother that his Russian teacher would be paying another visit the following evening. They were both in the kitchen. Madame Boulard kept pouring the coffee without showing any signs of interest.

"I've put your ham-and-cheese sandwiches in your satchel," she told her son.

Ever since his first day at school, in the previous century, the superintendent had set out every morning with his packed lunch.

As soon as Boulard had turned the corner at the end of the street, his mother put on her slippers and rushed downstairs to pay a visit to the concierge.

"It's me," whispered Madame Boulard through the glass. The door opened.

"It's set for tomorrow," she said.

They stared at each other and had an emotional holding of hands. The big day had come at last. Their plan had been ready for some time.

The next evening, at about ten o'clock, there was a ring at the Boulards' door.

The superintendent and his mother were finishing off their dinner. It was dark outside. Boulard seemed anxious and checked his watch.

"Is that your Rasputin?" asked his mother.

"It's too early."

"I'd better go and see."

"No. Wait."

Boulard pushed back his chair and went into the entrance hall. His mother strained to hear.

The superintendent returned.

"It's Madame Dussac. She says there's something she wants you to hear on the wireless."

For several weeks now, the concierge kept popping up at unexpected hours of the day and night to let Madame Boulard know about interesting programs on the radio.

"She enjoys getting me to listen to her favorite songs," Madame Boulard explained to her son as she stood up and folded her napkin.

"Take your time," said the superintendent, relieved that his mother would be out of the way during his interview with the terrible Vlad.

Madame Boulard and Madame Dussac headed downstairs to the caretaker's lodgings, where they turned out the lights and mounted guard.

At five to eleven, one of the main double doors opened.

"Here he comes," whispered Madame Dussac.

The Vulture walked past the two women, who remained hidden in the dark behind the net curtain. He was holding a hat. His head had been shaved, and the top of it gleamed under the light.

Vlad went through the glass door that led to the stairs, on the right. Every time he trod on a step, the handrail shuddered from top to bottom. He rang the bell. Up on the sixth floor, the door could be heard creaking open. The two women hugged each other to summon their courage.

When they emerged from their hideout, Madame Boulard had a crowbar on her shoulder and Madame Dussac had a bayonet gun from the 1870 Franco-Prussian War.

They tiptoed as far as the staircase, where they laid down their weapons. Madame Boulard was rather out of breath. They knelt in front of the first step and rolled up the hall carpet, whose screws had been removed in advance. A large double trapdoor appeared. It had been fitted into the parquet floor for coal provisions fifty years earlier and was no longer in use, since everybody had switched over to gas. The door led down to a cellar. Madame Boulard used her crowbar as a control lever, while Madame Dussac slid her hands into the gap. Five minutes later, the lid had been heaved to one side and there was now a lion trap at the bottom of the stairs: a gaping hole over a pit that was four meters deep, with a heap of sodden coal at the bottom.

Madame Dussac carried Madame Boulard on her shoulders in order to unscrew the lightbulbs in the stairwell. It was pitch-black between the second and ground floors.

"We're done; put me down!" said Madame Boulard, who felt a giddy turn coming on.

Stepping carefully around the hole, the women reconvened at the bottom of the stairs.

"Good luck. I'm going to my post," declared Madame Dussac, whose curly hair had come tumbling loose out of her bun.

Marie-Antoinette's dimples had also rediscovered their youth. The two women shook hands again, and their eyes shone.

Madame Dussac was now back at her lodgings, standing sentinel with the bayonet. Her mission was to prevent the return of the lovers from the second floor. Since four o'clock that afternoon, she had ticked off the names of all the residents as they headed up to their apartments, but, as usual, the lovers from the second floor still weren't back. They had married at the beginning of the summer and hadn't yet understood that an upstanding couple should be home by eight o'clock. They risked foiling the master plan.

Madame Boulard remained at the bottom of the stairs. The building was silent. As she grew accustomed to the darkness, the superintendent's mother was able to make out the dim glow from the bulb switched on in front of the concierge's premises.

She was thinking about what had led her to play cowboys and Indians at the age of eighty-seven. It had taken her a long time to realize that her son was no longer a free agent. At the beginning, she had assumed that he was caught up in some dodgy business. She had decided to give him a talking-to. She remembered doing exactly that when the young Auguste had been involved in marble trafficking on the school playground. There was no reason why it couldn't work again sixty years later.

But she hardly recognized Boulard after his recent visits from the Russian. This was altogether more serious than marbles. Her son was in danger; she was convinced of that. For as long as Rasputin was free, the superintendent could not be.

Madame Boulard clutched the metal bar firmly with both hands. She had just seen something pass by above her. A cat? Could cats cling to the ceiling? And anyway, where had it come from? There was no access to the small interior court-yard from the first three floors.

"Are you there?" A voice addressed her from a few paces away.

She hurled the crowbar as hard as she could in its direction. The bar could be heard spinning through the air, but it never landed. Madame Boulard held her breath.

"We mustn't make any noise," came the voice. "I can explain everything. I'm on your side."

"Who are you?"

"The person you're trying to trap isn't alone. There are two men waiting for him on the sidewalk. If your man doesn't come out, they'll destroy all of you."

"How did you find me in the dark?" whispered Madame Boulard.

"You wear the same perfume as my mother. I saw it on the chest of drawers in your sitting room."

"What? You've been inside my apartment?"

"Certainly not. I spotted it through the window."

"Heavens above! On the sixth floor?"

"Look, we've got to get a move on."

Madame Boulard's head was spinning.

"Tell me what I should do."

Very gently, the Cat put down the iron bar, which she had caught in midair.

"Why don't you tell me what you were intending to do?"

"I wanted to make him fall down a hole."

"A hole?"

"Yes, a hole."

The Cat smiled. A hole. A good old technique from the Stone Age. From her perch up on the roof, she had seen the comings and goings of Madame Boulard and the concierge, and she had guessed that they were up to something. But a hole! She would never have expected that.

"Brilliant. And where is your hole?"

"Right here. In front of me."

Just then, a door could be heard opening at the top of the stairwell. It closed again. The sound of footsteps on the stairs followed.

"We've got to block off that hole," whispered the Cat.

Vlad was already on the fifth floor.

"It's too heavy."

The Cat groped her way toward a trembling Madame Boulard.

"Come on!" she coaxed as she felt the giant lid beneath her hands.

The stairs creaked with each step of the Vulture.

He stopped on the second landing. The rest of the staircase was in darkness now. He continued his descent, but more slowly. Vlad was muttering something. He couldn't see anymore.

By the time he set foot on the ground floor, the trapdoor had been closed up again and two shadows had tucked themselves under the stairwell just in time.

Phew! thought the Cat.

The carpet! thought Madame Boulard.

Vlad took one step before going headlong.

He let out a raft of Russian swearwords, then stood up slowly. He kept cursing as he hunted for the exit, putting one foot gingerly in front of the other. Vlad suddenly realized that he was no longer wearing his hat. He let out another torrent of unrepeatable words and started groping around in the dark.

The Cat felt her elderly accomplice squeeze up against her, with something in her hands: the Vulture's hat had rolled as far as Madame Boulard. Seizing it from her, the Cat tossed the hat toward Vlad. He wasted no time in finding it, and was soon crawling off again on all fours toward the exit.

The light was stronger by the main entrance. Vlad stood up in a dignified manner and walked toward his reflection in the concierge's glass door, where he began to straighten up his clothes. His nose was bleeding from the fall. He wiped it clumsily, then dried his hands on his beard.

Invisible behind the glass, Madame Dussac was pointing her gun at him from the gloom. They were opposite each other, separated by a pane of glass and a net curtain.

As he leaned forward to adjust the angle of his hat on

his head, Vlad thought he could see the ghost of a woman with a bayonet.

His first reaction was to take a step backward, but then he pressed his eyes to the pane. He wanted to make quite sure. Madame Dussac was horrified at the spectacle of the Vulture's huge face crushed against the glass. Blood trickled down the pane. She was about to scream when the sound of giggling could be heard coming from the street outside.

"The lovers," whispered Madame Dussac gratefully.

The main door swung open, and the couple appeared. The Vulture peeled himself off the glass and turned his head.

There they were, arm in arm. The husband had a flower behind one ear; the young wife was singing. Madame Dussac made the sign of the cross. God bless the lovers.

Vlad turned around and hesitated a second before making for the exit. He crossed paths with a couple whispering sweet nothings into each other's ears. The young woman curtsied, holding her shoes in one hand. They walked past the concierge's lookout. The Vulture disappeared.

The lovers nearly tripped on the rolled-up carpet. When their sweet nothings had faded away on the staircase, Madame Boulard and the Cat rushed into the concierge's lodgings. They found her sitting at the kitchen table, deathly pale.

Up on the sixth floor, the superintendent had fallen asleep, crushed by the Vulture's latest threats. Vlad had given him one month to find Vango.

Down in Madame Dussac's lodgings, the night was spent preparing for the future. The Cat had convinced both women that Vlad's grip on Boulard was through his mother.

"Through me?"

"Yes. Boulard fears for your life."

"My little darling!"

By taking his mother out of the picture, everything would be easier. Madame Boulard shivered.

"Me?"

"Yes. You must vanish."

Madame Boulard rolled her eyes at the ceiling.

"Vanish? Heavens above, but where to?"

The Cat had an idea. She couldn't be sure about it yet and would have to make some arrangements. She knew somebody abroad.

"Abroad?" Madame Boulard balked, already imagining herself in the jungle, eating insects. She had never been abroad.

The Cat arranged to meet the women two weeks later.

On the agreed day, thanks to an excellent program on the wireless, all three of them convened again. The music covered their voices. To the tune of "You Who Pass By Without Seeing Me," sung by Jean Sablon, the Cat explained her idea. Madame Boulard heard her out and was clearly both won over and delighted to discover that she would also need to assume a new identity. It was her idea to become the Princess of Albrac in exile.

One Sunday at the end of the month of August, the superintendent woke up at ten o'clock in the morning. He leaped out of bed. His mother hadn't come in to wake him up for their weekly trip to the market.

"Mother?"

He stumbled toward the kitchen.

"Mother!"

On the table, he found a few words that, after a little advice about warm winter clothes (scarf, hat, woolen socks), concluded with:

> *Have no fear for my safety —*
> *just do what you have to do.*
> *Become the real you again.*
> *I'll be back, Auguste.*
> *Till then! Mother*

Superintendent Boulard bit his fist. He had done the same thing one morning in September 1879, when his mother had left him all alone at the gates of a boarding school in Clermont-Ferrand.

Boulard deliberately tore up the message and gathered a few belongings. How had his mother managed to understand?

He got dressed and put on his coat in front of the dining room mirror.

Yes, it was time to become the redoubtable Boulard once more. But he couldn't do it by himself. Still, he knew the person he could count on. The faithful of faithfuls.

An hour later, he knocked on Augustin Avignon's door.

LA BOHÈME

New York, November 1936

At the foot of the tallest tower in Manhattan, a small red van, boasting THE BEST DOUGHNUTS IN THE NEW WORLD in yellow letters, was permanently parked. An arrow pointing at a right angle indicated the direction of the shop, two streets away.

Gordon's Bakery, which had nearly hung up its oven mitts the previous summer, had doubled its customers in a matter of days. A mysterious donor had provided this free publicity, as well as paying for the parking place on Fifth Avenue. The baker and his wife had recruited three apprentices to meet the demand for doughnuts.

Zefiro licked the sugar from his fingers. He was polishing off his third doughnut of the evening.

"Well?" he asked.

Vango and Zefiro were hidden inside the red van, opposite the Empire State building.

"Nothing."

Vango's eye was pressed against a hole in the middle of the first *O* of Gordon's. He was sitting on a box of doughnuts.

Zefiro was behind the second *O*, spying on the main entrance on the other side of the street. They'd had the idea for the van after trying to follow one of Voloy Viktor's visitors. By the time they had rushed down every story of their tower under construction, the man had vanished into thin air.

So they now spent half their time in the new hideout. Zefiro had a notebook on his lap and a flashlight attached to his forehead.

"You can go up for a rest, Vango."

Vango didn't answer.

"I know you didn't sleep last night," Zefiro went on. "Where did you go this time?"

"Out for a walk."

"The man you're looking for is dead; you know that."

Vango took his eye away from the side of the van.

When he had visited Sing Sing prison, several months earlier, he had been told that Giovanni Cafarello had just been executed. Vango had asked to sit down in a chair. He had remained speechless for several minutes in front of the old guard, who had offered him a glass of water.

"Bad timing, my boy."

Gradually, Vango had perked up. He had explained that he wished to collect the prisoner's personal effects. He had come on behalf of his father, who lived in Sicily. The guard had entrusted him with a small parcel of clothes and an empty wallet. This was the sinister luggage with which Vango had left the penitentiary of Sing Sing.

As he was crossing the road in front of the prison, he had heard a voice calling out after him. He had turned around to see a short man whose double chin was propped by a stiff collar. The man had walked up to Vango and glanced at the clothes tucked under his arm.

"You haven't wasted your day," remarked the man, chewing a piece of gum.

Vango didn't know what to say.

"At least you've come out of this with a three-piece suit," the man went on. "You needed that to make the trip worthwhile."

"Who are you?" asked Vango.

"Lewis Lawes, warden of Sing Sing prison. I won't shake your hand. The prisoner had no family when he was in court. And no family in the visiting room. But now that he's dead, he's got family popping up all over the place. Are you the same person who came by yesterday?"

"No."

"A man came to collect his belongings. He'd gotten the wrong day. He didn't even want to speak with the prisoner—just said he would be back."

"I see."

"Some people are *that* impatient. . . ."

"I've come on behalf of his father," said Vango, "who lives on an island, in Sicily."

"You should all be ashamed of yourselves," declared Lawes through gritted teeth. "He needed you six months ago when his attorney did an appalling job of defending him. The worst attorney in the world, I'd say."

"I've come from Sicily," Vango explained in a thick accent.

"Cafarello didn't even know how to say hello in English. He only ever repeated the same words. So, tell your brothers, your uncles, and your distant cousins that I never want to see them at my door again."

Vango stared at the ground. Lawes spat out his gum.

"I've got a better idea now of why he kept saying what he said. I understand why he denied all of you right up until his final breath. Peace be upon him. And dishonor to grave pillagers."

Lewis Lawes turned on his heels and headed for the walls of his prison.

"Mr. Lawes!"

The warden spun around to discover that Vango had followed him.

"Mr. Lawes, just tell me what he kept saying against his family."

Lewis Lawes came to a stop.

"'I am not Giovanni Cafarello.' That's what he said, over and over again."

And, fixing Vango with his stare, the warden of Sing Sing prison had added, "He was ashamed of his name."

In the gloom of the van, Zefiro put his hand on Vango's shoulder.

"Your Cafarello is dead, Vango."

"He's not *my* Cafarello."

Zefiro sighed.

"Go and rest. I don't need you right now. The lawyer won't come out again tonight."

Acting as if he hadn't heard, Vango resumed his surveillance duties.

For several weeks now, the man they both referred to as "the lawyer" had been the main focus of their attention. Zefiro noted down his comings and goings in a black notebook. This log of his movements gave some odd results.

The padre had noticed that when the lawyer appeared each evening in Voloy Viktor's sitting room, he had not been seen, a little earlier, passing through the revolving door at the bottom of the tower. Zefiro had concluded from this that there must be another passage to gain access to Voloy Viktor's fortress.

Discovering the secret entrance was of paramount importance to Zefiro. Not only that, but according to the padre, the lawyer was Viktor's closest confidant. He arrived in the evening and very early in the morning, but never in the presence of other visitors. And during their meetings, Viktor gave him free run of the office while he remained screened from view by the bedroom curtains.

With the flashlight on his forehead, Zefiro was examining his notebook again.

"He's coming out!" Vango suddenly signaled.

Zefiro put on his hat.

"I'm off."

"No, Padre. Don't move. They know you too well. I'll follow him."

He half opened the rear door of the van.

"Vango!" whispered Zefiro, already having misgivings.

But Vango had disappeared.

Despite the late hour, the district was still busy. Nobody noticed the boy slipping out of the Gordon's Bakery van.

Vango immediately saw the lawyer turning down the second street. He quickened his step to catch up, staying discreetly on the opposite sidewalk. A chilly autumn wind gave him the perfect excuse to wear his collar up around his face.

The lawyer, on the other hand, didn't appear to be cold. He was wearing a long coat in gray cashmere with a hat to match. His patent leather shoes glided over the dead leaves. He walked briskly past all the night owls. Some were smoking in front of darkened shop windows. Others sauntered in groups of two or three. These were the last few nights when it was still possible to step out, before the first snow of winter arrived.

Vango didn't really know what he was looking for. He just wanted to find out more about the man. His name, his address, anything he could get hold of. Was he even a lawyer? Above all, Vango was determined not to let this character out of his sight, because he wanted to observe him entering the secret passage to Viktor's suite the following morning.

A hundred paces back, a small shadow was following Vango. It clung to the walls, not wanting to be noticed. It belonged to Tom Jackson, the young street urchin from midtown, and Zefiro's employee.

At eleven o'clock that evening, the lawyer walked into a restaurant on the corner of a square. Vango stayed outside for a little while. It was a French establishment, La Bohème, where, despite its frugal name, a glass of wine would set you back the price of a barrel of oil. Two porters guarded the entrance, subtly dressed as sapper grenadiers from Napoleon's army.

Vango was only fifty meters from the main entrance to the restaurant, but he still hailed a taxi.

"Are you going far?" inquired the driver.

"To La Bohème, on the other side of the square."

The man stared at him as if Vango had taken leave of his

senses. But the young man held out a bill. He guessed that it wasn't the done thing to arrive on foot at this sort of eatery. The taxi drove on for another few meters, did a U-turn, and proceeded to park in front of the two Napoleonic soldiers, who opened the doors.

Vango thanked the taxi driver in a French accent. He walked in as if he were a regular. Someone was playing slow numbers from light operas on the piano. Over at the back of the restaurant, Vango spotted the lawyer from behind: he was sitting with a couple. Vango particularly noticed the young woman, who seemed to be daydreaming rather than listening to the others.

Vango made his way over to a low table set to one side. A waitress, in a traditional peasant's costume from Brittany, was already trying to take his coat. He resisted.

"I'd just like a drink," he said.

He sat down on a long upholstered seat at the low table, next to a man who was asleep. The Breton peasant girl relaunched her attack. What did he want to drink? Vango pointed to his neighbor's glass.

"I'll have what he's having."

The waitress scowled and headed off.

Vango was pretending to listen to the music. He tapped the arm of the sofa in time to the rhythm, prompting the man to open an eye. Vango seized his chance.

"Do you come here often?"

"If it's required."

His response did little to encourage conversation. The man seemed rather unsociable: his face was expressionless and his right eye was weeping. But Vango persisted. In order to strike up some kind of connection, he pointed to the glass that had just been brought to him.

"I ordered what you're having."

"It's tap water."

Now Vango understood why the Breton girl had made a face.

"Tell me," he persisted, "the man who's got his back to us, over there, under the mirror, isn't that Wallace Bridges?"

Vango had made up the name on the spot. His neighbor's eye began weeping a bit more as he glanced in the direction of the lawyer.

"Don't know him."

"And the couple?"

"It's the Irishman and his wife."

"The Irishman?"

Vango had never seen the Irishman. He knew he owned the tower that was being built, and which Zefiro was occupying in order to keep Viktor under surveillance. The man was a banker, but there was no limit to his business interests: he was rumored to own a ranch in New Mexico and vineyards in California. For all Vango knew, he might even own the water Vango was about to drink.

"His wife looks very young," Vango remarked.

The man turned to face him, grabbed a napkin, and wiped his right eye, without taking the other eye off Vango.

"D'you want her address?"

"No," Vango replied. "I just thought—"

"Don't think."

And then something odd happened. The woman they had been talking about stood up and stared straight at Vango. She picked up her handbag and, without saying good-bye to her husband or the lawyer, walked slowly toward Vango's table. She looked annoyed.

Vango glanced away, but the woman was now standing right opposite him.

"He wants me to go home. They're talking business, and I'm bored. He says it's private. Will you take me home?"

Vango could feel his head pounding. He opened his mouth to speak, when a voice right next to him answered.

"Yes, ma'am. I'll bring the car around."

Vango's neighbor stood to attention, holding a black-and-gold cap in one hand. Now it all made sense. The man was her chauffeur, and her words had been directed at him.

The woman left first, followed by the chauffeur with the watery eye.

Vango let out a long sigh and sank back into his seat.

So Viktor's lawyer was also working with the Irishman. This was the only piece of information he had gleaned from the evening. Vango saw a table become free just next to them. He hesitated. Would it be dangerous to move any closer? The lawyer wouldn't recognize him. He might look after Voloy Viktor's business affairs, but he was unlikely to be familiar with the faces of each of his client's enemies. Vango signaled to the Breton peasant girl.

"I'd like to have dinner after all. Could you get that table ready for me, in the corner? I'll be over in a moment."

She nodded, aloof. The boy didn't look like the kind to leave tips in double figures.

At last, Vango stood a chance of hearing something. For two months, he and Zefiro had been distant spectators.

They had merely tossed a piece of meat into the anthill, then watched to see what happened.

The piece of meat in question was the promise of a huge contract.

It was Zefiro's great ruse to catch Viktor. He had forged a letter in which he had passed himself off as an intermediary, writing on behalf of the Nazi regime, to offer Voloy Viktor the most important armaments contract in history. The factories would be established in Germany, and Viktor was tasked with finding investors from across America to finance them. It looked set to be a highly lucrative deal, and the figures were astronomical. Madame Victoria had probably counted out the zeros on her ten polished nails many times over.

For every ten billion dollars' worth of investment, Viktor would be entitled to two, making this the greatest scam of all time.

The offer, which was completely fictitious, had been invented by Zefiro. Through their binoculars, he and Vango had been able to observe the fever that had taken hold of Voloy Viktor's penthouse suite in the Plaza Hotel. The anthill was humming. Visitors came from far and wide to this private club. Viktor showed his guests the letter of patronage accompanying the proposal. It was signed by Hugo Eckener, director of the Zeppelin Company, an irreproachable figure who was acting as guarantor for the contract. The *Hindenburg*-headed notepaper inspired everyone's confidence.

Around Viktor, glasses of bourbon clinked and checks circulated. But perhaps the guests were also talking about their Christmas holiday plans for the family, or how fast their children were growing up. They might have been talking about hare hunting and their country houses on Long Island. As they signed the contracts on the baize of the bridge tables, each of them conveniently forgot that they were dealing in tanks, guns, and the graveyards of the future as big as polo fields, planted with white crosses beside the sea.

As for Zefiro, he was trying to forget that he had used the signature of his friend Eckener, without asking him and in the knowledge that he was severely compromising him.

Just as Vango was about to stand up and go over to his table, one of the two Napoleonic grenadiers entered the restaurant. He scoured the room and spotted Vango.

"There's a gentleman outside who'd like to have a word with you."

"Me? I think there must be some mistake."

"He said 'the young man sitting by himself.' He doesn't want to come in."

"Did he give you his name?"

"He didn't give me his or yours."

Vango glanced at the two men who were talking at the other end of the room. He was about to miss his chance.

"Tell him he's got the wrong person," Vango said, standing up.

"I think it's urgent," said the grenadier.

"But who is it?"

"That's him."

And Vango saw a very pale Zefiro appear, his head sunk into his shoulders, and proceed to sit next to him, in the place vacated by the chauffeur.

"Sit down," he whispered.

Vango did as he was told. Zefiro held himself very stiffly. The soldier had disappeared.

"We've got to get out of here," said the padre.

His lips barely moved. An accordionist had joined the pianist, and together they were playing a soporific rendition of a French cancan.

"I've understood," Zefiro went on. "I've finally understood everything."

Vango, on the other hand, was completely baffled.

"When you left . . ." Zefiro trailed off.

"Yes . . ."

"I climbed back up the tower to keep an eye on Viktor's bedroom through the binoculars. There was a window cleaner at work, and I suddenly had a suspicion. I went back down and telephoned the Plaza Hotel."

"You're crazy."

"I asked for Madame Victoria's room. I let it ring for a long time."

"Did he answer?"

"No," said Zefiro, even more quietly. "He couldn't answer."

"Why not?"

There were beads of sweat on Zefiro's nose.

"Because he's sitting right opposite us."

Vango looked up.

He was staring at the lawyer's neck.

The mysterious man who went away when Viktor went to bed, the man who reappeared briefly first thing in the morning, who seemed to wake up Voloy Viktor before disappearing again . . .

That man was Viktor.

"We've got to get out of here," said Vango.

"I know that," echoed Zefiro in a voice from beyond the grave. "Our faces are etched in acid in his mind. I am the man who betrayed him fifteen years ago when I was his confessor. I am the man who tried to deliver him to Boulard. He hasn't forgotten me. He would recognize us even in a crowd, even in a stadium. If he turns around, we are—"

"Why did you come in here? You should have stayed outside."

"Because four cars heaving with men just pulled up and parked outside while I was waiting for you by the door. I know that they've all got a photo of the two of us in their wallets. They're by the exit."

Vango felt a shudder run down his body.

"How did you know I was here?"

"Thanks to someone I couldn't have done without: my friend, young Tom Jackson. He followed you."

And, majestically, as if waiting for his name to be announced in order to make his grand entrance, Tom Jackson stepped out from behind the curtain by the door. He was holding the hand of the exasperated sapper grenadier.

"Sir, you left your child outside; he's had a fall. He's crying, he's bleeding, he's asking for you, and I don't know what to do!"

Zefiro's eyes bulged. Tom leaped into his lap. Vango kept his eyes trained on Viktor's back.

The soldier clicked his heels and set off again.

"Take me in your arms," whispered Tom, "and leave, hiding your face in my neck."

"Jesus," breathed the padre.

He had never picked up a child before. And Tom had never been held. Just the idea of burying their faces in each other made them feel embarrassed. They stared at each other in a state of shock. Two of Viktor's men had just walked into the restaurant.

"Do as he says," muttered Vango. "The three of us can't leave together. I'll manage."

The padre stood up with Tom in his arms, hugging him close as they walked toward the door.

The lawyer hadn't moved. The Irishman was listening to him.

When Tom and Zefiro had disappeared, Vango surveyed the premises.

The kitchens were at the back, next to a painting of some clams on a beach in Normandy. He could have gone that way, but he was suspicious of kitchen exits, emergency exits, and back exits, which were always under as much surveillance as the main exits. To the right of the pantry was something more interesting: a stairwell disappearing into the gloom could be glimpsed behind two drapes. For Vango, escaping always meant moving upward.

He stood up very gently, as if he didn't want to wake anybody, and tiptoed toward the curtains.

"Your glass of water, young sir."

Vango turned around.

"You need to pay for your glass of water."

The waitress was staring at him with both hands on her hips, her Breton headdress rocking backward and forward. Viktor's men were up at the bar, just behind her.

Vango jangled his pockets and held out some change.

"You said you were going to have dinner," she grumbled.

"I've changed my mind."

"Well, in that case, the exit's the other way."

"I thought—"

"It's private, over there. That's for the boss."

"Ah, yes, the boss."

With her finger, she pointed somewhere behind him. He turned around and saw the Irishman bent over a plate of pasta. Vango could see only his wide forehead. So he was the boss. Vango's gaze slid across that forehead to meet the eyes of a man who appeared to be sitting next to the Irishman on the banquette, but this was in fact the reflection of Viktor in the mirror just behind the Irishman.

Voloy Viktor was staring hard at Vango in the mirror.

He even smiled at him, like an old acquaintance you stumble on somewhere unexpected. Then in one movement, Viktor took out a silver pistol from his belt, politely excused himself to his host, turned sharply around, and aimed at Vango.

Zefiro and Tom were already some distance away when they heard the gunshot.

"Was that him?" asked Tom, stopping under a street lamp.

Zefiro remained in the shadow. He didn't want Tom to see his distraught face.

Silence.

Zefiro gave the wall a few violent kicks. He took his head in his hands. If that really was the case, he would never forgive himself.

Tom went over to him.

"Padre?"

There was a final bang.

"Come on, little one," the monk said without turning around. "I don't know what it was. Come on now."

A GHOSTLY BEDROOM

Vango tried the doors on every landing, but they were all locked. He could hear the commotion down below as he climbed the stairs.

As soon as the first shot was fired, Viktor's men had appeared, half-crushing the Napoleonic security guards and their bearskins in the scramble. The customers had shrieked as they crouched down on the restaurant floor.

Voloy Viktor was already outside, safely in the back of a car with darkened windows. His instructions were terse but calm, delivered through gritted teeth to his henchmen: "That's Vango Romano. Don't kill him."

But underneath, Viktor was seething. By aiming to wound Vango rather than kill him, he had missed. He'd had no choice: the kid was a link in the chain that would lead to Zefiro, the man who had betrayed him and who still wanted him dead. More pressingly, because of Vango, Viktor had just compromised his conversation with the most important business partner he had ever approached.

The Irishman had long since disappeared, siphoned off toward the kitchens by two burly men who had been dining three tables away. Another car was waiting for him in the street at the back of the restaurant. The banker's security arrangements had for some time been worthy of President Roosevelt.

The men giving chase lost precious minutes from the outset. A first door, behind the curtains that opened onto the restaurant, had been locked by Vango. That door cut off access to the stairs and could be unlocked only from the inside. It took a while for the men to smash it down with a fifty-kilo block of wood on which whole suckling pigs were usually butchered. With each blow, the headwaiter protested, but he was under strict instructions not to interfere.

Next, the pursuers forced their way in tight ranks through what was left of the door. The stairwell wound around a brick column, scaling a modest seven-story building. Like Vango before them, the men tried opening the doors to the first few rooms. Fortunately, the wooden block wouldn't fit in the stairwell.

"He couldn't have gone in anywhere," the headwaiter called out. "All the rooms are locked, and I don't have the keys: it used to be a hotel. You'll need to look for him higher up."

Sure enough, there was a skylight above the top landing. And, despite its inaccessible height, it was wide open. Two men lifted a third man, while a fourth availed himself of this human ladder to reach the roof. After a few seconds, his head reappeared in the window frame.

"He came this way. . . . Look!" he exclaimed, holding out the brown cap he had just found.

"The rooftops are flat and adjoining, so he could have gone in any direction."

More men started to climb up in turn.

"We won't get him!" someone declared.

The others stopped and stared at him.

It was Dorgeles. His head bowed, he was already predicting Viktor's wrath when he reported back to his boss.

"Everyone back downstairs!" ordered Dorgeles. "I want you out of my sight."

The man on the roof wasn't sure what to do.

"As for you," said Dorgeles, "you can stay up there another hour, just in case."

Next, he turned to the headwaiter, who was about to follow everyone else.

"Hold on a moment."

Once they were alone, Dorgeles explained how matters would be handled.

"Tell the Irishman that our men will put everything back in order. A joiner is already on his way to repair the door. What time is the first sitting for lunch?"

"Midday."

"It'll be fixed before midday. What about the police?"

"They won't be coming," the headwaiter reassured him.

"Why not?"

"Because we've asked them not to."

"And the customers?"

"They won't talk."

"Why not?"

"The same reason."

Dorgeles nodded in silence.

"Above all," he added, "you can tell your boss that my boss doesn't want these events to jeopardize their discussions. This was a personal matter, and it won't happen again."

"I'll tell him."

Dorgeles gestured, thinking that he had heard something.

"Are you sure he couldn't have gotten in there," he whispered, pointing to a door.

"Positive. Everything is barricaded up. Look at the locks. Nobody's been inside those rooms for fifteen years. It's like a museum."

The headwaiter started walking down the stairs, with Dorgeles following. Their voices grew fainter.

"I don't know what that boy's done to you, but I suspect it's in his best interests to get as far away from here as he can."

No, thought Vango, who was very close by.

Sooner or later in life, it's good to stop running away.

Having made it up onto the roof, Vango had climbed down the outside of the building and entered one of the locked bedrooms via the window. He had gone over to the door to listen. Through the thick wood, he had kept track of his pursuers' indecisiveness.

When calm was restored, he turned around and took a good look at the room. It was a museum piece . . . like a tomb, with a layer of dust on the furniture and a bitter smell in the air. The ghosts of spiders' webs seemed to tether the bed and the bedside tables to the floor. The decor was illuminated by the light from the street. Vango took a few steps in this hotel bedroom outside of time. There was a calendar on the wall from 1922. Above the washbasin, the mirror no longer reflected anything. The contrast with the luxury on the ground floor was striking. A swish restaurant had been opened up on the site of a former seedy hotel.

An hour later, Vango heard the thud of someone taking

a tumble onto the landing by the stairwell, followed by a groan of pain. He had been expecting this. It meant that the man on the roof had left his post. He had been left all alone up there, so dropping down was his only means of escape. Vango listened to the sound effects as the man dragged himself downstairs. Then the path was clear.

He waited a little longer. Then, securing a foothold on the windowsill, Vango climbed all the way back up to the roof. There, he picked up his cap and took in the view of the city by night. The landscape was the color of ash and earth. Even on this raised terrace, he felt as if he were at the bottom of a pit, because the buildings towered above him. Smoke escaped from the chimneys. A few windows were still lit up, holding out against the night. Voices could be heard high up on a balcony, and there were songs wafting from a small basement window in a courtyard.

Vango headed off along the rooftops.

At dawn, he found Zefiro on the scaffolding of their tower. The padre was a terrifying sight as he leaned against a section of wall, his face drawn and haggard. All night long he had been afraid for Vango, and ashamed of having led him into the trap. He had just sent Tom Jackson away with a two-dollar redundancy package. Zefiro no longer wanted to involve these kids in his madcap scheme to take the law into his own hands. It was a matter for him and him alone. He had pleaded with the heavens all night long, begging for Vango to come out alive. The knees of his trousers were as worn out as a child's.

The padre greeted Vango as awkwardly as ever, because he didn't know how to express his relief at seeing him alive. He tilted his hat over his eyes.

"Take your belongings. I never want to see you here again. I don't need you anymore."

Vango stared at him. For the second time in his short life he was being thrown out by Zefiro.

"Get out. Now."

Vango gathered his belongings into a bag, leaving one of the precious stones in Zefiro's breviary, on the page for the evening prayer. He walked back toward him.

"Padre . . ."

"Not another word, Vango."

Vango left.

In the morning, the waitress from La Rocca restaurant, in the district of Little Italy, found a young man asleep on the doorstep when she arrived to open up. She rolled the body to one side and instantly recognized Vango.

He opened his eyes, and the young woman smiled.

"Hello, Lupo. I told you that you'd run into trouble. . . ."

Vango clutched his bag. Next, he stood up and brushed down his clothes. He had only met her the once, but he had thought of her right away. He didn't know anybody else in New York.

"I'm looking for somewhere to stay for a few days," he ventured without crossing the threshold.

She was already inside, grinding the coffee.

"Close the door!" she called out.

The delicious aroma enticed Vango inside. He watched the waitress at work as she concentrated on turning the coffee grinder handle.

"Miss, I'm looking for . . ."

She stopped and looked at him, her eyes emphasized by black eyeliner.

"I heard."

Then she picked up a coffee bean and crunched it between her teeth. She was glad he was there. She didn't want to let him go.

"My boss has two bedrooms upstairs, but he's a rat. He drives a hard bargain. You'll have to pay."

"That's just as well; I don't accept gifts from rats."

She smiled again and kept grinding.

"Wait for him here. He's called Otello. And my name is Alma."

She grabbed a bucket and mop and, for twenty minutes, she made the old wooden floorboards shine until Vango's chair became an island surrounded by water.

Vango kept drifting in and out of wakefulness, still dazed by the night that he had just spent. He understood that the padre was probably saving his life. But was his life worth saving? He had nobody now. Even Ethel, in a small parcel that he had collected from the post office, had told him not to write anymore. And, cruelly, she had sent back to him, neatly folded, the blue handkerchief that bore Vango's name and the mysterious phrase: *Combien de royaumes nous ignorent.*

He had just left the handkerchief with Zefiro, like a souvenir he no longer wanted.

A cup of coffee slid across the counter in front of him.

"He's dead, I saw," said the girl.

"Who?"

"The man you're looking for . . . Cafarello."

"Where?"

"At Sing Sing prison."

"Where did you see that?"

"Someone cut . . ."

Vango shuddered.

"Who got cut?"

"The article, someone cut it out of the newspaper."

"Ah!"

"An article with his photo. It was pinned up here."

She pointed to a wooden board beneath the liquor bottles.

"I threw it out with the trash yesterday."

"Threw out what?"

"The cutting from the newspaper. It was too scary."

"Why?"

"He used to come here sometimes. He would be right there, in front of me, just like you are now. And . . ."

She was leaning on her elbows in front of Vango, staring at her hands.

"And?"

"Well, when you think what he did."

"What did he do?"

"You mean you don't know? Then why were you looking for him?"

"What did he do?"

"It's why he was arrested, two years ago. He threw a girl off the new bridge above the Bronx Kill."

Vango stared at Alma. Why had he never wondered what

crime the condemned man at Sing Sing stood accused of? He stared down at the white halo floating on his coffee.

A girl thrown off a bridge.

The horror of this crime changed everything for Vango. Curiously, he had never wanted to accept that the now-dead man really was Giovanni Cafarello. But, on hearing Alma's account, he suddenly felt as if he recognized his parents' murderer. So perhaps the real Cafarello was dead after all, buried in the communal grave at Sing Sing?

Vango's confusion proved that his whole life had depended on revenge. The desire for revenge was what had kept him going. It was what he'd lived for. There are some very old houses still standing because of the ivy that is destroying them.

"Why did you want to talk with him?" Alma repeated.

"Who was the girl he threw off the bridge?"

"Her name was in the newspaper. I can't remember it now. Nobody knew anything about her. Maria, I think . . . or Laura. Yes, Laura. She had only come to America six months earlier."

Just then, the owner of La Rocca walked in. He was carrying a ham over one shoulder and rolling a small barrel with his foot.

"Help me, *bella*."

Alma went to help roll the barrel to its rightful place, and the two of them disappeared at the back of the kitchen.

"Who's your boyfriend?" the owner asked her.

"He's not my boyfriend."

Otello was surprised to see Alma blushing. After all, she had enough experience when it came to jokes. And boyfriends.

"He's a customer; he wants Wendy's room, upstairs."

"Does he realize that Wendy isn't in there anymore?"

He burst out laughing, presumably as he thought of dowdy Wendy, who had just moved out.

"Stop it; it's serious."

Otello screwed up his eyes mischievously.

"Ah, it's serious?"

Alma had done her boss a disservice by calling him a rat. He was a good man and, by and large, honest. He was kind to her. He liked to joke and was always quick to laugh. Otello was only a rat when it came to money.

"Right. Has he got the means, your boyfriend?"

The owner of La Rocca had become serious again. As a matter of fact, he resembled a hamster more than a rat.

"I don't know."

He went back into the bar. The discussion didn't take long. Vango agreed to the asking price, which Otello was only moderately pleased about. In the kingdom of the greedy, if the other person doesn't haggle, then you wish you'd asked for more in the first place.

"Sheets aren't included. Nor is gas. Did you want pillows?"

Vango signed up for all the optional extras.

He stayed in his bedroom for two days and two nights without coming out, tucked under two blankets that he had also rented, his head buried in the pillow for which he was paying. The feathers were extra.

When he finally got up, he had slept a lot and thought a lot. He stretched in front of the window. Two or three bills had already been slid under the door. He put them in his pocket and went downstairs. It was lunchtime. Vango had to go outside in order to access the restaurant. It had snowed, and the cars were passing by in slow motion.

Vango walked inside and sat down on one of the bench seats. The kitchen was bustling. Alma pretended not to have seen him. When he ordered an egg, she gave him a little wave from a distance.

The customers arrived in dribs and drabs. From the way they paused after walking through the door (to sniff the air as they shook the snow off their shoes, to greet Otello, who kept saying "Easy does it, easy does it. . . ." because he was worried about his doormat getting worn out), you could tell they were happy to be there, and that in a single step they had passed from the Atlantic to the Mediterranean, where they were at home again, in shorts. Sunday back in the home country.

"I'm eighteen, but they take me for their mother," Alma told Vango.

She put his fried egg down in front of him.

"What was he like?" he asked.

"Who?"

"Him. Cafarello."

Alma seemed hesitant.

"I don't know. Don't talk to me about it anymore. I mean, it takes you three days to come out of your bedroom . . . and then the only thing you order is an egg!"

"But you knew him."

"As a customer, that's all. I didn't even know his last name until he made the papers."

She went to take the hat of a man who had just arrived. As he crossed the threshold, the customer made it look as if he were still cold, whereas in fact it was the warmth and the aroma of fried bread crumbs making him quiver with pleasure.

Alma passed in front of Vango again. She stopped.

"I remember that he was kind. That's what scares me, thinking about it. Does everybody hide their cruelty? And the girl he killed is buried in Woodlawn Cemetery; I read that. Cafarello was a kind man. He didn't speak English. He was a bit lost in New York. I think he'd worked for a long time in the West, looking after cows. He knew all about meat."

"A kind man . . ." echoed Vango.

"That's what scares me," repeated Alma, before heading into the kitchen.

Vango didn't know what to think anymore. He ate his egg. The yolk was just as it should be, creamy. The white was merely fried at the edge, as crisp as a sliver of caramel. It had been sprinkled invisibly with white pepper.

Cafarello's kindness didn't surprise Vango. A girl like Alma tended to bring out the best in people. But why, with a fortune in his pockets—namely the treasure stolen from the boat—had he started out by looking after cows in the West?

Vango waited for Alma to reappear.

"Was he rich, your cowboy?" he whispered when she came to take his plate away.

"Yes. He always had money. A lot of it. And he couldn't count. The boss noticed that."

She seemed embarrassed by what she had just said.

"The boss notices those kind of things . . . but he *is* honest."

This time, it was all heading in the right direction. Vango was starting to believe in the evidence: that Cafarello was indeed Cafarello; that he had died because of his final crime, the murder of a girl on the bridge over the Bronx Kill.

Vango pushed back his chair and went outside. He took a few steps beneath the swirling snowflakes. Alma was watching him through the restaurant window.

There was no sense of relief in Vango's heart. In the act of dying, Cafarello had robbed him both of his revenge and of the truth.

He walked all day long. He stopped several times to sit on benches and watch the people passing by. He knew where he was going, but he was heading there via a thousand detours. Sometimes he lost a whole hour, just watching. Time moves to a different rhythm when it's snowing. And it's easier to fathom people against a white background.

Vango's footsteps had long been covered up. He left his bench when he felt too much weight on his cap and shoulders, just before he disappeared altogether beneath the snow.

He passed by several bridges, and each time he stared at the icy waters flowing beneath.

Vango reached Woodlawn Cemetery as daylight was beginning to wane. It was a huge field of snow dotted with trees. He went to knock on the caretaker's door, in the knowledge that his quest was ridiculous: the cemetery stretched to dozens of hectares.

The man who opened up had bandages on his hands. He was wearing a coat and a woolen hat.

"I'm sorry to bother you," said Vango. "I'm looking for somebody."

The man held out a spade.

"Follow me."

Feeling rather alarmed, Vango allowed the man to lead the way. They skirted the house. The man walked stiffly. It was snowing more heavily now.

"Dig there," he ordered. He had come to a stop and was pointing to a mound of snow.

Vango was speechless. He had no desire to bury or indeed to unearth anybody.

"I'm afraid I can't help you," the man explained, when he noticed Vango's reluctance. "I did my back in two weeks ago."

"But . . . who is under here?"

"Who?"

Vango took a step backward.

"You've got some very odd ideas," the man remarked. "I haven't been able to warm myself up all day," he added with a smile, "because my wood is buried right here under the snow."

Vango was embarrassed and uncovered the wood in a few shovelfuls.

"So, you're looking for someone?" the man asked him on the way back, when Vango was laden down with the logs.

"Yes. A girl who's buried here."

"Last name, age, date of death?"

"I don't know."

"You're joking. Not even her name?"

"She might be called Laura."

"Might?"

"Yes."

They came to a halt in front of the door.

"Put the wood down here. Keep the spade. There are

a hundred and fifty thousand graves to scrape the snow off. You'll find the right one in the end."

The caretaker had removed the bandages, which had been standing in for gloves. He went back inside his home.

"Wait," Vango called out after him. "You might remember. She was a young woman who was murdered last year, or two years ago."

The man reappeared. He went over to Vango and put his hand on the shovel.

"Did you know her?" the man asked.

"Yes."

"So why was I the only one digging her grave in the middle of June?"

He stared at Vango for rather a long time.

"All right, you rescued my logs, so we're quits. Take that path, just there. It's the fifth turn on the left. A wooden cross between two trees. Poor girl."

Vango nodded, already heading off in that direction.

"Did you hear about the murderer's attorney?" called out the caretaker, whose stiff legs couldn't keep up.

"No." Vango sighed.

"The worst attorney in the world. He pleaded self-defense. Do you know what he said?"

Vango didn't answer.

"He said that it was the girl who had attacked the man."

Vango let him talk, but he didn't want to listen anymore.

"He turned it into a whole saga. People were laughing in the courtroom. He showed a notebook that had been found with the girl, made out that it was a case of revenge for old crimes."

"Thank you. That's all," said Vango, standing very still.

The caretaker hobbled over to Vango and shook his hand.

"My condolences," said the man, and off he went.

Vango kept walking, his feet sinking into the snow for a few minutes more. He arrived in front of the cross. What had he come to do at this grave?

There was no particular spot where he could go and reflect on his parents' lives. So this young victim, murdered by the same man who had killed his parents, buried in the ground between two trees, had attracted him. And this cross inclining under the snow soothed him now.

He crouched down, searching deep inside himself for the prayers or cries that would help him reach the other side of his anger. He wondered why he had survived Cafarello's cruelty that night in 1918, in the waters of the Aeolian Islands. He thought about Mademoiselle. Was she also lying dead somewhere with her secrets? Was there a glimmer of life in anyone who could reveal Vango's past to him?

He glanced up at the caretaker's chimney, which was smoking now in the distance. He tugged on his coat sleeve to cover his hand, like a mitten. Leaning forward, he brushed away the snow on the stone that had been laid in front of the cross.

He saw Laura's name appear. He rubbed some more and revealed the boulder on which the paint hadn't yet flaked off, and read:

Laura Viaggi
Salina 1912 — New York 1935

Vango dug both knees into the snow.

● ●

"THIS NOTEBOOK BELONGS TO LAURA VIAGGI"

The man described by both a prison warden and a cemetery caretaker as "the worst attorney in the world" had his offices in a handsome building on Broadway.

There were life-size mythological characters sculpted across its facade. At night, by the light of the theaters that surrounded the building, there flickered an army of shadows, including Jason, Odysseus, Antigone, and Hercules. They had watched over the lives of ordinary New Yorkers down the years.

But this evening, in the midst of these statues, twenty meters above ground level, one face in particular might have intrigued an attentive observer. The eyes of this hero moved in the dark.

Vango was standing on a narrow ledge, waiting for the crowds below him to disperse after their big night out at the theater. Hot on the heels of the dancing throngs that emerged from the Ziegfeld Follies at the Winter Garden, came a wave of tragedians, followed by spectators in hoots of laughter, and then the sleepwalkers who had found the show too long. Finally, a calm began to settle again over Broadway. This time of night belonged to the artists. The lights shining onto the pediments were switched off. Dancers, still sporting hairdos from ancient Chinese dynasties, dived into snow-covered taxis.

Just opposite, a theater boasted: WALTER FREDERICK, SOLO ON STAGE, in letters that were four meters by two, alongside an outsize picture of the actor. And the performer himself had just appeared, solo on the sidewalk, a diminutive figure whistling a tune by the light of his name. Vango would never have guessed that three years earlier they had flown together, two stowaways aboard the *Graf Zeppelin*. After his arrival from Germany, Walter Frederick had quickly sprung to fame on Broadway and in Hollywood.

Vango stayed where he was, balancing on his heels halfway up a thirty-story facade. He was waiting for the lights to go out in the window above him. The worst attorney in the world was working late this evening.

But instead of the lights being switched off, the window opened and a man leaned out.

Hidden in the folds of a Roman goddess's plaster dress, Vango didn't move. The smell of tobacco wafted over to him. He could even hear the gentle sigh accompanying each puff.

"Snow, snow, snow," the man remarked, because you don't need to sound clever when you think you're alone.

For the same reason, he muttered stupidly, "There goes another one!" as he tossed his cigarette butt and shut the window.

The lights went out shortly afterward. Vango waited for the man to leave the building, and for the gray hat belonging to the worst attorney in the world to disappear around the corner of the street.

Vango put his hands on the windowsill and scaled the window. He took a sharp implement out of his pocket, and the lock soon gave way.

Once inside the office, he made for the desk, where he found a pile of Christmas cards ready for sending. He checked the name printed at the top: Mr. Trevor K. Donahue, Attorney—this was the lawyer he was looking for. The card showed Mr. Donahue wearing his court apparel and standing by a stream, holding an enormous salmon.

Vango opened a drawer. The paper clips had been arranged according to color, the erasers had been shaved with a knife to make them pristine again, and the pencils were arranged according to size. Vango deduced that he wouldn't have too much trouble finding what he was looking for.

In the second drawer of the desk, Vango found five identical and perfectly ironed cotton shirts. In the third drawer, there was a toothbrush attached to a tube of toothpaste by an elastic band. The toothbrush had the attorney's initials stamped on it. The word *teeth* had been handwritten on the elastic band, as if there were a risk of getting it muddled up with the elastic band for cotton balls or nail files. In another box were two new razors and some shaving cream. All that was missing was the shaving brush.

Where are the files? wondered Vango.

He also found a cigarette case filled with toothpicks, two playing cards, an address book that was mostly empty, a guide to fly-fishing, a menu from La Bohème restaurant, a key ring in the shape of an octopus, a detachable collar, a collection of theater tickets filed by title in alphabetical order, a diary for the coming year, a small painted soldier, and a raccoon's tail in a bag marked A SOUVENIR FROM THE ROCKIES.

Vango wanted to search the large piece of furniture at the back of the room, but it turned out to be a bar. Next, he opened two files that were completely empty. To the right, along the small but carefully ordered bookshelves, which even had a notebook hanging from a string so that any books taken out could be noted down, he failed to find a single file.

He went next door into what was presumably the secretary's office. The room was remarkably clean, but there was no sign of a file in there either. It looked more like a waiting room, with a few magazines, a painting on the wall, a telephone, and a fish in a bowl.

Vango sensed that he might have to leave empty-handed. The goldfish was staring at him. Where could he find what he was looking for? Vango was about to turn out the lights when the telephone rang. Curious, he waited a moment before picking up.

"Is that you?" came a man's voice.

When Vango didn't reply, loud laughter could be heard.

"I know you're there. I'm downstairs, in the café, and I saw the lights on. I've just come out of the show. I'll pop up. So stop pretending you're deaf, Trevor, old boy, and don't forget I've still got the key!"

Vango hung up. He took a step backward, knocked over the goldfish bowl, and crashed into the partition wall. The bowl smashed on the floor just as the painting came off its hook on the other side of the office. Vango watched the goldfish belly dancing on the carpet, and then he looked up. Behind the painting, a steel-studded safe had appeared. Vango went over to it. Shards from the broken bowl crunched beneath his feet. He stared at the safe. Opening it required six numbers, all between zero and nine. Vango had less than two minutes for a million combinations.

Vango tugged at the safe door. It was locked. He closed his eyes, took a deep breath, and tried to imagine himself in the shoes of the worst attorney in the world. After concentrating for twenty seconds, he rushed out of the office and back into the room next door, opened a drawer, and took out the address book. He went directly to the letter *S,* glanced through the different surnames written down there, and found what he wanted. After the telephone numbers for Simpson, Henry James; Smith, Philip; and Saraband, Plumbing, came Secret Code, J. Edward, followed by a six-digit number. Vango was appalled and thrilled.

He went back to the safe. Somebody was ringing the doorbell.

Vango set the first three digits.

"Open up, you idiot!"

More ringing.

The man was losing his temper.

"Watch out! I'm going to let myself in. Are you with someone, Trevor?"

The final digit on the safe combination.

"I can hear you, Trevor!"

The safe opened. There was the red notebook, next to a wad of dollars. Vango grabbed the notebook and ran toward the window. He could hear the jangling of keys now.

"I'm coming in," announced the voice.

Vango jumped onto the windowsill and slammed the shutter behind him.

"Trevor?"

The visitor took a step inside the lobby area and immediately spotted the goldfish lying among the pieces of broken glass.

"Andy!"

The man dived onto the carpet, caught hold of the fish, rolled with it toward the bar, grabbed two bottles of mineral water in one hand, rushed back into the lobby area, and emptied them into the umbrella stand. Then he threw in Andy.

No animal was mistreated or injured in the offices of Trevor Donahue that evening.

Vango scaled down the outside of the building as lightly as a snowflake. He headed back toward Little Italy, where he ran into Otello, who was closing the shutters at La Rocca.

"I didn't talk to you about the hot water," said the boss.

"Yes, you did. Five cents a pint."

"Well, it's six in winter. Good night, young man."

"Good night."

"Do you realize that Alma waited up for you until very late? Not that I suppose you take such things into account."

Vango didn't answer. He went up to his bedroom.

The handwriting was careful; the words were written in Sicilian without any mistakes but in a limited vocabulary. On the first page was the sentence *This notebook belongs to Laura Viaggi,* much as you might expect to find in the exercise book of a primary school student. Laura would have been twenty-two years old when she started to write these pages.

Vango was lying in bed, the notebook open in his hands.

I've decided to leave. I'm going to find him. Spoke to poor Pina Troisi. He is in America. That's what she says. She described his face and height for me.
Giovanni Valente Cafarello.
Giovanni Valente Cafarello.

Laura wrote his name everywhere in the notebook, as if there were a risk of it being washed away. She might even have written it somewhere on her skin.

I'm staring at the house I'm leaving behind. There's a storm, over there, by the lighthouse at Lingua. It's been four years now since my sisters left this world. Seven years for my mother. And sixteen for my father. Why wait? He killed my father, Bartolomeo Viaggi. He killed my father after trying to turn him into a murderer. He put a curse on the Viaggi family.
I'm going to catch two boats to start. Then I'll take a third from Naples. I've got the money for the crossing. I keep counting up all the coins and notes. I bought some new clothes from Buongiorno's. Someone told me you can work on the boat to pay for your first days in America.

Next came a few words written out in English to help her learn the language. Lists of words she would need: *eat, boat, work*. And phrases: *Hello, I'm looking for a friend of my father, Giovanni Valente Cafarello, from the island of Salina, in Sicily*. The names of the different districts of New York were scribbled in the margins, with maps, as in an explorer's journal, as well as sketched faces always with the same recognizable features: the photo-fit of Cafarello. And his name was in every corner of the book.

I'm sleeping down by the port tonight. I've sold the house. I'm setting off tomorrow. I've put a bit of money into a sock tied to my petticoats.

With each page, Vango was able to clamber deeper inside Laura's mind. With each page, he also recognized his own struggle. The memory of that small wooden cross at

Woodlawn Cemetery brought tears to his eyes: it was the answer to the glimmers of hope in Laura Viaggi's notebook. The trouble was that Vango knew the end of the story. The red notebook made for heartbreaking reading.

I'm in Naples now. It's cold. The tickets are much more expensive than they told me back in Malfa. I'm going to spend Christmas working in the fish market. I'll catch the boat in the middle of January.
Sold a pair of shoes.

There were lists of accounts, the price of a bowl of soup, of a night in a convent, then some new English words, and a few sentences addressed to her two sisters who had left her, sentences she had tried to obscure but that were still visible under all the crossings out:

I'm taking you with me. I'm doing what I swore I would. Stay close to me. Help me find him. Please, God, help me find him.

Vango was reading the notebook slowly. He had enough candles to get him through the night. He would simply have to pay Otello by the weight of molten wax.

Suddenly, between two pages, he saw Laura's face. It was a photograph taken on her arrival in New York, stuck to an official card. The photo was thumbnail sized. Vango held it up to the flame to get a better look.

She wasn't staring at the camera. She was glancing to one side as if on the lookout already, over the photographer's shoulder, for a glimpse of Cafarello. She looked young for her age. Her hair had been cut very short, probably during the crossing. A few pages back she had written about the fleas on the boat. And sometimes tiny insects appeared crushed between the pages.

Vango scrutinized Laura Viaggi's face. It was a long time before he turned the page.

The American part of the notebook was the most painful. The only place Laura knew was her islands: where a traveler could arrive in Salina or even in Lipari and give a name down at the port, and there would always be someone who could point to the house of the person she was looking for. But when she stepped off the boat in New York, Laura's first impressions were disastrous. How was she supposed to find anyone in this city of clouds?

No sign of Cafarello down at the port. No sign of Cafarello in her first ten days of looking. No sign of Cafarello by the end of the first month.

"Carello, my brother-in-law's called Carello," a young barber had told her on the fortieth evening. "But he isn't from Sicily. He's from Calabria."

And so Laura Viaggi had been to pay this Carello a visit, thinking that perhaps he had tried to disguise his name. But he turned out to be an old grocer. The sign on his store was enough to put Laura off: CARELLO, GOOD TASTE IN NEW YORK SINCE 1908. Ten years too early. All the same, she had asked for a bottle of wine from the islands of Lipari to gauge his reaction. Old Carello had made her repeat the name, but in the end he had brought out a bottle of Calabrian red, insisting it was the best.

Two weeks later, Laura had seen a man in the street

wearing two wooden boards, one in front, the other on his back, tied together with leather straps. Glued to them were posters advertising a brand of soap.

And, the next day, Laura Viaggi had walked the avenues of New York with two large boards that asked the crucial question:

Do you know Giovanni Cafarello?

People must have thought she was mad. This went on for weeks. Now Vango understood why, each time he had asked that same question nearly two years later, the name of Cafarello seemed to stir up muddled recollections. Very few of the city's inhabitants could swear that they had never come across Laura and her famous question during the winter of 1934.

In the early days, she watched the reactions of passersby. These ranged from amusement, to surprise, to suitors going down on their knees in the pathways of Central Park: "It's me; I'm Cafarello. I've been looking for you too!" But Laura's dark glare deterred them.

People's curiosity soon gave way to indifference, as happens in all big cities, where anything considered a novelty is quickly superseded by something newer.

In the final quarter of the notebook, Vango stopped at two pages that were stuck together. He couldn't separate them with his fingers. He left his room and tiptoed over the cold tiles to fetch a razor blade that he had spotted on the washbasin at the end of the corridor. As he was about to return to his room, he heard a voice close by.

"Is someone with you?"

"Alma?"

Alma was sitting on the floor in the corridor.

"I heard you talking to someone."

"What are you doing here, Alma?"

She was wearing a hat covered in snow.

Vango realized that he must have been reading out loud.

"Who's with you? What's her name?"

"There isn't anyone."

"I heard you. Come with me, Lupacchiotto. There's something I want to talk to you about."

"Not now, I can't. Tomorrow, Alma . . ."

Why did Vango have the feeling that someone was waiting for him in his bedroom? Laura Viaggi's notebook was breathing on the bed.

"Tomorrow," Vango said again. "All right?"

"What have you got in your hands?"

He showed her the rusty razor.

"You give me the creeps," she said. "What did you want from Cafarello?"

"He knew my family. I've got to go now."

"Good night."

Alma got up and walked away.

Vango went back into his bedroom. Through the window, he watched Alma heading off in the middle of the white street.

Down below, Alma was mulling over what she had wanted to say to Vango.

If he had made a little time for her, just a little bit, Alma would have told him about something she had just remembered. Cafarello's words, one day when he'd been drinking:

"I am not Giovanni Cafarello."

She turned around to look at her footprints in the snow and at Vango's window lit up at the end of the street.

Vango picked up the book again under the sheets. He slipped the razor blade between the stuck pages and separated them slowly. This left some rust on the paper, but he was still able to read:

May 17, 1935, eight o'clock in the evening. Rain.
Sitting on the steps outside the Law Courts. Short, bald man, brown eyes, came to talk to me. Saw him for one minute in total.
He gave me all the information about Giovanni Cafarello: staying at Hotel Napoli, Room 35. Then disappeared.
Still here, in the rain. I've come to the end of my journey.

Vango reread these lines. The attorney hadn't even tried to prize apart the pages stuck together by the May rains. And this, in turn, gave Vango a clear indication of how weak the defense must have been. Attorney Donahue probably had his mind on his trout river, up there in the Adirondack Mountains, where he would be going the following Sunday. In his head, he was already getting his boots, hooks, and flies ready.

It wasn't even a case of trying to pervert the course of justice; it was just laziness. Rather than reading the notebook all the way through to the end, Donahue had spent an hour trying out a new paper-clip sorting system, or writing "small envelopes" in Gothic script on the large envelope that contained them.

The next pages were an account of trailing Cafarello.

Laura was right behind him, step by step, for several days. His age and face fitted the bill. She was amazed by his stoutness, which was very different from what Giuseppina Troisi had described to her. Perhaps the change of climate had transformed him? She herself had become a lot thinner.

He wandered around the city, without a job, but he was never short of money. Surprised to discover a real man when she had been expecting a werewolf, Laura never let him out of her sight. One night, at the reception desk for Hotel Napoli, she had been able to take a look at the customer register. The occupant of Room 35, Giovanni Cafarello, had indeed been born at Leni, on the island of Salina, Italy, in 1885.

She closed the register. This was her man. The murderer of Bartolomeo Viaggi.

Vango found it hard not to tremble as he read the last pages of the red notebook. They were addressed to Laura Viaggi's family. There were childhood memories, tiny specific details that nobody else would have thought of writing down.

Vango appropriated them as if they were his own. This was the childhood he had never known. With these words penned in black ink, Laura was remembering.

The sound of footsteps on the roof at night, when her parents were stargazing. Fragments of invisible lives. When her father arrived home, and the children were already at the supper table, the steam from the soup would settle back down on the bowl because of the open door. Or again, after a storm, when they used to put the twigs of broken bougainvillea in her mother's hair. Papery flowers filled with drops of water. Or when it was too hot, the way the three sisters would sleep together with dampened sheets forming a tent around them. And silly memories: the tale of a beetle they tamed, of a cat locked by mistake inside the salting tub, funny moments, the day when this happened, the day when that happened, repainting the house white in June.

And then there had been the night when their father hadn't returned, when he had gone fishing with Gio, who was Cafarello's son, violent, unmarriable, and another man, the one with the donkey at Pollara, tall Mazzetta.

The three men had gone to sea. Laura Viaggi believed she knew what had happened. They had boarded a boat somewhere between the islands. There was much more on board than they had bargained for. Cafarello had turned crazy and bloodthirsty. And the next day, he had killed Laura's father to seize his share.

Vango recognized that night. It was his night too. This was what he shared with Laura Viaggi: a night of gunpowder and blood.

The notebook ended with the words *I'll go tonight.*

There was no period. And the word *tonight* trailed off in its last letters, falling below the line.

Holding the closed notebook, Vango imagined what must have happened next. The confrontation on the bridge, above the Bronx Kill, on the way back to Hotel Napoli that night. The victory of the wolf against Laura the goat. Perhaps there were witnesses, enough to condemn Cafarello. And to end the story, a flash of electricity in Sing Sing prison.

The next day at midnight, Vango left America. He had ventured to the foot of the scaffolding on Zefiro's tower.

He had gazed up to see a glow at the top. Then he had returned to the landing pier. By chance, the ship's departure had been delayed by twenty-four hours because of a breakdown. The atmosphere was festive: waiting turned into a party. Hundreds of passengers ended up dining in leisurely fashion down at the port, as a whiff of wine wafted among the suitcases and traveling coats. In every nook and cranny, children lay asleep. People were singing at the foot of the gangways.

The ship took to the seas at midnight, all lit up, waltzing and full of life again.

Dozing in his sitting room, which resembled a cigar box lined in walnut and leather, the Irishman woke with a jolt on hearing the ship's horn sounding. He got up out of his armchair and padded over in his socks to grab a bottle from the desk before going to the window.

"*Barcàzza,*" he said in Sicilian. Dirty boat.

He was weary of hearing the ships' horns sounding, and he disliked immigrants, so he would soon be moving away from Manhattan's docks in order to be nearer Midtown. But building work on his tower was still behind schedule.

The man they called the Irishman took a long swig from the bottle before catching his breath, like a seal emerging from the water. Apart from the origin of the whiskey, there was nothing Irish flowing in his veins.

He watched the lights of the ship disappear on the horizon until all he could see was his own reflection in the window. With his left hand, he stroked the Cossack scarf around his neck. In eighteen years, since the massacre on the boat in the Aeolian Islands, Cafarello had never parted with this bloodred scarf: it was a token of his spoils from the sea, and the fortune he had made.

PART TWO

EUROPE,
JANUARY–MAY 1937

THE CONSTELLATIONS

Paris, January 1937

Superintendent Boulard was pacing the corridors of the police headquarters in his underwear. It was five o'clock in the morning. The building was pitch-black.

"Perishing cold!" muttered the superintendent as he shuffled over the parquet floor in his slippers, trailing a woolen blanket behind him and cursing the arctic temperatures.

He was trying to find somewhere less freezing cold to sleep a while longer, as he had done in the early hours for several weeks now. It was always the same story: Boulard would doze off under his desk at eleven o'clock, only to wake up in the middle of the night with feet like blocks of ice. He would then stride energetically up and down the corridors for an hour before hunkering down somewhere.

This morning, he pushed open the door to the HQ archives and came to a stop in an aisle. The mass of paper seemed to be giving off a particular kind of warmth, and he felt if he could only lie down between the boxes he would soon drop off. In the end, he found a warm spot by the shelf for Homicides, under the archives for Crimes of Passion. He wrapped his blanket around him and closed his eyes.

Since his poor mother had gone away, Boulard hadn't set foot outside Police Head Office at the Quai des Orfèvres.

But before seeking refuge there, he had taken a stroll around the back of the Sorbonne University in order to knock on the door of his faithful second-in-command, Avignon, who had been extremely embarrassed. After half an hour of talking in the communal hallway, Avignon had agreed to let his boss step inside his small apartment.

Boulard was dumbstruck by what he saw. It was the first time he had crossed the threshold of the man he had been working with for twenty years. Augustin Avignon lived alone in three dark rooms. The walls were covered with documents and newspaper cuttings relating to every case he and Boulard had ever solved together. There was no sign of any personal belongings. A mattress lay in the corridor. The doors to the kitchen cupboards had been dismantled so that books and files could be stacked inside. Boulard pretended not to notice the large photograph of him that was displayed in the tiny living room.

"May I?" ventured the superintendent, sitting down beneath his own portrait.

Avignon cleared the clutter from the sofa.

Boulard ran his finger over a dusty table flap.

"Do you own this apartment?"

It was the only polite question he could think of, faced with such a pigsty.

"Yes."

"That's good. . . ."

Boulard pursed his lips enthusiastically and scanned the room, as if he thought Avignon were sitting on a gold mine.

"Have you got any coffee, my boy?"

Avignon's eyes bulged.

"Coffee?"

You'd have thought Boulard had asked for six bottles of Château d'Yquem 1921. Avignon headed into the kitchenette.

The superintendent began to explain his situation. The threats from the Russian, his mother's departure, his need to find a refuge, to get down to work properly again. And above all his desire to be done with the Vango affair once and for all.

From the other side of the room, Avignon avoided Boulard's gaze.

"Does anyone know you're here?" he asked suddenly.

The superintendent looked surprised.

"Why?"

Avignon seemed even more agitated. He rummaged about in a box, perhaps looking for a coffee press.

"I don't know. . . . Someone might have followed you."

"Relax," said Boulard, shaking his head.

Avignon stopped what he was doing and turned toward Boulard, who glanced briefly around him, taking in the closed shutters and the photos on the walls. He felt stifled. What was going on in this man's life? He understood Avignon's absences for the past few months rather better now. His deputy was in a bad way.

"You've been working too hard."

Such words had never been expressed before by the superintendent.

"Haven't you got a lady friend?"

He had never asked a question like that either.

"You take things too seriously. You should lighten up."

This was a feast of expressions that had never escaped Superintendent Boulard's lips before, of which the last was not the least.

"Can I sleep at your place, my boy?"

Avignon broke into a sweat. His eyes had glazed over. Boulard could sense his discomfort.

"Of course, if it would cause any problems with your neighbor . . ."

"Why do you mention my neighbor?"

"I bumped into him, and he said hello."

Avignon nearly leaped out of his skin.

"So someone did see you come in here?"

The superintendent went over to Avignon.

"You don't look well. Don't worry. Everything will be fine. I'll base myself at the Quai des Orfèvres. Don't mention to anyone what I've just told you. Let's have a meeting tomorrow morning, when we're both feeling calmer. I'm counting on you."

A few seconds later, Boulard was gone.

He had left Avignon lying on the kitchen floor, both hands stuffed inside a cardboard box, with the handle of a steel meat cleaver clenched between his teeth.

Avignon had intended to plunge this cleaver into his boss's chest. It was a unique opportunity. Voloy Viktor would have been pleased with him. But he couldn't bring himself to commit such an act against the man he had admired and betrayed for so many years.

And so Superintendent Boulard had taken up residence in the police headquarters. It was the only place where Rasputin the Vulture wouldn't come for him. Nobody, apart from Avignon, knew that Boulard stayed behind every night to sleep in this great building. One morning, a secretary had screamed when she discovered a pair of men's underpants in her desk drawer. Boulard had taken the precaution of not reclaiming them from lost property on the second floor.

On this particular January night, lying on his shelf at the back of the archive room, the superintendent couldn't get to sleep. For the thousandth time, he was piecing together what he called his "constellations."

It was his way of cogitating.

When he closed his eyes, he could make every element of his investigation appear in an imaginary night sky. In his head, he would draw all the links that might exist between the isolated stars. Boulard was now convinced that Father Jean, murdered in his bedroom at the seminary in 1934, had not been killed by Vango. No, the opposite was the case: Father Jean had died for refusing to hand Vango over to his killers.

So there had to be a connection between the bullets fired at the facade of Notre Dame Cathedral as the young man tried to escape and the murder of Father Jean, as well as to the Russian who was still after Vango's skin. The departure of the superintendent's mother on account of the Russian was a dark planet to add to this constellation.

From the outset, there had been a luminous triangle connecting Vango, Ethel, and the zeppelin in the middle of this sky. The triangle obsessed Boulard. He had gleaned some information from Ethel about the famous voyage around the world in 1929, but he knew that he hadn't yet probed that particular constellation enough to make her talk.

What he found interesting in this approach was the emergence of unexpected links from the gloom. And so, between one constellation and another, he might discover a connection—between Madame Boulard and Ethel, for example. Strange as it seemed, it was perfectly possible that such a connection existed. And in the same way, hopping from star to star, there might be a bridge between the predatory Russian and the round-the-world zeppelin trip.

But in the early hours of the morning, as he breathed in the smell of old paper, the superintendent wanted to make his sky look even bigger. Whenever an investigation came to a standstill, he would attempt to link it to other investigations. With his eyes still closed he would review the important cases from recent years, conjuring up other starry canopies. He would recall unsolved murders, holdups, swindles, and cases of organized crime. This morning he lay in the dark for an hour, trying to match up the cases with the witnesses and dates from the Vango mystery. It was as if he were asking the hundreds of suspects he had encountered in his life to try on Vango's glass slipper.

The room was almost silent. Right at the back, a gentle chewing noise was coming from the corner with the yearbooks: an archivist mouse was painstakingly at work.

Suddenly, the superintendent leaped to his feet. He ran over to the door and pressed the big switch: one after another, the overhead lights came on. A maze of shelves appeared before him, ten meters high, as Boulard strode toward the middle of the archives. An extraordinary choreographed dance began to take place from one end of the room to the other. The superintendent kept pushing around a ladder on rollers, climbing up it, rummaging through piles of paperwork, then climbing back down again. He transferred the files clamped under his arms to a box, then ran to the other end of the room and peered hard at the labels of archive boxes while hopping from foot to foot. He selected one, pulled out a wad of index cards that made up an old diary or record of admissions to the police headquarters for 1935. Out of breath and only half-satisfied, he scratched his chest through his undershirt and started pushing the ladder on rollers again, like a soldier moving his catapult at the foot of a fortress. On reaching the intended spot, Boulard threw his head back and commenced his ascent of the great wall.

Suddenly, between two aisles, he bumped into someone.

"Is that you, Avignon?" asked Boulard without bothering to stop. "Take this," he said, picking up the box he had just dropped, "and follow me."

"Superintendent."

"Take the box. I've found what I was looking for."

"But . . ."

"Leave the rest. This is the only thing that matters."

"It's eight o'clock; the staff are arriving."

"What's that got to do with me? Come on."

Avignon grabbed the box.

"It's all in there," said Boulard.

"Superintendent, I think you've got . . ."

"You can think what you like, my boy. Let's go to my office."

He switched off the lights and pushed the door shut.

They headed down the corridor together: Avignon out in front, carrying the mound of paperwork, while the superintendent followed. People hugged the walls to let them pass.

Boulard was on full display in his snugly fitting underwear. With his head held high, and the body of someone who likes tucking into his food, the superintendent took no notice of the astonished looks he was getting. He nodded at an archivist, who covered her eyes.

Avignon was attempting to pave the way with apologetic glances. But Boulard was parading himself, with his belly thrust out. After shaking hands with the chief commissioner, who walked past with some of his advisers, he turned right and took the final corridor. When he reached the office marked BOULARD in gold letters, he ushered Avignon inside and shut the door.

"Give me that."

The superintendent tipped the contents of the cardboard box onto his desk. Then he grabbed his trousers, which were hanging on the radiator.

A crowd of curious eavesdroppers had gathered behind the door.

"I may have found something, my boy."

Boulard was trying to do up his trouser buttons.

"I don't know where it's going to lead us, but it'll count for something."

First of all, he took out the thick register from the bottom of the pile and opened it on the table.

"Does this date bring back any memories?"

Boulard was putting on his shirt now.

Avignon read the first line: "'July 24, 1935.'"

He took a few seconds to think about it.

"No." The lieutenant shook his head.

Boulard went over to his door and kicked it. The eavesdroppers could be heard beating a retreat.

"Now we can put our minds at rest," he explained. "Right. Look at the twenty-seventh name on this page."

The document listed everyone who had passed through security at police headquarters on that day.

"'Ethel B. H.'"

"Quite so."

"And now look at number forty-two."

Avignon gave an almost imperceptible frown before reading, "'Drat That Rat! Pest Control.' That's—"

"That's Father Zefiro. Now, open this for me at the same date."

He held out a file. Avignon leafed through it and began to read the daily depositions.

"Go straight to the end. Our dear Mademoiselle Darmon—"

"'Mademoiselle Darmon, forty-nine years old (age as reckoned by the complainant herself), retiring in two months, secretary to Superintendent Auguste Boulard, declares that she saw a young man, who arrived via the roof, and who presented her with a letter signed Vango Romano.'"

"Very good. Now go back to the previous page, first paragraph."

"'Alert raised. Premises sealed off. Interrogation of a high-security defendant in the basement. See confidential files for identity.'"

"That's all, my boy."

"What?"

"Ethel, Vango, Zefiro, and Voloy Viktor, on the same day in the same place: doesn't that surprise you?"

Avignon gulped and shrugged.

"These things can happen."

"Yes, you're right. These things can and do happen. So, take a look at this for me."

Boulard held out three stapled pages to his lieutenant, who began to read. It was an old statement on yellowed paper, dating from the early 1920s. A man who wished to remain anonymous, and who signed using the initials M. Z., gave the description of arms dealer Voloy Viktor, together with all the necessary information to capture him in a church at Faubourg Saint-Antoine in Paris.

The pages quivered between Avignon's fingers. That day, in the parish of Saint Margaret, when the entire police force had believed the arms dealer was in their grasp at last, Avignon had betrayed Boulard for the first time by over-seeing Viktor's escape. And since that time, he had never stopped lying. It was he, Avignon, who thirteen years later had undone Viktor's metal belt so that, with one head-butt, the dealer had been able to shine the light on Zefiro. And it was he who had made Viktor's flight via Spain possible in a special train a few days later. For fifteen years he had filed weekly reports to this criminal, updating him on all the latest news from the French police.

Avignon had stopped reading. Boulard was staring at him.

"Are you going to go on?"

"Yes."

In a flat voice, the deputy read the list of accusations made by this anonymous priest against Viktor. The litany was terrifying.

"Can I stop n-now?" stammered Avignon.

"No."

He kept reading as Boulard paced to and fro in his office. Avignon had reached the end of the document. He fell silent.

The superintendent raised his eyebrows inquiringly.

"Well?"

"Well . . . I don't understand," spluttered Avignon.

"Well?" asked Boulard, beginning to lose his temper. "Aren't you going to read the last line?"

The lieutenant dived back into the pile of papers. Zefiro, the author of the document, had added a few sentences at the bottom of the page.

"'After the capture of Voloy Viktor, no contact is to be maintained with me. In the event of circumstances beyond my control, the sole point of contact should be: Commander Hugo Eckener, of the Zeppelin Company.'"

Superintendent Boulard looked serious.

"There it is." He sighed. "That's it: the missing star! The zeppelin! This final link leaves me convinced that the Vango affair is connected to the Viktor affair. As sure as my name's Auguste Albert Cyprien Boulard."

He tore the three pages out of his lieutenant's hands.

"And that link is M. Z."

"Who?"

"Vango knows Zefiro!"

Part of Avignon was relieved, but the other part was panicking. He had been worried that he'd been found out, which wasn't the case. This should have reassured him. But Boulard's discovery was problematic. Thanks to Viktor, Avignon had been aware for over a year now that Zefiro and Vango were close. He was convinced that the superintendent would make the most of this finding, which meant that Voloy Viktor's file risked being reopened.

More serious still, Boulard was going to hunt down Zefiro. And Zefiro had already discovered Avignon's betrayal.

A telegram denouncing the lieutenant had been sent from New York to Paris, although Avignon had managed to intercept it before it reached Boulard.

"Superintendent . . . I'm not clear about what you want to do here."

Boulard picked up a piece of chalk from the blotter in front of him. He turned to the blackboard and tore off the papers that were stuck to it. Then, launching himself at the board, he drew a large white cross.

"There you go. These are our options: the four routes to finding Vango," he declared, adding an arrow at each extremity of the cross before chalking up their initials: "Viktor, Ethel, Eckener, and Zefiro."

"Viktor to the west. Twice we've heard about him being in America. Ethel to the north. Eckener to the east. And Zefiro . . ."

Avignon was hanging on every word.

"Zefiro to the south."

For four years, Avignon had been trying to find out where Zefiro's base camp was situated. It was something that obsessed Voloy Viktor, who knew about the existence of the invisible monastery but had never been able to locate it.

"We'll have to set off in all four directions," the superintendent concluded.

There was a knock at the door.

"Come in!"

"Superintendent, your candidates are waiting for you in the blue room, sir."

"Is it today?"

"It's every Thursday, Superintendent."

"I'll be down," groaned Boulard.

"And the chief commissioner would like to have a word with you."

"What about?"

"The incident, I believe."

"What incident?"

"This morning's incident, sir."

Boulard didn't understand. Avignon, who was standing next to him, ventured a guess.

"Your attire in the corridors, perhaps, sir?"

"What about my attire?"

"Your . . ."

Avignon pointed vaguely at his boss's nether regions.

"Your . . . your underpants."

"What about them? Does the commissioner want to choose the color himself?"

The embarrassed envoy was shuffling from foot to foot.

"Right," Boulard continued. "I'm off to see my candidates. Avignon, you can handle this sartorial matter."

Superintendent Boulard arrived in the blue room in a cloud of dust.

For two years, he had been interviewing candidates to replace his secretary, Mademoiselle Darmon, who had retired to spend more time in her garden in Bagnolet. But he had suffered so badly during the Darmon years that he didn't dare pick a replacement. And so Boulard would interview four young candidates every Thursday, always in the hope that he wouldn't have to choose any of them.

On this particular Thursday there were five young ladies.

They were sitting on chairs, legs crossed, in the middle of the small waiting room.

"I'm warning you right away: I'm impossible to get along with," Boulard declared as he strode in.

He pulled out a chair for himself and sat down in front of them. He asked the first girl, a brunette in full evening dress and glasses, what she was reading at the moment.

She stammered, disappeared inside her handbag, and finally got out a big navy-blue book, which she offered up with trembling hands: the Police Code.

"You're reading that?"

She bit her lip.

"Is it any good?" he inquired, leafing through with a degree of curiosity.

He asked the second candidate how many fingers she typed with. He got the third one to do a mental arithmetic exercise and then recite the fable of "The Wolf and the Lamb." The fourth girl didn't feel well and had turned a shade of purple. She had to leave before it came to her turn.

So Boulard turned to the youngest candidate, sitting on his right. She was wearing a rather severe chignon, but it wasn't enough to make her look any older.

"Don't you have school on Thursdays?"

"No."

Her response was trenchant and insolent.

"Is your mother waiting for you downstairs?" inquired Boulard patronizingly.

"And what about your mother?" the young woman replied in the same tone of voice. "Where is she?"

Boulard rubbed his ear gently. The other candidates looked down at the floor.

"You do realize, young lady, that you are on police premises, and there is no guarantee you will leave here this evening."

"I won't be the only one staying late."

She was staring at him, but Boulard didn't react.

"How old are you?"

"Younger than you," answered the Cat.

"How did you get through the selection process?"

"Via the window."

This time, the superintendent stood up brusquely.

GUARDIAN ANGELS

He didn't call out.

Boulard would have felt ridiculous calling for reinforcements against a girl who weighed a fraction of what he did. He stood up and paced around her, trying to think of a more professional question that would calm the atmosphere.

"How do you envisage your role here?"

"Delivering the mail."

"And then?"

"That's all," said the Cat. "After that, I'd go back home. I've got other business to attend to."

There were two knocks at the door. Avignon entered and whispered something in Boulard's ear.

"Ladies," said the superintendent, "you may go now. We'll be writing to you."

He turned toward the Cat.

"Not you, young lady. Wait for me here."

The other three filed past the superintendent, who duly left with Avignon. The Cat was staring at the patch of sky through the window. Once outside the interview room, Boulard turned the key twice in the lock.

"Who was that?" asked Avignon.

"A candidate I'm interested in."

"Are you worried that she's going to fly away?"

"Quite so. What did you want to talk to me about? Hurry up."

Avignon glanced around before lowering his voice.

"I've just been thinking about what you told me."

"Is that a reason to interrupt me?"

"Hear me out. I'm the only person here—apart from you—to have seen Padre Zefiro, on the day when he came to identify Viktor."

"And?"

"I could set out to find him. I'm ready to leave right away."

"Now? Are you in need of a vacation, Avignon?"

"I'm trying to be useful. If you tell me the whereabouts of his refuge . . ."

Boulard pinched his ear. This was a state secret, and he had already jeopardized it one time too many.

"I'll have to think about it."

But he could tell that it was an interesting idea. With the Russian snapping at his heels, it was best to be careful. Avignon would do just as good a job of exploring Arkudah. And the superintendent wouldn't mind keeping the visit to beautiful Ethel, over at Everland, for himself.

"Come with me," he said. "I'm going to introduce you to someone rather odd."

He turned the key and pushed open the door. The blue room was empty.

"She told me! She told me!" complained Boulard, running over to the window.

"Told you what?"

"That she came in and out via the windows."

Both of them leaned out over the courtyard.

"It doesn't seem possible," said Avignon, staring at the void below them.

"But it's just the kind of thing she would do. What a she-devil! Who is she?"

The superintendent walked over to the only chair that hadn't been stacked against the wall. There was an envelope on its blue upholstery. Boulard opened it.

"Well?" inquired Avignon.

"It's personal."

Boulard put it in his pocket. He didn't have the strength to continue reading for now. It was a letter from his mother. It began with her recipe for chestnut soup.

Up on the roof, the Cat took off her high heels. She undid her chignon and strolled calmly on high until she reached the Palais de Justice, looking out onto Place Dauphine. There, she finally made her way back down to ground level. She walked along by the river. The waters were high after five days of rain. In some places, the river was overflowing onto the dockside. The Cat went to sit at the tip of the Vert-Galant, the island that divided the Seine.

Would the day ever come when she would be her own messenger? The Cat spent her life brushing against other people's destinies: slipping between them and imperceptibly changing their course. Vango, Ethel, Andrei, Boulard . . . She saved lives. She floated above the world. A guardian angel looking down from above.

But if she thought about herself, what did she have left?

She'd had a friend, Vango, but she hadn't seen him
years. She'd been in love with Andrei, but he di̇
know she existed. And as for her own family: it
ing apart at the seams. In the evening, before going   ⸱or
dinner, her mother would only touch her when wearing long
silk gloves that stretched all the way to her shoulders. Her
father was crumbling before her eyes. Nobody really cared
about her. Nobody stood by her.

She made a very good guardian angel, but this wasn't her
chosen vocation. She wanted her life to be down at ground
level.

The Cat wasn't counting the day and night she had spent
in Scotland, two months earlier. That was an extraordinary
memory.

She had stroked a horse for the first time. She had sat
down with Ethel by the fireplace at four o'clock in the afternoon and listened to music. She had thrown stones into the
lake and felt her boots weighed down with earth as she walked
in the grass. She had worn a hat belonging to Ethel's older
brother, who wasn't there. She had chased sheep. She had
cried with laughter as she dressed Madame Boulard for dinner
in the evening. She had almost choked with amusement on
witnessing the stiff upper lip of John, the head butler, when
one of the princess's fake diamonds had fallen into the soup.
She had paid a secret visit to Ethel in the aircraft hangar at
night, and had dreamed about it until the morning. She had
run in the first light of dawn to climb the copper beeches.
At breakfast, listening to the others interrogating her, she had
been surprised by their curiosity. She had even spoken a little
bit about herself.

"I'm often alone. It suits me that way."

Mary had given her plenty of shortbread to take back home, insisting she could always share it. "You must have someone, a younger brother, I don't know, perhaps even a lover, somebody. Yes, why not, a lover . . ."

And Mary had gone down on bended knee, begging the Cat to tell her whether she had one.

For the Cat, it was astonishing that anyone should imagine this for her.

"Just look at this young lady!" Mary kept saying. "With hair like hers, she'll have more than one after her."

And she had popped three more slices of shortbread into the guest's bag, just in case.

As the Cat was leaving, Madame Boulard, hidden behind the door, had entrusted her with an envelope for her son.

"You're going back to Paris. If you could give this to him in person . . ."

She had kissed the Cat on the forehead.

Ethel was waiting at the steering wheel of her car.

When they were alone, on the road that led to the boat, Ethel asked the Cat to open the letter carefully and read it.

"Why?"

"I'd prefer to err on the side of caution. I don't want her to have made the journey for nothing."

Not a single word could risk revealing Madame Boulard's whereabouts. The Cat read the letter at the top of her voice, over the sound of the engine. Both women were reassured and moved. The message was full of handy tips. It was rather like a letter from a mother to a son who had gone off to summer camp. Her advice was that he should eat well and not take any notice of anyone else.

The Cat stared at the Seine with its brown current. What was she going to do now? Vlad the Vulture had vanished into thin air since the end of the summer. He was in hiding. From the safety of his fortress, Boulard must have given out the Russian's particulars.

Andrei had disappeared even longer ago. The Cat didn't have the energy to stand up again. What was left for her?

Cats can survive on very little. They can be solitary, independent, and largely silent. But they do need something to keep them alive.

Meanwhile, in Moscow

Mademoiselle walked into the garage, accompanied by three children: a little girl had joined Kostia and Zoya.

"I wish to speak with Ivan Ivanovitch Oulanov."

"Why?"

"I'm looking after his children."

"He's at the back, soldering. But don't take the little ones in there."

The *tioten'ka* made them sit down on a bench, and Zoya held Setanka's hand.

"Wait for me here."

Next to them, Kostia was playing with a stick.

Mademoiselle strode through several workshops where cars were stacked like loaves of bread. The mechanics watched her as she passed by. In the last room, she saw Andrei's father, covered in soot, working under an engine that was running. She called out to him.

He didn't hear her right away. Two men were soldering metal a little farther off. He stood up and wiped his hands.

"Ivan Ivanovitch," she said, "I've got a problem."

"Where are the children?"

"They're here. It's because of Setanka, their little friend from Sokolniki Park. This morning, as we were setting off for school, she was waiting for us outside in the street, on the sidewalk opposite. I don't think she's told anybody she was planning to run away, and she doesn't want to say where she lives."

He switched off the engine.

"Is she here?"

Mademoiselle nodded, and they headed toward the front of the garage.

"Do you know her last name?"

"No. We only ever meet her with her governess, and always in the park. I've been to take a look, but the governess isn't there."

They were in front of the children now.

"What's going on?"

"She wants to live with us," Zoya told her father.

The mechanic sat down between the two little girls and sighed. Konstantin was still playing with his stick. Mademoiselle sat to one side, under a clock.

"What's your name?

"Svetlana."

"But we always call her Setanka," said Zoya.

"Setanka," Ivan repeated, putting his hands on his knees.

He was forty-five, but his hands looked as if they belonged to someone much older.

"Things not good at home?"

"No."

"We sometimes have trouble at home too."

He was staring at three men who had walked into an office with windows that looked out onto the garage. They were talking with the boss.

Ivan had cautiously taken hold of Setanka's hand.

"You're going to tell the *tioten'ka* where you live. She'll take you back home. You can come and play at our house another day."

Setanka glanced hesitantly at Mademoiselle, while Zoya gazed steadily at her friend.

Ivan Ivanovitch noticed the garage boss pointing at him. The three men all turned around at the same time. Ivan stood up.

Mademoiselle watched as one of the men stepped outside the office to summon him.

"Wait for me here," Ivan told the children.

He walked past a gray car, and then they saw him being ushered inside the office. The garage boss discreetly distanced himself.

Mademoiselle had moved closer to the children.

The office smelled of tobacco and gasoline. They made Ivan sit down. One of the men stayed back, near to the door, as if waiting for a bus.

"Ivan Ivanovitch, do you have any news of your son?"

asked the shortest of the three men, pushing away some tools and leaning on the table.

"No."

"We don't either."

Ivan stared straight ahead.

His interrogator took a worn-looking white handkerchief out of his pocket and blew his nose loudly. Through the glass, he was keeping an eye on the workshop.

"Have you always been a mechanic?" he asked, wiping his mouth.

"Yes."

"Didn't your son, Andrei Ivanovitch, want to follow in your footsteps?"

"He's a musician."

"I know. But there are plenty of workmen who are musicians by night. Is he lazy?"

"He's a great musician. He had to choose."

"Why?"

Ivan didn't answer.

The short man with the cold sniffed.

"I asked you why!" he barked.

"Because it was necessary to choose," said Ivan, putting his hands on the table. His blackened fingers were covered in scars; his index finger was wonky. This was his answer. Who can play the violin with hands like that?

A second interrogator took over.

"Andrei has been on the run for sixteen weeks."

"I'm not allowed to communicate with him," said Ivan, standing up. "I don't know anything."

"We don't trust him, Ivan Ivanovitch."

"He was in Paris for his music. All his papers were in order—"

"I'm not talking about papers. I provided him with those papers, you fool. He had another assignment."

"I don't know anything about that," said Ivan.

The short man with a cold signaled to his colleague and whispered in his ear. He wanted to be alone with Andrei's father. The two others left the office. He began to play with a brass bolt he had found on the desk.

"Ivan Ivanovitch Oulanov . . ."

"Yes."

The interrogator was still fiddling with the bolt.

"Your son knew what would happen to you if he disappeared. That's what I find so surprising. And you know what will happen too."

Yes, he knew. For two years now, the great terror instigated by Joseph Stalin had led millions of Russians—men, women, and whole families—to the camps. At this time of year, in the mines of Vorkuta, it was fifty degrees below freezing.

"Andrei will turn up again," said Ivan. "He'll be able to explain where he's been."

"That's not what the person who deals with him in Paris thinks. Four months . . . that's a long time. So there are two possibilities. The first is that he doesn't care about what will happen to you. He's saving his own skin, end of story. He's prepared to sacrifice his family."

Ivan Ivanovitch was looking down. The man turned back to face the workshop again.

"That's what my comrades think. And it is, of course, the most obvious explanation. But—I don't know why—I have another idea. . . ."

He wiped his nose again and glanced at one of his comrades, who was maneuvering the car into the garage, next to a pump. The other man looked like he was playing with the little blond boy.

"The second explanation," he went on, still observing the scene in the forecourt, "is that Andrei Ivanovitch is saving his skin because he thinks you're saving yours."

"I don't understand."

The man smiled.

"He knows you've got a plan for your family."

"A plan?"

"A trip abroad. Or some dirty con-trick."

"We're being spied on day and night."

"Which is why I'm anticipating a more refined plan from you: blackmail, some kind of conspiracy."

His piercing eyes were fixed on Ivan.

"I won't let you go."

Outside, the two others had parked their car in order to fill up the tank. A garage worker was serving them. The two men had approached the children to suggest they clamber into the car, just for fun. Mademoiselle declined the offer, but she couldn't restrain the children. Kostia was already in the back-seat, and the girls followed. They were laughing. Setanka sat at the steering wheel, her troubles forgotten.

Mademoiselle stayed on the bench.

Next to Ivan, behind the window, his interrogator was keeping a close eye on this scene.

"Who do those children belong to?"

"Me," said Ivan.

The man fell quiet and took out his glasses.

"They're yours?"

"Yes."

"What are they doing here?"

"They were passing by."

"And?"

"The woman is their *tioten'ka*," Ivan explained. "The one you gave us to keep in our home."

The man was still watching through the window.

"One, two . . . three."

"Sorry?"

"Three children."

"With Andrei, yes, but—"

"The little girl, in front . . ." said the short man, screwing up his eyes behind his glasses.

Ivan sighed softly, while his interrogator sat there on the desk, muttering to himself.

"The little one . . . the . . ."

Suddenly the man let go of the bolt, which rolled onto the ground. Then he walked toward the door, made his way over to the car, and crouched down so that he was level with the window. The little girl was pretending to drive.

He knocked once. Setanka turned toward him.

He signaled for her to open the window, as if they were at a wartime roadblock. The driver didn't move. Zoya and Kostia were sitting bolt upright in the backseat, and Kostia was wearing a hat belonging to one of the men. Setanka, who had both hands on the steering wheel, wasn't sure what to do.

The man tapped on the window again.

"Open the window, comrade driver," said Zoya, very seriously.

Setanka turned the handle and wound down the window.

"Hello," said the man.

Setanka was staring straight ahead.

"What are you doing here, Svetlana Iosifovna?"

"I'm setting off on a journey."

"Where to?"

"With my friends."

"Tell me where, Svetlana? Where are you going?"

"Italy."

In a flash, Ivan Ivanovitch Oulanov saw the man open the back door and shout orders, grabbing hold of Kostia's arm and dragging him out of the car. On the other side, the second man was doing the same with little Zoya, who was screaming. Mademoiselle rushed over and held the children close to her, while Setanka clung to the steering wheel.

The children's father ran out of the office, but they caught him before he could join his family. As he tried to defend himself, Ivan was elbowed in the face. He was thrown onto the backseat, where he was flanked by two men. In front, Setanka was huddled on her seat, having been pushed to the passenger side by the driver. The car started up with its headlights on full beam; it knocked over a cart, reverse-accelerated out into the street, and disappeared from sight.

Mademoiselle was left alone with the two sobbing children. Zoya kept repeating Setanka's name over and over again, and Kostia was calling for his father. Their *tioten'ka* couldn't stop trembling. Perhaps all this was her fault. The day before, in the park, she had finally entrusted little Setanka with her letter for Doctor Basilio, requesting that she post it as discreetly as possible. Had she been found out?

Mademoiselle hugged the children's heads in her lap as the garage boss stormed furiously toward her.

"Get out of here. I don't want any trouble."

In the car, Ivan had given up struggling.

"I knew I wasn't mistaken," crowed the man with a cold.

Ivan had sustained a bleeding lip and several broken teeth.

"But I hadn't imagined this sort of monstrous situation. You will explain to us what you were intending to do with the daughter of Comrade Stalin."

Ivan Ivanovitch Oulanov didn't understand anything anymore. Something was trickling down his neck. His mouth was a jumble of words and broken teeth. If the listener had carefully pieced together the fragments of his speech, he might have heard the name of Ivan's son and this one question, repeated over and over again: "Why are you doing this to us?"

THE RUINED GARDEN

Off the shores of Sicily, a month later,
February 16, 1937

Suddenly, Vango saw the islands.

A northwesterly wind had slowed their approach, and the voyage had been misty. But at last the Aeolian Islands appeared.

Vango didn't know how this rosary of stone, greenery, and fire in the middle of the sea had become the root of his life. These seven or so islands were the only place where he truly felt he could breathe.

He was hugging his knees as he sat beneath the mast pole. The sun in the sails reflected a saffron color around him. A woman was sitting next to him with some chicks in a wooden box. She gave them her finger to peck on. With her veil to protect her from the sun, she looked like the Virgin Mary. A dozen passengers were asleep around her, as if the splendid view was nothing new for them. Vango scoured the horizon for the plume of smoke from the volcano of Stromboli.

It had taken him a long time to get this far. He had collapsed along the way, back there in France, on another rocky island. He had come close to death.

After the ocean liner had pulled into Cherbourg, he had felt lost. Over in America, Cafarello had taken his secret to the grave with him. Vango didn't know how or where to begin his life again. He had spent several days in Normandy, wandering between the port and the station. There were boats leaving for England, and he could have continued on to Scotland. But he was afraid of what he might find at Everland.

And so he had headed south along the coast for several days, escorted by seagulls, forgetting to eat or sleep. A covering of frost crunched beneath his feet. In the villages, the children were frightened of him.

He had arrived at the foot of Mont Saint-Michel in the middle of the night.

High tides had swept the seabed. The rock rose up in the middle of a moonlit desert of sand. The tip of the abbey could be glimpsed high above, blacker than the night itself. Haggard and frozen, Vango headed up the little lanes. He wanted to knock on the giant door of the Benedictine monks and ask for their hospitality, as if he were en route to an imaginary Jerusalem. But he felt ashamed. He hadn't washed since leaving New York. He wasn't on his way to anywhere. He looked more like a piece of wreckage than a pilgrim. He climbed the wall and performed his high-wire act over the rooftops, his shadow flickering under the moon. He scaled the church and found shelter behind the zinc columns of the bell tower. In his exhausted state, he lay down, watched over by the archangel Michael.

Vango felt as if he were losing his mind. He could hear the canticles being sung, and thought he saw the glimmer of flares. He couldn't even feel how cold the stone was. He was barely breathing. Down below, the Night Office had begun. The monks had filed into the church singing, but it was as if they were traversing Vango's head and body, their flares in their hands.

He no longer had any strength left to make even the slightest gesture. He wanted to stay there for what remained of his life. The smell of incense wafted up to embalm him. For a moment, he was afraid of this numb feeling. Zefiro had told him not to flee anymore, and to make choices instead. But he dismissed any idea of resisting. It felt good to forget about being permanently uprooted. The cold and the hunger were carrying him off.

A monk had found him there the following day. At dawn, the gulls had made a racket under the spire. The brother responsible for masonry wanted to repair any damage, so he had climbed up despite the lashing morning hail.

A harsh winter was under way, and it was very rare for anyone to climb the bell tower, so the monk assumed that the boy had been dead for some time. The glacial wind brought all sorts of surprises: once, after a stormy season, he had even found some fish in the bell tower. So why not this bohemian swept off a cliff by the wind? The mason put his coat over Vango's body and blessed him. It was only then that he took the young man's pulse and discovered that he was alive.

Two men hoisted Vango down into the church using ropes. They found him a bedroom and some warm milk. Three days later, he was already doing better. He forgot about time and made the most of this gentle reprieve. He stayed there until Christmas, then Epiphany, and then Ash Wednesday.

Those winter months went by in a flash, like the first mysterious minute after waking up. Vango was simply aware of a freedom that reminded him of his childhood. His strength had returned. He deliberately kept a low profile with the monks, leaving the bay every morning and walking among the tall grasses. On finding a black horse, Vango didn't give it a name, but he taught himself to ride, like the first Amerindian in the world. His staple diet was bread and butter in the kitchen, as well as winkles. He walked out into the sea, against the freezing current, as the tide was rising. He went diving. He set off to climb the high surrounding wall at night.

Vango was waiting. He joined in the monks' worship by lying behind the stained glass windows.

One day, high up in the sky, he saw a falcon flying in circles. Heading back in the direction of the abbey, he thought of Mademoiselle, who had disappeared because of him, and of the invisible monastery, whose monks believed they had been orphaned by Zefiro. Had Brother Marco found a way of stepping into the padre's shoes? He thought of his home. He knew he needed to set out in that direction first.

Vango left a translucent sapphire in the salt box of the monks' kitchen, to pay for his bed and butter. Then he was off again. The horse with no name followed him as far as the first village, before they each went their separate ways.

A few weeks later, he arrived at Salina, by the western port of Rinella. His intention was to head off on foot around the wild coast and cliffs separating the village from the hamlet of Pollara, where he had grown up.

The Virgin with the chicks was greeted by a group of little girls. She gave the youngest one permission to take a chick in her hands.

Vango stayed on the dockside, watching them from a distance. He was thinking of Laura Viaggi and her sisters. They had grown up here, in the sweet sea air. And now there was nothing left of them.

"Don't hold it too tightly," the woman was chiding. "Treat it like a butterfly."

The little girl was so eager to do as she was told that she let it slip through her fingers. Laughter broke out. The chick hopped over the fishing net and Vango ran after it, sneaking between piled-up crates. The children applauded. They followed, calling out, but Vango was lying in ambush and signaled to them to keep quiet. Perfectly hidden behind two large floats, he waited patiently. The chick thought it was safe and stopped to catch its breath just three meters away from him.

Augustin Avignon was wearing a straw hat. He stumbled across a group of children, who seemed to be waiting for something to happen down at the port. There was a woman with them. The scene was like a painting. They were all staring hard in the direction of a chick snuggled against a tire.

One of the fishermen who was accompanying the lieutenant tugged on his arm. The other fisherman was already waiting for them in the boat. They had agreed on a price for the day. They couldn't afford to let nightfall creep up on them. Avignon climbed on board. The two men never stopped talking to him, even though he didn't understand a word of their language.

As they left the port of Rinella, Avignon heard a cry go

up. He could picture the excitement around the chick, which the children must have caught. They had formed a tight cluster around a boy who was obscured from view.

"*Avanti!*" said one of the fishermen.

"No," Avignon corrected him. "Not *'Avanti!'*"

Anxiously, he opened out the map of Sicily. He put his finger on a small gray dot (the island Boulard had ringed in red) and said clearly and slowly, "A-li-cu-di."

Vango was carrying two dozen eggs in a box. The Virgin with the chicks had given them to him. By midday he was above Pollara, staring down at those few houses scattered at the bottom of the baked-earth cupola, which split in half toward the sea. In this season, the sun didn't reach the bottom of the crater.

Vango headed down slowly. He stopped from time to time to stare at the white of his house. He would have liked to see a wreath of smoke emerging from it. If only Mademoiselle could appear on the terrace. Vango gazed out at the other islands on the horizon and spotted a tiny white sail that was heading into the distance. The stems of dry fennel plants snapped underfoot, and he was afraid of treading on the small birds that threw themselves at his legs. He could feel the humidity rising up from the crevices in the lava stone.

He paused in front of Mazzetta's former refuge. The entrance was blocked with branches, but the ring for tying up the donkey was still embedded into the stone.

Vango then headed for the two white cubes of his home. The cool and shade were spreading as he found the key in the hollow of the olive tree, put the eggs down on the terrace, and opened the door.

Avignon peered at the small boat with the lowered sail that was waiting for him down below. He hoped they wouldn't abandon him here. He had paid for everything up front. Avignon had been climbing for two hours, but the stone steps just kept multiplying ahead of him. There seemed to be no summit to the island of Alicudi.

He knew how much was at stake with his exploratory trip. Voloy Viktor referred to this refuge as "the burrow" and had gathered plenty of information about it, including the list of names of those who hid there and a letter from Zefiro to the Vatican explaining his project. But he had nothing on the whereabouts of the burrow. Viktor had ordered that the pockets of the pope and his secretaries be searched, and the unexplored limits of Europe visited, including every possible hiding place: eagles' nests, hollow mountain peaks, and disused mines. He would gladly have had two or three cardinals boiled like lobsters in order to make them talk.

Avignon hadn't said anything to Viktor about his expedition. Voloy Viktor hadn't forgiven him for sparing Boulard when the superintendent had visited his lieutenant's apartment to seek refuge. So Avignon was here on a reconnaissance mission. If he discovered the burrow, he would ask Viktor for his freedom back in exchange for revealing the whereabouts. The policeman might be able to start again from scratch and rediscover the joys of an innocent life. He'd had enough of being torn in two: serving and betraying at the same time, every moment of the day.

* * *

He had begun this double life just after the war, because of a Catalan petty criminal, a tailor, whom he'd caught and who had promised to deliver Viktor up to Avignon if he let him go.

The arrest of Voloy Viktor! At last, Avignon had found a way of dazzling his boss, Boulard, and gaining his respect. He had agreed. But the tailor kept putting off his promise. Week after week, he requested additional favors, which Avignon also granted. The cogs were turning. The Catalan met him in a cellar in Faubourg Saint-Martin. He offered him bespoke suits while whispering in his ear. Avignon stole files from Boulard's office, got messages sent into prisons, and covered up political stories.

On the day when Lieutenant Avignon was finally due to meet with Viktor face-to-face, he realized that it was already too late. Avignon was now the person to whom all the traffickers came. He had become corrupt to the bone. There was no going back.

When Viktor was finally presented to Avignon, he recognized the tailor he had tried arresting two years earlier and who had been manipulating him ever since. Voloy Viktor was the tailor. And the tailor was just one of his many disguises. The arms dealer had played the game perfectly. Avignon was caught in the trap.

Avignon picked up his pace. He looked at the island around him. Who on earth could live on this barren outcrop of scree? Boulard must have made a mistake.

The fishermen had tried to make him understand there was nothing to see on the rock. Nothing. Avignon had shown them his camera and taken three stones out of his pocket.

"Me geologist. Me not tourist."

He gesticulated at them, overpronouncing his words as if he were talking to the indigenous people of the Nicobar Islands.

Finally, he reached an area that was almost flat and that extended toward the north of the island. Two rabbits bolted in front of him. He had Superintendent Boulard's directions before his eyes. The sketched map was clear enough. He had to take this high plateau for a few hundred meters, with the mountain on his left. Finally, Avignon climbed a small steep slope, headed back down into the grass, and came to a stop. His heart began to beat very fast.

The rock formation below him was in the shape of a rectangle, just like the one Boulard had drawn.

Avignon tucked himself between two rocks and surveyed all around him. It was as if he were in the ruins of an ancient capital, a temple that had been returned to nature. The invisible monastery had become a jungle. Dense vegetation surrounded the stone walls, insinuating its way into narrow cracks. The wooden and terra-cotta irrigation system was broken in many places, and the water ran into the earth. Climbing plants choked the branches of the orchard. A rabbit was asleep beneath an almond tree that had collapsed onto a terrace. Not a single sign of human life remained, just the memories of an ancient civilization.

A few years earlier, in Paris, the temples of Angkor had been reconstructed at the foot of the Eiffel Tower for the Colonial Exhibition. Avignon had visited them several times. He felt the same fear now as he had back in Paris in 1931:

he was frightened of treading on snakes or of a tiger watching him through the palm trees.

Avignon dared to venture through a doorway, where he discovered dark and dank-smelling rooms that were completely empty. The floor was damp and the windows half blocked up; all that was visible was the moss invading the walls. Where had the builders of this place gone?

Avignon's mission was a failure. He stood there in the shadowy room, his horizons having just shrunk again. No Zefiro. Everyone had vanished.

The policeman flanked a wall and stopped in front of a stone shelf that had been inset under a window. His eyes fell on a small pile of orange-colored strips. He bent over and discovered that they were carrot peelings. Peelings that hadn't had time to turn black. Peelings that were less than an hour old. Avignon picked one up.

Rabbits was his first thought. The island was clearly overrun by them. But did rabbits peel their own carrots? Avignon had no idea. Paris-born and -bred, he had never set foot in the countryside. The work had been carried out with a knife, however, which meant this had to be a very resourceful rabbit. Now, there were books about certain primates being able to manipulate tools. . . .

"Don't turn around."

But Avignon did, and what he saw wasn't an orangutan. It was Pippo Troisi.

15

THE CITADEL OF WOMEN

The man stood in the shadow cast by the vaults, holding a knife in one hand and a carrot in the other. He was a short, plump fellow with a beard of a few days' growth: a sort of island tramp with a torn hat on his head.

"Clear off! You're trespassing!"

"I'm looking for some people who used to live here," said Avignon.

The man shook his head. They were each speaking in their own language, and neither could understand the other. Avignon uttered one of the rare words he had learned in Italian in order to ask where the monks were. *"Monaci?"*

"They're not here. Haven't been for a long time."

Avignon put down the piece of carrot peel. He had understood.

"Monks . . . where . . . are?"

He thought that by mixing up the word order, he would be easier to understand.

"Leave. Before I can say Arkudah."

"You . . . monk?"

Avignon wanted to get closer, but the other man took a step backward and brandished his carrot. This movement brought his face into the light.

"I told you to leave," repeated Pippo.

"What about Zefiro?"

"Who are you?"

"Me . . . friend . . . Zefiro."

"I don't know that name."

With the tip of his carrot, Pippo Troisi signaled to the stranger to make for the door, adding, "Go away. Don't tell anyone you saw me."

Avignon headed off, still inspecting the overgrown garden, before turning to face Pippo. With his trousers cut off at the knees and his threadbare shirt, this man resembled a hefty Robinson Crusoe who'd probably never known the time when Zefiro and his men lived here. A rabbit came right up to Pippo. He kicked it back into the bush.

"I'm off," said Avignon, raising both hands as if in surrender.

Pippo Troisi followed him for a few hundred meters. Avignon had turned around several times to contemplate the ruins. At one point, retracing his steps, he had asked, "What about Vango? You . . . Vango . . . know?"

But Pippo Troisi just stared at him stupefied, and he had given up.

When they reached the side of the island from where the tiny fishing boat was visible, Pippo sat down on a rock. Cross-legged like a Huron chief, he watched Avignon's descent.

The stones slid and rolled beneath Avignon's feet. From time to time he glanced back up at the man, who never took his eyes off him. The lieutenant was suffering far more than he let on. He had staked everything on this voyage.

Still a good distance above sea level, he made his way

down in less than an hour. The fishermen were sleeping under the sail, which they had rigged up like a tent canvas. Avignon had to shake them in order to rouse them.

Pippo Troisi watched the boat heading off along the coast.

He waited a little longer before going on his way. First, he walked for five minutes toward what remained of the invisible monastery, then he took a barely trodden path that climbed the side of the hill. Feeling very out of breath at the top, he checked that the white sail was still heading off into the distance, berated a few rabbits in his way, and scrambled over a maze of rocks. He pushed a pile of branches to one side to reveal a circular opening that had been dug into the ground. Pippo dived head-first into the tunnel and immediately got stuck, which was what happened every time. Due to his hips not being the slimmest part of his anatomy, his legs were left flailing on the outside. He tried to haul himself inside with his arms.

When he had finally squeezed through, he exploded into a tunnel that descended almost vertically and hurtled all the way to the bottom, where he was scooped up by two men. Two huge candles overflowing with molten wax illuminated a black stone crypt.

"They've gone," announced Pippo, standing up.

Brother Marco, the cook who had been left in charge following Zefiro's disappearance, turned toward the thirty monks from the invisible monastery.

"I don't know who he was," added Pippo Troisi. "But he was looking for Zefiro and Vango."

If you remove the queen from a bees' nest, you're left with a drone colony that goes into decline. The hive loses its get-up-and-go and returns to its wild state.

Since Zefiro's disappearance, the monks had lost their get-up-and-go. They lived in fear. They had abandoned their monastery, allowing nature gently to erase all traces of them, and had taken refuge in this underground tunnel. Pippo's job was to play the role of a crazy Robinson Crusoe if a stray visitor appeared.

They called their new shelter "the citadel of women," after the women who used to hide there in ancient times, when pirates pillaged the islands. The men would stay on the shore, defending their houses. Beneath the dark lava vaults, thirty monks in homespun cowls had now replaced those women.

At night, they couldn't help thinking about the mothers, young women, and children who had waited in the darkness, just as they did, singing perhaps and afraid, just as they were, of the murderous hordes rising up. For as long as they didn't know what had happened to Zefiro, the monks were frightened of invaders.

During the day, however, they ventured out into the open. They had given up growing any produce and had emptied the hives, moving the swarms of bees into holes in the cliffs. Pippo Troisi's worst day came when he had to open up the rabbit enclosure. He watched their cheeky behinds disappearing off into the thickets. He despised those animals with a vengeance, and they in turn worshipped him more than ever for liberating them.

The monks lived like Stone Age hunter-gatherers. They had switched civilizations. At dawn, they set off to gather rotting fruit and vegetables from the former kitchen gardens, collect prickly pears, hunt the rabbits with bows and arrows, and fish for what they could. They left no trace of having passed by, covering over with earth any fires they had lit. In the evenings, Brother Marco was suspended from ropes to harvest his honey from the cliffs. He gave one spoonful to each monk, as a remedy.

The fruit trees provided for them when they were in season. But come winter, the survival of these thirty monks on the rock proved tricky. The sea was too rough for fishing. They caught birds with traps set on the rocks. Twice a week, a small team of pilferers took to the sea at nightfall and set off for the other islands, to raid the barns and henhouses. The next day, breathing in the smells of sizzling bacon and maize bread in the embers, they confessed in turn to one of their fellow monks, who, with his napkin already tied around his neck, forgave all their pillaging with the sign of the cross.

A few islands away, in his house in Pollara, Vango was staring at two objects on the table: a flask and a book. He had lit a fire in the fireplace and closed a few shutters.

Having just washed his face in a bucket of water, he was drying himself off using a towel embroidered with rose-bushes. It was dark. For two days, he had scoured the house of his childhood and its surroundings for any clues left by Mademoiselle or her captors. He had found nothing apart from a book he didn't recognize under the sink and a metal bottle floating in the well.

The flask was empty and had a stopper held in place by a metal lever. It might have been tossed there by a passing hunter who had come to sit by the edge of the well. There was nothing distinctive about its shape; it contained no cry for help rolled up like parchment with a secret address. And its insides smelled of nothing except old metal.

But there was a bear engraved on the neck, which was why Vango had put it down on the table. The animal seemed exotic. He stared for a long time at the snarling bear, which was standing on its hind legs.

The other object, the book, was a Russian dictionary. Vango realized that just because the book was there, this didn't necessarily mean anything. He had never seen it in the house before, but Mademoiselle had lived here for three years without Vango. She could speak Russian, and might easily have obtained it for herself.

There was little chance that one of the thugs would have arrived wielding his dictionary like a handgun, only to toss it under the sink in his hasty departure as he carried off Mademoiselle. This book wasn't a clue to anything at all, but Vango held it, opened it, and went into a long meditation.

He pictured himself with Mademoiselle, washed up on Scario beach, two castaways. He suddenly realized that what had survived of their past, the only things that hadn't disappeared into the sea, were languages and songs, recipes and gestures. He had inherited words and flavors from Mademoiselle. But it had never occurred to him to find out any more about his inheritance.

Why did he understand the words in this Russian dictionary? Why did Mademoiselle cook that particular soup better than anyone else? Why had he always fallen asleep to the sound of Greek lullabies? Where did those thorny roses come from that she had embroidered on the towels but that didn't grow on this island? They all came from the past, clamoring the secrets of his life, but he had never heard them before. Each moment of his childhood was a small parcel wrapped in a layer of tissue paper: it had never been opened.

And the treasure? He had one third of it: the share belonging to Mazzetta and his donkey. Like a pirate, Vango had hidden it on his island in a cave that no one else would find. The remaining two thirds had disappeared with Cafarello.

Vango picked up the dictionary and the book and made his way over to the window.

Suddenly, diving headfirst to the ground, he rolled into a ball by the fireplace. This took less than three seconds.

He put the two objects down next to him and waited for his heart to stop racing. Scanning the room, he sat up slightly before moving toward another window, still crouching low. He peered through one of the gaps in the shutter, then bent down again.

Vango crawled toward the door. This time, he didn't even need to take a peek. A crackling noise could be heard in the undergrowth from that side too. The house was surrounded. He had seen at least five shadows, and there were likely to be two more at the back.

No doubt about it. They were on his trail again. He turned the key in the lock.

Vango took the bucket of water he had used to wash his face, emptying its contents onto the remaining embers, which barely sighed as they were extinguished. The room was plunged into darkness. Vango heard the door handle squeaking. He had locked the door just in time.

Someone was walking on the roof. Vango knew that he hadn't taken any precautions on reaching the island. He hadn't been able to resist playing with the children, who had carried him in triumph: and all because of the tribulations of a chick! He had calculated that by arriving into the small port of Rinella, he wouldn't be spotted. He could have made immediately for the wild coast, staying close to the sea. But he had clowned about first, to win the smiles of three little girls, in memory of Laura Viaggi and her sisters.

How was he going to escape now? He knew this whitewashed cube like the back of his hand. There was no way out. All the windows were being watched. The chimney flue was barely wide enough to squeeze an arm up it. There was no cellar or attic or hidden nook. All he could do was fight back.

A few paces from him, he saw a wooden lever smash through the first shutter. A small pool of starlight spilled through the glass, which immediately shattered. Then a hand burst through the hole and turned the handle. Vango had swiftly crouched beneath the window, where he remained hidden in the gloom.

A shadowy figure stepped through the window. Noiselessly, Vango grabbed hold of it and pinned it to the ground. He struck the man on the back of the head, and his victim promptly fainted. When a second shadow chanced its luck, Vango put it out of action in the same manner. All that was audible from the outside was the rustling of clothes. A minute went by. Vango could hear the sound of muffled voices on the other side of the house. Despite the cold, he was drenched in sweat, and the sensation of those two bodies pressed against his legs made him feel panicky. His eight years as a fugitive had sharpened his survival instinct: he feared what his own hands were capable of doing.

The third man got away from him, and they rolled together toward the fireplace. Vango had gagged the man's mouth with his hand, but his opponent was putting up a real fight. On feeling the Russian dictionary against his shoulder, Vango grabbed hold of it and, with one heavy blow, knocked out the enemy. The man slid to the ground. Vango also picked up the metal flask and crawled back under the window, armed with these two weapons.

A voice was mumbling at his feet. One of the men was coming around, but he was talking gibberish. Vango was about to acquaint him with the heavy dictionary when he recognized what the man was saying.

It wasn't Russian, but ancient Greek: the beginning of the Gospel according to Saint John. "In the beginning was the Word . . ."

Vango put the dictionary down.

"Brother John?"

"Vango?" gasped the man, wincing in pain. "Is that you?"

When another voice called through the window, Brother John replied, "I'm here. It's Vango!"

A fourth man hopped over the windowsill.

"Vango? What are you doing here?"

"I could ask you the same question!"

"We're hungry over there."

"Hungry?"

"Pippo Troisi told us this house had been lying empty for ages. We're on the hunt for anything to eat. Where are the others?"

"Over there."

"And what about Brother Pierre?"

"I think he took a knock to the head. I'm sorry."

"Who did that to him?"

Vango shrugged. The monk understood.

A final shadow appeared. There were five of them. Five monks turned gentleman-burglars, with sacks over their shoulders, clad in the color of the night.

"Fill the bucket in the well," ordered Brother John. "I'm going to try reviving the others. We've got to carry them as far as the boat."

"I'll lend a hand," offered Vango. "I want to talk with Brother Marco."

"Have you got anything to eat?"

"Eggs."

"How many?"

"Two dozen."

"Pippo will be waiting for us down on the beach."

Pippo wasn't on the beach. He had sailed around the cliffs to the port of Malfa, in order to tie the boat to a mooring buoy. Next, he had slipped into the sea and swum over to the dock. Now he was sitting with his back against the hut belonging to the lady of the port, Pina Troisi, and he was listening.

Pippo Troisi did this every time he ferried the pilfering monks. On Christmas Eve he had dared to get close for the first time, and he had heard his wife talking to somebody: Doctor Basilio. She was telling him about what it was like to wait, to be patient. She had talked about the boat that would bring Pippo back to her one day. Basilio got her to recite the boat timetables, together with the ports of departure, and Pippo would listen in, feeling confused.

Whenever he came by in the evening, he nearly always heard the doctor's voice. Pina and Basilio had become firm friends, and the doctor was always ready to listen to Pippo's wife. He was interested in understanding her world and what had brought her to this point. And he in turn would talk about his patients.

She would prepare a light supper for him, its aromas assailing Pippo Troisi's nostrils. Tonight he recognized the smell of the pasta-style dish she was making from zucchinis. Pippo was salivating. All he could hear was the flame inside the spirit lamp, behind the thin wooden wall, like the sound of a sheet being unfurled.

"I'm just back from Lipari," Basilio declared.

"I saw you arriving this morning, on the nine twenty-seven."

"There's an old man over there who lives under house arrest. He's spent seven years in the former penal colony. He's about to die."

"Are you looking after him?"

"Yes. He's a Communist from Venice. Signor Mussolini doesn't like him, so he put him there, seven years ago."

"I've never met a Communist," Pina admitted. "What are they like?"

On the other side of the partition, the question made Pippo smile.

"He's not even really a Communist anymore. He spent four years in Moscow, and that changed him. But he kept pretending he was one, just to annoy the authorities."

He wiped his mouth.

"If your Pippo comes back one day, he'll be different too. He'll have changed a great deal."

"So will I," mused Pina. "Which is just as well."

Pippo Troisi strained to hear.

"Aren't you afraid?"

"Yes, I'm afraid. Which is just as well."

And then she added quickly, as an afterthought, "What about you, weren't you afraid at first, with her?"

The two friends sometimes talked about the woman Basilio could never stop thinking about. Mademoiselle.

"I barely shook her hand, you know."

"How long has it been?" she asked.

"I'm not counting. What about you?"

He knew how much Pina loved numbers. "If I don't count the days," she would say, "then what's the point of one day more?"

"Well?" Basilio asked again.

"He left one hundred and twenty-two months, two weeks, and three days ago."

Pippo Troisi headed off, feeling emotional, as he did every time he dropped by. He ran down to the sea and swam out to his boat, nearly capsizing it as he climbed on board. He was sopping wet as he began to row beneath the stars. He was thinking about Pina.

"You know that letter I told you about—the letter she sent me?" Basilio had said, in Pina Troisi's tiny hut.

"Yes. How did that sentence go again that you liked?"

"'Being far away from our home makes me feel rather differently about things.'"

"Yes, 'far away from our home.' I remember."

"Well, there was also an envelope for the boy. Vango."

"Vango, the wild kid from Pollara," she said.

"He hasn't lived here for a long time now. Anyway, I don't know if I did the right thing, but I opened the letter."

"Today?"

"No, weeks ago."

"You didn't mention it to me."

Basilio gave an embarrassed smile.

"The letter is written in Russian."

"So it's as if you hadn't opened it." She tried comforting him.

"The old man from Lipari translated it for me today. The Venetian. He speaks Russian."

There was a pause from Pina Troisi, and then she asked, "What does she say in the letter?"

He didn't answer her right away.

"She says everything. She tells Vango the whole story. In five pages. I wrote it all down. You can't begin to imagine. . . ."

Basilio seemed to be of two minds about going on.

"Do you remember how they arrived on the beach, and then at Tonino's inn, one stormy evening?"

"Yes, I remember. Pippo was there."

"She tells him all about where they came from, the little one and her. Vango's parents . . . You can't imagine, Pina. You can't imagine what's in that letter. She tells such secrets."

"Well, then keep them to yourself."

Pippo Troisi could make out six figures on the narrow beach at Pollara. Most of them were lying on the pebbles. As he drew close, he recognized Vango, who was standing in the sea with the water up to his knees. Pippo got everybody on board, both injured and able-bodied, and shook Vango's hand vigorously. The sails didn't even quiver.

"You vanish, but you always come back," said Pippo.

They pulled away from the beach in order to navigate the rock of Faraglione.

"Life has become very difficult," Pippo added as he rowed.

"Has Marco taken over for Zefiro?" asked Vango.

"Not really."

"Who's replaced him?"

Neither Pippo nor any of the monks had an answer. It was cold. A long silence accompanied their voyage toward the islands. In the end, a voice from the back replied, "Fear. Fear has replaced him."

They were the words of Brother Pierre, who was coming to his senses again. As the boat headed for Arkudah, the only sound was that of the oars slicing through the water. The sail was redundant.

"I've come to speak with Marco," said Vango. "I have news of Zefiro."

16

BACK TO EVERLAND

Inverness, Scotland, three weeks later, March 1937

An odd-looking person walked into the shop to shelter from the rain. Andrei recognized him instantly, and proceeded to stare at him.

Boulard was wearing a square-framed pair of glasses with thick lenses that made his eyes look strangely close together. He sported an oilcloth rain hat and a matching custard-colored raincoat. The superintendent had stuffed the bottoms of his trousers, which were too long for him, into a pair of black ankle boots. No doubt about it—he was in disguise. Incognito. And to prove it, he was whistling.

With his hands behind his back, he started looking at the color samples.

Andrei had been working in the shop ever since he'd left Everland. He had stopped here, in the first town he had come to, rather than return to Vlad the Vulture. He had been hired to work as a stockroom-cum-delivery boy for the paint shop opposite the station. His boss was getting a good deal, since he only paid a part-time wage despite Andrei working non-stop and even sleeping at the back of the shop.

The boss appeared from behind the cash register and headed over to Boulard. Andrei stayed at the back.

"Are you looking for something?"

"Yes."

"Are you French?"

Boulard bristled. How could anyone tell?

"*Well* . . . Ah, some of my ancestors came from France," explained the superintendent, trying to speak the Queen's English as airily as if he were a member of Oxford University's Bullingdon Club. "You have a sophisticated ear, Mr. . . . Colors."

He had just spotted the shopkeeper's name on the notice above the till: GREGOR'S COLORS.

"Mr. Gregor," said the boss, putting him right. "Francis Gregor. *Colors* is the name of the shop."

"Yes, of course. Now, I'm on my way to see a charming young lady friend of mine on the other side of Loch Ness. It's a surprise visit."

Boulard tried winking, but his heavy glasses slipped down his nose, and he ended up jabbing his finger in his eye as he tried to push them up again.

"I'm sure she'll be delighted!" commented Gregor, taking in the superintendent's old-dog look, his cardboard suitcase disintegrating in his grip, and the excessive amount of trouser fabric spilling over the top of his boots.

"I've been waiting for a car since this morning," said Boulard, "but I've rather given up hope."

"There are no taxis."

"I was thinking as much. Might you be kind enough to take me a little closer to my destination?"

"There are no taxis," repeated Mr. Gregor, who owned the only shop outside the station, but who regretted daily that he had opened up a paint shop instead of a bus station.

Boulard turned to glance at the road, where the rain was pelting down.

"I do believe I can see a vehicle with your name on it alongside the curb, Mr. Colors."

"Mr. Gregor."

"Gregor, yes."

"That vehicle is for deliveries only."

The superintendent nodded.

"Of course. Deliveries. What a pity. Well, it only remains for me to wish you a pleasant afternoon."

Boulard walked toward the door.

"But I can sell you an umbrella," Gregor called out brazenly.

"Well, well," said Boulard, turning around. "An umbrella? Good idea!"

Francis Gregor took out an umbrella and demanded an exorbitant price.

"Gracious me," said Boulard, rummaging in his pocket. "What's your umbrella made of? Amaranth? Or ebony from Makassar?"

He took out the money and put it down on the counter before heading once more for the door, whose glass was all misted up from the rain. The umbrella had stayed on the till.

"You've forgotten your umbrella." Gregor sneered at the superintendent.

"Not at all. I won't be taking it with me now."

Gregor's eyes bulged.

"As a matter of fact, I didn't specify my requirements," added Boulard, retracing his steps and folding up his glasses. "I should like it to be delivered."

The boss's jaw dropped. Andrei was riveted.

"A delivery . . . for the umbrella?"

"Yes."

"To which . . . address?"

"I told you, to the house of a charming young lady on the other side of Loch Ness."

"But—"

"Now, as for how to get there, it's rather complicated to explain. So I'd better accompany you, Mr. Colors."

Mary and the Princess of Albrac had broken down by the side of the road. Mary had left the princess in the car. The open hood was steaming in the rain. There had even been the beginnings of a fire, which the housekeeper had put out with her coat. As a result, Mary was standing by a ditch, in the pouring rain, waiting for a car to help them out. She had draped her charred coat over her head. Each drop of rain was like a water bomb. In the Scottish Highlands, the rainfall can achieve levels of two or three meters in an especially wet year. Enough to drown the frogs.

Mary was ruing getting them into this mess. A few hours earlier, the princess had run out of knitting wool. She had been offered all sorts of balls of wool at Everland, but none of them were right. She was very fussy about texture and color. And so, without telling anyone what she was doing, Mary had sat the princess in the car. She wanted to take their guest to the mill where the wool from the Everland sheep was spun.

"Your Highness, you're going to choose your wool on the animal itself!"

The aging princess was excited by this prospect. On the animal! Madame Boulard gave a little round of applause from the backseat. The two women got on so well, and the jaunt had been very jolly for a while. They had forgotten that neither of them knew how to drive.

Mary could have kicked herself for not having alerted Ethel before setting off. She was agonizing over what might have happened if the car had gone up in flames and she had returned the Princess of Albrac in cinders.

The road was muddy and slippery. Andrei was at the steering wheel of the van, where Boulard had tried to engage him in conversation, but the boy gave only the briefest of answers. No, he hadn't been working there for long. Yes, Mr. Colors was a good boss. No, he had never heard of Everland Castle. And yet he had driven fast, avoiding all the potholes as if he were familiar with them. With each bend they could hear the umbrella, which was the only item to be delivered, rattling about in the trunk.

Suddenly, half a kilometer away, they saw a car that had stopped.

Andrei began to slow down. He felt overawed, returning to these parts after an absence of several months. But he hadn't needed any persuading when his boss had assigned this delivery job. Everland still held an irresistible attraction for him. He had glimpsed Ethel only once over the winter, when she had come into the shop to choose some paint, no doubt for the airplane. Nicholas had been waiting for her in the car outside. Andrei had hidden in the stockroom while the boss served Ethel. She took her time. He had heard her reading out the names of the colors: "Cobalt Blue, Burnt Umber, Naples Yellow . . ."

She was whispering the names as if they were a poem. "Caramel, Nymph's Thigh, Sumac . . ."

Andrei felt his head spinning, and it wasn't because of the solvents.

When Ethel left the shop, he had nipped out of the back of the stockroom to keep watching her. He suspected that Nicholas had recognized him as they drove off. Deep down, perhaps that was what he had been hoping for. But Ethel never came back.

As he drove along the road toward Everland, all he knew was that he wouldn't go as far as the main entrance. Nobody should know that he was still in the region.

Andrei braked a little more.

"Those poor people must have had an accident," tutted Boulard. "Pull up just after them."

They were less than fifty meters away. Steam was rising from the car, and somebody was sheltering under a cape.

Andrei leaned forward to have a look. It was rare to see a breakdown on this stretch of road.

"There's someone inside the car as well," he pointed out.

"Are you sure?" asked Boulard.

A face appeared to be pressed to the back window. The van belonging to Gregor's Colors paint shop was now almost level with the broken-down vehicle.

"Well, I never," whispered the superintendent, shuddering. "The woman signaling to us, beneath that coat, is Mary!" He hadn't yet had a chance to recognize his mother, who was sitting in the back.

Andrei slammed his foot down on the accelerator, and the car skidded for a moment before shooting off at top speed. The mud churned up by this spurt of acceleration splattered Boulard's window, just as his passenger door came level with his mother's. All that the superintendent glimpsed was a gray shape flickering like a ghost.

"Are you mad?" bellowed Boulard.

Andrei put his foot down even harder. Had Mary had enough time to recognize him? He covered the remaining distance on his hubcaps, to the sound of Boulard's reproaches.

"A poor lady in distress on the side of the road! Young man, you're a savage! I demand that you turn around."

Andrei dropped his passenger off at the bottom of the drive, at the exact spot where he had arrived two years earlier.

"Philistine! Lady splatterer! Umbrella deliverer! You're worse than your boss!"

The superintendent's barrage of names for his driver continued, but the van had already departed via a different route.

Back at Everland, everyone was in disarray. The shouts rose up from all quarters. They had searched the estate high and low, including in the hydrangeas. The princess was nowhere to be found.

Ethel could have kicked herself for not taking more precautions.

"Someone's carried her off; I'm sure of that," she told Scott.

The cook was wide-eyed. He was remembering stories from his childhood about princesses carried off by dragons. But who carried off eighty-eight-year-old princesses? Elderly dragons?

228

Ethel leaned against the window. Where should they look for her? Glancing up, she noticed a small figure virtually swimming in the middle of the drive as it failed to open its umbrella.

"That's him!" she exclaimed on closer inspection. "That's Boulard!"

She tore downstairs and rushed outside. The superintendent was waiting for her, as upright as possible. His boots made a squelching noise every time he moved. She was convinced that Boulard had gotten his mother back.

"What have you done with her? Where is she?" Ethel shouted at him.

The superintendent wasn't sure how to react.

"It was for her own good!" Ethel went on. "She's so attached to you. I know she wrote to you in Paris. Tell me where you've taken her."

Boulard was at a loss. Who was this young woman talking about? Suddenly, Mary sprang to mind.

"Wait," he said, thinking he'd understood at last. "You're mistaken. I haven't taken anybody. It's pure coincidence. She's on the road, in a broken-down car. You need to get her out of there."

Incredulous, Ethel made for her own car, with Boulard following.

"Yes, she wrote to me in Paris," he admitted. "Don't tell anyone, Ethel. How did you know? Her words expressed powerful feelings. Yes, I admit my heart stirred. But do you really think I would come like a desert tribesman to carry her off? Me, Superintendent Boulard? No, I didn't come for her."

"Out in the rain," muttered Ethel. "The poor woman, by the side of the road . . . at her great age."

"I think you're overstating it a bit," he protested, trotting along behind. "Of course, I'm considerably younger than she is. But she's a very handsome woman."

Ethel stopped. She had a doubt. Was he really talking about his own mother?

"I'm sorry, Superintendent. We are talking about . . ."

Boulard looked down, and the rain from his hat dripped onto his feet.

"Emotions . . ." he said. "We're talking about emotions."

"But whose?"

He was all fired up now.

"The emotions of a policeman who is also a man. Of a heart that beats beneath its Legion of Honor medal and its military cross. Of a——"

"What about her?"

"Mary? Oh . . . I think she's understood that I'll always be a veteran bachelor. Our story won't go much further."

Ethel seemed so taken aback that Boulard felt obliged to offer an explanation. "Don't worry; I won't put it to her like that. She'll understand."

"Was Mary the only woman you saw at Everland?"

"What do you take me for? A lady-killer? Do you think I seduced all the servants?"

"I meant, did you see anyone else by the broken-down car?"

"There was a female passenger, I believe, in the back, but I couldn't——"

"Thank goodness for that."

"Who is she?"

"A guest. Miss . . . Turtledove."

"Turtledove?"

"Yes. We had no idea where she'd gone."

The three days that followed were like the three acts of a farce. First of all, there was the reunion between the superintendent and the housekeeper. This involved a long silence with lowered gazes and fluttering eyelashes. As chance would have it, Madame Boulard had caught a cold, so she stayed in bed, cloistered in her bedroom. Mary and the rest of the staff were instructed that under no circumstances were they to mention the superintendent to the Princess of Albrac. Mary's curiosity was piqued by this mystery. But when Ethel explained to her that it was on account of a very old and private bond between the princess and Boulard, Mary was deeply moved.

"The wound must not be reopened," Ethel had told her.

The idea that she might be rival to a princess was, for Mary, a feather in her cap. She no longer walked in the same way. She felt great compassion for this broken woman and was prepared to defend her secret like a guard dog.

As for Boulard, he was informed that the guest on the first floor, Miss Turtledove, was highly contagious. He should have no contact with her.

All this resulted in an intricate piece of theater. Doors could be heard banging. And shadows roamed the corridors at night.

But alongside this theatrical comedy, something completely different was being played out.

"Ethel, I'd like to speak with you about Vango."

The superintendent had closed the door of the small

library after dinner. They were alone. Ethel wanted to leave, but he was blocking the way.

"This time," he declared, "I'm here for his own good. Things have changed. I can't be certain about Vango anymore."

"You're the only person who ever was certain about him."

"Mademoiselle, before you stands a hunted man."

"You poor thing."

"I left the police headquarters via the drains."

"What a shame."

"Do you hear me? By the drains!"

"Yes, I heard you, and I can smell it too. Let me out or I'll scream. Your Vango no longer interests me."

"Sit down for a minute. Hear me out."

"I don't like sitting. I stand or I lie down."

"Ethel, I've come to ask for your help. I have to see Vango. I think I know who's after him. I can help him, Ethel. He's in danger."

"In danger?" she echoed sarcastically. "That's not his style."

"I know that he is linked to a man named Zefiro. Have you heard of Voloy Viktor?"

No answer.

"Voloy Viktor is a killer," said Boulard.

"You enjoy scaring the ladies, Superintendent Boulard."

"Vango can help me find Viktor."

Ethel pointed an accusing finger directly at Boulard.

"You see. You came here because you want to use him."

"No."

"Let me go to my bedroom."

"Zefiro tried to attack Viktor, and now his island has been ravaged. There's nothing left. I recently sent someone over there. You heard it from me; there's not a single survivor. Just ruins. That's what awaits Vango."

"As I say, you enjoy scaring the ladies."

Boulard sighed.

"Give me an address; tell me where he is."

"My parents are dead, and my brother, Paul, might be dying in battle in Spain for all I know, so if I really could save my one friend, don't you think I would?"

There was a long silence. Boulard observed every tremor on Ethel's face. He himself had experienced neither personal tragedy nor passion. The only hand he had held tenderly had belonged to a little girl from the Aveyron when he was ten years old. But he did understand the human soul.

"But what if I believe you know where he is?"

"Let me through."

"One day," said Superintendent Boulard, opening the door, "you'll receive a cry for help from him, and it will be too late. And then you'll remember me."

He looked at her again.

"You'll remember me."

Boulard headed off in the direction of his bedroom.

Ethel watched him climb the stairs at the end of the hall. She remained in the library. As always happened when she was alone, those feelings hidden from the eyes of others came flooding in: fear, doubt, and loneliness. What could she do? Yes, there was a place, at the intersection of two streets in New York, that had been Vango's last address. He could still be there.

Until the very last moment, Ethel was of two minds about telling Boulard what she knew of Vango's whereabouts. A few weeks later, and for many years to come, she would regret not having done so.

The following day, the comedy was in full swing again. A lovesick Mary was weeping in the kitchen. Letters had been slid into the superintendent's bedroom. He was waiting for them, down on his knees, just behind the door.

There had been missed trysts on the stairs, and a game of hide-and-seek played out on various landings. One night, Offenbach's arias were heard being sung with gusto. Luckily, Boulard was sleeping soundly and didn't recognize his mother's voice.

When the superintendent eventually left Everland, everyone hoped for calm again.

But Mary shut herself in her bedroom with the umbrella that Boulard had forgotten. Her sobs could be heard all the way down to the cellars. The Princess of Albrac sang to cover these lamentations. Ethel knocked on Mary's door. She was worried about the housekeeper staging her own death with that umbrella, like Dido falling on the sword of her fleeing lover, Aeneas.

Two days later, in the morning, Mary reappeared. She brewed a pot of tea for the princess and buttered some slices of toast. The curtain had fallen for the end of the performance. The fever had departed the walls of the house, but inside Ethel there was a growing sense of unease.

BLOOD AND HONOR

Berlin, Germany, March 25, 1937

Hugo Eckener took a shortcut through the zoological gardens. This was an hour that belonged to babies, nannies, and old men basking in the sun, their feet in the daffodils. The rest of Germany was at work. It was eleven o'clock in the morning.

Commander Eckener stopped to watch the repairs under way on an aviary. Carefully, he observed the wire meshing being assembled. As a rule, he found everything around him interesting: the welding on an old cage, the flight of a sparrow, the canvas covering the arbors. He took inspiration from everything. The gigantic *Hindenburg* airship had barely been flying for a year, and Hugo Eckener already had new projects in mind. But this morning, his gaze cut discreetly through the aviary netting and focused on a young man who was waiting farther off, his hands in his pockets, cap on head.

Eckener had already noticed the lad the previous day, on the other side of town. The commander was frequently trailed by the authorities, but not usually by an eighteen-year-old kid. He started to walk again, in the direction of a brick pavilion. The young man followed close behind. Eckener felt exasperated. He had a meeting in a café a stone's throw away, and he had no desire to turn up with this leech sticking to him.

He entered the reptiles' enclosure, which smelled of

rotting meat. The walkways were deserted. A lackluster boa constrictor was asleep in a heap behind a glass wall. Hugo Eckener made his way across the room as swiftly as possible, leaving via an emergency exit that gave onto two vivariums packed with lizards. He closed the door quietly behind him. Because of the nightmare that his country was experiencing, he was still playing cat and mouse in the park at the age of nearly seventy. Dictatorships keep you young, he reflected.

As he took a few moments to catch his breath, he spotted three young women pushing baby carriages. They were exactly what he needed, and Eckener joined them. They headed off together, with the commander leaning over the babies, playing grandpa, smiling at the women, performing magic sleights of hand, and showing them how he could make the swastika appear and disappear beneath the eagle on a two-reichsmark coin.

"Ta-da!"

One of the women looked thoughtful and inquired if he wasn't the balloon man.

"Me?"

Eckener apologized profusely, muttering that he often got asked the same question and pointing out that the man in charge of those airships was much older than he was and had less hair. No, truth be told, he was in the cigar business. And he promptly took a cigar out of his pocket.

"You really look like him."

"A little bit, yes, but he's got a bigger nose, hasn't he?"

The commander advanced with this baby lotion–scented convoy until they reached a hedge, at which point he disappeared behind it. He waved good-bye to the company and lit a cigar. When he walked toward the park gates, there was no one behind him.

Eckener walked down the first street and entered a restaurant that was almost empty.

At the only occupied table, a man was reading a newspaper. It was his old pal Esquirol, the doctor from Paris.

Hugo Eckener took a good hard look at him. He remembered the first time they had met up in the café on rue de Paradis, one winter's evening, together with Zefiro and Joseph Jacques Puppet, the boxer-barber from the Ivory Coast: these founding members of Project Violette had made a pact for peace in the trenches. Back then, the Great War was over at last, and everything seemed possible in their eyes. But they had been wrong. Ever since that day, each time they met again it meant that a fresh danger was looming.

Eckener sat down opposite his friend.

"Can you read German, Doctor Esquirol?"

The other man lowered his newspaper.

"No, I'm looking at the pictures."

He pointed to a photo of Chancellor Hitler carrying a child. Eckener didn't even glance at it. He shook Esquirol's hand warmly.

"How long has it been?" asked Eckener, blowing out the smoke from his cigar.

"Two years, at least."

"Where is Puppet?"

"On the Côte d'Azur, working on his suntan."

Eckener signaled to the waiter. They ordered two hot chocolates and stared at each other in silence through the smoke.

"It frightens me when you come to see me," said Eckener. Esquirol smiled.

"Any news of Zefiro?" added the commander.

"None."

Eckener was always worried about Zefiro.

"Well?"

"Well nothing," said Esquirol. "Paris is good. Likewise, my patients. I'm looking after the prime minister, who sends his regards."

"How kind of him," Eckener replied suspiciously.

"I just wanted to ask you a small favor."

Commander Eckener put out his cigar. Everything began with a small favor. They saw their cups of hot chocolate arriving, with the whipped cream overflowing into the saucers.

"I'm getting ready for a trip," Esquirol announced.

Eckener was watching his friend.

"One of my patients needs to be treated by a colleague abroad, in America. This patient gets dreadfully seasick if he travels by boat. . . ."

"Poor thing."

"He's an important man."

Eckener didn't know what *important* meant. He had already flattened the nose of a celebrity who had been caught secretly smoking in the *Graf Zeppelin*.

"Important in what way?" asked the commander. "He's too big to fit through the doors?"

Esquirol tasted the cream before declaring, "I want him to take your *Hindenburg*."

"When?"

"On the earliest departure for New York."

"There aren't any at the moment."

"What's the date of the first flight?"

"The third of May. Departing from Frankfurt."

"In that case, he'll wait until the third of May," stated Esquirol.

"I thought he was seriously ill."

"His illness can wait."

Eckener licked some chocolate off his finger and stared at his friend.

"I know you have a new cabin," said Esquirol, "with an external window and four beds. This gentleman is traveling with two people he requires close by at all times."

"And would he like the shirt off my back while we're at it?" asked Eckener.

"No."

"That's just as well. I won't even be on board."

"What?" asked an alarmed Esquirol.

Eckener was carefully buttering a slice of brioche.

"I'll be in Austria that week. Max Pruss will be in command of the airship."

Doctor Esquirol sank back into his chair.

"This Mr. Valpa I'm looking after," he insisted, "wanted to shake your hand."

"I beg your pardon?"

"He won't embark unless he's shaken your hand."

"Really?"

"Yes."

"What sort of disease has he got? It sounds rather alarming."

"I'm telling you that he's got to shake you by the hand."

"Well, I hope it's not contagious."

Eckener seemed resigned. He held out the butter knife to Esquirol before baring his right wrist.

"Cut it off. And give it to him."

"Stop it, Commander. This is deadly serious."

"Yes, that's just what worries me. It's serious. And I don't believe I can help you."

Eckener stared at his friend in silence.

"I saw the pictures of your Olympic Games last summer," remarked Doctor Esquirol, pushing his chair back a little.

Hugo Eckener stirred his hot chocolate with a teaspoon.

"A hundred thousand people in a stadium, each hailing the balloon with his arm outstretched," Esquirol continued. "That was your hour of glory, wasn't it?"

In August 1936, the Berlin Olympic Games had put the seal of approval on Adolf Hitler and the *Hindenburg* airship. The zeppelin, decorated in the Nazi colors, had flown over one hundred thousand spectators in the Berlin stadium.

"Be quiet, Esquirol."

"Why should I?"

"Hitler wanted the *Hindenburg* to bear his name. . . ."

"Adolf, what a nice name for a balloon."

"I refused. So I had to make a gesture of appeasement. But I've never detested the regime so much."

"A gesture of appeasement!" Esquirol sniggered.

"Stop it. You understand what I'm talking about."

"No. I don't understand. I'm simply asking you to shake this man's hand. I shall pay for the cabin for him and his friends. Just as I shall pay for my own."

"Yours?"

"I'll be sharing it with Joseph Puppet."

Eckener stared deep into Esquirol's eyes.

"Is he sick too? This sounds like an epidemic."

"He's never been to New York. So I'm taking him."

"How sweet."

Eckener sighed. What were his friends up to this time? He tapped his thumb against the tabletop, while Esquirol glanced around. There were still no other customers in the restaurant. Two waitresses were eating lunch near the entrance.

"You've got a friend outside," remarked Esquirol.

Eckener didn't turn around.

"Where?"

"He arrived just after you did. He's sitting on the bench opposite the restaurant window, on the pavement. He's wearing a sailor's cap."

"How old?"

"Under twenty."

Hugo Eckener cursed, then turned and called to one of the waitresses, "Go and get that lad for me, over there, and drag him in by the scruff of his neck!"

A few seconds later, the young man was deposited in front of the two friends. He appeared to be standing to attention and he swayed gently backward and forward.

Eckener mopped up the bottom of his cup with some bread.

"Get out of my sight, and take your tramp's cap with you."

"Yes, Commander."

"Who sent you?"

The boy's eyes flickered.

"Who sent you?" roared Eckener, as Doctor Esquirol looked on.

"I . . . sent myself, Commander."

Eckener had put his large hands on his knees.

"What?"

"I sent myself."

"What do you want?"

"To come with you," volunteered the boy.

"I don't need anyone. Get out."

"I have a letter."

Hugo Eckener felt a tremor in his chest. Years earlier, a boy had uttered those same words, *I have a letter,* and he had produced the note from Father Zefiro commending the boy to Eckener.

"Give me that letter."

The boy opened his jacket, briefly revealing its woolen lining covered in Nazi insignias.

From his pocket, he removed a piece of paper that was curiously folded into the shape of a triangle.

Hugo Eckener turned the object over in his hands. Then he unfolded it.

There were just a few jotted words, but Eckener seemed to take a long time reading them. He glanced at the young man.

"What is your name?"

"Schiff."

The boy started rattling off the words of a Nazi song. They referred to "closed ranks" and "brown battalions."

"That's enough, thank you," interrupted Hugo Eckener.

"I'm in your camp," declared Schiff, taking a knife out of his pocket.

Esquirol stood up, but the commander indicated for him

to sit back down again. He prized the knife out of the boy's hands. The words BLOOD AND HONOR were engraved on the handle: the motto of the Hitler Youth movement.

"You see, I am with you."

"Yes. Put that away, right now."

Schiff started reciting another poem.

"Be quiet."

To Esquirol's astonishment, Eckener took out a name card. While he was scribbling on it, the commander kept on talking, like a doctor writing out a prescription.

"What can you do, Schiff?"

"Anything."

"Can you carry heavy loads?"

"Yes."

"Go to the air terminal at Frankfurt. Do you know where it is?"

"Yes."

"Show this note to Herr Klaus. He'll give you work. Go straight there, all right?"

"Yes."

"Right away. Catch the train. Ask for Herr Klaus and stay there."

The young man took the letter, clicked his heels, and went on his way. He had left behind the knife with BLOOD AND HONOR engraved on it.

As he watched him go, Eckener felt as if he were still glimpsing the figure of Vango from a few years earlier.

Doctor Esquirol was sitting bolt upright opposite him.

"It seems there are some requests you don't refuse, Eckener."

"Indeed."

"You've changed," he said.

"Yes, I've changed," agreed Eckener, taking a deep breath. "Everybody changes at one time or another."

"You disgust me. . . ."

"Did you know, for example, that I studied psychology in Leipzig?"

"That's irrelevant, Commander Eckener."

"I wanted to become a psychiatrist. I earned my doctorate, then I changed my mind. What matters is knowing when to change, Esquirol. I realize now how much I would have suffered: they no longer look after the sick in our psychiatric hospitals; they eliminate them."

"That's not what I'm here to discuss," said Esquirol, standing his ground.

Among many other shocking laws, the doctor knew about the measures taken by the Nazis against the mentally ill. Hitler had been talking for more than ten years about suppressing "life unworthy of life."

"You're muddling everything up," declared Esquirol.

"No, I'm telling you what I see and you haven't experienced."

"You are complicit in all of this. You're giving work to this lad who's come to see you, because he's been recommended by people in high places."

Eckener gently scratched the tablecloth with his thumb. Wearily, he slid the piece of paper from the boy toward Esquirol.

"Do you want to see the recommendation from someone on high?"

"No."

But the doctor reached for the piece of paper all the same. It was a carefully presented letter, signed with an illegible name. Esquirol couldn't read German.

"Who wrote this?" he asked.

"He did. Schiff."

"Is it a fake?"

"No, it's a real recipe for pork with cabbage."

"I beg your pardon?"

"Pork with cabbage, allow one and a half hours' cooking time. Do not stir."

"Is he crazy?"

"Yes, chronic schizophrenia with atypical features. Didn't you notice anything? What do they teach medical students in Paris? To stroll around the Latin Quarter with pretty girls?"

Doctor Esquirol was a bit lost.

"Did you see his eyes?" Eckener went on. "The way his head moved? You didn't notice anything? Luckily, that boy has never set foot in the Hitler Youth. Otherwise, a man in a white coat would already be experimenting on his brain in a laboratory somewhere."

"So—"

"I'm sheltering him. He may have been sent by some of my university friends. Or by chance. It doesn't really matter. He'll lift gas bottles and boxes in our hangars at Frankfurt. It's better for him that way."

Unable to utter a word, Esquirol was still holding the letter.

"I'm sorry," he said eventually.

"I have to choose between blood and honor every day, Doctor."

Eckener stood up, put a note down on the table to cover the bill, thrust the knife into it, and headed for the door.

"Wait. When can we see each other again?" Esquirol called out.

Eckener looked surprised.

"What about May, and the embarkation of the *Hindenburg*? Are you telling me it's not a serious appointment after all?"

He stepped outside. In the street, he was a sight to behold with his white mane of hair and his alpaca coat. Esquirol watched the commander stopping the cars with a wave of his hand, like Moses crossing the Red Sea.

Esquirol drank a glass of water and thought for a few minutes.

He asked for the telephone, and was pointed toward the basement. Ten minutes later, after battling with a telephone operator using the few German words he knew, he finally managed to connect with a number in Geneva.

He asked for Vincent Valpa.

"Mr. Valpa? It's me, Doctor Esquirol. I'm in Berlin. Everything will be ready for the beginning of May."

Not a word from the other end of the line.

"Can you hear me? We're leaving from Frankfurt on the third of May."

The person on the other end hung up.

It was always the same story.

Whether he was disguised as Vincent Valpa, Madame Victoria, or any of his other avatars, Voloy Viktor never spoke on the phone. He listened and he hung up.

18

FOUR WORDS IN A TELEGRAM

Moscow, April 20, 1937

A bare-chested stranger stood on the stairs, wearing only a pair of trousers. He was staring at Mademoiselle, who had just opened her front door and looked taken aback.

"Is Ivan Ivanovitch Oulanov in?" asked the stranger.

"No. Who are you?"

"When will he be back?"

Mademoiselle didn't answer, but the man wouldn't let it drop.

"What about his wife?"

"She's been working nights in the factory now that Mr. Oulanov isn't here anymore."

Mademoiselle felt uncomfortable standing opposite this man in the middle of the night. He seemed rather stiff, and he kept his hands firmly by his sides. She had opened the door the moment she heard the knocking because she still hoped that the father of Kostia, Zoya, and Andrei would be safely returned to them.

"I'm the neighbor from the first floor," the man informed her. "I know the family's got some problems."

"Please don't worry on their behalf," said Mademoiselle, trying to shut the door.

"Wait."

The man blocked the door with his foot.

"Please," whispered Mademoiselle firmly. "The children are asleep."

She pushed the door against the man's shoe and managed to shut it.

"Open up," he called out.

"Come back tomorrow. I'm alone with the children. I'm not allowed to open the door."

"Wait," he whispered. "Hear me out! I've just received a telephone call from Andrei. He wants to talk to his father. He's going to call back in a few minutes."

There was a long silence, and the door opened very slowly.

"Andrei?"

"The Oulanov son. Sometimes he sends messages via us. Andrei got on well with my son. He wants to talk to his father."

"I've told you: his father isn't here anymore."

"Well, come with me, then. He's going to call back for news of his family."

"I've never met Andrei. What am I going to say to him? He had already left when I arrived. I've taken over his bedroom."

"You're the only person who can answer him."

"But the children . . . I can't leave them."

"They're asleep."

Mademoiselle thought back to what Andrei's father had told her about their linked destinies: what Andrei did determined their lives.

The man took a broom from the landing and propped it across the doorway.

"Come with me. The door will stay open."

"I don't know what I'm supposed to say."

"Come on."

"I can't."

But as she spoke she was already making her way downstairs, and turning around to check on the door. She walked into the first-floor apartment. The telephone was in the kitchen. They made their way along a gloomy corridor to find an old woman sitting at the kitchen table.

"This is my mother. My wife is asleep in the bedroom, next door."

All three of them sat around the table. A cup of tea was poured for Mademoiselle. The old woman served the tea just like in the grand houses Mademoiselle had once known. They waited. The telephone was fixed on the wall near the door.

"We'll leave the room when he calls," the man announced. "I don't want to hear what you say to him."

On the wall, there was a brand-new poster celebrating the twentieth anniversary of the revolution. Mademoiselle looked at the faces depicted on it. A child carrying bricks in his arms, a woman pointing to the horizon with a trowel. Opposite Mademoiselle, the old woman sat very still, her hands on the table, as she stared at the visitor.

"Are you French?" the woman asked in French.

"Yes," said Mademoiselle.

The woman smiled.

"I grew up and worked over there, in Paris," explained Mademoiselle. "But I haven't been back home for a very long time."

It had been years since she had last divulged such simple facts about herself.

"I've never been to France," replied the old woman. "But I used to speak good French. And I haven't forgotten it. I talk to myself in my bedroom."

"Be quiet, Mother," said the man, who couldn't follow the conversation.

They didn't say another word until the woman rattled off, "You need to return to Paris. People need to go back home one day. My husband died in exile, sadly."

To avoid her son's wrath, the woman stood up and carried the teapot over to the sink, before heading for the kitchen door. Just as she was in the doorway, the telephone rang.

The man offered his arm to his mother. They left, closing the door behind them. Mademoiselle was next to the telephone. On the fifth ring, she picked up.

"Hello?"

"Hello."

The voice sounded very far away and unsure of itself.

"Mother?"

"No."

Mademoiselle was panic-stricken. What could she say?

"Hello?" came Andrei's voice again. "Who's there?"

"This isn't your parents, Andrei."

"Who's there?

"I am the *tioten'ka* who looks after your brother and sister."

"Where are they?"

"Your father's been taken away. I don't know why."

At the other end of the line, the voice had gone quiet.

"Hello?" said Mademoiselle.

Perhaps the line had been cut off. Confronted with this loud silence, she suddenly felt bolder and began to talk.

"I don't know why your father's been arrested, Andrei, and I don't know where you are or what you're doing. I don't know anything. I don't know you. Can you hear me? Your violins are under my bed. Under *your* bed. I came here by chance. No one tells me anything."

She listened to the crackling of the line before continuing.

"But I want to warn you about something. It is my belief that your actions are being watched by someone, that your actions affect what happens here. That's what your father explained to me before he went. I'm afraid they may have taken your father because of you."

Not a sound in the receiver. Perhaps Mademoiselle was talking to herself in the kitchen, just like the old woman every evening when she recited Verlaine's poems to the empty table, the big poster, and the samovar.

"Andrei, can you hear me? Tell me if you can hear me. Think this over. Is there one thing you could do that would help bring your father back? He needs you. Your brother and sister need you. Your mother needs you. Are you still there, Andrei?"

She clung to the telephone and whispered, "Good luck, if you can hear me . . ."

The line hadn't been cut. Andrei had heard everything. But he was speechless. He was in Inverness, Scotland, in Gregor's Colors paint shop, and it was the middle of the night. He had dared to make this phone call.

The crackling grew louder. Then nothing. He replaced the handset and put his head in his hands. His father . . .

He no longer had any choice. His plan had been ready for a long time. Four words in a telegram. All he had to do was take it to Everland. But he had wavered for weeks about using Ethel in order to save his family.

Andrei stared at the telephone on the desk: there couldn't be many calls to Moscow made from it. In any event, he would be far from here by the time his boss received the bill. And Vango would already be in the Vulture's clutches.

As she returned to the apartment and tucked in little Kostia, who was crying in his sleep, Mademoiselle didn't realize the gravity of what she had just done. In those few words to Andrei, she had relaunched the hunt for Vango.

Sochi, on the shores of the Black Sea, the next day,
April 21, 1937

Setanka was locked in her father's study. She was listening to her nurse, Alexandra Andreyevna, shouting at her from behind the door.

"He'll be here any moment and he won't be happy. Come out, or I'll break down the door."

Setanka knew that her nurse would never break down the door of Joseph Stalin's study. She even felt a bit ashamed making the woman she adored, who was like a surrogate mother to her and much more besides, resort to such threats.

"He's holding me prisoner in this house. I want to go back to Moscow! It's not fair making me stay here when I'm only eleven!"

Sitting in the desk chair, she opened a drawer.

Setanka had been at the dacha in Sochi for almost four months, ever since she had been rescued from the garage where the father of her friend Zoya worked. The political police had referred to a kidnapping attempt. Setanka would gladly have been kidnapped, but as it was, she explained to everybody that she had simply tried swapping families. She didn't mention the envelope, which she had mailed to Italy on behalf of the *tioten'ka*. She loved secrets.

"Setanotchka, open the door for me. . . . Your father's coming."

Sometimes, in order to make Setanka come out when she had spent the whole day hiding behind the furniture, the nurse would toss two handfuls of sugar into a hot pan and wait. The sweet scent of caramel was too delicious to resist.

From the drawer, Setanka took out a letter that she often came to look at. The paper was very old and the handwriting seemed to have been blown sideways by the wind. It was a very mysterious letter. Addressed to *Dear Mother,* it had always seemed to Setanka as if she could have written the opening sentences: *I am alive. I know that you haven't forgotten me. . . .* Setanka would have liked to address these words to her own mother, who had died in the year Setanka had turned six. Why did her father keep a letter in his drawer that was written by a stranger who gave his *Dear Mother* an appointment on a bridge in Moscow and who also told her: *Please don't get out of the carriage; don't even stop. You'll see me beneath the sculpted horses on the bridge, and you'll know that I'm alive.*

Setanka was particularly staring at the drawing that served as a signature: a word that wasn't written in the Russian alphabet—*Romano*—and a capital *W* just below.

"This time he really is coming, Svetlana. Come out quickly!"

A door slammed downstairs. Setanka put the letter back

and closed the drawer. Alexandra Andreyevna could hear footsteps on the wooden stairs. Then she saw Joseph Stalin appear on the landing.

"Comrade, the little one is locked inside your study. The key must be jammed."

"Poor, poor little one . . ."

The nurse could immediately tell that he was in a good mood.

"Didn't you try climbing in through the window to rescue her, Nurse?"

He was smiling. She didn't answer. Stalin took a large key out of his pocket and went over to the door.

Setanka was waiting on the other side. She saw the key she had used fall out of the lock and land on the carpet. A second later, the door flew open.

"There we go, rescued!" declared her father.

He scooped Setanka up in his arms as if he wanted to rescue her from a fire. But she wasn't laughing.

"I want to go back to Moscow," she said.

Joseph Stalin put his daughter down on the landing.

"I want to go back to Moscow."

"Yes. I think you'll be able to go back soon," he told her with shining eyes. "The little problem has almost been sorted."

The little problem had been bothering him for exactly twenty years. The problem was called Vango.

Setanka headed off along the landing.

Her father went back into his study, closing the door behind him. He stared through the window at the mournful rosebushes beyond. He had neglected them for some time now. He opened the drawer of his desk and took out the letter. There it was. He would soon be done with this obsession: this perpetual hunt. He would soon be able to tear up the letter his men had found in a ransacked palace in Petrograd, among family photos and holy images.

Back then, he had been young and had recently returned from several years of exile in Siberia.

It was the revolution of 1917, and Stalin was back in the capital of the tsars. He didn't want anything of the former empire and its descendants to remain. And then this letter had been thrust into his hands. It mentioned a child who was going to be born.

In 1929, two of his men, Kakline and Antonov, who were Moscow's official representatives for the zeppelin's world tour, had discovered the same signature on board, but this time it was embroidered on a handkerchief belonging to a fourteen-year-old boy. Stalin had immediately been informed. Having just assumed full powers in his country, he had only to give the order. The manhunt had been going on since that summer's day. The Bird seemed impossible to catch.

But at last he was going to be shot down out of the sky.

Paris, a week later, April 28, 1937

In the private mansion of Ferdinand Atlas, from the cellar to the attic the party was in full swing. But his daughter, the Cat, was on the roof.

Down below, they were playing the foxtrot and a new fast waltz called the java. Couples danced opposite each other, making the glasses on the tables clink and the marble floor vibrate. There were two orchestras. Upstairs, a string quartet brought couples closer together. People were whispering on the banquettes. There were candelabra on the mantelpieces. The doors to the wine cellars had been flung wide open, and guests headed down to serve themselves. Some of the elegantly dressed men hid bottles of wine in their wives' handbags to take back home with them. Madame Atlas pretended not to notice.

The Cat was watching her father as he sat on the balcony below her. He had carried a wooden kitchen chair outside and was keeping an eye on the guests continuing to arrive in the courtyard. Nobody could see him behind the stone railing. He was like the punished child everyone has forgotten, but who doesn't dare to stand up from his chair.

The Cat had abandoned her bedroom when one of the guests had tried forcing her door. It was an invasion. They were everywhere.

The Cat still regretted not following Ethel when she had met up with her that same morning in Montmartre. They had spoken for only a few minutes before going their separate ways. The news was worrying. They ought to have set out together in search of Vango. At least that way the Cat wouldn't be here defending her bedroom against marauders.

She had pushed the wardrobe against the door to stop anyone from entering. An hour earlier, she had heard laughter on the landing.

"That's their daughter's bedroom. . . ."

"They've got a daughter? You're joking."

In the end, the Cat had grabbed her blanket and taken refuge on the roof, from where she could observe her father.

Someone appeared behind Ferdinand Atlas. The Cat recognized the chauffeur.

"It's very kind of you to have come up, Pierre. Put the parcel down on the table."

"Good night, sir."

"Pierre," her father called out to the chauffeur, who was already on his way again, "what was the name of the small town you were talking about this morning?"

"Guernica."

"Is that where you come from?"

"It's on the other side of the border, but it's my country. I'm Basque."

"Guernica."

"Yes."

"Have they destroyed it?"

"Hitler wanted to test his planes. It happened yesterday."

"How many dead?"

"I don't know."

Ferdinand Atlas nodded in silence.

"Pierre, do you believe that this is the beginning of a war?"

"The war has been going on in Spain for nearly a year now, sir."

"But why are the Germans in Spain?"

"I don't know."

The Cat saw her father loosening his black tie around his neck. He waved at Pierre.

"Thank you. You can go to bed now. I'm jealous. I've got to go back down and join all these people."

When the chauffeur opened the door, the bedroom was

filled with laughter. Three or four people rushed in, led by Madame Atlas.

"There he is, dear old Ferdinand. Look, he's sulking!"

The Cat's father got up off his chair.

"Ferdinand, these ladies wished to see our bedroom and the balcony."

The guests let out shrieks of amazement before trampling a tiger skin rug and rushing out onto the balcony.

The Cat crouched on the roof. She watched her father calmly lift his wooden chair and raise it above his head. The merry shrieks stopped. He hurled the chair with all his might toward the bedroom: it went through the French windows, which shattered.

"Ferdinand!" exclaimed his wife.

But he had disappeared.

Attracted by the noise, clusters of guests turned up and entered the bedroom. The Cat watched her father, down below, striding across the courtyard.

After a few minutes of people walking around the bed and slipping on pieces of broken glass like tourists on a battlefield, the orchestra downstairs lured nearly everyone back onto the dance floor by playing "Tout va très bien Madame la Marquise," a song that was all the rage in the open-air cafés and dance halls.

The Cat thought she was on her own at last, but three men had stayed behind to smoke on the balcony.

"There's trouble ahead," said one of them.

"Let's enjoy ourselves while we can. There won't always be parties in this house."

It wasn't possible to hear the third man, whose words

were muffled. But someone answered him, "Yes, his name has been cited in the Chamber of Deputies by Monsieur Vallat or one of his friends. . . . There was a terribly witty pun about his extravagant business dealings; I can't quite remember how it went."

"If they go for Atlas, they won't leave him in peace."

The man with the muffled voice must have suddenly remembered the play on words, because he said something short and punchy that prompted his friends to burst out laughing. The only thing the Cat heard was the word "Jew": the same word she had seen scrawled on the gate one morning, before it was painted black again, a word she had never heard spoken at home. She removed a piece of slate from the roof.

Out on the balcony, they were talking about the paintings they had seen in the drawing room, about how charming Madame Atlas was despite everything, and about the quality of the champagne. Someone mentioned a debt of loyalty to their host, who had always been so hospitable. Indeed, he wished to discuss the matter with the deputy of the Ardèche region.

"Loyal, yes, I'd defend him!"

"At least until the champagne runs out!"

The others pretended to be shocked. But they were tipsy, and it was hard to stop laughing.

Just then, the three men saw a piece of slate appear out of the night sky, spinning in their direction. It decapitated a champagne glass and grazed the cheek of the man with the muffled voice. Then it splintered on the parquet floor of the bedroom. The Cat, who'd had enough, jumped onto the neighbor's roof.

The orchestras were enjoying a break, which meant that

the slate could clearly be heard skidding over the wooden floor like a piece of ice hurled onto a frozen lake.

The Cat was already running over the rooftops. No sooner had she thrown the slate than she noticed somebody rise up and begin to chase her. She had taken to the rooftops when she was seven. Usually, it was easy for her to throw someone off her trail. She outran the gutter cats and feared nobody on this terrain. The person following her, however, was cut from the same cloth. He didn't exactly tread in her footsteps, but he followed her at the same speed, slightly to the right, as if he knew that a stampede on the rooftops meant that bits of metalwork or tiling might work loose, and the person behind in the race would risk slipping.

The Cat couldn't believe that one of the three men had managed to react so quickly. Luckily, a bit farther off, in a courtyard between the buildings, stood a chestnut tree in which she could shelter. There were just two more buildings to traverse: the first had a large roof terrace, while on the second there were three stacks of chimney pots that she had to climb one after the other. When the Cat turned around as she stood on the gutter opposite the tree, her pursuer was no longer behind her. The highest branches were below her now. She took a deep breath and jumped. While she was in midair, she saw a shadow burst from the other side of the courtyard and throw itself into the branches.

It was as if a pigeon fight had broken out in the leaves of the chestnut tree. The branches were shaking. The two opponents chased each other from one end of the tree to the other, and then everything went very still.

"Are you going to stop?"

Silence.

"Who's there?" asked the Cat eventually.

"It's me," answered Vango.

The Cat quickly climbed to the top of the tree and found herself face-to-face with Vango. They hadn't seen each other for three years.

"What are you doing here?"

"I came to the party hoping to find you."

"You were there?"

Their hands didn't touch. The Cat was trembling and out of breath.

"You barricaded yourself in when I tried to come into your bedroom," Vango told her.

"I did?"

"Yes."

"That was you?"

"And when I climbed onto the roof, you ran away."

"I didn't realize." The Cat smiled. "It wasn't because of you."

She was happy to see him. She grabbed hold of his sleeve, which was the most affectionate gesture she had ever made.

"So, have you seen Ethel?" asked the Cat.

"No. I'm on my way to her place; I just wanted—"

The Cat pulled away.

"But didn't you see her today? Does she know you're here?"

"Don't worry. I know she doesn't want to see me any-more. . . ."

"Vango . . ."

"I must talk to her."

"Vango!" exclaimed the Cat, raising her voice. "She's already gone."

"Who has?"

"She received your message. She's set off to find you."

Vango twisted the branch above him to let in some light. But it did little to shift the shadow over the Cat's face.

"Where is she?"

"She'll have left Paris this evening."

"But where has she gone?"

"You wrote to her, telling her to join you."

"What are you talking about? She'd asked me not to write to her."

"She showed me the telegram. Four words in a telegram. You were asking for her help."

Vango felt his heart racing.

"They're going to follow her," he said. "They'll follow her in order to find me. Where is she?"

"She mentioned an address that you gave a long time ago, an address on the corner of two streets, in a building under construction. Ethel has left for New York."

Vango immediately thought of Zefiro. Ethel would lead whoever was after him to Zefiro.

And, just as happened every time, in a flash the Cat was alone in the branches. Without so much as a good-bye.

Vango arrived to find an empty station. The last train to Cherbourg had just left. He woke the engineers, one of whom pointed to the end platform, where Vango jumped onto a goods truck bound for Caen.

In a state of torment, Vango bedded down between some blue sacks. He didn't sleep a wink. At dawn, in front of Caen Station, he climbed onto the roof of a truck, jumping off at Valognes, where he borrowed a bicycle for the last twenty kilometers or so.

He entered the Port of Cherbourg and ran toward the dock. Too late.

The *Europa* had set sail that night.

19

"WRITE TO TELL ME HE'S WELL"

Frankfurt, Germany, May 3, 1937

Sleep, Hindy, sleep a while longer.

Schiff was pushing a cart of empty gas bottles, while technicians whirled about the hangar. Above him, the *Hindenburg* had gobbled up its two hundred thousand cubic meters of hydrogen. Schiff couldn't take his eyes off it. The balloon's belly was full to bursting. It was a giant, as long as twelve tennis courts end to end, and appeared dust colored in its lair. Schiff talked to it from morning until night, moving his lips soundlessly. He called it Hindy, as if it were a friend.

Sleep until this evening. . . .

Hugo Eckener had asked Schiff to talk inside his head, and the boy was doing his best to obey him. He worked hard, and that way people forgot about him. It took hundreds of gas bottles to satisfy Hindy's hunger. Schiff transported them one by one, day in and day out.

The Zeppelin Company workers were doing the final checks. Two or three of these men were still suspended from the arches.

The *Hindenburg*'s departure for America was set for that same evening. It had already made several crossings to Brazil at the start of the season. But this was its first flight to New York in 1937. A dozen cabins had been added over the winter. It wasn't fully booked on the outbound journey, but every cabin was already reserved for the return leg from New York. The *Hindenburg* zeppelin could now digest seventy-two passengers and nearly as many crew members. It was an ogre.

Captain Pruss walked past Schiff, who stopped his cart to gawk at the four golden stripes on the sleeves of the captain's jacket. Pruss was accompanied by an assistant, who was running through a list of problems still outstanding. The captain was used to this kind of inventory: the kitchen generator had broken down; the cabin boys didn't know how to make the beds; the thousands of tons of water were taking too long to load; the chief engineer's wife was about to give birth. . . .

"What d'you want me to say? Get another engineer, or else bring his wife along too!"

The assistant was taking notes.

"Just tell me there isn't a storm forecast," growled Pruss.

"Not tonight, no. But the piano—"

"What's wrong with the piano?" asked the captain irritatedly.

An aluminum baby grand piano covered in yellow leather had been installed in the starboard saloon of the airship, on the upper deck. Schubert could be played over Cape Verde or Ellis Island.

"The piano tuner is by the door. I don't know what I'm supposed to say to him. You've asked him—"

"I haven't asked him anything!" protested Pruss. "Don't you think I've got better things to do? Does it sound out of tune?"

"I'm not an expert, sir, but when I . . ."

The man sung a nocturne very badly while tinkling his fingers over an imaginary keyboard.

"All right, all right," interrupted Pruss. "Have him tune it."

Schiff's lips were still moving as he stared at the captain's four stripes.

"Is he still here?" asked Pruss, noticing the boy.

"The commander wants to keep him."

"Heil Hitler!" fired off Schiff, raising his right arm.

Pruss continued on his way.

"Apparently Commander Eckener is in his office."

"Apparently so, Captain."

"I thought he was supposed to be in Austria for some meetings."

"I don't know about that."

The two of them headed off. And Schiff pushed his cart toward the exit.

At eight o'clock that evening, at the far end of an airfield in the middle of nowhere, two cars arrived from opposite directions. The first was a black German car with a Swiss license plate. The second was a big shiny red Bugatti, which flattened the grass with its fenders.

The cars came to a stop at a respectable distance from each other. Once their engines were switched off, silence descended again.

Then two men got out of the first car, keeping their right hands under the left armpits inside their jackets and their eyes trained on the other vehicle. They were ready to pull out their weapons at any moment. The airship was already outside the hangar, gleaming in the evening sun less than a kilometer away.

The doors of the red car remained shut for another minute.

Over on the other side, the two men were waiting. From time to time they said something to the person inside the black car. They didn't want to betray their anxiety. Suddenly, three doors of the red Bugatti opened simultaneously. The driver stepped out first. He was an old man in white leather gloves and a chauffeur's uniform. He looked as if he had spent the last couple of hours shining his shoes, which were such a dazzling black they almost looked white. His face was dignified and expressionless. You could tell he had an English accent before he even opened his mouth.

Behind him, another man appeared. It was Esquirol, looking more elegant than ever. He wore a long jacket over a pair of striped wild silk trousers. He was fiddling with his hat, which boasted a claret-colored ribbon. His black hair was turning gray at the temples, and he had slicked it down with a subtle eau de parfum.

Doctor Esquirol was leaning on the car door, his hand raised slightly to protect himself from the sun. Even the small flies in the evening light were getting on with their business in silence. All that could be heard was an occasional creaking from a cylinder cooling down.

Finally, the third person appeared: a short black man with broad shoulders, which he squeezed through the open door one at a time. He was dressed like an Andalusian prince. He wore an emerald-green jacket with a purple collar, a pearl waistcoat, a wide black tie that was almost undone, and trousers with a braided trim. Perhaps Joseph Puppet had gone a little over the top. But he had been told not to skimp, and he had followed his orders to the letter.

His eyes were hidden by dark tortoiseshell glasses, he

sported three rings on each hand, and he carried a walking stick with a carved knob depicting a sparrow. He wore no socks inside his Italian shoes, which had been made from a single piece of leather. On his wrist was the lace from the left glove of his final boxing match, in which he had knocked out an American in the Buffalo Stadium at Montrouge before calling an end to his career. J. J. Puppet looked like a prince, but a sophisticated, fashionable prince. On his other hand, he wore a slim wristwatch that could have belonged to a lady. There was brocade on his elbows and a pair of rosewood buttons at each cuff; and the ivory clip on his black suspenders appeared beneath his waistcoat when he leaned on the car hood.

Doctor Esquirol took a few steps toward the black car. He was approached by one of the two armed men. Esquirol raised both arms. He was frisked carefully.

"And the others!" ordered the man.

Puppet and the English chauffeur stepped forward. They were frisked in turn.

The bodyguard went back to the car and opened the passenger door.

A man stepped out. He strode across the grass toward Esquirol and Puppet, clad in a dull suit that couldn't have contrasted more sharply with their fashionable attire. He looked tense.

"Where is Mr. Eckener?"

"Mr. Valpa, there's a problem with Commander Eckener. He's not with us."

"I am here to speak with Eckener," insisted Valpa.

"I'm afraid I wasn't able to let you know in time, but

Commander Eckener won't be on board the *Hindenburg* with us tonight."

Vincent Valpa took a handkerchief from his pocket and pressed it to his mouth.

"You've made me . . . come from Geneva for nothing?"

"Certainly not," said Esquirol. "Have you heard of Joseph Jacques Puppet, the boxer?"

"Yes, I think so," said Valpa, staring at the Andalusian prince.

"He's here for the same reason as you. He is part of the great contract. He is suspicious, and wishes to meet Eckener before signing."

"I'm not suspicious, Doctor." Puppet smiled. "You are overstating the case. But I've only seen Eckener's name at the bottom of the page. I need to feel his hand in mine before I can believe him. I am investing a great deal of gold in this contract, equivalent to the combined weight of your two bodyguards, Mr. Valpa. And, like you, I want to be sure of what I'm doing."

Valpa turned to assess how heavy his bodyguards were. It would appear that this man's investment amounted to three hundred kilos of gold. He looked at Puppet with rather more respect.

Puppet smiled, because he knew that the only gold he possessed on this earth was the tiny ray of sunshine that had just come to rest on his patent leather shoes. He didn't even own a pair of scissors in the hair salon where he worked in Monaco.

But he had been asked to play the role of a wealthy retired boxer who invested his money in arms trafficking. And Puppet was proving to be an excellent actor.

"You're about to meet Commander Eckener, gentlemen," said Esquirol. "He's not able to fly to New York with us, but he is waiting for you in his office."

After a few seconds, Vincent Valpa folded his handkerchief. Puppet tucked the sparrow head of his walking stick under his arm. Each of them returned to their cars, which proceeded to crawl toward the *Hindenburg* as if part of a funeral convoy.

In the first car, Esquirol leaned toward the chauffeur.

"Harry, drop us here and return to Monte Carlo."

"Yes, sir."

"Please thank Madame Solange again."

Madame Solange, who was a customer at Joseph Puppet's salon, was married to an ambassador. She had lent her husband's red Bugatti and his chauffeur, Harry, in exchange for twenty free wash-and-dries.

Esquirol was taking the most insane risk he could possibly imagine. Hugo Eckener had no idea about any of this. They were going to have to improvise.

There was a slight fuss at the foot of the airship. A lady traveler who had arrived from Italy had just found out that she would have to pay five marks for every fifteen kilos of excess baggage. She hadn't been informed of this until now, she complained. Air hostess Imhof, the only female member of the zeppelin's crew, was trying to calm her down. But the lady kept insisting that she weighed at least twenty kilos less than most of the passengers, and she pointed at Madame Kleeman a little farther off, the wife of an important motorcycle manufacturer.

Inside the zeppelin, Kubis the headwaiter was striding through the lounges to check that everything was in order. It was almost quarter past eight, and the passengers would be appearing in a few moments.

One of the young chefs, Alfred, was putting vases of flowers on the tables. Kubis noticed that he was limping. Porters passed by in the corridors, as they started to take the luggage to the cabins. There was a scent of lily in the stairwell. Kubis found the cabin boy sitting on the piano stool.

"What are you doing here?"

Werner leaped up, knocking over the pile of bath towels he was supposed to be laying neatly by the basins.

"It doesn't work," he explained.

"What?"

"The piano."

Kubis went over and played a chord. The piano made a dreadful noise.

"Where's the tuner?"

"He must have gone already."

Kubis played a few more notes.

"He's left this piano in an appalling state."

"Do you want me to find him?"

"Certainly not. Deal with those towels."

Kubis checked his watch. There was no time to call for another piano tuner. He would handle this matter on their return. There would be no piano music on the outbound journey, which was no bad thing as far as the headwaiter was concerned, given that Captain Lehman would be on board. Lehman spent his time either at the accordion or on the piano. This delighted the passengers and tortured Kubis. Indeed, the previous winter he had argued the case for not having the piano at all.

One minute later, Kubis walked down the footbridge to greet each of the passengers individually. There were still five missing. They hadn't caught the bus from the hotel and were supposed to be arriving under their own steam. Kubis ordered the removal of a cart of empty gas bottles that was lying around, realizing that it was a cause of alarm for a mother of three children.

"Stay away from there, Irene," the woman told her eldest daughter.

"Those bottles are empty, madam," a steward explained.

Nobody was in any rush to point out to this lady passenger that there would be one hundred times the quantity of explosive gas directly above her head throughout the voyage. That was the risk with these balloons, for as long as the United States refused to sell helium to the Germans. Hydrogen was a slightly more load bearing gas, but extremely flammable. Out of superstition, the danger was rarely mentioned on board. There had been no serious accidents for a very long time in the Zeppelin Company.

The passengers were eager to climb on board. Captain Lehman, who was embarking as an observer, was speaking with two people over to one side. He looked rather self-conscious: the Berlin journalists were supposed to be writing a book about him. Lehman had become an increasingly important figure as an airship commander because, unlike Eckener, he wasn't fiercely allergic to Nazi power.

At the bottom of the footbridge stood Joseph Spah, an American acrobat who had come to the end of his European tour. He had jumped out of a taxi with his dog Ulla moments before. He was telling his life story to a Swedish man in a black coat and hat. When he spoke, Spah rose up on his tip-toes, like a dancer. He had missed the boat from Hamburg, but he had a show the following week and so he had raised the hundreds of dollars required for his ticket to the sky.

Hugo Eckener was in his office, staring out the small window with its view of the airship.

"I'm not worried, so nor should you be. You'll under-stand everything in three days' time."

He was talking to somebody who was sitting in the shadow. Eckener looked nervously around him before head-ing for the door. Just as he reached for the handle, the door opened wide. In walked the young in-flight medic, Doctor Rudiger, who was bright red.

"Kurt?"

"Commander, I've got some people here who say they have an appointment with you."

"Whatever happened to the courtesy of knocking, Kurt? Is this your new approach?"

"The thing is, they're about to —"

Esquirol's face appeared over the doctor's shoulder. Eckener made Rudiger step aside.

"I thought it must be you, with your French manners."

When Eckener saw J. J. Puppet appear in his luminous suit, he was stunned. Esquirol rushed center stage and hur-riedly began to speak.

"Commander, here I am, as arranged. Perhaps a few min-utes late. And here are the friends I told you about."

Three other men had entered behind Puppet.

"You know how important these gentlemen are for us. Allow me first to introduce you to Mr. Vincent Valpa, whom we discussed at great length in Berlin."

Valpa wanted to shake his hand. Eckener stared at Esquirol, who cast him an imploring look. The commander took Valpa's hand and shook it.

"Pleased to meet you," said Valpa.

"Yes, my friend told me about you," growled Eckener. "I don't know what he's like as a doctor, but should you feel unwell you can always see Doctor Rudiger, who will be our onboard physician for the crossing."

Young Rudiger nodded.

"I hope to remain in good health as far as New York," said Valpa, sounding rather surprised.

"I hope so too," agreed Eckener compassionately. "In any event, you have a very handsome cabin. It's brand-new. I understand that you have company."

He gave a forced smile to the two strapping men waiting behind.

"And next," Esquirol told Eckener, "I hardly need introduce you to J. J. Puppet. You know what a great champion he was. And you know that he is now our partner in our splendid venture, of which you are not . . . unaware."

They shook hands. Eckener couldn't understand what was going on. Puppet beamed and wouldn't let go of his hand. The commander opened his mouth to say something, but Esquirol leaped in immediately. "You have no doubt followed the career of our friend, his fights. . . ."

Again, Eckener felt the urge to bellow something like

"What on earth is all this song and dance about?" But while Puppet was crushing his fingers, Esquirol plugged the gap.

"Yes, you must recall his great era, Commander. If I tell you that——"

"I recognize him," came a voice from the back of the room. "I've seen him in action."

There in Eckener's chair, behind the desk, all eyes landed on a young woman nobody had noticed until now.

Puppet finally let go of Eckener's hand.

"I remember very well," she added.

The commander was gently rubbing his wrist.

"You haven't given me a chance to introduce this young lady," he pointed out.

Ethel stood up.

"We were in the middle of a discussion," Eckener explained, "when you arrived with such a——"

"Such a vote of confidence," declared Esquirol, loudly finishing off the commander's sentence as he went over to greet Ethel.

But she had eyes only for Puppet.

"This young lady will be on the same flight as you," said Commander Eckener. "She has just informed me of this, having arrived only now. She is my goddaughter, and she is going to New York, where she hopes to join . . ."

He hesitated.

"To join my fiancé," concluded Ethel.

Clearly, everybody felt a need to finish the commander's sentences for him.

"Yes, Mr. Puppet, I recognize you very well," she whispered with a smile.

Eckener frowned.

"I saw you at the Holborn Stadium in London," Ethel went on. "I was five or six years old. My father used to take me to boxing matches."

They shook hands warmly. On the other side of the room, Vincent Valpa pulled on Esquirol's arm.

"We talked about a one-to-one appointment with Eckener," he growled.

"Of course, and that's what we've scheduled," Esquirol reassured him. "The commander is greatly looking forward to it."

He took a step toward Eckener, then pricked up an ear. The *Hindenburg*'s horn was being blasted. For Esquirol, that sound was as sweet as the bells of the Armistice, the soldier's peace, the boxer's gong, the reprieve of the condemned man. It was time to go.

"Good God," exclaimed Esquirol, glancing up at the sky. "We've run out of time! It's leaving!"

Crestfallen but delighted, he turned toward Valpa.

"I do apologize."

The next two minutes were full of confusion.

There was a general surge toward the office door. Rudiger bumped into Valpa's henchmen. Eckener tried grabbing Esquirol by the collar to demand some kind of explanation, but the doctor dodged him. Vincent Valpa kept complaining.

Only Ethel took her time.

Eckener walked behind her in the corridor.

"Write to me when you find him," the commander called out.

"I will."

"Write to tell me he's well."

The footbridge was about to be raised, so they ran across the grass.

Ethel was the last to climb on board. The moorings were released and the balloon took flight.

20

THE SMOKING ROOM OF THE *HINDENBURG*

On board the Hindenburg, *from Frankfurt to New York*

With only thirty-six passengers when it could accommodate double that number, the *Hindenburg* felt like an out-of-season grand hotel. The setting could have been Deauville or San Remo in the spring, when the hospitality trade chugs along in slow motion: umbrellas are restitched, there are plenty of empty tables, and the beach attendant has time to talk to the guests. The sixty-one crew members were able to attend to every request, however small. There were five chefs for the three dozen passengers. So it hadn't been difficult for Eckener to find a cabin for Ethel when she had sprung a surprise visit two hours prior to takeoff.

On taking her leave of the Cat in Paris, Ethel had planned to drive to Friedrichshafen in order to catch the zeppelin rather than the boat.

Intending to gain a few days, she had in fact lost a lot of time. The car had skidded on a tree-lined road and turned over. In the next village, she had been promised a speedy repair, but two days later Ethel was still at the Golden Lion Hotel, waiting for miracles that didn't happen. As chance would have it, the hotel, which was empty, belonged to the garage owner. He had to travel no farther than the end of the street to repair the car. But the engine had given up the ghost. And so Ethel abandoned the handsome but crumpled Napier-Railton and had jumped on a train instead.

At Friedrichshafen she had found the hangars empty. The *Graf* was on a stop-off in Brazil and the *Hindenburg* was leaving from Frankfurt the next day. So Ethel had caught the train back to Frankfurt, arriving just in time. She had lost a week.

Eckener gave her a warm welcome.

Ethel had showed him Vango's telegram, and the commander had stared at the piece of blue paper:

EMERGENCY. MEET ME. VANGO.

The commander read the four words over and over again, and tried to be as reassuring as possible.

"He's a brave boy, my dear. He knows how to fend for himself."

This was exactly what Ethel was worried about. A cry for help from a brave boy was by definition an act of desperation. Eckener had the office alerted immediately so that a cabin could be reserved for the young lady. Someone replied that two tickets had just been unexpectedly purchased by some travelers from Norway. With a bit of luck, they would end up being full.

Ethel was in the first cabin at the top of the stairs to the upper deck. When she arrived on board, she had discovered that the *Hindenburg*'s cabins were spread across two floors. There were fifty berths upstairs, and twenty had been added below, on the port side. No sooner had Ethel walked into her cabin than she lay down and fell asleep. It was nine o'clock in the evening. She awoke at midnight, dabbed her face over the washbasin, glanced again at the telegram, which she had tucked by the mirror, and then went out.

Ethel almost got lost. This wasn't the small family-run hotel she had known on board the *Graf Zeppelin*. It was a flagship. The cabins were in the middle of the gondola, and two handsome promenades with glazed views ran along both sides. The premises seemed deserted. Everybody was asleep. Ethel found the baby grand piano, which she stroked. A notice that read OUT OF ORDER had been put on the music stand. Intrigued by this ban, Ethel wanted to try playing a note. She pressed down on a B-flat, which sounded like a grumbling stomach, and then played an appalling F-sharp. Abandoning the piano, she pushed open a door and entered a reading room hung with paintings. A man was poring over an illustrated newspaper that he had spread out on a small table. He looked up and lowered his glasses on his nose. Ethel indicated that she didn't wish to disturb him and went to survey the view from the large sloping window. The sky was overcast and dark. Only the occasional glimmer could be seen from the earth.

Ethel would have liked all the lights on the balloon to be switched off, so that she could contemplate the night. She was recalling the evening when she and Vango had followed two small headlights flickering far down below them. It was when they were flying over Russia, during their world tour in 1929. Back then, Vango used to invent stories at the window of the *Graf Zeppelin*. Two bicycles on a country road in the middle of the night: they must be returning after a party. Vango made up names for them. The girl was called Yelena. She was cycling a little ahead. The boy was following behind.

When the lights sped up, Vango said it was because they were going down a steep hill, and he asked Ethel to strain her ears. According to him, shrieks of joy could be heard as the bicycles made their descent. And then the lights slowed and drew closer together. They came to a stop. Ethel was looking at Vango. Everything had gone dark.

"What now?" she had asked.

Vango had smiled.

"What do you think's happening now?" she had pressed him.

But he couldn't give an answer.

Ethel left the window. She walked toward the reader, who had fallen asleep over his newspaper, his cheek squashed against a photograph of an ocean liner being approached by a submarine. She switched off the light and left the room.

Ethel blamed herself for not having joined Vango earlier. She had wanted to let him plunge into his past alone, so that one day he would return free. She had waited dutifully, channeling all her impatience into restoring the tiny plane. But she wondered if she wasn't inventing dangers around her in order to justify Vango's absence. She had even stopped writing to him, in order to protect him, and had ordered him to do likewise. Still, every morning she tore the post out of Mary's hands, searching for his handwriting on the envelopes.

Ethel walked down the staircase in front of her cabin. The atmosphere on the lower deck was much more lively. The small bar was still open. Three men were deep in conversation on the banquettes. The barman was slicing lemons on his counter. Behind a high-security door was the famous smoking room, which comprised the most popular twenty square meters in the airship.

Ethel stepped inside the smoking room and Max the barman followed, closing the pressurized door behind her. A dozen men sat around in armchairs swathed in smoke. It took a few seconds to recognize J. J. Puppet beneath the cloud on the right. He smiled at her. He was alone near the picture window, with an enormous cigar.

"Do you smoke?" he inquired when Ethel came over.

"No, but even the carpets smoke here!"

Ethel felt that without lighting a cigarette, she had still inhaled a cupful of tar just by opening her mouth.

Puppet was keeping a discreet eye on one of Valpa's men, who was sitting near to the door.

"So," he ventured, "your father enjoys boxing?"

"Yes," replied Ethel.

"And what about you?"

"I don't know."

Ethel didn't want to mention that boxing made her cry because it made her recall the sound of her father's voice whispering in her ear as he explained the fights.

"It's not a little girl's sport," declared Puppet.

"Oh, yes it is. But I'm a grown-up now."

He looked at her.

"What are you going to do in New York?" Ethel asked him.

"No idea."

Puppet was watching Valpa's man, who had just stood up.

"Don't tell anyone," he went on, "but I'm not even sure what I'm doing here. I'm just doing a friend a favor."

"Is he here?"

"I hope so. I haven't seen him yet."

Ethel didn't seem surprised. She liked mysteries.

"Where is he?"

"I don't know. He might be hidden in the piano, upstairs."

Ethel laughed.

Little did she suspect that at that very moment in the empty lounge above them, the lid of the piano was slowly being raised. Two eyes scoured the room. Nobody. The piano lid opened a bit more. A man got out. He was completely numb. It was the piano tuner.

"Aha, so now I understand why the piano's out of tune!" declared Ethel, back in the smoking room.

"Have you tried it? You shouldn't have. The hammers strike my friend when you press down on the keys."

Joseph Puppet half stood up.

"Max!"

He gestured at the barman, who approached with a tray.

"I hadn't forgotten you," he told Puppet.

"No, I'd rather you gave that glass to the gentleman who's about to leave."

Puppet indicated the man who was standing close to the door.

The barman did as requested, and Ethel saw the man sit back down again with his glass.

"I don't want that guy hanging around the corridors," Puppet whispered to Ethel.

One floor above them, in the empty lounge, the piano tuner was gently closing the piano. He was in so much pain that he could only just manage to stand up. To pass the time from four o'clock in the afternoon until two o'clock in the morning, he had been reciting the breviary. He stretched his body and cracked his fingers.

His hands weren't those of a pianist but of a gardener.

They belonged to Zefiro.

The door opened behind him.

"Excuse me?"

He didn't turn around. Somebody had just emerged from the reading room, his face puffy with sleep.

"Excuse me?"

"Yes?" said Zefiro.

"Are we here yet?"

Zefiro turned to take a look at the man, who held an illustrated newspaper in one hand.

"I shouldn't think so. The crossing takes three days."

"Were you the person who switched my lamp off?"

"No. You should get some sleep."

"Where are we?" inquired the man, wandering over to the far end of the lounge.

Zefiro let out a long sigh.

Back in the smoking room, Ethel finally sat down.

"Do you know anybody on board?" she asked Puppet.

"Not really. Have you noticed those two men pretending not to look at you?"

"No."

"Can't you see that everybody's staring at you in here?"

"No."

"A woman in a smoking room is like a black man in a German airship. People stare."

Ethel was interested in Joseph Puppet. She listened carefully to what he had to say.

"Those two over there, for example, the ones I just mentioned, who are staring at you even more closely than the rest, I'm slowly getting to know them."

"Well?" Ethel pressed him.

"They say they're Norwegian."

She shot a quick glance, while Puppet made progress with his cigar.

"Have you ever been to Norway?" he asked.

"No."

"Me neither, more's the pity. And nor have they."

"What do you mean?"

"I don't believe they've ever set foot there."

"Why?"

"Because they're speaking Russian."

She shooed the smoke away with her fingers, as if she were turning the page of a book. Puppet had Ethel's full attention now.

"I made mincemeat of a Russian in 1919 in a boxing ring in Belgium. I swear he was speaking the same language as them."

"You made mincemeat of him?"

"Well, steak tartare."

Zefiro tapped four times on the partition wall of the cabin. The door opened. Zefiro and Esquirol fell into each other's arms.

"You're out of your mind," said Esquirol. "You have no idea what you're getting us into."

"You gave your word, just as I did."

Both of them remembered the pact they had made in the

clearing at Falbas, and which had become Project Violette. A communal promise made in the midst of all the fighting. An Italian priest soldier, a German aviator, a French doctor, and an Ivorian infantryman.

"Is Voloy Viktor here?"

"Valpa is here," Esquirol corrected him.

"I don't care what name he's going by these days." Zefiro shrugged.

"He's in his cabin, down below. His two men are taking turns guarding him. He doesn't come out. His meals are brought to him."

"What about Eckener?"

"I don't think it went too badly. It was a crazy situation. Valpa shook his hand. That was the best we could do, seeing as you refused to explain your plans to Eckener."

"He wouldn't have played our game."

"You never know, Zefiro."

"Is Viktor in the large cabin at the back?"

"Yes. A family with three children was expecting to go in there. But I held firm. All the other cabins along the corridor are empty."

"And what about the cabin boy?"

"He knows not to go into Valpa's cabin or ours. We've come to an arrangement."

"Good."

"When will it be?" asked Esquirol, looking Zefiro straight in the eye.

"The last night, before landing. Where is Joseph Puppet?"

"It was rash of you to make him play the part of a heavy weapons investor. It's madness."

"Did you have someone else in mind?"

"Puppet is known far and wide for his pacifist appearances."

"Where is he?" asked Zefiro.

"He was keeping an eye on the other bodyguard in the smoking room. Now that you're safely out of the piano, I can liberate him from his duties."

Esquirol turned toward the door.

"Bring me something to eat," called Zefiro.

The padre lay down on the floor and closed his eyes.

"Don't you want a bunk?"

"I'm a monk, Esquirol. I sleep on hard floors or inside pianos."

When he saw Esquirol appear at the door to the smoking room, Joseph Puppet stood up.

"I think someone's come for me."

He took Ethel's hand and bowed so low that his forehead touched it.

"Good night, miss."

A few passengers eyed them disapprovingly.

Puppet was reveling in the attention. He knew that, the previous summer, after beating Joe Louis—a black American from Alabama—in the twelfth round, the great German boxer Max Schmeling had caught this same *Hindenburg* back to Germany. For the Nazis, his triumphant return had been symbolic of the superiority of the German race.

With a smile on his lips, Puppet gave a little bow to the assembled company and left.

Ethel stayed behind only a few minutes longer, but she took the time to observe the two Norwegians. They had openly turned their backs on her now. She noticed that they had brought their own metal flasks with them, which appeared to contain something strong, because with each swig the men winced.

One of them was tall, strapping, and bearded. He had a shaved head and he didn't speak. The other was a small nervous man who chain-smoked cigarettes. He rolled them on his knees using mild tobacco. He muttered things to his colleague, who nodded every time he paused for breath.

Walking past them on her way out, Ethel noticed, on the neck of their flasks, the outline of a snarling bear.

A northwesterly wind rose with the day. Captain Pruss had chosen to steer a course that took them toward the North Atlantic, with the result that the airship was now in a headwind. It was difficult to navigate. Not that the passengers even realized. The *Hindenburg* was remarkably stable in all weather conditions. But the crew could tell that Captain Pruss was preoccupied. He didn't linger at the table, and spent most of his time in the cockpit. The airship was running late. Pruss knew that among the numerous passengers on the return flight were many English travelers who wished to embark in New York in order to return to Europe in time for the coronation of King George VI the following week. They couldn't afford to be late.

The piano being out of order didn't improve matters. A little music might have created a more relaxing atmosphere. A few months earlier, Captain Lehman had made the passengers forget all about a thunderstorm thanks to his piano recital, which had lasted an hour and a half.

* * *

Just before the second night, Esquirol went to knock on Vincent Valpa's cabin door. The cabin was situated at the end of a long corridor in the keel of the balloon. It was one of the few cabins with an external window, and the only cabin large enough to accommodate four bunks.

"Who's there?" someone called out through the closed door.

"It's me," said Esquirol.

One of the two guards nudged the door ajar.

"What do you want?"

"I should like to invite Mr. Valpa to a glass of something in the dining room."

What Esquirol really wanted was to empty the cabin for a few minutes, in order to scope out the premises prior to Zefiro's operation.

"No," muttered Valpa without putting in an appearance. "I'm not thirsty."

"He doesn't want to come out," relayed the henchman.

"There's a bottle of champagne that Commander Eckener has left for us."

"Drink it."

The door closed again.

Esquirol found Zefiro waiting with Puppet on the banquette in the cabin.

"He won't come out."

Zefiro was already in black combat dress.

"Well, in that case I'll get him in his hidey-hole. You need to make sure that all three of them are in there."

"I thought you only wanted Viktor."

289

"Nobody must raise the alert before the zeppelin lands in Lakehurst."

In front of him, Zefiro laid down a Luger Parabellum loaded for three shots.

21

THE WHITE FLAG

At one o'clock in the morning, on the sixth of May 1937, an inexplicable phenomenon occurred high above the North Atlantic.

Ethel was lying on her bunk, but her eyes were wide open. She hadn't been able to sleep since that first evening. Boulard had warned her that one day Vango would ask for help, and it would be too late. Her stomach was in knots, and she couldn't stop thinking about him.

Suddenly, she heard the sound of the piano. Someone was playing a Bach fugue, and the notes were pitch-perfect.

She sat up in bed and listened attentively. Then she got up, put a coat on over her nightdress, and went out into the corridor, where she saw many of her fellow passengers surging past. Captain Lehman's hands were roaming over the keyboard.

An idle traveler must have pressed down on one of the ivory keys before going to bed, only to discover that the piano worked perfectly.

What could have happened? How had such a turnaround occurred? Nobody guessed that the piano had been relieved of eighty kilos in body weight. Someone swore they had found an olive-wood rosary among the strings. This story had the makings of a miracle.

While everybody was gathered around the piano, Esquirol went to warn Zefiro, who was still hidden in his cabin.

The monk immediately removed the square he had cut out of the plywood ceiling and hoisted himself up into the forest of metal. Zefiro could hear the piano below him: the music of Bach filled the air as he made his way through the dark on the ceiling of the upper deck. He was trying to follow the girders so as not to lose his way or put his foot through the ceiling and land in a cabin. Zefiro counted the rows as he went. He must be above the staircase by now. Taking a left turn, he began to slide down an aluminum pole with holes punched in it. The piano was just on the other side of the partition.

Zefiro was now walking above the new cabins on the lower deck. He knew that the tenth one belonged to Voloy Viktor, but the padre stopped just before it. He checked the weapon on his back and removed a razor-sharp blade from his belt before cutting a hole and lowering himself down through it. Viktor and his men should be just there, in the next-door cabin. A small amount of light seeped through a narrow window to the side: this was the beam from the zeppelin's headlights as it traveled into the black clouds ahead.

The cabin was as noisy as Zefiro had hoped, because it was so close to the engines. He would be able to go about his business undetected. By gluing his ear to the partition, and despite all the noise, he could just make out the sound of people moving about. Somebody was definitely in Viktor's cabin.

Zefiro checked his watch. It was twenty past one in the morning. Esquirol and Puppet knew that the operation was planned for half past one. It was their job to make sure the two bodyguards had rejoined their boss by that time.

Zefiro had ten minutes in which to prepare his lightning attack. He needed to cut through the partition under the bottom bunk. This hole just above the floor would remain invisible. All he had to do was push the wall at the last moment. At half past one, he would finally be able to enter. He had rehearsed every movement. He knew which firing angles he should adopt to avoid a stray bullet damaging the hydrogen balloons of the great airship.

The operation he was about to perform was as delicate as if he were removing a tumor wrapped around a vital organ. The zeppelin was a bomb ready to explode. But Zefiro had waited more than eighteen years to reach this point, and he felt capable of anything. He lowered himself into the gloom and disappeared under the bunk.

Just as his palm made contact with the floor, a damp hand grabbed his wrist. The padre almost screamed when he felt someone's nails digging into his forearm. His aggressor rose up from under the bunk and trapped Zefiro with his legs, squeezing with all his might as if he wanted to choke the monk. Zefiro was trying to resist, but he couldn't reach his knife or his pistol. The two of them rolled over as far as the basin on the other side of the cabin. Not a sound had been made; there were just the stifled movements of the struggle. Finally, Zefiro managed to free one of his arms, but he was now on his back and his weapons were out of reach. Grabbing hold of the curtain that hung across the wardrobe, he tugged it off. Then, in a single movement, he passed the curtain around his enemy's neck like a rope. In seconds, Zefiro had seized control of the situation. The other person stopped putting up any resistance when he felt the curtain tightening around his neck.

Zefiro had assumed he was dealing with one of Viktor's guards, but when he turned his aggressor's face toward the window, he saw a young man who couldn't have been older than twenty and who stared at him with imploring eyes.

"Who are you?" whispered Zefiro.

"Heil Hitler!" said the other person.

Zefiro put his hand over the young man's mouth. When he took it away again, the boy was muttering a jumble of words from which could dimly be distinguished "Reich," "race," and "blood."

"Your name?" asked Zefiro.

"Schiff."

The padre had let go of the curtain, and the young man was no longer putting up any resistance.

"What are you doing here?"

"Hindy ate me."

"Who's Hindy?"

"The balloon. Hindy."

Schiff's eyes flitted around the room, terrified. Zefiro couldn't catch his gaze.

A stowaway.

He must have been hidden in this hole for three days. Zefiro released his grip and sat down on the bunk, where he took out his watch. He no longer had enough time to get through the gap in the partition: the three targets wouldn't stay together in the cabin for long.

"Hindy ate me," Schiff said again.

Zefiro clenched his fists. The previous year, in New York, he had missed Viktor because of Vango. And now this boy, who was barely twenty years old and looked so much like Vango, was going to pull the same trick on him.

"Do you know how to count to a thousand?"

"One, two, three, four . . ."

"I want you to count all the way to a thousand without moving."

"Five, six . . ."

"Stop! You're going to start counting when I tell you to."

Schiff stared at the padre.

"If you move, Hindy won't be happy. Understood?"

Schiff nodded.

"Go back into your hiding place and count."

The boy did as he was told.

"One, two —"

"Quieter."

"Three, four —"

"Quieter!"

Upstairs, in the great lounge, the piano had stopped.

Zefiro approached the window, bandaging the curtain fabric around his fist before smashing the glass. He waited. No reaction next door. A freezing wind blew in through the broken window. The previous evening, the passengers had glimpsed chunks of iceberg floating on the sea. Zefiro smashed three more windows and then removed the strips of wood separating them.

"Seventy-six, seventy-seven . . ." Schiff rattled off behind him.

Zefiro laid the aluminum ladder down on the floor in front of the window. He removed his weapon from his belt and held it in his hand. Leaning out of the hole he'd made in the window, he was hit by the extreme cold. Despite the wind, the balloon was traveling at a hundred kilometers an hour, so Zefiro had put his legs through the ladder to stop himself from falling out.

He pushed his body outside all the way to the waist. The ladder was now jammed against the window. Slowly, he raised himself up to take a look at the neighboring cabin. The wind was whistling in his ears.

To begin with, he couldn't see anyone through the windowpane. Then suddenly, twisting a little farther, he saw him, from behind, standing in front of the window. Where were the other two? Zefiro wanted to fire without waiting. He hadn't got this close to Viktor in a very long time. But he was mindful of Esquirol and Puppet, who were also risking their lives. Just then, to the left, he spotted the foot of one of the two guards sticking out from under the blanket on the bed. He was asleep. So there was only one missing.

In the smoking room, Esquirol had just approached Valpa's second man.

"Mr. Valpa is asking for you."

"What?"

"Mr. Valpa," Esquirol repeated.

"What does he want?"

"Your colleague informed me that Mr. Valpa is asking for a glass of water."

The man stared at him for a moment, incredulous, then

headed for the door. It was twenty-nine minutes past one. Esquirol glanced at Puppet, who was staring at the anthracite clouds through the window.

"They're forecasting bad weather," he told Max, the barman.

"Mr. Spah's dog is howling in the hold. He gave her the bones from the beef with morel mushrooms yesterday, but that hasn't calmed her."

"She doesn't like the storm," said Puppet.

"Captain Pruss says we'll wait above the coast for it to pass."

Still hanging out his window, Zefiro saw Valpa's door open. The second of his henchmen entered with a glass of water and said something. The padre couldn't hear a word. Valpa closed the door. Zefiro was trying to flex his frozen fingers. He had to fire three shots. His index finger would need to press down three times on the release mechanism. The other guard had gotten up from his bunk. All three of them were standing in the cabin. Voloy Viktor still had his back to him, and Zefiro had yet to see his face. He was waiting. The engine was growling a few dozen meters in front of him.

As one of the two men passed in front of Viktor, the arms dealer turned around and was visible in the electric light of the cabin.

Frozen tears appeared around Zefiro's eyes. Valpa was staring at the glass of water he had just been given. But he wasn't Voloy Viktor.

Dorgeles! thought Zefiro.

Vincent Valpa had never been Voloy Viktor. Viktor's

right-hand man had replaced him for this European trip. So they had all been duped. Viktor's instinctive distrust had deceived them once again.

Zefiro was weeping in the wind. He could feel his legs losing their strength. He let go of the pistol, which hurtled into the abyss.

He thought of letting himself drop as well. For the second time in his life, he railed silently against the sky, against God. He had done this once at Verdun, during the Great War, when ten men had been blown up only two paces from him. And now he was doing it again, four hundred meters above sea level, on seeing evil triumph once more. Who would come to his aid?

Just then, very close to him, a voice called out.

"It's over."

Schiff's head had appeared between the bars of the ladder.

"I've counted everything. All the way to a thousand."

"Pull my legs, my boy," said Zefiro, looking at him. "Pull me inside."

Esquirol and Puppet were waiting. They had sat down next to the piano, which Kubis had covered with a black cloth to give his ears a rest. Both men were surveying the far end of the saloon.

Puppet saw him first.

"Look!"

Esquirol held his breath.

The man approaching them was Vincent Valpa's body-guard. He made his way over and stared at each of them in turn. Puppet was wearing a blue organza dressing gown, while Esquirol was dressed in a simple suede waistcoat and wide-legged trousers.

"Mr. Valpa didn't want a glass of water."

"No?" said Esquirol. "Are you sure?"

"Why did you ask me to take him some water?"

"I thought that with the dry weather . . . Can you feel the storm brewing?"

Valpa's guard knocked over the glass and deliberately smashed it on the piano, before turning his back on them.

Puppet and Esquirol went to lock themselves in their cabin. What could have happened to Zefiro?

"We're going to delay landing by a few hours," Captain Pruss told the passengers the next day at breakfast. "There's a storm above Lakehurst, and we've got enough fuel for a little sight-seeing trip over the beaches of New Jersey. We should arrive in the afternoon."

"My wife is waiting for me with our three children," complained Joseph Spah.

"She will be informed."

"She'd better make the most of her final moments without that mutt," remarked a lady who hadn't slept on account of the raucous barking from Spah's dog.

A man explained that he hoped to be able to catch a glimpse of his house, which was farther up the coast.

"We'll do our best, sir. I'll send the navigation officer to have a word with you."

There was barely a disgruntled murmur from the group. They were keen to arrive, but the bread was warm, the bacon was making the eggs bubble, and a delicious aroma was wafting out of the silver coffee pots. They couldn't complain.

Only Ethel was devastated by this delay. She followed Pruss to the stairs.

"Are you sure we can't land now?"

"Yes, I'm sure, miss. Is someone waiting for you as well?"

"Yes. It's important."

"Would you like us to let anyone know?"

"No."

Just behind her, she noticed one of the Norwegians whom Puppet had claimed were Russian. It was the tall one with the beard. He looked like a textbook portrait of Rasputin. She had a sense that he had never let her out of his sight.

Ethel went into her cabin and slammed the door. She lay down on her bunk.

Meanwhile, two hunched figures remained deep in the hull of the zeppelin: Zefiro and Schiff were hiding between the hydrogen balloons.

"What are you going to do afterward?" asked Zefiro.

Schiff didn't answer. He didn't even seem to understand.

"I'd like to drift like you," said Zefiro. "Drifting instead of swimming against the current. I'm tired."

But when his eyes met Schiff's, he realized his mistake. Schiff's life had been just as much of a battle as his own. This boy wasn't a piece of bark drifting along in the stream. He had been forced to learn to swim from very early on.

"If you like, I can take you back home with me."

Schiff looked up.

"I live with some friends in the middle of the sea. I keep bees."

Schiff smiled. And once again, Zefiro recalled Vango's first days at the invisible monastery.

"I'll take you there, and we'll never have to move again."

The monk removed a ball of blue silk embroidered with yellow thread from his pocket and wrapped it around his wrist. The *V* for Vango appeared in a fold of the handkerchief.

"And think of this, my boy: one day, I'll introduce you to a friend of mine who's rather like you."

Lakehurst, New Jersey, two hours later, May 6, 1937

The airship was turning gently above the crowd.

At the edge of the landing field, a gray wooden hangar stretched for nearly thirty meters. The ground floor was cluttered with metalwork. Up above, the hay was stored when the field was mown once or twice a year. But since airships don't eat hay, not even in winter, the stock increased year on year. No one knew what to do with it anymore. Bales of hay were stacked all the way to the roof.

Close to a small window, on the second floor that smelled of dust and dry grass, a space had been cleared. Voloy Viktor was watching the *Hindenburg* through a pair of binoculars. Next to him, a man had assembled the different pieces of a wide-ranging rifle. Down on the floor, he had opened up a double-bass case containing a complete arsenal.

"Watch out for the last window on the right flank. That's where they'll give the signal," explained another man, who looked like an Argentine tango dancer.

Viktor lowered the binoculars and turned dismissively toward him. He knew about which side; he just wanted silence.

Voloy Viktor had sent Dorgeles to Europe, under the name of Vincent Valpa, to bring back proof that the transaction was a bona fide venture. The Irishman also required proof. The latest news was that Dorgeles had received all the necessary confirmation during his trip. But he had yet to report on the meeting with Hugo Eckener, and this was the only valid guarantee in their eyes. If Commander Eckener had indeed welcomed Valpa, then Dorgeles was to raise a piece of white cloth at the window of his cabin. A scrap of red material, however, would mean Dorgeles had evidence that the deal was a hoax.

The elite marksman, who was counting his cartridges, was here for the second scenario. Several of his fingers were broken, but he needed only one to kill somebody. In the event of a red handkerchief, Viktor would have Mr. Puppet and his mysterious colleague destroyed the moment they set foot on American soil.

The *Hindenburg* continued its descent. It had performed one final large maneuver and was now presenting them with its nose and cockpit. At last, they would be able to see the right-hand side of the balloon.

"Well?" asked the tango dancer.

Viktor's eyes were glued to his binoculars. He knew that if he was being deceived, it would cost him thousands, the biggest contract of his life. A red piece of cloth at the window would result in a lot of bloodshed to wash his honor. The marksman was waiting beside him. The balloon turned a little more.

"White," said Viktor. "White."

"Bravo," cheered the Argentine from behind. "Everything is now confirmed. Congratulations!"

"WEEP FOR HUMANITY!"

Five hundred meters away, on the other side of the airfield

"Ethel . . ."

Her name leaped from his heart and lips. Vango was sprinting toward the *Hindenburg*.

His boat had dropped him off in New York two days earlier. He had rushed to the tower, where he climbed the scaffolding. Building work had still not resumed. Vango found Zefiro's lookout post deserted and the huge steel letters abandoned. Nobody had lived there for some time. There was no trace of the padre. Had Ethel led the enemy to Zefiro? Had she been captured with him?

Vango had waited there for one night. Then he had crossed the street and recklessly presented himself at the reception desk of the Plaza Hotel.

"I have something for Madame Victoria in the suite on the eighty-fifth floor."

"I beg your pardon?"

"Madame Victoria."

The man had scrolled through his registers.

"There's no customer under that name. Never has been."

"Somebody occupied the eighty-fifth floor for several months this winter. I may have their name wrong. Please check."

"No," the receptionist had assured him. "The eighty-fifth floor has been under construction for three years now. There are no rooms on that floor."

"I can assure you—"

"Please. That's enough. Go away now."

So Vango had set off to wander the city at random. And then he had found a newspaper that someone had left behind on a bench in Grand Central Station. On the back page were a few lines announcing the arrival of the *Hindenburg* close to New York. Vango had glanced up at the clock.

Ethel would be on board. He was sure of that.

As he ran across the field toward the balloon, Vango felt as if he had set a trap for Ethel. She would be there, pursued by murderers, far from home, because of him. When he had left her alone among the cornfields of Lakehurst nearly ten years earlier, following their world tour in the *Graf Zeppelin,* it was to spare her the death that Vango felt hovering over his shoulder at all times. When he had abandoned her on the dockside at Southampton, it was because she meant more to him than anything else in the world.

A two-tone Ford coupe sped past him. The tires skidded, leaving ruts in the damp grass.

In the airship, Ethel kept her tiny suitcase by her feet. She was waiting next to the window in the lounge and leaning forward as, little by little, she saw the earth draw closer. Already, the people on the grass looked less like miniatures. She could see children. She could even make out the feathers in the ladies' hats and, over there, a black-and-white car approaching a hangar.

* * *

The Ford coupe parked in front of the door. A man got out and climbed the exterior staircase of the warehouse.

Voloy Viktor was watching the marksman dismantle his weapon. For once, Viktor was relieved that the weapon wouldn't be used. He had sometimes doubted this game of poker that he was caught up in, with tens of millions of dollars at stake. But he was starting to believe in it now.

"Mr. Viktor . . ."

It was the man with the Argentine accent again. Viktor turned around brusquely to make him pipe down.

"There's somebody here for you," announced the man, whose hair gleamed as much as his pointy shoes.

Viktor turned another ninety degrees and saw a figure appearing between the bales of hay. It was the Irishman. He was brushing off his jacket, which was covered in dry grass.

Viktor gave a weak smile: something he wouldn't have done for anyone else in the world. A weak smile that was vaguely respectful.

"Your men let me through down below," commented the Irishman. "They're not very careful."

"They recognize my friends just as I recognize them."

The Irishman had gone over to the window. He was watching the airship, which was still a hundred meters above ground level.

"You've got a nice view."

Viktor nodded.

"What's the news from on board?" added the Irishman.

"It's good."

"Meaning?"

"My men have been able to confirm everything in Europe. It's a clean deal."

"Oh, yes?"

"I would never involve you in a dodgy one."

"Is that so? And who are your men on board?"

"Dorgeles and two others. Dorgeles has been working with me since the beginning."

"Is that meant to inspire confidence?"

The Irishman was still brushing his jacket nervously, even though there wasn't a shred of hay left on it.

"Can I go now?" asked the marksman, who had closed his double-bass case.

"No," the Irishman said softly before Viktor could even reply.

Voloy Viktor was mildly startled, but the Irishman went right up to him.

"Can I ask you a favor?"

"Yes," said Viktor.

"I've got filthy hands because of this pigsty. Could you take out the photo from my inside pocket? I don't want to get my shirt dirty."

Viktor moved his hand toward the Irishman and thrust it into his jacket, where he fumbled about a bit. He felt rather uncomfortable standing next to him, and had never before had such a close-up view of the red scarf worn by his business associate. Once, the Irishman had told Viktor that it was "a present from a friend who disappeared."

Viktor rummaged around some more in the pocket and felt a piece of paper.

"Here you go," he said, taking out the photo.

"No, you look at it. I told you, I've got dirty hands."

Voloy Viktor went over to the window to take a look at the photo.

"It's J. J. Puppet," he exclaimed.

"Yes."

The engines of the *Hindenburg* were roaring less forcefully now, and the airship was flying lower and lower. Viktor took a careful look at the picture.

In a flash, he understood.

Puppet wore his boxer's gloves around his neck in the photograph. He was in the middle of a field of white crosses: the cemetery of Douaumont near Verdun. Fifteen thousand graves and ten times that number of unknown soldiers. The caption was written in italics just below:

The boxer J. J. Puppet, world champion and advocate for peace

"How well do you know your friends?" asked the Irishman.

Voloy Viktor remained silent. He was staring out of the window. He had just lost a fortune, and he was about to lose his wealthiest partner. So he needed to give a powerful and rapid response that would turn the situation on its head.

"Prepare the rifle," he ordered.

The marksman put his double-bass case down again.

"You told me this was a clean deal," the Irishman reproached him. "But it's a rat trap. And I was about to get my leg caught, just like a rat, because of you, Mr. Viktor. Puppet is a regular in this kind of conspiracy. We've been framed. I don't know the name of the other guy, but he's a

Frenchman of the same ilk. And as for that Dorgeles of yours, the man's incompetent."

"I'll put this right," said Viktor in a flat tone of voice. "Puppet, Dorgeles, and all the others. I'll make them history."

And he bent down to select a long thin bullet from the top of the elite marksman's holster. He held it out to him, while the Irishman looked on.

"That's an incendiary bullet. . . ." pointed out the marksman with the broken fingers.

"Load it up."

"I've only got one. And I can't kill a man with a bullet like that."

"I know. You're just going to fire the once."

Viktor turned toward the balloon, which had dropped half a ton of water so as not to descend too quickly.

"Hurry up," he ordered.

"But . . ." protested the marksman, "we've got three men on board; there's Dorgeles——"

"I don't know anyone called Dorgeles," retorted Voloy Viktor, threatening the marksman with a gun he had just taken out of his pocket. "Do as you're told."

This attempt at winning the Irishman back was met with some success. He gave an amused smile as he made his way between the bales of hay. But he wasn't hanging around. He headed downstairs, got into his car, and drove off.

Vango was now at the edge of the area where the *Hindenburg* would touch down. Cables had just been cast from the zeppelin. A sprinkling of water also fell. For a moment, he thought he saw Ethel's face at the window. He tried to force his way forward but got pushed back. Men lunged to catch the moorings, which had reached the ground, but the *Hindenburg* was still a good forty meters up.

Suddenly, a flash of light burst from the back of the zeppelin.

Flames. A cry rose up from the crowd. Vango couldn't even tell if he was shouting as well.

It took a few seconds for the balloon to become a flare. Next to Vango, a journalist was still clinging to his microphone, trying to file his report: "There is smoke, there are flames, and everything is collapsing! Yes," his voice kept breaking, "everything is collapsing to the ground! Weep for humanity!"

All Vango could think of in the middle of this blaze was Ethel. Was this the trap for her that he had always feared? He felt as if he had lit the match that had sparked these flames. As if he were responsible for this field reduced to ashes. The prow of the *Hindenburg* had just touched the ground, but in a vertical position. Vango began to run toward the fire as hordes of shadowy figures were trying to escape from it. They were the same men who had wanted to pull on the cables to bring the airship down to the ground. Disaster had struck.

"Ethel!"

At last he could hear his own voice calling out in the roar of the flames.

"Ethel!"

It had only taken one minute. And now almost everything was destroyed.

"Ethel!"

The hydrogen had caused the fire to spread like lightning. And yet, as he drew closer, Vango could make out a few ghosts emerging from the flames. Survivors. There were survivors! Vango gathered up the first person, who was black with smoke. Vango led him to one side and signaled for someone to take him. Figures rushed over to help.

On the other side, not far from there, a man had just extracted himself from the inferno. Half his body was burned, but he couldn't feel anything. He was clutching a lifeless, unrecognizable body, which he laid down in the close-cropped grass before collapsing alongside it.

"Schiff," pleaded Zefiro, shaking the body.

But Schiff was no longer alive. As Zefiro fell to the ground, he understood that he didn't have much time left either. He could feel the painful beating of his heart slowing down. His eyelids no longer moved. And yet he thought he saw a face leaning over him.

"Padre . . ."

It was Vango.

Zefiro tried to move his lips.

"Is that you, Padre?" whispered Vango.

He leaned even farther over him.

"Stay alive. . . . Go away and live, Vango. Leave everything. Start again."

"Padre —"

"Forget."

Zefiro gave a numb smile.

"I didn't know how to. Promise me. Abandon arms. Forget."

Vango hesitated.

"Promise."

He promised.

And Zefiro raised his right arm slowly. Vango spotted his blue handkerchief tied around the padre's wrist.

"Take it," ordered the monk.

Tenderly, Vango obeyed. He stared at the fabric, only one corner of which was burned, with the charred section petering out just before the star.

"It's yours. But you're going to give it to this young man who looks like you. It would have made him happy."

He pointed to Schiff.

"Do it, Vango. It will save you. They will all think that Vango is dead. And that way," added Zefiro, "you will live."

Vango had placed his cheek next to Zefiro's, and the padre was whispering into his ear. Vango's tears ran down his friend's face.

"Leave." Zefiro sighed. "Go somewhere no one will recognize you. Where you'll no longer be a danger to anyone."

The Irishman had stopped two kilometers away in a field, just for the fun of it. He was smoking in front of this spectacle, sitting on the hood of his car, as if he were watching the sunset.

Ethel emerged barefoot from the debris. She had walked over embers, and one by one she had pulled out anything with a human shape from the flames around her. Strangely, she was soaking wet in the middle of this furnace. Water reserves had saved her life, by bursting just above her the moment the fire had broken out. It was as if she had been hurled, screaming, into the Victoria Falls. Now that help was at hand, she only wanted one thing: a car to New York. It was a matter of life and death. Someone noticed a severe burn that began at her right shoulder. The firemen were trying to catch her, but she was thinking of Vango and managed to escape them. She kept running toward the shell of the *Hindenburg*. Perhaps there would be a car on the other side.

When she spotted the blue handkerchief on the burned body, she didn't stop right away. She tried to erase what she had seen and keep on running.

A car. New York. Fifth Avenue. Thirty-Fourth Street. That was all that mattered.

But she could feel herself slowing down, then retracing her steps. Very slowly.

She knelt down next to the faceless corpse and, silently, she took the handkerchief in her hands.

At that instant, Vango saw her from far off. He called out to her, but she didn't hear him. He started running. Twenty meters away, he came to a stop.

A man was watching Ethel. He wore a burned coat. He didn't take his eyes off her for several minutes. The survivor, who looked like Rasputin, seemed very calm. Vlad the Vulture was drinking from a small metal flask.

The man drew closer, tossing his bottle far behind him in Vango's direction. Ethel was paralyzed in front of this unrecognizable body on the ground.

"Vango . . ."

Vango picked up the flask from the grass. He recognized the snarling bear engraved on the neck. They were still after him. He was convinced that his death alone could bring everything to a halt. Only then would he no longer be a danger to anyone.

A group of rescuers had gone over to Ethel. They were talking gently to her, but she didn't even notice them. She clutched the handkerchief as they took her by the arms; she tried to put up a struggle, but there were four of them. She was screaming.

Other men were busy transporting the bodies of Zefiro and Schiff on stretchers. They had already counted twenty-one dead and twelve missing. There were sixty-four survivors, which was a miracle.

Vango kept his eyes trained on Ethel through the cloud of smoke. She was repeating his name over and over again.

Vlad the Vulture made his way slowly toward the main arrival building. He needed to let Moscow know. It was all over.

Vango made directly for the deserted field.

A man stopped the two stretcher bearers who were carrying Zefiro.

"I'm looking for my brother," he said, and they allowed him to lift the cloth that covered the padre's face.

"Is that him?"

"Yes."

"My condolences. Give us his name. It will help."

"He was called Padre Zefiro."

For the first time in his life, Voloy Viktor took great pleasure in pronouncing his former confessor's name.

While the vultures hovered over the ruins of the most recent zeppelin, Vango was walking through the grass. Flashes of lightning streaked the sky toward the north.

He had torn off his shirt. He was leaving everything behind him, even his love.

He didn't know that his father, at the end of the preceding century, had experienced something similar. A rebirth.

Mademoiselle had told him all about it in the letter that was waiting for Vango, in Basilio's home. One morning, his father had forged a new path. Taken for dead by the rest of the world, he had started again from nothing. And like his father, Vango sensed the same hunger and terror surging through his body that is felt, perhaps, though nobody knows, by newborn babies.

Vango began to run toward the fire as hordes of shadowy figures were trying to escape from it.

PART THREE

PARIS UNDER OCCUPATION,
1942–1944

AN ENCOUNTER BY THE SEA:
WEEPING WILLOW

Abbas Tuman, Russian Caucasus, July 10, 1899

The setting was a wooden palace with colorful rooftops, balconies, and turrets rising up between the pine trees. All around were wooded hillsides. The fairy-tale palace looked deserted, but the low waters of the river Otskhe could be heard singing over the pebbles or pausing in the nooks and crannies behind the rocks. It was nine o'clock in the morning and the dew had already evaporated from the grass. It was going to be a scorching-hot day.

A man was contemplating this landscape from the roadside. He wore a pale jacket, which hung so loosely he appeared to be float-ing inside it, together with a pair of white trousers in the style of the Uhlan Cavaliers. Behind him was an extraordinary-looking machine: the first model of motorbike invented by the De Dion-Bouton workshops a few months earlier, consisting of a tricycle with a three-hundred-cubic-centimeter engine. The man had brought it from Paris by train.

He had spent eight years living in this valley in the Caucasus, arriving as an invalid in 1891. Tuberculosis had seized him during a grand tour around the world, which he had embarked on with his brother. They were in Bombay when he had spat up blood for the first time: he had been forced to leave Nicky behind and return home.

Out of the dozens of palaces that his family possessed, he had chosen to live alone in this one, guarded only by a few soldiers. The waters of the region were supposed to have healing properties, but they hadn't healed him.

In the shadow of these forests, the man known to his sister and his mother as Weeping Willow had become even more of a wild romantic figure.

They had given him this nickname back in the days when his English teacher, Mr. Heath, had taught him fly-fishing. George had become solitary and lugubrious, spending whole days beneath the willows at the water's edge. His sister, Xenia, used to say that he would take root, like the willow posts planted by the riverbank that instantly turned green.

Now, all these years later, he was weak; and yet he ran around the countryside until dusk. He was solitary but would sometimes hold celebrations for which the entire region arrived in costume. The guests would dance and bathe in the river before sunrise. Weeping Willow often slept out on the mountainside, watching the stars. He lived far from the capital and had embroidered on a handkerchief, which he never took out of his pocket, a phrase that he liked from the philosopher Pascal:

Combien de royaumes nous ignorent

Everything was contained in these words, written by Pascal as a reflection on mankind's modest place in the universe, but which Weeping Willow applied chiefly to his life's dream: living apart from the world. How many kingdoms know us not.

However, no kingdom was really unaware of him. There were always rumors about him. He had been claimed as dead on several occasions. There had even been an article in the New York Times announcing his disappearance. Imaginations ran riot about him taking a mistress among the princesses of the Caucasus. Hidden children and secret marriages were invented for him. And this twenty-eight-year-old man, who was solitary and sick, was the subject of all these myths.

His mother, Maria, loved him more than her other children. Sometimes she would pay a surprise visit from Saint Petersburg. He would pretend to be convalescing sensibly and doing well, spending three days on the wooden terrace with her, sipping lukewarm tea. But he would creep away to cough into a pillow. And when Maria Fiodorovna, who looked more youthful than her son, disappeared as her carriage reached the other side of the bridge across the river, he blew her kisses with his slender hands. He always believed it would be the last time. He would stay there, listening to a bird, watching the trout in summertime, or noticing the snow falling off the tops of the pine trees in winter.

But on the morning of the tenth of July 1899, his farewells to this valley in the Caucasus were for good. Lieutenant Boissman, guarding the main entrance, had allowed him to drive off on his motorbike, against the advice of his family and doctors. The only thing the officer had mentioned was the bear.

"Someone spotted it higher up, on the river. Take my gun."

Weeping Willow had declined with a smile.

Moments later, directly above the palace, he switched off the engine on a path strewn with pine needles. After surveying the world he was about to leave behind, he drove off at top speed westward, his shadow gently ahead of him and the roar of the engine deafening him. He overtook a horse-drawn cart transporting milk cans. The motorbike flashed past with the ten-liter fuel can that he had attached at the rear. He wanted to drive to the Black Sea and head along the coast as far as Constantinople. He had organized a boat there, in secret. His plan was to vanish.

After two kilometers, Weeping Willow slowed down, then stopped. He could feel some thick liquid in his mouth. When he tried to spit it out, his white jacket was splattered with blood. He turned off the engine by a ditch and bent over to cough.

He could barely get back on the motorbike. The cart laden with milk was trundling toward him. He knew he didn't have many more days left to live, but he wanted to die alone, at sea. He had set it all up. He didn't want to disappear into this ditch, in the middle of the mountains. He needed a few weeks of freedom, the only such weeks of his life, far from the gaze of onlookers.

The motorbike edged its way forward in slow motion, tracing a loop and sliding backward. The woman driving the horse cart saw the young man wobble from side to side as he clung to the handlebars. The engine cut out. Having recognized him when he had smiled and overtaken her a few minutes earlier, the milk woman climbed down. She didn't know whether she had the right to approach him or not, but arrived just in time for him to collapse into her arms. He was covered in blood.

"What should I do, Your Highness?"

"Nothing," he answered. "Nothing."

His face was turning pale and his hands no longer had any strength left in them.

Horrified, the milk woman laid him down on the ground. She turned toward her cart to fetch a container of water. She wanted him to drink it, but he kept his teeth clenched. In the end, she washed his face instead. Then he lost consciousness. And yet, from the depths of his blackout, he heard her sigh, "He is dead. The tsarevitch is dead."

She left him there alone in order to announce the news, abandoning cart and horse.

Half an hour later, twenty soldiers from the Palace Guard

returned with Lieutenant Boissman. They found the motorized tricycle, the cart, and traces of blood on the ground. But the tsarevitch's body had disappeared. The milk woman's tears were flowing thick and fast.

"He died in my arms!"

The horse was no longer there either, having broken free from its harness. Meanwhile, Boissman was hunched over the bloodstains. The earth had been churned up and the bracken trampled by the side of the road. The lieutenant's first thought was of the bear.

When he opened his eyes again, George couldn't taste the blood anymore. He was breathing calmly. On hearing the milk woman's words, he had experienced a deep sense of relief. The tsarevitch is dead. A sense of peace worthy of the great hereafter. His lungs were still filled with a burning sensation, but he was alive. And he was no longer the same person.

Five years ago, his older brother, Nicky, had become Nicholas II, tsar of all Russia. It was then that Weeping Willow's disease had taken a turn for the worse. He hadn't even been able to attend his father's funeral. From that day on, he had become the crown prince, the next on the list: for Nicholas II had no son.

George the Weeping Willow might succeed his brother at any moment.

Ever since, he had been haunted by the desire to depart, to flee or to die. His tuberculosis had returned with a vengeance. The crown hovered above his head like a threat. All he wanted was to be able to watch the stars and to lie down on the heathery earth. He didn't want to be emperor.

"The tsarevitch is dead." These words had given him back his life. He thought of the Tsarevna, or Little Princess, the boat belonging to his grandfather Alexander. It was waiting for him on the Bosphorus,

rescued at the eleventh hour from the scrap yard where it was due to be destroyed.

He considered how free he was as a dead man, and got back on his feet.

George was barely able to stand. He stared at the motorbike lying across the path. The woman hadn't yet returned with the palace guards. He made his way over to the horse and undid its harness. Too weak to climb on its back, he whispered softly to it and made it kneel down slowly instead, like a circus horse. No sooner had Weeping Willow hoisted himself onto its back than the animal stood up. It was a draft horse that had never been mounted before, and it reared up as it tried to throw off its rider. Weeping Willow kept whispering, his arms wrapped around the beast's neck. He gave a kick of his heels and together they galloped off, taking the path to the west.

Nobody recalled seeing a rider lying prostrate on his horse passing by. He didn't stop for more than one hundred kilometers. The animal's coat was covered in blood, but Weeping Willow was too far gone to notice. He was riding through the forests of Georgia.

At Chakva, on the shores of the Black Sea, he slid onto the sand in the middle of the night. The sound of the waves was music to his ears.

A little girl found him the next morning. She spoke Russian with an accent and stayed on her knees, singing to him, while her brother set off in search of grown-ups. Weeping Willow watched her without coughing: he didn't have the strength. He could see giant bamboo canes above her.

The women finally arrived. They were on their way to work in the tea fields that covered the hills. They could tell at a glance that George was in agony. The families that lived in Chakva, on the eastern shores of the Black Sea, belonged to the Greek-speaking minority that had come from Anatolia. The mother of the little girl settled him into their house, in the heart of the bamboo forest, where everyone spoke Greek among themselves. Weeping Willow stood up several times to leave, but he never got farther than the door. He spat into a bowl, which the little girl rinsed out ten times a day.

It was the end, and he knew it. He had dreamed of dying on the waves, alone with the gulls. But he would have to make do with a simple view of the sea between the bamboo canes, and an eight-year-old girl instead of cawing birds.

The climate in this part of the Caucasus was almost tropical. The tea plantation was magnificently maintained. It was run by a Chinese man, Mr. Lao, who had left his country in order to manage one of the first plantations in Russia. He was never without the medal that one of the tsar's ministers had awarded him for services to the Russian Empire.

When Mr. Lao came to see the sick man he had been told about by his workers, a woman raised the curtain with the invalid lying behind it and said, "He's dying."

"No," countered Mr. Lao. "He's not dying yet. He will die tomorrow."

Next to him, the little girl shuddered.

The Chinese plantation manager stared at George, pushing his eyes open with his fingers. He tore off the sick man's shirt and put his hand to his heart. Then he went away again, followed by the little girl.

That evening she returned with a cloth bag containing some small folded squares of paper. She opened them one by one, to reveal that each was filled with a fine powder. These were Mr. Lao's remedies.

The first sachet contained a mixture of indigo, powdered bones, and gardenia. The second blended the roots of blackberry bushes and licorice with crushed-rice powder. The little girl boiled up a few pinches of these powders, and the water turned dark.

The next day, George was still alive. And the day after too. A week later, he wanted to sit on the steps and stare at the bamboo forest. After that, he was able to go and observe the workers in the tea fields. People wondered what he was doing still there.

He pinched himself when he woke up, to find out whether he really was still alive.

He could speak some Greek and most of the European languages. He made everyone laugh by asking why, in this plantation, only the women and children worked.

"What about you?" they asked.

And he shrugged.

"I'm convalescing, ladies."

In reality, he had never thought about working. His only job was being born and then, every morning of his life, trying to come to terms with his birth.

One morning he went to take a look at Mr. Lao's house. George hid between the trees to view the handsome white residence that gave onto the sea. One day, he would ask the plantation manager about the secret of his powers. Was Weeping Willow being cured? He heard a noise.

Mr. Lao was standing behind him, bowing, his head level with his knees, holding out a little red box as an offering.

"Take this for another fifty days."

When George approached him, Mr. Lao knelt down, his gaze still lowered. He put the box on the ground, where it rested on a sheet of printed paper folded in four.

"Another fifty days."

George tried to help him to his feet again, but Mr. Lao pressed *his forehead into the grass, so that he was even lower. Then he stood up and walked slowly backward, inclining his head until he disappeared between the trees.*

George picked up the red box. On opening it, he discovered further supplies of the remedies he was taking. Then he unfolded the piece of printed paper, which turned out to be the front page of a Moscow newspaper. The picture showed a coffin covered in flowers in the middle of Saint Petersburg Cathedral. A wide border in the color of mourning surrounded the article, which took up the entire page. The only printed words read: GEORGE ALEXANDROVICH ROMANOV IS DEAD.

So Mr. Lao knew who he was.

Weeping Willow never returned to the house in the bamboo forest. He left without saying a word to anybody. Barefoot and with a heavy basket under her arm, the little girl, whose name was Stella, watched him walking toward the sea.

STELLA

Chakva, Caucasus, fourteen years later, 1913

The boat, which was all lit up with flares, had cast anchor two hundred meters from the shore. On the beach, dozens of shadows watched its reflections. Some sat on the sand, others were up to their thighs in the water. No one dared speak. There was no moon and no stars, only this incandescent launch on the sea.

"I told you," a young woman whispered breathlessly.

"Has it just arrived?"

"Two hours ago. It was still light. We saw a flag I didn't recognize to the rear. Perhaps the sultan of Constantinople is fleeing."

"Don't talk nonsense, Rhea."

"It's all-out war. . . . Look, the other side!"

Rhea thought her sister was referring to the flashes of war on some invisible shore. But she was pointing to the back of the boat. A dinghy had just been thrown into the water, making the reflections of light ripple. Two men clambered on board with a lantern and proceeded to row toward the beach.

"Come on, Rhea."

The girls made their way over to the spot where the boat would come ashore. The other spectators kept their distance, fearful. One of the sailors stepped into the water and grabbed the lantern from the fore of the boat. As he raised it, the flame alighted first on Rhea's face. She was only thirteen and felt intimidated, turning her gaze toward her sister as if she didn't want to be there, preferring people to look at her sibling instead. Her older sister's hair flowed all the way down to her hips. She must have been at least twenty. Her face was barely visible because she was shielding her eyes from the dazzle of the lamp.

"I'm looking for Mr. Lao Zhenzhao," said the sailor.

"You speak Greek! Are you Greek?" asked the young woman.

"I'm looking for Mr. Lao."

Even in Greek, he had an odd way of talking.

"He's probably asleep," she replied. "He lives in that house over there. He runs our plantation."

"I need to bring him on board."

"Why?"

"To drink tea with my master."

"Mr. Lao has enough tea to brew up the Black Sea," said the young woman. She seemed hesitant but, staring at the lights from the boat, she added, "My little sister will accompany you to Mr. Lao's house."

Rhea led the way for the visitor.

The other sailor stayed in the boat, having stashed the oars. Small rolls of waves broke against the hull. The young woman sat on the gray pebbles, staring at the silhouette of the boat with its three masts linked by garlands of lights. Fifty meters of fine gold. Who did it belong to? She thought she could hear music on board.

"Is he a prince?" she asked.

The sailor smiled and smoked his tobacco from Argos.

"Perhaps. I don't know, even though I've been sailing with him for ten years."

"Has he got a family?"

"No."

Mr. Lao arrived at the beach. Having dressed hastily, he was wearing his medal of the Order of Saint Stanislaus back to front. Rhea went to sit on the sand next to her sister. The curious bystanders had all gone, and there was just a dog left sniffing around the algae. Disconcerted, Mr. Lao clambered into the back of the dinghy. The two sailors also climbed on board and made for the open sea with strong oar strokes.

"Go home, Rhea."

"Me?"

The beach was deserted.

"Go to bed."

"What about you?"

Stella was staring intensely at the play of light on the sea. When the dinghy became invisible behind the boat, she stood up and took a few steps toward the water's edge. She hitched up her skirt and tied it around her waist.

"Go to bed, Rhea."

"What are you doing?"

Rhea saw her big sister keep on walking: first her feet, then her knees, and finally her waist disappeared beneath the water. Without disturbing the surface of the sea, Stella dived in, reappearing farther off, where she began to swim. She turned back toward Rhea and signaled again for her to go away. She dived once more and vanished into the liquid night.

Rhea fled toward the trees.

Mr. Lao sat on the floor, holding his cup in his right hand.

Weeping Willow was at the far end of the carpet, pouring from a large samovar. He wore a red blanket over his shoulders.

"I'm sorry for disturbing you in the middle of the night."

The candles gave off an ecclesiastical scent in the boat's long cabin, as Lao bowed his head respectfully.

"I wanted to wait until tomorrow. But there are skirmishes on the sea toward the west. I have to leave, so as not to be trapped."

The Chinese plantation manager bowed his head again.

"I wanted to thank you," said the stranger. "I left without thanking you for healing me."

Mr. Lao opened his mouth to give a response, but then thought the better of it.

"I know what you were going to say," offered George. "By your reckoning, it's the first time that a dead man has returned to thank his doctor."

Lao nodded, and a long silence fell between them, before he ventured, "According to the newspaper, your mother suffered greatly in grief."

"I had no intention of living. I wanted to die. It's not my fault."

"In that case, it's mine, Your Majesty."

"Don't address me in that way."

Lao hadn't yet sipped his tea, but he inhaled its aroma.

"Perhaps you should let your mother see you, one day," commented Mr. Lao.

"Nobody misses me anymore."

"Just your mother——"

"Be quiet."

George was staring at a candle as the boat swayed.

"You have also come to ascertain whether I've told anybody," said the plantation manager, wetting his lips in the tea for the first time. "This tea is Ottoman," he declared.

"Yes."

"I haven't breathed a word," continued Mr. Lao. "I haven't

spoken about it to anyone. I'm always on my guard. My tea merchant often repeats a proverb from his home village: Tell your secret to a friend, but your friend also has a friend."

Weeping Willow nodded. The wick of a candle spluttered as it drowned in wax.

"Perhaps I'll go to see my mother," he said.

"Promise me."

George had learned that his mother hadn't stayed until the end of his funeral service. She had left the cathedral, distraught. After his departure from the palace at Abbas Tuman, Weeping Willow had guessed that nobody would mention the fact that his corpse had never been found. There were enough curses hanging over his family already. George Alexandrovich was dead. That was enough. A coffin was buried containing no body, but filled with books.

"Look at me, for example. I left my country," explained the man, "without ever seeing my mother again."

Weeping Willow glanced at Mr. Lao, who was smiling. Only the light trade winds rippling the surface of his cup of tea betrayed his emotions.

"And then my mother died," said Lao.

Somebody pushed open the glass door that gave onto the deck.

"I said nobody was to enter!" growled George.

The sailor took a step backward.

"Forgive me."

"Go outside."

"We've netted something out the back," declared the sailor, looking pale.

"I told you to go outside."

"I—"

"Out!"

Defying his master, the sailor dared to go over to him and whisper in his ear. George was taken aback. The red blanket slid off his shoulders.

The crew on the boat was from Cyprus. In every sea of the region, as far back as antiquity, fishermen had harbored a secret dream of one day catching a fantastic creature in their nets. And the sailor had just uttered the magic word in Greek: Leucosia, meaning fair maiden, and the name of one of the three sirens.

George stood up. Perhaps he too had been looking for a fairy or a siren during his fifteen-year odyssey? He had searched all the gulfs and rocks of the Mediterranean as far as Gibraltar. But there was still no woman by his side.

He went out on deck and made his way toward the aft of the boat. The sailors were huddled near the tiller, with two lanterns flickering above them. They had formed a circle around somebody whose guilty demeanor, clenched fists, and sopping-wet hair and skirt were more reminiscent of a drowned cat than a mermaid. She hid beneath her hair. Nobody dared approach her.

George wasn't sure whether to cover her in his blanket. He leaned gently over and noticed that the mermaid had two bare feet where a tail should have been.

Mr. Lao had followed George outside. He parted the sailors and surveyed the scene, standing next to the boat's Russian owner.

"Stella?" he called out.

A face streaming with water appeared between the locks of hair. Two eyes found those of Weeping Willow. She had changed a great deal since the man with tuberculosis and the little girl from Chakva had first met.

"What are you doing here, Stella?" asked Mr. Lao.

But there was no reply.

*   *   *

Despite the threat of war, the boat remained in the bay for ten days. And when it sailed off, one cold morning, there were many tears shed on the beach. Stella was going away with Weeping Willow. Their marriage had taken place at night. The priest had placed the Orthodox wedding crowns on the heads of the bride and groom, and George had flinched at the weight on his head.

At dawn, on the shore, Stella's mother had kissed her eldest daughter good-bye, as Mr. Lao held a black umbrella over them and the sand was whipped up. Little Rhea stayed hidden in the bamboo forest. She had climbed to the top of a thatched roof, in among the leaves and the wind, from where she watched the gathering on the beach as if it were a funeral. Stella forgot to seek her out and kiss her.

George had the front of the boat emblazoned with a gold star, after his wife's name. The sails swelled. They promised they'd be back, but the following summer the straits leading to the Black Sea were closed off with a sinister din. War broke out across the Dardanelles and the Bosphorus.

The boat and its new star never returned to Chakva.

That said, one day, even though armored soldiers roamed the region, the boat dropped anchor off the shores of Constantinople. George had entrusted the care of Stella to his crew. It was 1915 and the baby she was expecting might arrive at any moment. He promised to return before the baby was born. For the first time, Weeping Willow went back to Saint Petersburg.

He saw his mother on a bridge, behind the Anichkov Palace. He kept the promise he had made to Mr. Lao. It only lasted for a moment.

He had arranged a meeting with her in a letter on which was reproduced, in freehand, the motif of his blue handkerchief, to prove *that it was him. It bore the refrain of his youth:* Combien de royaumes nous ignorent. *And, embroidered in gold thread, the signature he had created for himself, when he was fifteen years old, by carving it into a tree. The word* Romanov, *the name of his dynasty, was written in the Latin alphabet. But the V had been doubled, and was separate from the other letters, one line below.*

ROMANO
W

W, *as in Weeping Willow.*

In the letter to his mother, George told her about what had happened to him, about being cured and his new life. Dear Mother, I am alive. I know that you haven't forgotten me. *If she wanted to see him, to be sure that it really was him, all she had to do was drive past at five o'clock. He would be beneath the sculpted horses on the bridge. She mustn't stop.*

He also announced that he was going to have a child.

Standing in the rain, George heard the sound of horses' hooves first. Then he saw the carriage pass by with its misted-up windows.

Stopping off in Moscow, he found Mademoiselle in a railway station. He noticed her red eyes, her suitcase, her upright figure, and he heard her French accent. He followed her discreetly as far as the post office and offered her a job. He was looking for a nurse for his child. He was sure that it would be a little girl.

But it was a prince. Vango. A prince without a kingdom.

To begin with, George's mother kept safe the letter he had written her. But when the revolution broke out in Russia two years later, in 1917, it was found in one of the deserted palaces.

* * *

In the boat, sitting on the carpet-covered deck and listening to Stella singing, Weeping Willow had carefully used his knife to pull out the golden thread on the second V. Only one remained now: V for Vango, his son.

ROMANO
V

It was ten o'clock in the evening, and Mademoiselle was pouring pitchers of hot water into a copper bath. Vango lived in his mother's arms. For several days now, the boat had been far from the war. Weeping Willow folded the square of blue silk. He had no idea that one day the signature on this handkerchief would identify his son, delivering him into the hands of his enemies.

As they spotted the first lighthouse of Crete, a gust of wind was all it would have taken to blow the handkerchief out of Weeping Willow's hands, drowning it in the sea, and changing Vango's destiny forever.

The five pages written by Mademoiselle to Vango, but which had never reached him, recounted much more and in a style that was simple yet powerful. They also mentioned the treasure, which the tsar's mother had stored for safekeeping in Weeping Willow's boat when the great revolution had begun. Mademoiselle described the little fishing port where one night they loaded on board a padlocked barrel with the seal of the tsars.

Doctor Basilio read and reread these pages for many years. When he had first opened the letter, a long time ago, he had bought a Russian dictionary that he left in Mademoiselle's deserted house in Pollara, in order to check how some of the words had been translated by the prisoner of Lipari.

There was even a short paragraph about Mademoiselle's youth in Paris, and it contained a former address, which was enough to make Basilio dream. It was the address of the place where she had worked before setting off for Russia in 1914. When would Vango come to collect Mademoiselle's letter, which filled in the blanks of his life?

For Basilio, many of the sentences addressed to Vango remained incomprehensible and even poetic sounding.

You see, the truth is I remember everything. And the star I embroidered on your blue handkerchief marks the exact spot where we were shipwrecked, on the big V *of our islands.*

These words surely meant nothing, even if the Aeolian Islands did form the shape of the letter *V* over the sea. The translator must have made a mistake. But Basilio liked this poem, which he kept just for himself.

23

THE CAPITAL OF SILENCE

Paris, December 20, 1942

It was pitch-black at nine o'clock in the morning. For two years now, the clocks in Paris had been moved forward to Berlin time.

Two men were walking up the Champs-Élysées. The first was called Augustin Avignon. He wore a black woolen scarf and a hat pulled down over his head to protect his ears from the biting cold. He was followed by a young man, who carried a heavy briefcase in both arms. Avignon was issuing a barrage of short sharp orders, as if to hear his junior respond as frequently as possible.

"Yes, Superintendent."

Avignon had been superintendent for nine months, and he still hadn't gotten used to it.

"His name's Max Grund?"

"Yes, Superintendent."

"Find out what grade he is for me."

"Yes, Superintendent."

"I've only ever addressed him as *offizier*. I must look like a fool."

"Yes, Superintendent."

"I beg your pardon?"

"Sorry, Superintendent. The Germans are establishing

new offices every day. It's hard to keep up."

The city was dark. The street lamps along the avenue were off. They came across some men pushing a cart full of wood.

"Is it a little farther up?"

"Another hundred meters, Superintendent."

"I'm going to give them a piece of my mind, I can tell you. The sparks will fly."

"I understand, Superintendent."

"So, are you taking any vacation, Mouchet?"

"Just for Christmas."

"To do what?"

"My wife wants to visit her family in Nice."

"And when does this vacation of yours start, Mouchet?"

"Yesterday."

"Perfect."

Whenever he listened to himself speak, Avignon was always hoping to catch the intonations of the great Boulard. He imitated his former boss as best he could, as he tried to punch above his weight. To be a bit stronger, a bit tougher, a bit more generous than he really was. But he often fell short of the mark.

"My regards to your wife. Is it Monique?"

"No, it's Elise."

"Lise, yes, of course."

"Elise, Superintendent."

"Don't split hairs, Mouchet. And merry Christmas to your children."

"Yes, Superintendent."

Mouchet didn't have any children. Avignon had chosen him as his assistant because he was young and had never known Boulard. With luck, the copy wouldn't seem so pale to him.

"Here we are," declared Mouchet.

"You can say what you like, but they've got good taste," commented Avignon when they stopped in front of a set of large metal gates. The Nazi flag was draped from the balcony of a handsome private mansion with a courtyard. France had lost the war and Germany was occupying the country.

"Superintendent Avignon, for Offizier Max Grund," they announced, showing their papers to a soldier who was guarding the gates.

They walked across the courtyard and went into the entrance hall, where they reported to a woman who asked them to wait. She then disappeared upstairs. It was deliciously warm inside. Men tramped in and out of doorways carrying files. A workman was replacing the glass on the front door. The Gestapo had recently requisitioned these magnificent premises. Mouchet sat down on a banquette, but Avignon remained upright. He went over to a large picture frame that had been covered with a sheet and propped against the wall.

He hitched up the sheet slightly. There, painted on the canvas, was a man standing in a drawing room, with a lion skin at his feet. The man was consulting his pocket watch.

"Is it interesting?" Max Grund called out from the top of the stairs. Mouchet leaped up off the banquette, but Avignon kept examining the picture.

"Is that you, in the painting?" he asked.

Grund didn't respond. He signaled abruptly for the superintendent to join him upstairs, and Mouchet also tried to follow.

"Wait for me down here," muttered Avignon, removing two documents from the leather briefcase.

"I've got the statements as well. And the other photos."

"All right. Follow me."

Mouchet flew into action. While they climbed the stairs, Grund barked at a removals man who had just appeared at the doorway, close to the painting. Mouchet understood German perfectly, and Max Grund's instructions for the canvas to be disposed of weren't difficult to follow. Referring to the man with the pocket watch in the portrait, the German officer ordered, "Get rid of that Jew once and for all." Presumably, this wasn't the first time he had been mistaken for the house's previous owner.

Mouchet and Avignon walked into the office.

"What seems to be the problem?" Grund wanted to know. "I'm very busy."

He sat down at his desk, leaving his visitors standing. The woman who had greeted them downstairs was now sitting behind a typewriter by the door. Mouchet studied the room carefully. Only a little while ago, this must have been a bedroom: a velvet-and-wooden ornamental headboard was still fixed to the wall. Three huge windows let in the dim light, and a balcony gave onto the courtyard.

Avignon stepped forward with the two photographs. "Armand Javard and Paul Cerrini," he announced.

Grund lit a cigarette. With each word spoken, the typewriter clattered.

"Yes?" asked Grund.

"Do you know them?"

Since his early days in the Gestapo by the shores of Lake

Constance, Max Grund had never lost his flair for memorizing and being supremely organized. As a result, in ten years he had risen through the ranks, culminating in his appointment to the Paris posting a few months earlier. He had learned to speak French in four weeks.

"I can give you their dates of birth, if you like," crowed Grund. "Javard was born on the fifteenth of September 1908 —"

"Are they yours?" Avignon wanted to know.

Grund shook his head, indicating, over on the wall, a picture of a small brown mustache and a well-combed part.

"They're his."

"So what am I supposed to do with them?" pressed Avignon, who had no difficulty recognizing the portrait of Adolf Hitler.

"Leave them alone."

"They attacked a bank in rue de la Pompe."

Mouchet took out the statements from the briefcase.

"Leave them alone," repeated Grund.

Avignon smiled tersely. Since the occupation had begun, he found himself in this kind of predicament on a daily basis. Half of the gangsters in Paris had put themselves under German protection. Just fifteen minutes' walk from this address, a cavern of brigands reigned over the city with impunity. Avignon's work was becoming impossible.

"Anything else?" barked Grund.

"No. Thank you. Come on, Mouchet."

They headed for the door.

"Wait," commanded Grund.

Much to Avignon's horror, the secretary was typing every word.

"Did you receive my little invitation?"

"No, I—"

"Superintendent," interrupted Mouchet. "Offizier Grund must be referring to New Year's Eve. . . ."

"I don't know what you're talking about." Avignon scowled.

The typewriter was recording them again.

"I had your invitation delivered to police headquarters," said Grund. "There will be a dinner with friends on the thirty-first of December, for foreigners I wish to thank. I should like to offer a positive image of the collaboration between our two peoples."

Avignon retraced his steps.

"Offizier Grund, let me be frank with you. I am a very young superintendent. In deference to the chiefs of police, Monsieur Brinon and Monsieur Bousquet, it would be a breach of etiquette for me to accept the honor of being your guest. Might I suggest that you invite one of them? I'm sure they would be delighted."

"You are the person who is invited, Superintendent, and nobody else. Good day. I am counting on you."

When they were back out on the sidewalk, Avignon turned to Mouchet.

"You nearly discredited me in front of Grund."

"Yes, Superintendent."

"I told you to forget about that invitation."

Avignon was speaking through clenched teeth.

"I'll have you transferred to the guardroom in Drancy if you continue in this vein."

"Yes, Superintendent."

"You've got to fix this, Mouchet, and fast. Find me the guest list. I have no wish to be perceived as a fraternizing collaborator. I do my job as best I can. This is a war, after all."

"I'm catching my train in an hour, Superintendent."

"Oh, no you're not. You're not going anywhere. You can tell your wife it's your own fault."

"Sir——"

"Enough of your prewar Christmases! All that's over now."

"I'll have to go to the station, to let her know. I'm the one with the passes."

"I want you at the Quai des Orfèvres by midday. I've warned you, Mouchet!"

"Yes, Superintendent. I'll be back shortly."

Mouchet stopped in the middle of the street. There was full daylight now, but the silence remained oppressive. The superintendent's footsteps grew fainter.

Since the summer of 1940, the city had fallen silent. The rare cars that passed through made that silence vibrate. Some inhabitants had pressed their old horses back into use, pulling antique carts and bringing the smells of the countryside into the city.

Mouchet crossed the avenue and went down into the Métro, to catch a train in the direction of Vincennes. On the platform, he waited next to a man who was reading a doorstop of a book wrapped in newspaper. They got into the carriage at the same time and sat down on the same wooden bench.

"I'm not leaving anymore," said Mouchet.

"Why?" asked the man, keeping his book open on his knees.

"I'll tell you later. We need someone for the suitcase."

"We're meeting the others at the station, in the bistro."

At the next stop, Mouchet switched carriages. He got out at the Gare de Lyon. As he walked into the station bistro, he saw a small group of people waiting for him: two men and a young woman. They all greeted one another like long-lost cousins.

They were served a black liquid that faintly resembled coffee. Mouchet paid immediately. The man with the book covered with newspaper entered and sat down at a neighboring table. Glancing discreetly toward the bistro entrance, he listened in on their conversation.

"I'm not leaving anymore," repeated Mouchet. "Avignon needs me."

"What about Grund?"

"I went there this morning. The plans are accurate. Right down to the number of steps on the staircase. And yes, the office is in the room with the balcony. Marie's done a great job."

They turned toward the young woman, who was sipping a glass of water.

"What are we going to do about the suitcase?"

"I can try to free myself up for Christmas Eve," said Mouchet.

"It'll be too late."

Outside, soldiers in green uniforms were checking the departures board opposite.

"I'll have to take it myself. I've got papers from the Ministry of the Interior. That way, it's sure."

"I can go there with an ordinary pass," said one of the men.

"No," the man with the book countered softly, without looking at them. Sitting to one side, he was participating secretly in their meeting.

"We can't take any risks," he added. "That's what Caesar told us. So we'll wait for the twenty-fourth after all."

And with that, the meeting's clandestine participant stood up and walked out. A minute later, two others followed with the suitcase.

Mouchet remained sitting next to Marie. They were watching two young women saying their good-byes a little farther off.

"How come you're so familiar with Grund's offices?" whispered Mouchet.

"I knew the people who used to live there," said Marie.

Mouchet nudged a newspaper toward her.

"There are three messages inside: one for Sylvain and two for Caesar. Avoid the mailbox at Sylvain's place. The concierge can't be trusted: she's got the key."

Marie used her little finger to remove a feather from her glass of water. Caesar was the code name for the leader of their network. Neither of them knew his real identity.

"And we need to move Sylvain at the end of the month," said Mouchet.

"I've got three new empty bedrooms in the same district, if you like."

"Where do you find them?"

She twirled her fingers as if plucking the rooms magically out of thin air.

"There will be more mail," said Mouchet. "Meet me tomorrow, Odéon Métro station, on the platform. At six o'clock."

"I'd rather meet aboveground," said Marie, who suffered from claustrophobia.

"In front of the newspaper booth, then; we'll go to the cinema."

"What about those documents I asked you for?"

"I'll have them tomorrow as well," said Mouchet.

Marie stayed behind on her own. The German soldiers in front of the departures board smiled at her through the window. She dived back into her glass.

She left the station toward eleven o'clock. An hour later, she was running across the rooftops by the gardens of the Palais-Royal. She tucked the first envelope into the gap in a shutter that opened onto leafless trees. The neighbors of the mysterious Caesar kept two chickens on their balcony. One of them raised the alarm by beating its wings. But by the time someone appeared, Marie was already jumping over the rue de Montpensier.

Marie had been known as Marie since September 1940. Before that, she had been called Emilie for a little while, but mainly she went by the name of the Cat. She had delivered mail for the Paradise Network from the first day, ever since the word *resistance* had sprung into life.

She had so little to do with her parents—any ties to them having worn loose—that she had been very surprised when, just before the summer, her father had slid two yellow triangles edged with black under her bedroom door. She had stared at them for a long time, reconfiguring them in every possible shape, from a diamond to a sailing boat, before tidying them away. The next day, in the street, the Cat had passed a woman leading her daughter by the hand. On the left-hand side of their chests, firmly stitched in place, both of them wore those same two triangles forming a yellow star.

The Cat had followed them for some time, until the woman had noticed her and shooed her away.

"This isn't a freak show. Leave us alone."

The Cat kept on pretending she didn't know what was going on. The fact that people like her were banned from parks, museums, and cafés . . . For the first time in her life she almost tried her luck in the Métro, just for the thrill of entering the front carriages, where Jews were forbidden. On the twelfth of June, she chanced on her father walking with his chauffeur along Avenue Montaigne. It was a fine day. The chauffeur, Pierre, was carrying four new suits on coat hangers. They were on their way back from the tailor, and Ferdinand Atlas wore the yellow star on his white linen jacket. The Cat crossed over to the other side so as not to look him in the eye.

Three days later there was a phone call for her, which the Cat took in the kitchen.

"It's Marie-Antoinette."

The voice belonged to an old woman.

"Who?" asked the Cat.

"It's me, Madame Boulard. I've got my son next to me. He wants to speak with you."

"Hello?" boomed Boulard, grabbing the phone. "Do as

I tell you, young lady. Make sure you're not at home next week. Something's going to happen."

"What would you know about it? You're out of the loop now."

The Cat had fallen out with Boulard a year earlier, when he had been moved from the Quai des Orfèvres. Boulard's presence at the heart of police operations had been a stroke of luck for the Paradise Network. He was more useful to them on the inside than he was on the outside.

But from the start of the Occupation, the superintendent had done everything to be kicked out: incendiary letters to the minister, refusing to obey orders. He had left like a hero, slamming the door and putting his life on the line. He had even abandoned Paris for his village in the Aveyron, in the desert of Aubrac. The Cat had never forgiven him.

She nearly hung up.

"Take your parents with you and disappear for a few days!" bellowed Boulard at the other end of the line.

"So you're interested in me all of a sudden? If I'd known that you were going to drop us, Superintendent, I wouldn't have reunited you and your mother. She would still be in Scotland."

The Cat knew that Boulard was very grateful for what she had done a few years earlier to make sure his mother was safe.

"I did everything I could to help you," said Boulard.

"You shouldn't have left your job."

"Don't be so naive. There was no sense in it. If I freed three people for you, the next day I brought in fifty for the chief of police."

Boulard had been courageous from the outset. Two days before the arrival of the Germans, in June 1940, he had attempted to move all the files referring to the origins of French citizens. With his troops, he had organized a chain to transport the boxes from police headquarters to two barges. But the boats were intercepted before reaching their destination.

The Cat heard Madame Boulard wrestling the telephone from her son.

"Hello? Auguste is a blockhead, I'll grant you. But today, you really must listen to him, my dear. Your address is on the list."

"Which list?"

"They're going to arrest more Jews."

"What's that got to do with me?" quipped the Cat.

And she hung up.

That same evening, however, she had put her pride to one side and spoken to her parents.

They had smiled at first. Yes, everyone had heard the rumors. Ferdinand Atlas trusted the state. His family wasn't clandestine: they were French and, what's more, they had been French for generations. Not only that, but he had made sure he was reregistered every time it was required. The police were just trying to pacify the Occupier. This was understandable.

Ferdinand took out his wallet, containing his identity card with JEW stamped on it in big red letters. He held out the card for his daughter to see. All his paperwork was in order with the authorities. It was as if he believed the stamp protected him. He had nothing to hide.

But when the Cat explained that this recommendation came from a former police superintendent, Ferdinand Atlas shot his wife a confused glance.

And so all three of them caught the train to Trouville the day after Bastille Day. The Cat had never traveled with her parents before. She spent two weeks walking on the beach, wading out into the waves, and watching her mother sleep in the sun, an open book on her face to protect her fair complexion. They returned at the end of the month.

"There! You see! Everything's as it should be! Nobody came after all," declared Ferdinand, striding through the rooms of his house.

There were tears in his eyes, and he felt ashamed for having doubted his country.

The Cat resumed her clandestine life, and never went back home.

But one Sunday in September, French police officers came to knock politely at the door. They escorted the Atlas parents off the premises. It was only when they were in the car that Ferdinand noticed he was still wearing his slippers.

"I'll just pop back upstairs for my shoes."

In the backseat, his wife gripped his arm.

"You won't be needing them," said the officer.

The Cat found out three days later. She entered her house via a skylight. The household staff had fled. On a tray at the foot of the unmade bed were two croissants as hard as fossils. Through Mouchet, at the prefecture, she tried to obtain information without revealing that these were her parents. In early December, Max Grund set up his offices in the house.

Paris, the Odéon crossroads, December 21, 1942

Mouchet kissed Marie on the neck as if she were his girl-friend. She had a student's satchel slung over her shoulder. He led her into the cinema. On the screen, two soldiers on horseback were trotting up a mountain. A few spectators were smoking three rows in front of them. Another was sleeping at the back.

"Give me the mail; I've got to go," she whispered.

"Wait. I need to speak to you. An airplane is going to parachute in a Frenchman on Christmas Eve, in the night, near Chartres. He's coming from London, and he's going to train three of our men for radio transmissions. It can't be done in Paris."

"So?"

"Caesar is thinking of sending all of them to Saint John."

"I don't think Saint John would like that."

"I want to meet this Saint John."

"I'll ask him. He only talks to me. Let me go now."

"Ask him. It's very urgent."

As she stood up, Mouchet grabbed her hand. Their neighbor was watching them. Mouchet started whispering into the Cat's hair as if they were lovers.

"Those people you wanted to find — the Atlases — they're no longer at the camp at Pithiviers. They left on the twentieth of September."

"Where?"

"They're still taking them eastward. We don't know where. They're not in France anymore."

Some medieval music was now accompanying the film.

"One of the envelopes is for Caesar again; it contains some very important documents. The other one is for you—it's about your friends."

"They're not my friends."

"Silence, up front!" called out the man who was dozing in the back row.

"I've put in everything I could find out about the Atlases," whispered Mouchet. "There's a form with all the places they've been to. One last thing, Marie. I need to speak with Boulard as well. Where is he?"

"I don't know."

She left, without mustering the strength to open her own package. That evening, she was back on the roof of the Palais-Royal. After sliding the new piece of mail through the gap in the shutter, she warmed herself up for a moment against the clumps of terra-cotta chimney pots that jutted out from the rooftop. Beneath her woolen vest was the envelope from Mouchet. She still couldn't bring herself to open it.

La Reine Morte was playing at the Comédie-Française. Tonight's performance was over. Some of the spectators lingered in the foyer, making the most of the warmth.

The Cat spent the night in the theater's attic, where she was reunited with a violin. She had hidden it there, a long time ago now, between the beams. She didn't touch it.

In the morning she took a train to Le Mans, then caught the express Manche-Océan ferry, which dropped her off in Nantes.

The day passed by in a flash, and by six in the evening she was walking along the exposed path that linked the mainland to the island of Noirmoutier at low tide. It was dark.

She avoided the German guardrooms, whose lights she could spot on both shores, and cut across the sandbanks instead. Saltwater pools were bristling with life. She heard the crabs scuttling away.

The Cat knew that she couldn't turn up on Saint John's doorstep in the middle of the night. So she slept in a tiny hut between the salt marshes, warmed by three donkeys huddling below her.

24

SAINT JOHN THE EVANGELIST

La Blanche Abbey, Noirmoutier, off the shores of western France,
December 22, 1942

Mother Elisabeth (all one hundred kilos of her beneath a spot-less habit) was the most terrifying force known to the island of Noirmoutier since its invasion by the Vikings in the ninth century after Jesus Christ. She had reigned over the abbey at La Blanche for forty years. No bishop had ever dared mention the word *retirement* to her. And not even the German soldiers who had set up headquarters in the château a few kilometers away were prepared to take any risks inside the abbey's high walls. They had trampled over three quarters of Europe, but they took off their boots at the threshold when they turned up timidly at La Blanche in order to buy a small pot of honey or some radishes.

Everyone was frightened of Mother Elisabeth, but she was universally admired. The large walled garden at the abbey fed a good proportion of the island. Three of the sisters ran a health center in the mill to the south of the abbey, which had a better reputation than some provincial hospitals. The choir was magnificent. The services for Christmas and the Assumption attracted the whole diocese.

People would have been even more amazed if the public had been able to glimpse, at nightfall, the fiercely contested soccer matches that the nuns played on the beach, or the midnight swims on Easter Sunday, after prayers. Hallelujah! The shrieks of joy from the waves must have traveled all the way up to the Loire estuary.

And yet, aside from these openings onto the world, La Blanche was a citadel that no one could enter. The few children who had tried scaling the wall in order to steal a Z pear — allegedly the juiciest pear in the west, and a sub-species of the classic Williams Bon Chrétien variety — bitterly regretted it. They had received an almighty walloping on the backside from the holy mother.

The Cat rang the bell at the main gates. Two black eyes appeared behind a small grille.

"Our holy mother is in the chapel. She's singing."

"Tell her that the Cat wishes to speak with her."

"The Cat?"

"Yes."

"As in —"

"As in the small furry animal."

"Don't you have a name that's a bit more . . ."

"Serious sounding?"

"I'll have to interrupt the Christmas rehearsal. The sisters will all be staring at me. So, if I announce that the Cat —"

"Are you new here, Sister?"

"Yes."

"Tell her it's about Saint John."

"The Evangelist?"

"Yes."

"That's better. That's what I'll say. And you can talk to

her about the Cat, if you like. Take a seat on the bench. I feel bad about leaving you out in the cold."

Sister Bertille walked across a former lawn, which had been transformed into a potato field when war had broken out: a fine example of the nuns' pragmatic approach. She headed along the cloister and pushed open a door. Strains of Christmas carols could be heard. Sister Bertille crossed a courtyard and entered the chapel.

Fifty nuns were singing "Mid the Ass and Oxen Mild" in six- or seven-part harmony, their eyes raised heavenward, with enough emotion to make the listener forget that this was hardly a masterpiece of religious music. The carol's thousand divine angels could be heard hovering beneath the vaults. Mother Elisabeth was standing on a box before the choir, stirring the air convincingly.

It took her a while to notice Bertille blushing by the door. She conducted until the end of the refrain before bringing the choir to a halt.

As Mother Elisabeth turned around, there was a splitting noise from the wooden crate beneath her clogs.

"Well, Sister Bertille? Is it the general?"

"No, Mother Elisabeth."

The question "Is it the general?" was Mother Elisabeth's stock-in-trade. She requested not to be disturbed unless General de Gaulle was landing with the English. It was her only way of ensuring peace and quiet. Whenever someone came to ask her a question while she was meditating in the garden, whenever someone interrupted her while she was at work, whenever someone raised her hand in the course of the nuns' silent meals, she always responded with: "Is it the general?"

"So, Bertille, you're not guarding the gates?"

"There's a young lady who wishes to speak with you."

Bertille didn't dare pronounce the Cat's name.

"She says it's about Saint John."

"Sister Marieke, would you kindly replace me?"

A pretty nun stepped out from one of the rows and helped Elisabeth get down off her crate before climbing up onto it herself. The abbess was now reunited with her walking stick, and she began issuing instructions as she made her way toward the chapel door.

"It's not working with the twelve sisters at the front; we can't hear 'Sleep, sleep, sleep, my little child.' So, Sister Marieke, you've got a choice: either make them sing more loudly, or remove the basses. I'm thinking of Sister Véronique, right at the back, who would be most useful in the kitchen when it comes to peeling the Jerusalem artichokes."

Everyone turned toward one of the choristers in the back row, who went pale beneath her freckles.

"Do your best, my sisters. May I remind you that Christmas is in three days' time, and I'm counting on the collection to mend the roof. Be brilliant. I don't want to leave you in abject poverty when I die. Which won't be long now: I'm nearly as old as Marshal Pétain."

The door slammed shut.

Bertille and the abbess crossed the first courtyard and headed back along the cloister before skirting the potato field.

"Open the gates, Sister."

Sister Bertille did as she was told. The Cat appeared, and Mother Elisabeth kissed her on the forehead.

"Come with me, my daughter. Given the hour, we'll have to go this way."

The nun led the new arrival beyond the enclosure, and the Cat offered her arm. Bertille watched them heading off, flanking the exterior wall, in the direction of the sea.

"Those aviators you sent us last time were charming. My sisters would have liked to keep them forever. But they didn't have a calling for our way of life."

The Cat smiled.

"I hope you'll find us some French Canadians. With the English, I can't speak their language. But I managed to convince the swarthy handsome one with a head wound to repaint the chapel. He wasn't allowed to be outside in the sun, so at least he wasn't wasting his time."

They had reached the woods and were strolling beneath the green oak trees. It was ten o'clock in the morning, and a cold pure light slid beneath the trees without illuminating them.

"Did you know that I found a bicycle? There are no more inner tubes for a hundred kilometers around, but we put hay in the tires. It works very well. Are there inner tubes in Paris?"

"I don't know."

"If you find any, would you mind sending them to us? I'll pay you in eggs."

Mother Elisabeth had extraordinary energy. As she strode along, she beat the undergrowth with her stick. The Cat was holding her left arm.

"And what about eggs? Do you have eggs in Paris?"

"No."

The nun's face lit up.

"I was just thinking last night that if I sent two of the sisters to Paris with a hundred eggs every Sunday, to sell them in the parishes, we'd be as rich as Rockefeller. That way, I could afford to put fifty French Canadian airmen in the refectory and machine guns in the bell tower, and the Boche wouldn't last long!"

They emerged from the woods to find the sea opposite them. The Cat took off her socks.

"My daughter, tell me first of all whether Saint John is bathing," pleaded Mother Elisabeth, covering her eyes.

The Cat scoured the beach.

"No."

"Too bad."

The twinkle in the abbess's eye reappeared from behind her hands. She was staring at the horizon.

"Do you have a fiancé?"

"I think so."

"That's good. Wait for our Saint John here. He'll be back. And remember to pass by the kitchen before you leave. Ask for some brioche. We hear they're so hungry in Paris that people eat their own cats."

"Thank you very much, Mother," said the Cat, sitting down in the sand. "You won't get lost on the way back to the abbey?"

"Unfortunately not," called out Elisabeth as she headed off. "Take good care of yourself, my daughter. And if you ever decide to become a nun . . . We're full up here until the end of time. But for you, I'd make an exception."

And with that, she vanished. The Cat was very much in her thrall: she would have taken the veil just for the pleasure of hearing Mother Elisabeth solving the world's problems every morning.

For a few minutes, she had forgotten about her parents' fate. And now it was the sound of the sea that kept her outside of time. She was thinking of Andrei.

The Cat hadn't really lied to Elisabeth about having a fiancé. She had seen Andrei reappear one morning in the summer of 1937, in the same student boardinghouse on the rue du Val-de-Grâce, in Paris. He clearly wasn't in hiding, and she had followed him for a while through the city.

One day, he had met a man on the terrace of a café on the Grands Boulevards.

"The Bird is dead," the man had announced.

"The Bird?"

"Back there, that's how they refer to the boy."

"Which boy? Vango?"

"Be quiet."

Andrei appeared stunned.

"What about my father?"

"You came to your senses just in time. If you hadn't finally led us to the Bird, your father would be dead. But he is free, and he has been reunited with your family."

"I want to join them too."

"Do what you like," said the other man, standing up.

"You've fulfilled your mission. I've told Vlad to leave you alone."

"I'm going back to Moscow."

The man walked away, but Andrei stayed on. The Cat was sitting at the next table and, just as on that first day when she had approached him years earlier, she was having an ice cream. The Cat didn't dare pick up her spoon because her hand was trembling so much. Andrei left the terrace. Luckily, he forgot his violin.

The next day, she had glued a note to his window.

I've got your violin.

She had spent the night staring at the violin, its case open in front of her. She knew that for as long as she had the violin, he wouldn't leave. She dropped off another note the following week.

I might return it to you.

When she tried to leave a third note, there was a response from Andrei already on the window.

I don't want it anymore. Keep it.

This message worried the Cat. The next day, she returned via the gutter to deliver the several pages she had written. But the room was empty. He had fled, leaving an address in Moscow.

She hid the violin and mailed her letter.

A reply arrived two months later.

For two years, they had corresponded via these enigmatic letters. It took him four letters to grasp that the violin thief was a girl. And three more for her to write that the thief in question had been in love with him for four years.

When the war started, her letters no longer received a

reply. But the Cat kept on writing, adapting her tone according to her understanding of relations between France and Moscow. The first letters began with *Dear Enemy,* and the later ones with *My Fine Ally.*

And in his last letter to her, Andrei had addressed her as if she were his fiancée, telling her that he was enrolled in the army and that he was setting off for combat. *Farewell, my Emilie.*

For a few months now, the Cat had been hearing about the battles taking place in Stalingrad. The Soviet army was putting up an indefatigable resistance against the German assaults. The Cat horrified herself by imagining her fine ally fighting in the bloodstained snow.

In the middle of this daydream, in which Andrei's features became those of a messenger from the steppes, with his fur hat and frosty horse, the Cat, staring blankly at the sand, heard the seagulls cry and a voice next to her saying, "Emilie."

She opened her eyes. Vango was the only person, apart from Andrei, who was allowed to call her by that name.

"Saint John!" she called out.

She hadn't yet mastered the right body language to accompany such an exclamation. But she stood up and walked toward him with a cautious smile. The birds flew up.

"Hello, Saint John." She smiled, stopping a few paces away. He was carrying a wooden fishing pot and a large cork float.

Vango had come to the island of Noirmoutier in the immediate aftermath of Zefiro's death. Barefoot and with tousled hair, he resembled his seven-year-old self, even though he was almost four times that age. In the old days, the padre had often talked to him about La Blanche, where he had spent two decades. Zefiro's refuge at the beginning of the century had now become a refuge for Vango as well. Here he was known as Saint John the Evangelist. It was Mother Elisabeth who had given him this name, inspired by his full name: Evangelisto.

"I'm glad to see you, Emilie."

And he really was, because these days he had no other links with his past. She alone knew that he was alive. As far as the rest of the world was concerned, he had perished when the *Hindenburg* had gone up in flames. At last Vango had achieved what he had always craved: to erase all trace of himself, shaking off his pursuers in the burned grass at Lakehurst. He lived almost freely. He had renounced solving the mystery of his own life.

Farther along, in the shadow of the oak trees, were the graves of Zefiro and the unknown young man who had died alongside the padre in the *Hindenburg* explosion, and whom Vango had passed off as himself. The nuns had arranged the transfer of their remains.

On stormy days, the sea rose as high as these sandy graves, and Vango defended them with his spade, building walls, digging ditches, like a child entrenched in his sand castle.

A yawning noise could be heard coming from inside the wooden crate, which Vango had put down on the sand.

"It's for Christmas," he explained. "Will you be here?" He went over to the crate, and the Cat saw that it was teeming with greenish pincers and articulated bodies. She tried to poke a finger between the wooden bars, but Vango pulled her away sharply.

"Lobsters."

She followed him as they headed back through the trees.

The Cat had appeared at the beginning of the war, to ask for his help. Over time, Vango had agreed to become a correspondent for the Paradise Network. As far as Caesar, Mouchet, Sylvain, and their colleagues were concerned, Saint John was no ordinary agent. None of them had ever seen his face. He imposed certain conditions: Saint John would have nothing to do with any acts of violence, and he never left his refuge. This was the promise he had made to Zefiro.

One day, early on, he had been given a suitcase to hide, without any warning about its contents. On discovering that it was full of dynamite, he had refused to hand it back: he wanted to teach the other members of the Paradise Network a lesson, so that they never forgot his terms again. The explosive suitcase and its timer were still stashed away in the nuns' henhouse. Vango hadn't left this island since the summer of 1937.

When he and the Cat were close to the walls of La Blanche, at the edge of the forest, they climbed an enormous green oak tree and crept between its leaves. The gulls lost sight of them. Vango had tied the crate to his back. Then they made their way down a long branch that straddled the wall.

"Do you remember?" he asked the Cat.

She knew that he was picturing the chestnut tree above the park fence of the Jardin du Luxembourg, which had so often stooped to let them down into the deserted park at night.

The garden inside the abbey grounds was enormous. During the summer, the nuns even grew wheat and corn there. The enclosure wall continued farther than the eye could see. They took a path that flanked the wall. Despite being in the depths of a wartime winter, the garden was far from austere. Fragments of broken seashells glinted in the furrows of perfectly turned earth.

The Cat breathed in the smell of the algae as she followed Vango. The abbey buildings were behind them now, and after a few minutes' walk, they reached a greenhouse that was at an angle to the enclosure wall, propped up against a tiny house.

Ducking inside, the Cat was relieved to discover that the greenhouse was lukewarm. Crates of onions had been placed on the trestle tables. They closed the door behind them and entered the tiny house itself: this was where Vango lived.

"Tell me your news," he said.

The Cat went to sit close to a wood-burning stove, in which the fire had almost gone out.

"Mouchet's got a radio instructor who needs to be parachuted in on Christmas Eve night."

"Where?"

"Close to Chartres, I think. He's coming to train three men. It can't happen in Paris."

"And it can't happen here. The Germans have cars to help detect radio transmissions now. There was an alert with the last batch of Englishmen."

"This time they're French."

"It doesn't make any difference. I don't want the nuns in any danger."

Vango refused to negotiate. He had managed to break the

curse that had seemingly condemned all those around him to death. He only took risks for himself now.

"When your last batch of Englishmen was here, the Germans wanted to search the abbey. On one occasion, Mother Elisabeth had to keep them at bay with a hunting gun. She won't get away with it a second time."

The Cat fell quiet. The abbess hadn't mentioned this to her. Vango put some more wood in the stove, and the kettle started whistling.

"You want to protect people," she said.

"Yes."

"But they're all dying from being protected."

"Who?"

Vango was staring at her.

"The whole country," she said, "and beyond."

"Who?"

"Ethel."

He looked away.

"She's dying because you don't want her to suffer," the Cat continued. "She's dying of sadness."

Vango went outside. The Cat stayed on her own for several minutes by the fire before joining him. He was sitting on the stone wall of a cistern.

"You know what you're saying isn't true," he insisted. "Some people were saved by my death. Count them! And then count all the deaths in my life!"

The Cat knew all about this: Boulard and Andrei had been spared. If Vango hadn't disappeared, Ethel would doubtless have been eliminated, just like Father Jean before her, and

Zefiro, and perhaps Mademoiselle. Could Vango keep leaving a graveyard behind him?

"Ethel has lost everything," said the Cat. "All she has left is her brother, Paul."

"Is he better?" Vango wanted to know.

"Yes. He's serving as a pilot again for the British Air Force."

They looked at each other and smiled. By tallying up their friends like this, they counted a stubborn bunch—each individual keener and more headstrong than the next—and they found this comforting. They remained there together, out in the cold. They could smell the smoke from the fire, which the wind from the west blew back toward them.

Vango rubbed a pear against his jacket before giving it to the Cat. It was a Z pear, the variety that Zefiro had created by crossing the best strains in the orchard.

The Cat glanced at Vango's clothes: woolen vest, trousers with knees that had been mended a thousand times. The sisters fought among themselves to darn his clothes and stitch on patches like flags. Saint John was their convent's secret.

"Stay here until tomorrow," said Vango. "I'll have a think about your request for the parachutist."

The Angelus bell calling the nuns to prayer tolled above the chapel.

"What about your violin player?" added Vango. "Still nothing?"

The Cat shook her head. No news on that front.

Vango was cautious about asking the next question:

"And your parents?"

This time, the Cat turned her back on him and began to remove the dry thistles that had stuck to the bottom of her coat. Vango noticed her head rocking, and then he spotted some round blotches appearing on the stone. He had never seen her cry before.

"Where are they?"

"Nobody knows."

"Surely we can find out."

"No."

Her shoulders had stopped shaking.

"Mouchet has given me some mail that I haven't looked at yet," she added.

Vango gently reached for the envelope and opened it. He was silent as he scanned the bundle of papers and photos.

"This isn't about your parents," said Vango. "He's made a mistake."

The Cat was taken aback.

"In that case, I'm the one who's made the mistake. I've got to go."

"Wait. . . ."

"I must've muddled up the packets. I was supposed to give one to Caesar."

In the middle of the bundle, Vango had paused on a photo.

"Look, it's New York."

The postcard was of the heart of Manhattan, as seen from the sky. The tops of the towers rose up out of a sea of clouds. Vango leaned over to get a better view, just as he would have done from the window of the *Graf Zeppelin*.

Once again, he was walking at a height over the familiar sights of the city.

And, gently, the card with its serrated edge started moving. Vango couldn't keep it still in front of him.

"Put it all back in the envelope," the Cat told him.

"No. Wait!"

She held out her hand.

"Wait," repeated Vango.

A hand-drawn mark indicated the top of the Empire State Building. Above this mark was scribbled *1937,* in the same handwriting. But one single detail attracted his attention.

"What's wrong, Vango? Look at me!"

He wouldn't let go of the card.

"You're trembling, Vango."

When he finally turned to face her, the Cat scarcely recognized him.

THE LIST

In the large brown envelope, which had traveled in the Cat's belt, were two days' worth of investigation by Inspector Baptiste Mouchet. The results had been sufficiently interesting for him to inform Caesar, the leader of their resistance network, before officially handing his findings to Superintendent Avignon.

Returning from his clandestine meeting at the station, Mouchet had set to work. At the Quai des Orfèvres, his police colleagues had sniggered as they inquired about his vacation. He hadn't taken any leave for six months now. In order for him to remain beyond suspicion, his work record had to be spotless. So he concentrated on Superintendent Avignon's orders. He needed to find the list of guests to Max Grund's New Year's Eve party. Mouchet was glum about this assignment, which summed up the workload at headquarters: the police force divided its time between drawing room etiquette and crimes of state.

And so, on this particular morning, Mouchet was tasked with establishing the guest list as if he were the personal secretary of a marchioness.

He began by telephoning the restaurant.

La Belle Étoile was the rising star of Parisian restaurants: a small bistro in the Temple district that had become a force to be reckoned with in less than five years. The war hadn't interrupted its burgeoning success, even if the restaurant made no concessions to the occupying forces.

Mouchet got the brush-off when he called.

"Don't talk to me about that dinner!" roared the restaurant owner on the phone. "It's blackmail!"

And he had hung up so angrily that the inspector's ear was still ringing for several seconds afterward. Mouchet was about to try again when he noticed a line on the New Year's Eve invitation about the evening taking the form of a musical celebration. The singer's name was famous. He dialed the operator again.

"Put me through to La Lune Rousse in Montmartre."

Seconds later, he was connected to a weary-sounding trumpet player in the cabaret. The man, who was still sleeping off the previous night's show, told him to call a hotel on the rue de Rivoli.

"She should be there." He yawned. "But if you want her to show any interest," he added, "I'd advise you to put on a German accent."

The trumpeter burst out laughing and must have knocked himself out with the receiver, because a dull thud could be heard, followed by snoring.

Calmly, Mouchet telephoned the hotel. His call was transferred to room number twenty-two. It rang several times before a voice finally answered, "Allô?"

"Mademoiselle Bienvenue?"

"Put the small dog in the bath. I'm coming."

"I'm sorry?" said Mouchet.

"With bubble bath."

"Mademoiselle——"

"I was talking to the chambermaid."

"This is Inspector Mouchet speaking."

He was surprised at how cooperative Nina Bienvenue was. Despite all the commotion in the bathroom, despite the chambermaid shouting at the dog, despite the noise of the shower and Archibald's yapping, she didn't have to be asked twice to dictate the guest list for him. There were only twelve guests. She explained that she always requested the names of the guests, in order to prepare her songs.

"For example, does Offizier Grund appreciate 'Where Are All My Lovers?' Are you familiar with that song, Inspector?"

And she started humming into the receiver with her beautiful voice, which made Archibald bark for all he was worth. The chambermaid screeched in concert (she must have been bitten by the dog), but Nina Bienvenue sang on in heartrending tones.

Mouchet noted everything down and thanked her.

He put the list on his desk. Avignon had asked for very specific information, as a result of which the inspector had to research each individual guest. The first five names posed no difficulty: they were high-ranking German officials, including Max Grund and the chief of the Gestapo. The next four guests were French, and Mouchet was familiar with them. They were the Occupier's best friends in Paris, and they reported to the Vichy government every week. The Paradise Network had been keeping them under surveillance for two years.

The tenth guest on the list was one Augustin Avignon.

Mouchet began to wonder what his boss was doing in the thick of this rabble. Yes, Avignon had seized every opportunity to advance his career, and he referred to members of the resistance as "terrorists," but he didn't belong to the same species as the other individuals on the list. Mouchet had even, on occasion, found himself defending Avignon to his friends by explaining that his boss was only doing what most French people did: trying to get by while limiting the damage.

But from now on, in the police force, this sort of arrangement was becoming impossible. You had to choose. Six months earlier, thousands of police officers had organized a terrifying roundup. For Mouchet, the arrest of thirteen thousand Jews, from one Thursday morning to the following afternoon, had been an earthquake. And it was because of Caesar's rigid orders that he had agreed to stay at the Quai des Orfèvres after this nightmare, as a double agent.

Mouchet stared at the two last names on the list. The first was the Baron de Valloire. The second was a friend of the baron's, a foreign banker whose name Nina Bienvenue didn't know.

Mouchet began by researching Valloire. He couldn't find anything about the subject in his files. He simply opened an old Paris telephone directory for 1938 and found a Valloire *(Virgile Amédée de),* on the rue d'Anjou. Out of curiosity, he picked up the telephone directory for the following year. Valloire had disappeared.

He spent his lunch hour visiting the rue d'Anjou. The building gave onto a handsome paved courtyard. The concierge explained that the Baron de Valloire still owned the building but no longer lived there himself. She had never seen him. He rented the premises to the sales department of a cheese maker.

That afternoon, back at the Quai des Orfèvres, Mouchet cast another eye around the archives room. By pursuing his investigation in this way, he was no longer merely working for the satisfaction of Avignon. He was convinced that this meeting of Nazi officers and collaborators might interest Caesar. In the archives, under the letter *V*, he could find nothing for the name of Valloire, apart from three lines about an incident involving the theft of a goat in the commune of Valloire, in the department of the Savoie.

He was about to abandon his research when he noticed a short man in a gray shirt rummaging around in the boxes. It was André Rémi, a former inspector who had been demoted to his current job because he had effectively become deaf in 1940 during the Phoney War.

"What's in those boxes?" Mouchet called out loudly.

"Are you looking for something?" asked Rémi, turning around.

Mouchet wrote "Valloire" on his hand.

"Valloire? No, don't know that name. But take a look at the Boulard boxes before we throw them out."

"Boulard boxes?"

"No, I said: the Boulard boxes."

Rémi pointed to the pyramid of boxes he was stacking.

"Superintendent Boulard's paperwork amounts to our only legitimate archives. And it's being cleared out on Avignon's orders. Did you know Boulard, my boy?"

"No, I'm sorry to say. I arrived here from Marseille at the beginning of the year."

Rémi was becoming misty eyed.

"So, just like me, you know what a great man he was."

"No, unfortunately . . ."

"Please. The pleasure is all mine."

And he shook Mouchet warmly by the hand.

Mouchet found the name of de Valloire on a thick spiral-bound notebook. His last name was followed by a number. And this number led to a file. The file turned out to be a locked box, which he carried to his office. The box must once have contained some decent red wine, but it was now full of papers. Mouchet opened it and discovered these three strange words on the first document he came across:

VOLOY VIKTOR'S CONSTELLATION

Just below, among the forty-seven names Voloy Viktor sometimes went by, could be seen: Baron Virgile de Valloire.

The Viktor file had been definitively closed by Augustin Avignon in February 1942, on the same day that he had been appointed superintendent, but Mouchet was familiar with the arms dealer's name.

Boulard had continued doggedly with his investigation until the bitter end. He had kept track of Viktor from town to town, continent to continent, even during the war. In the box was a photo of one of Viktor's houses in Italy, and a postcard from New York with an arrow over his base for the year of 1937. There were lists of his contacts in each country, his associates, his friends . . . As for the foreign banker who would accompany Viktor on the evening of the thirty-first of December, Mouchet could make a reasonably informed guess as to who that might be.

The inspector put the most important photos and papers in an envelope. Then he encoded the guest list provided by the singer.

La Blanche Abbey

At the bottom of the garden at La Blanche Abbey, the Cat stared at the spot Vango's finger was pointing to on the post-card. The skyscraper was brand-new, with four spires covered in gold. It was taller than the Empire State Building and all the other towers.

"I spent months up there with Zefiro, spying on Viktor," said Vango.

The Cat couldn't understand what had come over her friend.

"I lived and slept in that tower, before it was completed," he went on. "One day, I even glimpsed the man who commissioned it to be built."

The Cat raised her eyebrows questioningly. She had never seen Vango in this state.

"Explain," she said.

"Finish what you're doing first."

She was decoding Mouchet's list.

"I shouldn't be doing this," protested the Cat. "This is a personal message for Caesar."

"Don't worry. I swear that it's for me too. You'll take it to him afterward."

When she had finished, she held out the piece of paper.

Vango took it and ran his eyes over it, before putting it back on the table.

The letter merely stated the information that Mouchet had pieced together: the party organized by Max Grund at La Belle Étoile restaurant on the thirty-first of December at nine o'clock. And at the end, in eleventh and twelfth places, were the two guests of honor: Voloy Viktor and a financier friend.

Mouchet's examination of Boulard's boxes had led to the conclusion that the financier in question was probably the man who had become Viktor's associate toward the summer of 1937, for industrial projects in Nazi Germany: the business-man known by everyone as the Irishman, and who signed by the name of Johnny Valence O'Cafarell.

Johnny Valence O'Cafarell.

Boulard had gone to investigate him in New York during the summer of 1939. It was the first time the superintendent had taken advantage of a novel idea that was now three years old: paid vacation. During his two weeks on the other side of the Atlantic, he had found out a lot more than the New York cops ever had. The Irish associate was every bit as much to be feared as Viktor.

Boulard had even heard a story that spoke volumes about the Irishman's reputation. According to one of his former chauffeurs, O'Cafarell had led a previous life in Europe, before arriving in America and making his fortune there. Learning that a young woman from his native country was looking for him and risked unmasking him, the Irishman had paid some poor worker from his ranch in New Mexico to assume his old name. He had eliminated the girl, and then had the man who now bore his name accused of the crime. The ranch worker was sentenced to death.

In one single crime, O'Cafarell had gotten rid of the girl who knew too much and ensured that his own past had been dissolved officially and before witnesses. It was a masterstroke.

Boulard wanted to meet with a New York judge in order to give him the results of his investigation, but war was grinding into action back in Europe, and he had returned hastily to Paris.

On seeing how shaken up Vango was, the Cat read the twenty lines of Mouchet's message, then glanced back at the postcard and at the name O'CAFARELL spelled out in giant metal letters on top of the tower with four spires. She blinked and read the message again.

"I slept under the letters of his name," groaned Vango. "And I didn't recognize it. I slept under the letters of his name."

The Cat would have liked to console her friend. But the truth was she didn't understand a word of what he was saying. Not a single word.

"I'm coming with you to Paris," said Vango.

He took a deep breath and almost smiled.

He was rediscovering feelings he thought had been buried. A seagull called out to him as it passed by. He looked up. For one last time, Vango was about to renounce his pledge to abandon the world and its violence forever.

BEFORE THE STORM

London, December 24, 1942, midnight

She was wearing a gray coat that came down to her feet. The bells of Saint Paul's and all the churches around had begun to ring out, at the same time as the warning sirens had gone off. Planes were flying over the blacked-out city. All the inhabitants had disappeared into cellars, but the sound of lone footsteps could still be heard in the street. The churches had been abruptly emptied on this Christmas Eve, and now the strains of carols floated up through the small basement windows. It was enough to rally the armies of mice in the basements of London with the Christmas message.

Ethel had been wandering around for hours. Having no desire to go to bed, she had visited various spots where people were dancing. At seven o'clock in the evening, she had passed by the hotel where she was staying and noticed that her own window was lit up on the second floor. It was raining. She had stood on the sidewalk outside, trying to recognize the shadow behind the window. It was bound to be her brother, keen to lecture her again about returning to Everland instead of remaining at the mercy of the bombs.

Ethel had been stopped during an alert the night before. She was found walking in the middle of an icy road in a summer dress. The police must have informed Paul. His air base was in Cambridge, but he had friends in London.

And so, seeing her window lit up, Ethel had fled. She didn't want to listen to any more reproaches from Mary or Paul, let alone from people she barely knew. The night porter at the hotel checked his watch and tutted when she came back late, and the garage mechanics had complained about the state of her car after she had reached speeds of nearly one hundred miles an hour traveling down from the north.

"That's no way to behave on the road. And look at the mud in your hair."

Hearing the mechanic give her a telling-off about her hair had put Ethel in such a temper that she had skidded twice as she sped off in the new Railton.

Ethel often reflected on what Joseph Puppet had said in the zeppelin about the way people looked at women. She had appreciated Puppet's freedom, his lightness of spirit. But the boxer had been killed when the airship went up in flames. What was left on this earth to keep her going?

Men pursued her with their best intentions. For a while, there had been attempts to introduce her to serious-minded young suitors. The previous summer, against her better judgment, she had agreed to attend Thomas Cameron's wedding. The results had been catastrophic: Ethel had looked sublime and the bride had made a scene, exploding at Thomas about the girl in the emerald-colored Indian outfit with little silver bells at her heels. That evening at the ball, two Cameron cousins had courted Ethel. After a dance or two, the first one began crying on his mother's shoulder over by the cloakrooms. The second had more luck. Ethel gave him her arm, led him into the woods, and lost him. He didn't return until noon the next day, by which time Ethel was already in Glasgow watching an air show.

Only a few realized that her arrogance, intensity, effrontery, and silence weren't simply part of her allure. Paul, Mary, and the Cat knew about her despair. Ethel's life had been in free fall for six years now.

On several occasions, Paul had tried talking to her about Vango's death. One evening, when he was looking for her, he had come across in his sister's bathroom the blue handkerchief that she had taken from the charred body on the grass at Lakehurst. She could only smile coldly in the mirror and shake her head, as if her brother were incapable of understanding the first thing about such a dreadful story, about a feeling of such complete emptiness. All grief is contemptuous, unassailable, perched at heights that nobody can reach. Perhaps we're too afraid of any comfort erasing what is left of the memories.

And yet this night spent roaming the streets of London was not the worst Christmas Eve of Ethel's life. She had collected a great many of them since her parents had died. No, this Christmas Eve was fine by her. Ethel was playing at dodging the groups of soldiers who were on duty because of the alerts. She wasn't afraid of the bombings. The few nights she had spent in air-raid shelters at the beginning of the war were happy memories. People shared stories, finally sitting next to neighbors they never greeted in the stairwell, as bottles of wine were dug out from the cellars. Ethel enjoyed these brittle moments. Her life was being protected. But one day she realized that she had nothing left to protect. She had tried to explain this to Paul with an odd question: "Do we bring the sand from the rivers indoors when it starts to rain?" And that was why she had made the decision to stay outside when the air-raid siren was sounded.

Suddenly, Ethel came out into a dead-end street and saw three soldiers behind the sandbags. She recognized one of them and deflected her gaze.

"Ethel!"

It was Philip, a friend of her brother's. She turned her back on them and headed off, flanking a brick wall. Philip had jumped over the barricades.

"People are looking for you, Ethel!"

She took the first road on the left. She knew that people were looking for her; that was why she was on the run. But it was hard to disappear in the deserted streets. Philip had spotted her turning the corner. When an airplane flew very low over the rooftops, Ethel couldn't hear Philip calling out anymore. She climbed a few steps, made her way between two buildings, and emerged into another street, only to spot that both ends were guarded: there was nothing she could do. Philip's voice wasn't far behind her. She advanced hesitantly, before a new siren sounded. In a matter of seconds, the doors of buildings were flung open and lights switched on. It was the end of the alert.

Men and women streamed out onto the pavement in their dozens. Ethel joined one of these groups. She saw poor Philip, who was puce in the face, going around in circles looking for her. She had known him in the old days, when he had studied in college with Paul. But now he was a family man with three or four children, or so she had heard, and he seemed very old as far as she was concerned.

She set off again in the direction of the hotel.

Two shadows could be seen moving behind the curtains in her room. She dug her heels into the cobblestones and tucked her fingers inside her sleeves. She was tired, and it was beginning to snow.

She wanted to be left in peace.

Paris, in a tower of Notre Dame, two hours later

Beneath the bell, Vango watched Simon the bell ringer toasting bread over the coals in the stove. His thick fingers were unafraid of the glowing embers, which he flicked away so the toast wouldn't burn.

"Whenever I see you, it always marks a big occasion." Simon smiled. "You should come more often."

He stirred two earthenware bowls filled with broth that were waiting by the corner of the fire.

"Do you remember the first time?"

"Yes," said Vango, recalling his ascent of the facade of Notre Dame, with the crowd at his feet.

"Well, a week later, I married Clara," said Simon. "It took the bishop five minutes to bless us in the sacristy."

The bell ringer held out a warm bowl and a piece of toast.

"The second time," he went on, "you looked just as lost to me. It was before the war, in thirty-seven. And my daughter was born eight days later."

"I didn't know."

"You spent at least two nights here. You said you were trying to find someone. . . ."

"The Cat."

"That's it. And you were going to disappear forever."

Simon slurped a mouthful of broth.

"And now here you are again."

"I'm not very reliable."

"I had a sense you'd be coming back, because I thought of you yesterday."

Vango seemed surprised.

"The reason my wife can't be with us," Simon announced proudly, "is that she's expecting in January."

"Really?"

"Our second child. Clara is with her mother in La Bourboule."

"Bravo!"

"Each time you appear, a child is born a week later!"

Vango smiled.

"I'm relaxed about it," said Simon. "It could be another girl. They've installed a motor for the bell. There won't be another bell ringer after me. So two girls would be fine. . . ."

He dunked his toast in the broth before adding, "And anyway, they don't make so much mess."

Vango nodded absentmindedly. A small gust of wind had crept inside the tower at Notre Dame.

"I won't ask what you're doing in Paris. . . ."

"No," said Vango.

"You can stay for as long as you like. I'd be delighted."

They watched the flames die down as Simon's eyes lit up.

"D'you remember how I hid you in the spire up there?"

"Yes."

"The police don't know it's hollow."

They each wrapped themselves in a blanket, on either side

of the stove. They could barely discern the bell in the gloom above them.

"I'll stay until the last night of December, if that suits you," said Vango. "There are some things I need to get ready. The Cat will pass by from time to time. After that, I really will go away."

"Really? Forever?" asked Simon.

Vango didn't answer.

"Luckily, I wasn't planning on having a big family," the bell ringer muttered to himself.

From time to time, in the darkness, the beating of pigeon wings could be heard. Each sound resonated inside the bronze bell.

Vango was thinking about the days that remained before New Year's Eve.

He slept very little. At half past four in the morning, the Cat arrived from the top of the south tower and woke him gently.

"Vango . . ."

"Emilie?"

"Yes, it's me. Is he asleep?"

"Listen!"

They could hear slow breathing. Simon was sound asleep.

"What have you got?" Vango wanted to know.

"I went to give the documents back to Caesar. There was a message for us in the shutter. The French agent has been successfully parachuted in from London. His code name is Charlot."

"Has he reached La Blanche?"

"No. He called Caesar from a village."

Nobody telephoned Caesar. Nobody ever met him.

Nobody knew who he really was. He led a public life that couldn't be compromised.

"Charlot managed to jump in time, but the plane was hit just afterward by the German antiaircraft fleet. He saw it fall."

Vango stiffened.

"The pilot has been reported missing. The plane plunged into a forest toward Mornes."

"Is there any chance of him making it out of there?"

"Very little. Caesar says we shouldn't do anything. The Germans will start looking for him there. And it's marshy too, so even if he's alive, he'll have a hard time shaking them off."

Vango was remembering the English aviators he had hidden. They were very difficult to transfer out secretly. The English were spoils of war for the Nazis.

"Charlot is coming to Paris tomorrow morning," said the Cat, lowering her voice. "He has a package for the network. We need to give him instructions for La Blanche. Nobody knows that you're not there waiting for him."

They fell quiet. Simon mumbled something and Vango strained an ear. The bell ringer was singing "Frère Jacques" in his sleep.

"Eight o'clock tomorrow morning in the cathedral, the chapel of the holy Virgin," ordered the Cat. "You'll be given the parcel. I'll collect it tomorrow evening."

"Wait!"

But the Cat had gone.

Vango hadn't signed up for this kind of mission. He had come on personal business.

He didn't sleep a wink for the rest of the night.

It was here, almost ten years earlier, that he had nearly

become a priest. What was he going to do now? Where was his path?

And yet he had never stopped believing. He felt as if he were in a deep valley flooded by a dam, where entire villages, paths, and hedgerows had vanished. Only the towers of churches appeared above the surface of the water. These bell towers were all that Vango had left.

At half past seven, he made his descent via the cathedral chevet. He walked around the square and passed the Portal of the Last Judgment.

London, at the same moment, dawn, December 25, 1942

Ethel walked into the hotel and requested her key at reception. A woman was busily eating biscuits, which she had crumbled into some milk. It looked rather like the porridge that was prepared for Lily the doe back at Everland, but the hotel proprietor could hardly be said to have doe's eyes. Instead, they were hidden behind lenses as thick as aquarium glass. She half stood up to take a disapproving look at Ethel's shoes, which were soaking the carpet.

"People have been waiting a long time for you."

"People?"

"There was one at first, then another. And a third's just arrived," the receptionist informed Ethel without blinking her fishy eyes. "They're upstairs. I gave them the key. They're officers. I don't want any trouble. And kindly remove your car from the sidewalk!"

Ethel climbed the two floors slowly. She followed the

landing all the way to the end, paused for a second, then turned the door handle.

There were two men smoking in her room. One of them was standing in front of the window. The other was sitting on the bed. They wore Royal Air Force uniforms. As they turned to face her, water could be heard running in the bathroom.

Paul must be washing his hands, thought Ethel, striding angrily into the room.

"Paul?"

"Good evening, Ethel."

It was Philip. He closed the bathroom door behind him.

"We've been looking for you since yesterday evening. Why did you run away when I called out to you?"

"Where's Paul?"

Philip turned somberly toward the officer standing by the window. The most senior of the three, and a colonel, he stubbed out his cigarette and took a deep breath.

"Paul's plane was shot down in France."

Ethel froze.

The colonel pursed his lips before adding, "You should prepare yourself for . . ."

Philip tried to put his hand on Ethel's shoulder, but she stepped away.

"The man he parachuted in is alive," said the other man. "Paul fulfilled his final mission. He was a tremendous pilot."

"Get out."

"I'm dreadfully sorry."

"I'll accompany you, Ethel," said Philip.

"Get out."

The men looked at one another, unsure how to react. Then the colonel gave a signal and all three of them headed for the door.

"If you need anything at all, please come to Cambridge. We'll be there for you. You will always be most welcome at the base."

Ethel stood alone in her room, listening to their footsteps as they headed downstairs, before she went over to the window. She wasn't crying.

The Napier-Railton was waiting for her just below, on the sidewalk.

Paris, Notre Dame, at the same time

Vango sat down next to a shadow that was kneeling in the chapel. The pair of them stayed there, motionless. They were alone. The last of the candles from the previous night were still alight, melting and dripping onto the floor.

The man looked very contemplative. He had put his leather briefcase behind him on the chair. Vango was wary of speaking to him.

When the man tried to sit up again, his briefcase was in the way.

"Is this yours?" he asked.

Vango only wavered for a second.

"Yes," he said, tucking the briefcase between his knees. The man was Charlot. Footsteps could be heard in the choir behind them. Somebody was drawing near.

"Are you due to meet Saint John at La Blanche?" Vango dared to whisper quickly.

"Who?"

"Saint John. He won't be there. Ask Mother Elisabeth. She'll explain."

"Thank you."

Charlot stood up and made the sign of the cross.

"Do you think the pilot is still alive?" Vango asked the parachutist as he was about to leave.

Charlot looked around and sat down again before speaking in hushed tones.

"The plane exploded. I saw it in flames. I've annotated the map of the zone with the location of the exact spot where the plane fell. That piece of paper is in the parcel you've got."

The footsteps were heading farther away now. Vango recalled the burned bodies from the *Hindenburg*: the chances of survival after a fire in midair were next to none.

"But I know the pilot," Charlot added. "To my mind, if he's still alive, he can get out of there."

Sounds of chairs moving in the cathedral choir. He lowered his voice.

"He had just recovered from his war injuries. I had already fought by his side."

"When?"

"During the Spanish Civil War, close to Madrid."

Three women, who sat down right in front of them, began reciting the rosary very quietly. It was impossible to carry on the conversation.

Charlot stood up for the last time. Vango couldn't let him go. He had one final question to put to him.

"Well, I shall pray for your friend," he called out in a clear voice.

"Thank you."

"What was his name?"

"Paul B. H."

Charlot headed off.

Vango put his head in his hands. He was imagining the burning plane spiraling over the forest in France. He was thinking of Paul. He tried to let himself be transported by the devotional chanting of the women in front. But Ethel's eyes haunted him. Would she be able to survive this?

THE SAUCEPANS OF ETERNITY

Paris, La Belle Étoile restaurant, December 27, 1942

"It's not what's supposed to happen," complained Bartholomew as he folded his duster. "You can't introduce a new character in the final chapters."

"Why not?" the restaurant owner called out from the other end of the dining room. "I could even introduce two of them if I liked!"

"I think it shows a lack of respect."

"I don't give a stuff about respect, Bartholomew. Clean that window and let me get on with my work."

Casimir Fermini resumed his furious bashing on his typewriter. He was approaching the end of his first novel. Bartholomew and all the restaurant staff had read each page as it was written. They offered opinions and suggested changes. They were already convinced that their boss would become a luminary writer elected to the French Academy.

Fermini was working at the back of his restaurant, on a table with a red-and-white-checked tablecloth. From time to time he looked up and watched Bartholomew cleaning the window across which the words LA BELLE ÉTOILE appeared in an arc. Viewed from the inside, the golden looping letters were back to front, a sort of negative image written in an oriental script.

Casimir Fermini had inherited the establishment on the death of his aunt in 1929. She had raised the young Casimir. Until the outbreak of the First World War, she and her husband had run a small but highly reputable café-restaurant on the premises, which didn't yet bear the name of La Belle Étoile. Uncle Fermini was an impressive cook. Business was good. They even had ten tables outside in summer, a menu with four main courses to choose from, and, for years, a very pretty waitress who was a sign of the restaurant's prosperity and who produced wonders as a chef's assistant.

In 1914, at the first sound of cannon fire, Monsieur Fermini died. Panic-stricken, his wife, who had never touched a saucepan, closed the kitchen and nailed up the door. Fifteen years followed in which the word *restaurant* was banned on-site. The establishment turned into a simple café. There were tears when the pretty waitress was sent away; the menus were withdrawn, and the tables removed from the pavement. Young Casimir spent those years serving glasses of fortified wine and liqueurs. On his aunt's death, the first thing he did was to reinstate the word *restaurant* above the window. But, to begin with, he only served omelets.

Shortly before the war, the food took off without warning. Omelets went by the wayside, with or without bacon, and customers lined up on the sidewalk for a table to become available. It was now called La Belle Étoile. And since this odd-shaped lane in the Temple district had very little passing traffic, Fermini set up tables in the middle of the street. When a car was heard approaching, everyone stood up and pushed their chairs to the side, complaining. The police closed their eyes in exchange for a taste of olives or wild asparagus.

The following year, weary of bringing the tables in with every downpour, Fermini also rented the premises opposite. And so the restaurant was spread over two buildings. A large dining room was opened on the other side of the street, up on the second floor. The kitchen also moved, to the ground floor opposite. There were fifty covers in total, with the historical dining room remaining at number eleven. Six waiters spent their lives crossing back and forth bearing trays.

The war and the Occupation were a new challenge for the establishment. To begin with, Casimir Fermini was faced with the temptation of contraband. For a price, you could get any product you liked, even though the city was hit by famine. Trafficking made a mockery of ration tickets. Foie gras and plump chickens were easy enough to find. But, from the autumn of 1940, La Belle Étoile flaunted itself as one of the rare eateries that rejected the black market outright. The list of dishes was divided by five and the length of the line doubled. On Saturdays, it extended as far as the Carreau du Temple market.

These days, there was only one menu at the restaurant, with starring roles for rutabagas, Jerusalem artichokes, potatoes, and dozens of herbs and wild leaves, which the waiters set off with the chef to pick in the countryside by the gates of Paris before daybreak. They returned on bicycles laden with crates of greenery and seeds, like a florist's wheelbarrow. Back in the kitchen, miracles took place. The Jerusalem artichokes were transformed beyond all recognition, as were the dandelions.

The restaurant afforded itself only one luxury. A luxury that arrived by horse and cart twice a week. A luxury that was stored in a vat and closed with a padlock. Butter.

A farm in Normandy had three dedicated cows whose job it was to provide this butter, and Casimir Fermini himself, on the request of his chef, took the train in order to pay a surprise visit and inspect the eating habits of these three cows. They lived in a peaceful valley with grass above their shoulders. They drank from a pond of clear water that was barely interrupted by frogs. They had no idea there was a war on. In their left ears, a silver ring engraved with LA BELLE ÉTOILE served as a reminder of their noble and exclusive calling.

Casimir may have been the restaurant owner, but he knew what he owed his chef for making La Belle Étoile's success possible. And so he respected the chef's whims. For some time now, however, the small matter of butter had served as an excuse for the German authorities to poke their noses into the kitchen.

The Nazi officers sniffed out everything that was fine and good in Paris. They always had perfect taste. And they wasted no time in tracking down this extraordinary eatery, far from the areas of Paris they were accustomed to frequenting. But the occupying army received no special treatment at La Belle Étoile.

The restaurant was always full. When a table became free, customers would rush in from all sides to stake their claim before the overdisciplined soldiers had a chance to sit down. In the summer, Fermini paid for two musicians to play in the street, for the enjoyment of those waiting for a table as well as his customers. Each time a green uniform appeared at the end of the street, the musicians would play a song from before the war that proclaimed: *"Everything passes in life, everything passes with time. . . ."*

The German military command had paid a visit to the kitchens, on the hunt for rationed products. The *kommandantur* had been surprised to find cheap boxes of root tubers, onions, garlic, two chickens barely big enough to make enough stock for the entire week, and bunches of wasteland plants soaking in bowls.

But at the back of the kitchen they found the butter.

To be strictly accurate, there were sufficient quantities to butter everyone's toast in the Department of the Seine. Casimir described his cows lovingly. But he realized, when faced with the stiffness of the *feldkommandant,* that he would have to make some kind of concession if he didn't want his restaurant to be shut down for good.

Casimir agreed to provide the large dining room on the second floor for the New Year's Eve party. In exchange, he would be left in peace for another year. This gave rise to arguments with his chef, but the smell of butter melting on the stove and the sound of spinach sweating in a frying pan got the better of both the restaurant owner and his chef. There was a war on. People could do without almost anything. Except butter.

Sitting behind his typewriter, Casimir asked Bartholomew for a café crème. The waiter put down his duster and disappeared briefly before returning with a cup on a tray. Because of the restrictions, there wasn't any real coffee, but the barley was roasted in-house and ground with three grains of pepper. The result was, if anything, superior to the coffee of old.

"Tell me, Bartholomew, how would you describe the ear of a young lady?"

"The ear?"

"At the end, you see, Marcel sits Rosalinde on his knees . . ."

He scrolled the paper in his typewriter back up in order to read the last few sentences. In his book, he had given himself the name of Marcel. He was telling the story of his restaurant as he had dreamed it.

"Listen: *'Sitting in the kitchen, Marcel had her chignon in one eye. But with the other eye, he had a good view of the ear of his fiancée, which was like a . . .'* That's the bit I'm not too sure about. Like a . . ."

"A flag?"

Casimir Fermini stared at his employee.

"Genius. Like a flag."

"The idea just came to me," Bartholomew admitted modestly.

"Now, in that case, I should introduce some wind a bit earlier; it'll read more powerfully that way. *'Sitting in the kitchen, with the window open, Marcel had her chignon in one eye. The wind was blowing forcefully. But with the other eye, he had a good view of the ear of his fiancée, which was like a flag.'* Yes, that's good. But I can do better."

He hunched over his keyboard. A man knocked at the door.

"It's beautiful," said Bartholomew, who was already picturing his own name under the boss's name on the title page of the book.

Outside, the man squashed his nose against the glass and peered in.

Bartholomew waved frantically.

"Look at that. He's going to make a mess of my window!"

The waiter rushed over to the door and stuck his head outside.

"We're closed until midday."

"It's about a reservation."

"We don't take reservations here, monsieur."

The man spoke with a foreign accent.

"I've come from a long way away; I'm off to explore the countryside. I won't be back until the evening of the thirty-first of December. I'm worried the restaurant might be full."

"The restaurant is always full."

Casimir Fermini stood up and went over to join them.

"Bartholomew, kindly treat this gentleman with due respect."

The gentleman in question gave an embarrassed smile.

"Dear friend, you are very lucky. I've never taken a reservation before. Never, I swear on the memory of my aunt Régine. But today, I'm going to do so for the first time, because less than one minute ago I completed my life's work: my first book."

"Congratulations," said the customer, who was visibly touched.

Bartholomew also seemed rather emotional. Casimir Fermini slid his right hand inside his suspenders, to the side. He was looking forward to stroking the ceremonial sword he would receive upon his investiture as a member of the French Academy.

The Saucepans of Eternity," he said.

"I beg your pardon?"

"That's the title."

"Bravo," said Bartholomew.

The customer was blushing. He had always admired

French culture, its fashion, its literature, and its cuisine. And now here he was in Paris at last!

They shook hands.

"Follow Bartholomew; he'll write your name on the slate."

"My name is Costa."

"You can have the little table at the back, where I work."

"That would be an honor for me."

"You'll be very comfortable there, Monsieur Costa. There's going to be a fancy-dress party in the dining rooms opposite. I hope they won't make too much noise."

The waiter escorted the customer to the door, then retraced his steps.

"A fancy-dress party?" whispered Bartholomew.

"It's better for the restaurant's reputation. We'll say they're wearing fancy dress."

Unconvinced, Bartholomew headed off. Casimir Fermini pulled the page out of the typewriter. And, very softly, he read the last lines: *"Sitting in the kitchen, with the window open, Marcel had her chignon in his eye. The wind was blowing forcefully. But with the other eye, he had a good view of the ear of his fiancée, which was billowing like a flag. And the flapping noise joined with that of his own heart."*

Lower down, the rest of the page would remain blank. He had finished his book.

Everland, Scotland, at the same time, December 27, 1942

Mary could finally hear Ethel's car in the distance, the sound of its engine muffled by the thick mist.

She had been waiting anxiously since Christmas Eve. The

Royal Air Force officers had telephoned the castle when they were looking for Ethel. They had informed Mary of Paul's disappearance. She had managed to stay calm until they had hung up, at which point she had let out a long howl as she ran down the corridor.

That night, Mary went outside barefoot. Wearing a shawl that trailed behind her in the grass, she made her way over to a tree, to the grave of Ethel's and Paul's parents. Mary railed against them with all her might. She hurled everything she could find: sticks and frozen clods of earth. She said horrible things to them. They had abandoned their children and now they were going to reclaim them one by one. Then, weeping, she picked up her shawl and reinstated the bunch of flowers she had knocked over, before turning her back on them.

When she heard Ethel's Railton, more than twenty-four hours later, she was asleep on a chair in the entrance hall. Mary headed out onto the steps. The car pulled up in front of her. Ethel switched off the engine but remained sitting behind the steering wheel. She stared at Mary, who nodded, to indicate that she had heard the news.

Ethel's face was unrecognizable. It was ten o'clock in the morning but still fairly dark. She started up the engine again and drove off, not reappearing until the evening. All the staff stood in a line in the entrance hall. No sooner had Ethel kissed Mary than she shut herself in her parents' room. The housekeeper opened the door in the middle of the night and scooped Ethel up off the sofa in front of the fire, which had gone out. She managed to carry the only surviving member of the B. H. family to her own bed.

* * *

The next day, when Mary brought her a cup of tea, Ethel was gone.

They searched for her all day. She had left her car behind. Peter the gardener and his son, Nicholas, combed the woods. Mary scoured the attics. That evening, when Nicholas returned to the castle, he had an announcement to make:

"The plane . . ."

"What plane?" asked Peter.

Nobody knew that Ethel's plane even existed.

"The plane has disappeared."

Later that night Mary noticed, open on the bed where Ethel had slept, a book that Paul had brought back from India for his sister years earlier. She read a few lines. The chapter was entitled "Jatinga." It was about some species of birds that, in a valley in Jatinga, northern India, hurl themselves against trees and cliffs during some seasons, in order to die. The author concluded with the words: "How great must be their despair."

Mary knelt against the bed and wept.

Outside, the moon was rising. Lily the doe trotted between the box hedges, keeping an eye on the darkened castle. Everland resembled a tree struck by lightning, bereft of what had kept it alive, with only the mournful hooting of an owl behind its hollow bark.

Paris, December 28, in the evening

The wind and rain were lashing against the towers of Notre Dame. The Cat found no one below the bell, but the fire was still alight. She tried to dry off her clothes in front of the flames, turning slowly like someone on a spit. Then she heard the wooden staircase creak, and Simon the bell ringer appeared. He was carrying a bundle of sticks covered in feathers, so he must have been foraging for firewood from the old birds' nests under the cathedral roofs.

He saw the Cat and immediately tossed a few twigs onto the fire. Then he climbed up to retrieve an armful of fabric from the bottom of a suitcase. He had only met the Cat on one occasion, when she had shown up with Vango a little before Christmas.

"These are my wife's clothes. Put them on."

"No, thank you. I'm already drying out."

"I can go downstairs if you're embarrassed."

"I'll be fine. Where is he?"

"He said he'd be back."

"Can I wait for him?"

"You can."

Simon stoked the fire with some more nest remains.

In Caesar's shutter at the Palais-Royal, the Cat had just dropped off the parcel from London brought over by Charlot. She had seen the boss for the first time. He had come out onto the balcony.

"Hello, Marie."

"Are you Caesar?"

He held out some papers.

"I believe these belong to you. Mouchet told me that you were interested in the Atlas family."

"I got the mail muddled up. Yours is in the shutter now. I'm sorry."

"I'm the one who's sorry," the man replied. "I'd have liked to have been able to do something for those people. But it's too late."

Clearly, he had figured out the Atlases' relationship to the Cat.

She gave him the map that traced the descent of the English airplane that had been hit. And, from the balcony shutter, he picked up the details about the New Year's Eve party at La Belle Étoile.

He opened the packet in front of her and cast his eye over the guest list. When he had finished reading, she thought she saw him stagger for a moment.

"Do you need me?" asked the Cat.

"No. Good evening, Marie."

The Cat felt as if she'd been living a secret life since she was born. She was used to it. She had nothing to lose. But him? She wondered how such an elegant man experienced his double life. Caesar looked like an important Parisian, the kind she saw when she climbed the fronts of buildings in the chic districts. There were bound to be ten guests waiting for him downstairs, feasting on oysters. None of them knew who he was. He had wandered away from the dining room to read his messages. But in spite of his sandalwood eau de cologne and his double-breasted silk jacket, Caesar would be gunned down within the hour were he to be unmasked.

He waved seriously at the Cat and left the balcony.

She headed off over the rooftops.

* * *

The Cat was watching the blaze of twigs beneath the bell at Notre Dame, as the smoke escaped via a metal pipe, which vibrated with the air currents. The bell ringer was feeling ashamed about the state of his den. When Clara was there, she made everything look more homey. He busied himself gathering up scraps of food onto a chopping board.

"Would you like an egg?" he asked. "I've found one."

"No, thanks; I'll be off soon. I just need to tell Vango something and then I'll leave."

"You've got time for an egg."

"Really?"

"Vango told me it would take two or three days."

The Cat leaped to her feet. "What?"

"He set off to find a friend in the provinces."

"A friend?"

"Yes. He showed me the map. In the middle of a forest. I'm not sure what kind of friend he's talking about. A weasel or a bear . . ."

"Whereabouts?"

"Near to Chartres. But he said he would be back in three days' time at the latest. He's expected at a New Year's Eve party. I think he wants to take his bear to it."

The Cat was furious. She had fallen into Vango's trap. He had copied Charlot's map before giving it to her, presumably with the aim of finding the pilot. She wished she hadn't wrenched him away from his island.

Saint John was out of control.

28

HORSES FOR SLAUGHTER

Mornes Forest, northern France, December 30, 1942

It was at the forest edge: a pretty log cabin with hearts cut out of the shutters. A ribbon of smoke escaped from the chimney. Birds played in the snow on the roof. The entrance was via a door that was too low, next to a window with patterned curtains. But instead of seven dwarfs in the living room, there were seven strapping men in German uniform and, in front of them, a woman sitting on a stool with a glass of water in her hand.

The log cabin served as the German headquarters in the hunt for the pilot who had disappeared.

Madame Labache didn't look much like Snow White. She was short and toothless, with two red braids wrapped around her mouse-gray face. Beneath her skirt, she wore boots with steel spurs. In her lap, she clung firmly to a brand-new handbag.

She lived a few kilometers away, in a tumbledown farmhouse that smelled of old kennels. Three years earlier, she had graciously rounded up the horses of all the owners who were leaving for the free zone. Madame Labache kept these horses by a barn and sold them, one by one, to a butcher in Dreux. The price doubled each year because meat was in such short supply.

A soldier stepped forward. He was interpreting for his superior.

"The woman can confirm that she heard the engine."

The leader shouted back that this woman had been wasting their time for twenty minutes now. She had said she had an important revelation to make, had insisted on having a glass poured for her, had spent a long time rearranging her skirts, and had then proceeded to talk about her work, her barn, and the necessity of finding hay as quickly as possible.

"My animals can't live on thin air. I'm short of hay."

"Lieutenant Engel is informing you that everybody for fifty kilometers around heard at least one engine on Christmas Eve," explained the interpreter, "because three planes were giving chase to a fourth for an hour. And he would also like you to know that he does not sell hay."

"The lieutenant is quite right about the noise on Christmas Eve," agreed Labache, sounding too friendly. "I have twelve horses and none of them got a wink of sleep that night. As for the hay, we'll talk about it later. He's not wrong when he says it's been a problem for me this winter. I see that Monsieur knows all about horses. . . ."

She gave a sly smile while twiddling with her red hair.

"I am providing you with this information with no thought of personal gain. Far be it from me to waste anyone's time by telling you about my problems with my neighbor who has a ton of hay but refuses to sell me any of it, because such stories won't interest you. And I wouldn't dream of mentioning what kind of people he hosts in secret, at what time, what sort of company he keeps, and all the rest of it. . . . No. I don't get involved in politics, me."

The soldier was of two minds about translating these overtures. His superior slowly smoothed his jacket collar in order to remain calm.

"I wouldn't have come all the way here today to talk to you about that, or about the airplanes at Christmas," Madame Labache went on. "I'm busy enough as it is. And it's a good forty-five minutes' walk from my house, if you take the short-cut. Or an hour, if you walk around the woods and the marsh over by La Crapaudière."

"Madame," said the translator, "I would advise you to cut—"

"I am cutting, young man, and straight to the point. But you keep interrupting me. I'm an honest woman, trying to help out as best she can!"

The wooden floor creaked beneath the weight of the soldiers. They had occupied this forest hut since the day after Christmas in order to direct the hunt for the pilot and the plane that had disappeared. The searches hadn't yielded anything. A large part of this vast forest was flooded, which complicated their task. There was no trace of either the aviator or the plane.

They'd had high hopes for this woman horse-rearer. But not anymore. Then, just as they were about to send her packing, she paused for dramatic effect before announcing:

"Gentlemen, I am here to tell you about the airplane engine I heard last night."

"What?"

"Translate!" she ordered.

The interpreter was pressed back into action. And the lieutenant finally stopped rocking on the table.

"Last night?" queried the interpreter.

"Yes, monsieur," confirmed Madame Labache, stroking her handbag as if it were a little rabbit.

"A big plane?"

"No."

"Madame," said the young soldier, leaning over her, "during the past three days, there have been cars patrolling the paths by the felling area at night."

"I am perfectly well aware of that."

"You have been confused by those engines," he whispered. "The plane fell on Christmas Eve. . . ."

The lieutenant uttered one word in German: *"Beweis."*

"Evidence," translated his interpreter.

She shrugged.

"In that case, you'd better come back with me, and I'll show you."

"So you've got an airplane in your bedroom, Madame Labache?" said Lieutenant Engel slowly, with a smile on his lips.

"Not exactly, Lieutenant. In my barn."

The silence thickened as she scratched her spurs on the floor. The lieutenant sighed. He had no confidence in this woman, but that was probably a good sign. Ever since he had been in the role of Occupier, he knew that he should only count on the most underhanded of individuals. Everything that he hated in life—bitterness, jealousy, cowardice—he now had to seek out and cultivate on a daily basis, among those who might further his cause.

"The airplane landed opposite my house," Madame Labache told the soldiers in the hut. "I had switched off all the lights, so they probably thought the farm was abandoned. The horses were tethered under the trees. And in the morning, I found the airplane hidden in the barn."

"What about the pilot?"

"No pilot."

The lieutenant issued a few orders. Someone should be sent. A soldier was duly assigned. Madame Labache wanted to talk about her neighbor's hay again but realized this wasn't the moment. The lieutenant was already hunched over his maps.

And so she left with her soldier, her boots, and her handbag.

The lieutenant remained with his men. He pointed to the eastern part of the zone on the map, and the thirty hectares of enclosed marsh area in the middle of the woods. The answer surely lay there.

Tentatively, Vango entered the house. The smell was disgusting, but the farm seemed to be inhabited. A yellow straw mattress had been left on the floor in front of the fireplace. Clothes were drying on a line and there was a bowl, some hard bread, a hammer, and a leather whip on a stone table.

Vango touched the whip. He also found two new horseshoes and some nails. A horse. That's what could save him.

He went outside again and noticed a barn a bit farther off. Many of the roof tiles had fallen into the grass. Perhaps he would find a horse there. The place where Paul's plane must have crashed was still several kilometers away. There could be no better means of exploring the forest and the marsh than on horseback.

As Vango was approaching the barn, the sound of whinnying diverted his attention toward the woods that started a hundred meters behind him. He turned back and ran toward the forest edge, where he saw some horses tethered to a tree. Perhaps twelve of them, bunched up like grapes. How long had they been there? They looked famished. Vango went over to one of them and stared at it.

He wanted to untether the horse, but the rope had been obsessively tied to the trunk. Without any kind of pocket-knife, it took him several minutes to undo the cluster of knots. A dangerous maniac must have spent hours tying up the horses. The final knot gave way.

All the other horses turned toward the happy chosen one. Vango led it over to the grass, where he let it graze. The horse's companions were becoming restless. Vango spoke softly into its ears and climbed onto its back. Sated by the rich grass, the animal didn't put up a fight. Vango had managed to assemble a makeshift bridle from the rope. The horse responded perfectly, as if rediscovering old reflexes. They were ready to go.

But on seeing the doleful looks from the other horses, Vango made first for the barn. Surely he would find an ax or a sickle in there to give the herd its freedom. His horse was enjoying galloping again. The barn door looked closed, but some of the boarding had fallen down on one side, and Vango made for the opening. Horse and rider crouched at the same moment to squeeze through. When they stood up again, there in the half-light of the barn, Vango saw an airplane.

It was a small white biplane with its two sets of wings, one on top of the other. It didn't look like a fighter plane, or the Whitley two-engine planes out of which soldiers could jump at an altitude of two hundred meters, but Vango couldn't help thinking of Paul's plane. How, given that it had been struck down in midflight, could it be here, intact, with its angel's wings? And what about Paul? Where had he gone? Slowly, Vango circled the vehicle. The other horses were whinnying in the distance.

Vango was on the verge of conceding that this plane wasn't the one he was looking for when, painted against a white background near the propeller, he noticed the following small red letters:

EVERLAND B. H.

A door creaked behind him. The horse turned around.

"Halt!"

A short red-haired woman was staring at him with a glint in her eye. Next to her, a German soldier aimed his submachine gun at Vango.

Three kilometers away, Paul's body was floating in the marsh water of what appeared to be a flooded forest. A single piece of metal was visible on the surface, a little farther off. It was all that remained of the plane.

From time to time, a few bubbles rose up out of the silt.

Paul's fingers moved on the surface of the water. He was wiggling them ever so slightly to feel what strength was left in his hands.

He had ejected himself from his seat, on Christmas Eve, a split second before the wings caught fire. But the blast from the explosion had prevented his parachute from opening properly. It was a horrific fall. Crashing into a tree, he had broken both legs as he rebounded from branch to branch. The marsh water had saved his life.

The first night, he managed to tie himself to a trunk, using his parachute cords to keep his head above the water. In the morning, he had to make a choice. It was raining, and his legs hurt with every movement, but thanks to the shallowness of the marsh, he could crawl about. So Paul set off, not knowing where he was going, with only his arms to propel him, covering a few dozen meters each hour. He was eking out the three portions of survival rations he had in his parachute. At night, he still slept a little, tied to a branch. He suffered from the cold as soon as he stopped moving. So as not to poison himself with the marsh water, he stretched his waxed cape across some branches. He waited and collected the rain for his drinking water.

On the morning of the twenty-eighth of December, Paul reached a spot where the forest gave way to dry land, and he thought that he was saved. But when he tried to stand on the ground, he realized the game was up. With his broken legs, it was impossible to move about on dry land. He was turning into a fish. He fell back into the water and felt his last ration in his pocket. He knew that the hunger and the cold would kill him soon.

He thought of the provisions still inside his plane. And so he set off again, backward this time, crawling once more through the black water. He no longer recognized the shredded skin hanging off his hands. It took him a day and a night to find the wreck. Most of it had been engulfed in the mud as a result of the impact. The airplane was no longer visible from the sky. Paul managed to open the boxes. He wept as he ate and drank, lying on the vehicle's flank.

He had fallen asleep there and now, floating on the water, he didn't know what to do next. The Germans would explore the marsh. In the end, they would find this wreck. But he would no longer be alive. He stared up at the trees above him.

Paul remembered a trip he had made to France as a child, with his mother, who was pregnant at the time. In the middle of winter, they had eaten lunch together by the banks of a river. There was a war going on back then as well, but they were far away from the front. They tried in vain to catch fish with their hands between the rocks, then ran to warm their fingers over the car engine. He still dreamed about that warmth and his mother's hands next to his. When they reached the villages in the evening, the hoteliers—on seeing a woman who was eight months pregnant braking abruptly in front of the door and holding out the keys to an imaginary valet—would run to wake up the midwives. Paul took his place behind the steering wheel and moved the car. He was eight years old.

His father met them in Paris on Christmas morning. But Ethel waited a while longer inside her mother. She wanted to be born in Scotland.

These were Paul's first memories of France. And he now knew what his last memories would look like: a canopy of branches in a white sky.

He heard a noise in the water a few meters away from him. They were coming. This time, he didn't have the strength to escape. He stayed where he was, and felt he was slowly disintegrating like a water lily into the water.

The noise was getting closer. Small waves rippled up to his

cheeks. Someone was running through the water now toward him. He felt himself being lifted up, and he let out a cry.

It was Ethel.

He hadn't seen that smile for a long time. It belonged to an Ethel from another era. It didn't even occur to him to wonder where she had come from, or which marsh creature had made her rise up out of the silt. She was there, a will-o'-the-wisp emerging from the water.

As for Ethel, she could see only one thing: her brother's face telling her he was alive. She could feel the pressure of his hand on her arm. From far away, she had caught sight of him motionless. She had assumed that she had arrived too late. Throughout this adventure, she knew that she had defied common sense: entering France at impossible altitudes, lack of oxygen, navigating at random in a plane that looked more like a paper toy. Ethel was equipped with nothing more than the two sets of numbers telegraphed by Charlot from the base in Cambridge, which she had traveled to collect before returning to Everland. Two sets of numbers: the coordinates of Paul's wreck. She had told the colonel that she wanted to have them engraved on her parents' headstone. Touched by this romantic gesture, he had even given her a map of the operation rolled up in a tube.

"This will be for your children, one day."

But she hadn't waited to have children before looking at the map. From the outset, she was haunted by a single image, which was of a butterfly crossing a battlefield, twirling between the bombs and the barbed wire. To succeed, you had to be a butterfly rather than a tank or a foot soldier.

"I can't walk," said Paul, shivering.

"I'll help you."

She tried to get him to stand up, but he stopped.

"No. Forgive me."

He looked at her sorrowfully, ashamed of his lack of strength. She didn't force him. She was smiling because he was still alive. They stayed like that for several minutes, without moving.

And then Ethel said, "A horse."

Vango was sitting against the wooden slats of the barn wall, still under threat from the soldier with his weapon. The horse's rope was tied to the propeller. The madwoman with red hair and silver spurs had disappeared almost an hour ago, in order to fetch German backup from the forest hut. The reinforcements wouldn't be long now.

The soldier stared at Vango, convinced that this was the pilot they were looking for. Vango had addressed him in German, denying everything and claiming that he was a Parisian student who pilfered from the countryside over the holidays. But the soldier reckoned that Vango would only speak such good German if he were English. He arrived at this conclusion while dangerously teasing the trigger on his gun.

As for Vango, he was thinking of Paul. They still hadn't found him, so all was not lost. The plane was in one piece and bore the name of Everland in small red letters. Vango's thoughts also ran on to Cafarello and Viktor, who would already be in Paris by now. In just over twenty-four hours, it would be too late. The shadows of his parents, of Zefiro, and of so many others haunted the silence of this barn. But could he be certain that these shadows were clamoring for revenge?

Briefly, Vango closed his eyes, then opened them again. His gaze came to rest on the mysterious white plane. And there, beneath the machine, huddled up against the wheel, he saw someone.

He saw her, but his mind refused to recognize her.

And yet Ethel was staring at him with those piercing green eyes of hers.

The man with the submachine gun had one ear cocked. He was hoping to hear the lieutenant's car approaching. His arms were growing weary under the weight of the weapon. He had never asked to be here, a thousand kilometers from home, wearing this uniform or wielding this piece of metal. Back in his hometown, he was a tailor. And yet he knew that he would open fire at the slightest movement. He would become the man who had killed the Englishman. Perhaps he would be granted leave before Easter.

Ethel let the terror inside her slowly subside. Before going to untie one of the horses from under the trees, she had entered the barn to check on her plane. She'd had no idea that by poking her head through the planks, she was crossing a holy line. Vango had been dead for six years, and yet here he was, sitting in the straw in front of her. Vango was dead, but his arms were around his knees. By poking her head into the hole in this boarding, she had found life again. And so she had crawled as far as the plane, where he had seen her, in turn.

In what amounted to barely a few seconds, a turbulent wave flowed between them: a surge of life, fears, memories, navigating a narrow path. It was as if they were part of the human tide that had formed the exodus in June 1940, along the main roads heading out of Paris, when the Germans came.

But all this happened without a sound, without a cry, without a Klaxon blast, as if in a silent movie.

Being face-to-face turned Vango's heart inside out. His life was right there watching him; his life was crouched down under the white wing of an airplane. Here was his true desire. Ethel had knocked at the door, on the eighth of August 1929, when she had walked into the kitchen of the *Graf Zeppelin* in the New York skies. Now, years later, he was finally opening that door for her. Ethel was also seized by a powerful energy. She could sense Vango's world being turned upside down.

The soldier stood up. A car! He had just heard a car. As he lowered his weapon, he was struck by a log at the base of his neck. He collapsed.

The assailant was Ethel. The log rolled on the ground. The rumbling of the cars was drawing nearer.

Vango rushed toward Ethel but she had already jumped onto the horse. She pulled a knife out of her belt, cut the rope tethering the horse to the propeller, and held out her hand to Vango, who climbed up behind her. They left on horseback through the gap in the wall where the planks had been ripped out.

The car was armor plated and mounted with a machine gun that fired ammunition belts of fifty bullets. Three other cars followed. The first burst was intended for the horse, but it set the barn on fire. Shrieks of horror could be heard from old Labache, who had jumped out of one of the vehicles.

"My barn!"

Ethel was galloping toward the woods with Vango, his arms around her waist and his forehead pressed into the back of her neck. He could feel the drenched warmth of her body.

Fresh shots rang out. Thick hedges of brambles forced the cars to swerve. As for the horse, it was making straight for the rest of the herd, which was whinnying.

When they reached the forest edge, Vango mounted a second horse. Ethel had cut its rope, and she freed all the others with one chop of her knife. The soldiers were firing at random. The liberated horses reared up before veering joyously in all directions. They would never see the butcher's hook.

Ethel glanced back toward the blazing roof of the barn in the distance, caving in over her plane. It was for the best. As the smoke rose upward toward the firmament, she was safe in the knowledge that her parents' plane wouldn't become enemy property. Her gaze met Vango's, and an inexplicable feeling of joy seized the pair of them, despite so much fire and death in the air. The foamy flanks of their horses brushed against each other for an instant. Then they plunged into the forest. Around them, stray bullets pumped the white trunks of the trees full of lead. But not a single bullet had their name on it. The forest ramparts stopped their pursuers.

At nightfall, two horses galloping hard caught up with the train from Dreux to Paris. A young woman held on to the wounded man strapped behind her. The other rider, a few meters behind, was hunched over his horse. A little farther on, the train stopped in a countryside station, surrounded by a wall of steam. There were a few travelers on the platform, and the passengers leaned out the windows. The inspector saw three people climb on board: they were young and covered in dust, and one of them appeared to be in a very bad way.

He had fallen off a bridge into a precipice during a horse race in the hills. That was the official version. His horse, which had died on the spot, had softened his fall. The man had gotten away with broken legs. He and his sister were in such shock that they couldn't speak about it. The third, who was more talkative, acted as their spokesperson. They needed to go to Paris, where the man would be treated at the Hôtel-Dieu Hospital. The train set off again.

For a long time, through the windows, Ethel, Paul, and Vango watched their horses galloping alongside the railway tracks.

The three passengers stared at one another, incredulous. They had found an empty compartment. Paul's pain was numbed by his astonishment at being alive. Night had fallen. He fell asleep on the banquette.

The horses disappeared around a bend in the river.

Ethel and Vango were the only ones awake in the semi-dark. They breathed to the same rhythm, supported by the swaying of the train. Occasionally, they would see a lit-up window in the countryside flash past at high speed, and shadows would hover over their intertwined hair.

They didn't know where they were anymore. Their skin was touching. When the train took a tight bend, they swung out at the same time, sliding all the way to the window. An acceleration on the rails was accompanied by a squealing noise that sounded like a cry.

And then there was nothing but the trees racing past and the kindness of the night.

29

MIDNIGHT

Paris, La Belle Étoile restaurant, the next evening,
December 31, 1942

They were thirteen at the table. But by counting Nina
Bienvenue and her pianist as well, they made it fifteen to
stave off bad luck. In any case, the atmosphere was less one of
distrust than of festive spirit. There were no holds barred as
far as the guests were concerned. The sound of their laughter
could be heard throughout the Temple district. Downstairs,
soldiers guarded the restaurant door.

As the night wore on, and they approached curfew hour,
the streets were increasingly empty. The second floor of La
Belle Étoile was the only place where the party was allowed
to continue up to the threshold of the New Year.

The rest of the city had its eyes firmly on the clock. By
eleven, everybody was supposed to be indoors. In some theaters, tickets had been sold with a room in the hotel opposite
thrown in for good measure, to avoid the curfew. Bold youths
planned to feast until very late. They carried a change of shirt
with them in the knowledge that they might end up at the
police station: the cheapest and most dangerous hostel in the
capital. When a German was killed, it was often among these
overnight detainees that lots were drawn for a victim to be
shot in reprisal.

But for now, according to the clock at La Belle Étoile, it

was only ten in the evening. Nina Bienvenue was singing, and only the pianist had his eyes glued to the keyboard. Everybody else was feasting their gaze on the singer.

The thirteenth guest had been added to the list a few hours earlier. He was a Frenchman in his fifties, very elegant, with a polka-dot tie: Max Grund's personal doctor. He seemed on familiar terms with most of those attending the party. He raised his glass but didn't drink. Accustomed to society life in Paris under German occupation, he knew Nina's songs by heart. Indeed, she even went over to finish them on his knees.

But by far the greatest part of the celebration was being played out on people's plates. The proprietor, Casimir Fermini, who hadn't flashed a single smile since the start of the evening, couldn't help going upstairs with each new course to observe the mood around the great table. Voices petered out at the first spoonful of soup. Grund ordered the pianist to be quiet. All that could be heard was the clinking of porcelain and the sighs of delight.

And so Fermini passed the armed guards roaming the landing and headed back downstairs to report to the kitchen, which occupied part of the ground floor immediately below the dining room.

"They're happy, chef," he said, pushing the door open with his shoulder. "If you could only see them. It's infuriating."

Astoundingly, all that had gone into the soup was a few carrots, a bucket of pink turnips, a chicken leg for the stock, and two or three wild herbs.

"Chef, you've drawn tears from the Third Reich."

And Fermini crossed the street to visit his more respectable clientele in the restaurant's other dining room. There, the first seating had ended at half past nine, and the tables were filling up again.

Fermini apologized profusely for the noise from the New Year's Eve fancy-dress party on the other side of the street.

At the back, seated at the small round table, was the lucky foreigner, Monsieur Costa, who had taken full advantage of his reservation. He had turned up at seven o'clock, having just spent two days in the deserted châteaus of the Loire, wine tasting. He had no intention of leaving, and Fermini gave him preferential treatment.

"You are my guest of honor!"

He got him to taste the wines he was opening for the neighboring tables. Monsieur Costa was in seventh heaven. He had just lost his fork in a buttery cabbage compote and was weeping with pleasure into his napkin.

Fermini remained attentive to each guest. He ran after the waiters, pointing out a customer who had been forgotten in a corner.

"And what about the young lady at the counter? She's been waiting for an hour out in the cold. Pour her something nice and warm before she orders."

On this particular evening, the young lady in question was called Ethel. She had just sat down with Vango. They had waited on the sidewalk at first. But at the darker end of the counter there was space for two diners, and so they had sat down.

Ethel knew that this would be no ordinary dinner. Vango had told her that he had to finish something, once and for all. He had even tried to discourage her from coming.

"Stay with your brother. I'll join you at midnight, and we'll set off."

But she had laughed as if she didn't understand what he was saying. She wasn't going to leave him now. She wasn't going to leave him now. She wasn't going to leave him now.

She looked fresh and well dressed, despite having been drenched in airplane grease, silt, smoke, and horses' sweat. Only the smell of brown earth lingered a little.

Ethel wasn't allowed to speak. Her accent would have betrayed her. Not that she minded at all. She had lost the habit of speaking, along with so many other habits. She needed to start all over again.

Fifty meters away, in a black Citroën, Paul and Simon the bell ringer were waiting. Soon they would head south with Vango and Ethel. Simon was standing in for the chauffeur.

"Does it hurt?" whispered Simon.

Paul was lying on the backseat.

"I'm fine."

He was lying through his teeth.

"You know that my wife gave birth to little Colette this morning?"

"Yes, you must be very proud."

"That's why the bishop has lent me the car," Simon explained. "So I can visit her. You're going to drop me off at La Bourboule, and I'll explain everything to the monseigneur on my return. You must keep going all the way to Spain."

"Please extend an invitation for the monseigneur to visit my home in Scotland, so that we can be pardoned. After the war."

The street was dark and silent around them. The market shutters had been lowered.

* * *

Vango stared at Ethel. He hadn't said a word. Indeed, they had barely spoken to each other since the previous day. They communicated via the strange and silent current that flowed between them: their reunion in the barn, their escape on horseback and then by train.

Reaching between them to set down a bowl in front of the young lady, Bartholomew could detect their magnetism. The waiter's movements slowed as a result of the air, which seemed thicker here than elsewhere in the room. Perhaps this is how ghosts talk to one another? This night was the crossroads of so many desires, fears, and secrets.

Vango was thrown off balance by the restaurant owner's friendliness. He had been expecting a collaborators' den rather than the warmth of this establishment, with not a word of German on the menu slate. Over by the door, there was even an old English advertisement for boats crossing from England to Calais—*Bienvenue, welcome*—which couldn't be innocent.

Vango had just tasted the piping-hot creamy soup Ethel had been served. Quickly, he pulled his lips away from the cup. The liquid had scalded him all the way to his heart. It was a heat that took him right back. The taste of rosemary . . . What was it about this soup?

Ethel held Vango's hand. Her nails dug into his palm. Vango suddenly wanted to whisk her away with him, without waiting.

On the second floor opposite, Max Grund stood up. It took a while for everyone to fall quiet around him. Grund cleared his throat like a tenor.

Augustin Avignon felt ill at ease and couldn't sit still. He was cross with Inspector Mouchet for taking so long to provide him with the list. Avignon had only received it the day before, at which point he had finally understood why he was invited: Viktor wanted to be remembered to him.

Avignon glanced at the two men at the other end of the table. Voloy Viktor and the Irishman shared the same smug smile, while their eyes smarted from the smoky room. Viktor was relishing being in Paris without needing to hide.

Voloy Viktor had succeeded in making a reality of Zefiro's fiction: a colossal arms deal with Germany, invented several years earlier by the padre in an attempt to ensnare the arms dealer. The contract had just been signed. The Irishman, supremely confident since the airship had gone up in flames, was prepared to follow him blindly. Viktor would gladly have put flowers on Zefiro's grave to thank him. After all, this was originally his idea! It was as if Viktor had killed him for a second time.

Grund stood there stiffly, his fingertips touching the tablecloth.

"*Messieurs,* this evening I shall address you in French."

Viktor leaned into Cafarello's ear to translate.

"In French, for the sake of a number of our friends around this table," continued Grund, "and because the gratin I have just eaten also speaks to me in this language."

Nina Bienvenue seized the opportunity to slip away for a moment. She signaled to the pianist and made her way down the spiral staircase.

"Among us this evening we have two gentlemen, I should say two friends, whom our führer has decorated with the

Grand Cross of the Eagle, two gentlemen who, without seeking honors or the limelight . . ."

Nina Bienvenue glided between the armed guards waiting downstairs. She walked into the ladies' room but immediately reappeared, accosting Fermini as he emerged from the kitchen.

"Monsieur, just now I left a lady's item in a little box, but it's not there anymore."

"I'm not surprised, Mademoiselle Bienvenue. We clean these facilities after every visit."

Casimir Fermini spoke drily. He knew about Nina's reputation and had no time for her.

"I thought I was the only lady here. I do beg your pardon."

She reached out and slowly pretended to remove a speck of dust from the patron's tie. He tried to maintain his composure.

"You are indeed the only lady on the second floor. But there are kitchens just behind this door, and perhaps a lady worthy of availing herself of these facilities after you, with your permission."

Nina Bienvenue flashed a disarming smile, unshocked by the democracy of the ladies' lavatory.

"Could you tell me where I might find my box?"

"In the cloakroom, behind the gentleman who is staring at your legs."

Startled at being caught midstare, a German soldier promptly stood to attention. Fermini moved him off one of the checkered floor tiles, like a pawn on a chessboard. He opened a curtain.

There was indeed a small box next to a large leather suitcase.

"Doesn't that case belong to you?" inquired Fermini as Nina picked up the small box.

"No, I use very little makeup. Thank you."

She disappeared into the ladies' room. The patron tried lifting the suitcase. It was full.

"Did one of your men arrive with this suitcase?" he asked, turning to face both soldiers.

They didn't appear to understand. Fermini leaned over to open it, but the case was locked. He hesitated for a moment before closing the curtain and heading upstairs.

Grund raised his glass in the air.

"To the greatness of our industry, the might of our tanks, the radiance . . ."

Fermini sighed. This wasn't the moment to talk about luggage. He went back downstairs, crossing paths with Nina Bienvenue, who now gave off a scent of frangipani.

"Perhaps it's for a honeymoon," she said. "Newlyweds always have a suitcase. You never know; someone might have a surprise in store for me!"

Fermini gritted his teeth. Nina, meanwhile, returned to the dining room to the sound of the applause for the end of Max Grund's speech. The pianist played the first few notes of a song, and Nina Bienvenue broke into German, *"From my head to my toes, I was made to love . . ."*

At eleven o'clock, the metal shutter on the other side of the street was pulled down so that it was three-quarters closed. Fermini had come to an arrangement with Grund the day before. Despite the curfew, he wouldn't send away any of his customers from the dining room opposite until the New Year's Eve dinner on the second floor had finished. A small victory in exchange for such an invasion.

And so thirty privileged guests remained in the restaurant with its shutters almost closed, which only heightened the diners' delight: just as when a lid is put on the cooking pot. Less shouting could be heard coming from opposite now, just a few notes from the piano. The food traveled via the cellars, which ran underneath the street: a tunnel lined with bottles. Plates and aromas arrived in waves. The waiters kept emerging from a trapdoor just behind Ethel and Vango.

Vango repeatedly checked the clock to stay in touch with reality. He had expected to be thrown out with the curfew, so he wouldn't be able to keep an eye on the premises right up until the fateful hour. But this hadn't proved to be the case, and now he was hoping to stay until the end. The suitcase was timed for midnight. He would be in the car, at the end of the street, when he heard the explosion.

And then it would all be over.

Ethel was staring at him intensely. For once, she allowed herself to be led by him.

Vango knew that he was breaking the promise he had made to Zefiro, as well as the one he had made to himself: to renounce warfare and death. This place, which he was warming to, would be affected as well. But it was the dining room opposite that would be destroyed. He had checked each name on Grund's list several times. Which of these criminals would anyone miss? If necessary, Vango would dig up Mazzetta and his donkey's treasure, the fortune hidden in a cliff on his island, in order to rebuild these walls so they looked exactly the same.

A small group next to the couple sipped at their herbal

teas. Vango could detect a whiff of aniseed in the air. Tonight, the whole world was conspiring to throw him off balance.

Slumped over the steering wheel, Simon was worried: the agreed time had long since passed. Paul was asleep behind him. Police officers walked past the car without seeing them. The bell-ringer-turned-driver was wondering whether he should get out.

At eight minutes before midnight Vango stood up, as if getting to his feet after a dizzy spell.

"We must leave."

Casimir Fermini rushed over to him.

"Please, a final dish for the young lady."

"We can't stay."

"One last dish, in the chef's honor. And then I'll grant you your freedom."

The patron clicked his fingers, and Bartholomew approached with a tiny plate beneath a copper bell. Vango glanced at the clock and sat down again.

"This is our great specialty," said Fermini. "Of course, we haven't served it on the other side of the street. I still have my honor."

Hearing him speak this way, Vango felt ashamed of the damage he was about to inflict. Ethel was watching every flicker on his face.

Fermini raised the bell. On a bed of melted butter lay eight little potatoes, no bigger than quail's eggs and peeled so that they had eight facets, like diamonds.

There was a first tiny explosion in Vango's heart.

"Your chef . . ." he said, with tears in his eyes.

Fermini had placed the bell against his chest so as not to let the steam fall back onto the plate.

"Is your chef a woman?" asked Vango.

The patron stared at him.

"Monsieur, you are the first person to guess that."

"She *is* a woman?"

It was five to midnight. The patron lowered his voice, as if he were talking about treasure buried in his garden.

"Not only is she a woman," Fermini corrected him, welling up with as much emotion as Vango, "but she is a marvel."

He seemed to be of two minds about going on.

"She used to work here before the First War. She was very beautiful, and I was still a child. She learned everything from my uncle."

He was shaking his head. Vango turned once again to check the clock.

"She disappeared, a long time ago. And then she returned, barely five years ago, to set to work again in the kitchen. She named the restaurant La Belle Étoile. It's a fine name, but she won't tell me why there has to be a star in her restaurant's title."

Fermini smiled before adding, "To us, she's only ever been known as Mademoiselle."

"Where is she?"

"In the building opposite, just over there. The poor woman has to cook to the sound of boots above her head."

Ethel saw Vango turn abruptly toward the clock, then fix his eyes on the trapdoor that led to the cellars. In a flash, he had disappeared.

He bumped into a waiter in the gloomy tunnel beneath the street. A few seconds later, he emerged on the other side. The trapdoor opened onto the corridor in front of the kitchen. He pushed open the first door and found himself face-to-face with the soldiers.

For a second, Vango stopped breathing. Then, slowly, he caught his breath again and managed to say to the soldiers, "My suitcase."

He went over to the cloakroom and lifted the suitcase, without appearing to take any strain. He probably had about two minutes left. He walked slowly past the guards and made for the door marked *Messieurs* under the staircase.

He reached out for the handle, but the door was locked.

Twenty seconds went by. The soldiers stared at him suspiciously.

"There's someone in there," Vango explained pointlessly.

Vango stood there waiting for the tiny click of the detonator at the bottom of the suitcase, but it was the lock in the door that grated first. The door opened and a man appeared.

Vango took a step backward.

It was Cafarello.

He wiped his hands on his jacket.

"It's clogged," the guest of the German high command muttered in Sicilian, staring at the man carrying the suitcase.

"It doesn't matter," replied Vango in the same language.

They stared at each other, and Cafarello didn't budge from the door. He checked that his suspenders and fly were in order. He was drunk.

Upstairs, the countdown to midnight had begun. Emerging from the trapdoor, Fermini appeared next to the guards.

Finally, Cafarello began to stagger toward the staircase. He turned around for a second to look at Vango, as if he reminded him of something.

"Sicilian?" he asked, holding on to the handrail.

"Sorry?" replied Vango in French.

"You spoke to me in my language," said Cafarello.

Vango shook his head to indicate that he didn't understand.

Climbing back up the stairs, Cafarello cursed French wine and all the vermin on this earth.

Vango pushed open the lavatory door and locked himself in.

He took a key out of his belt and turned it twice in the locks on the suitcase, which gave way. Upstairs, they were stamping their feet to mark each second. Vango had grabbed an iron box with a clock dial. Above all, he mustn't break the wire. With the same key, he attempted to undo the box's screws. They wouldn't turn. And then it happened: he accidentally snapped the rectifier wire. Upstairs, a great cheer went up for the New Year. It was all over. But the alarm clock that activated the bomb was five seconds behind German time. Vango jammed his finger into the mechanism and stopped it.

The walls were trembling.

A minute went by.

Vango didn't hear Fermini knocking on the door to the gentlemen's lavatories, or the military hymns wafting down from the great dining room. He was sobbing and staring at something left behind by the previous occupant, over there on the washbasin: a piece of red fabric.

A Cossack scarf, worn out by the century.

He went over and picked it up.

* * *

By the time Vango reappeared with his suitcase, Casimir Fermini was beside himself with worry. He'd been convinced that Vango wanted to kidnap his chef. He spoke quietly and urgently, complaining that he'd been given such a fright.

"You left just like that! It was so fast. And you were talking about my chef."

But his words didn't register with Vango.

"Is that your suitcase? You know, there are lavatories back on the other side too, as well as a cloakroom. Tell me, are you on your honeymoon?"

Casimir was whispering so as not to be understood by the two soldiers. He kept talking about how worried he'd been. What he wasn't admitting, his secret, was that he was madly in love with his chef. Even as a twelve-year-old boy, he hadn't been able to take his eyes off her setting the table. Now he lived in fear of losing her, even if she pretended not to pick up on any of his hints.

"Dinner was on the house! I'm sorry, but we have to ask our guests to leave now. You gave me such a fright. I must warn you not to go into the kitchen. Mademoiselle doesn't allow visitors."

All Vango heard was the final sentence.

"In that case, I'll come back," he blurted.

"Where is the young bride?"

Bartholomew opened the door for them, to reveal Ethel waiting out on the sidewalk.

"Here she is."

Upstairs, they were still singing. Vango clenched the red

scarf in his hand. He had failed on every count. Ethel ran toward him. Sensing how weak he was, she tried to take the suitcase, but he wouldn't let her.

"Wait!" the patron called after them. "If the police pick you up, tell them you were at La Belle Étoile."

They headed off down the street, hugging each other tightly.

"Bon voyage!" Fermini called out.

And they disappeared.

Next to the patron stood Costa, the foreigner, who had witnessed the whole scene. He seemed shaken.

What's the matter with everybody tonight? wondered Casimir Fermini, as he watched Monsieur Costa running after Vango and Ethel.

Fermini leaned against the wall, listening to the last German tunes. A moment later, the foreigner was back, out of breath and very pale. Fermini put a hand on his shoulder. Together, they walked into the downstairs dining room, where Monsieur Costa returned to his table. They sat down next to each other. There was no one else left.

The sounds of the New Year's Eve party opposite were abating.

"Did you never think of marrying?" inquired Fermini.

The man seemed to wake up with a jolt.

"What?"

"Are you Spanish?"

The foreigner smiled.

"No."

"Are you married?" asked Fermini.

"Not exactly."

"I like that kind of answer."

"I loved a woman," said the man, "back home, in Italy, on an island. She left."

"For someone else?"

"Not even that."

They both stared at the candle, which had melted right down but was still alight.

"One day, I received a letter from her, a long letter."

"A letter for you?"

"It was for a boy she had raised, but he never came back either. I opened it, and someone translated it for me. It tells the story of the boy's life, and of the woman's too. In five pages. You'd never believe what five pages could contain."

For once, Fermini didn't have the strength to go in search of his own manuscript, which was as heavy as a crate of apples, but he did confide: "I write novels."

"Even in a novel, the events wouldn't be credible. In the letter, in among all the other details, she mentioned that a long time ago, when she was still a young girl, she used to work here as an assistant, in the kitchen."

"Here?" asked Fermini, his voice cracking.

"Yes."

"In France?"

"Here, yes."

"In Paris?"

"I said: here."

And twirling his Sicilian fingers, Monsieur Costa pointed to the walls, the ceilings, and the tables of La Belle Étoile.

Casimir Fermini downed his glass in one and stared at the foreigner, who kept on talking.

"So, I said to myself, 'As sure as your name's Basilio Costa, one day you'll go to see it with your own eyes.' That's what I told myself. 'You'll pay a visit to the establishment that knew her as a girl.' And I told myself all this because I loved her."

Fermini put his hand on Costa's.

"Next, I learned French like a schoolboy," Basilio went on. "I wanted to wait for the end of the war before making the journey. But as we grow old, we run out of patience."

"Yes."

Basilio seemed overcome. He had waited for this day for so long, when he would visit Paris for the first time, and the place where she had spent her youth.

"And that letter, well, I've just given it to the person it was originally intended for."

He paused for a moment.

"It seems unbelievable, but there he was, with you, on the sidewalk opposite. I saw him. The boy, Vango. I went after him to give him the letter."

Fermini was listening to Basilio. He didn't know what to say to this story. He would never have dared to write it in a book.

"As we grow old, we run out of patience," Basilio repeated. "And what about her? Who knows what has become of her?" He sighed, putting his hand over his eyes.

Just then, a head popped up from the trapdoor, a head wearing a white scarf.

"They've all gone, thank goodness," announced Mademoiselle, without looking at the two men. "The Germans have all left!"

Out of sheer exhaustion, she began to laugh. She had stopped at the top of the ladder, and her shoulders were still shaking with laughter.

"Yes, chef. It's all over," agreed Fermini.

"Don't ever make me go through that again, Casimir," she said, turning toward them.

Basilio couldn't stop staring at the face that had emerged from underneath them.

Fermini watched each of them in turn, and he knew that it was all over for him.

"Basilio?" she whispered.

"Mademoiselle."

One street away, Max Grund was talking to his French doctor.

"Are you sure you . . . you're happy to accompany these gentlemen?"

Grund was drunk, and his driver had to help him into the car.

"Of course," said the doctor. "My car is parked a little farther off."

Just behind them, Cafarello and Voloy Viktor looked more robust than their host. They were able to stand upright with a degree of dignity. Doctor Esquirol stepped gaily between the two men, linking arms with each of them.

"*Messieurs,* allow me to lead you to my car. I'll take care of you."

And he started singing Nina's most famous song: *"Welcome to Paris. Glad to know you're alive. . . ."*

Viktor gently started singing along with him. Cafarello moved like a sleepwalker. They walked for several minutes, unaware that someone was following them along the roof gutters.

On entering a narrow street, Esquirol let go of both men's arms and admitted, "I think I must have lost my way."

Viktor and Cafarello came to a stop. Esquirol walked a few steps farther before turning around. He held a pistol in his hand. He was calm and collected, and his eyes were almost closed.

The two arms dealers stared at him blearily.

"In the old days," said Esquirol, "I used to stroll the streets of Paris with two friends. Just like tonight. Those were the good old days. One of them was called Joseph Puppet, the other Zefiro. We made promises to one another, and we loved each other."

High up on the rooftop, the Cat had come to a stop.

"Neither of my friends is still with us," said Esquirol. "Everything has come to an end because of you. My life has changed. The world has changed."

His hand didn't tremble.

The Cat heard two shots. She leaned over and saw the bodies on the ground and a man standing. Then the man walked away, passing into a beam of light and undoing his polka-dot tie.

She recognized the great boss. She recognized Caesar.

At the gates of Paris, a black car had just passed a barrier. The driver had presented an Episcopal authorization, which was all in order.

"And in the back?"

"That's my family," said Simon.

The police officer didn't appear surprised. He moved his flashlight and looked at the three passengers. Only one was awake. He wore a red scarf around his neck. A young woman was asleep on his shoulder. There was a letter open on his knees, and there were tears in his eyes.

"Thank you, Your Excellency," said the officer, returning the papers to Simon the bell ringer.

The car started up again. Three kilometers later, without the car slowing down, a window was opened and a suitcase hurled into the ditch. It rolled in the grass and slid on the remains of the snow, taking three seconds to come to a stop.

One, two, three.

The suitcase exploded.

A gigantic spray of light illuminated the night sky and the trees, and made the chrome on the car sparkle as it headed south between the plane trees.

BARBARY FIG TREES

Salina, Aeolian Islands

There were dark years ahead: struggles throughout Europe, families torn apart, places where death became a way of life. There were betrayals, acts of revenge, and beaches stained black with blood.

And many would later discover that they had only glimpsed the surface of the nightmare.

There were dark years ahead.

But there was also Simon, with tiny Colette in his bell ringer's hands, waving as the car set off again. There was the fire in the hearth at Auguste Boulard's house, in the middle of the snowy plains of the Aubrac. There were Vango, Ethel, and Paul around his table, and old Mother Boulard standing on a stool, unhooking sausages from the ceiling. There was their crossing of the Pyrenees on foot, the passes, the chamois, the snow, and then the view of Spain and freedom. There was the Cat's impossible quest for her parents, the hopes, the dead ends, the nights spent in theater attics sleeping next to a violin; and later, when she understood that she really did need to be afraid, there was the arrival of the young Sister Marie-Cat, disguised in the large white headdress known as a nun's cornet, and welcomed at the Abbey of La Blanche by a beaming Mother Elisabeth. There were

Esquirol's journeys back and forth to England to keep alive the Paradise Network, which he had founded in the first days of the war in memory of his friends from rue de Paradis. There was Eckener's melancholy as he stared at the reflection of the sky in Lake Constance. There was the good doctor Basilio's return by boat to the Aeolian Islands, with a lesson learned in his heart. There were the flowers he changed every day, while he waited, on the table of the house in Pollara. There was the revival of a monastery across the waves, with enough honey to make gingerbread again, with bells tolled on stormy evenings; but without Pippo Troisi, who had returned to his capers and his wife.

Then came deliverance for Paris: flags, and yet more tanks, with Superintendent Avignon fleeing on the day of Liberation, joyous shots fired into the air, and the crowd braying around Nina Bienvenue. There were Mademoiselle's farewells on the sidewalk outside La Belle Étoile and the tears of Casimir Fermini. There was a very young Russian soldier, named Andrei Ivanovitch, entering a camp in the south of Poland with his regiment, searching for two people he had never met before among the deportees he had just liberated.

"Monsieur and Madame Atlas?"

And, in front of him, the gazes that wanted to say yes.

There was so much waiting. But some returns were impossible.

At last, there was a fine autumn, the bells of Notre Dame ringing for no reason, fit to burst, and two figures holding tightly to each other at the top of a tower. There was a dinner to celebrate at La Belle Étoile, where everyone ate their fill of omelets. The Boulards were there, having traveled to Paris as guests of honor, as well as Paul in his uniform, covered in medals; there were speeches, there was white wine, and, at the end of the table, the Cat, very pale, because a letter had just arrived from Moscow.

And then there was a journey. Isn't it customary to set off on journeys after such occasions? There was a walk toward the bottom of a crater that fell away into the sea, a hamlet, and, at the end, a house made of two white cubes. There were Vango and Ethel walking between the Barbary fig trees, over-whelmed and breathless, but nothing could stop them from approaching their destination. There was a falcon in the sky.

There was a woman coming out of the house close to the cliff, a beautiful figure with a red scarf over her white hair, watching attentively, her hand shielding her eyes, looking to see who was heading down between the Barbary figs. Two beings were coming toward her; there was nowhere else in the world they could be going.

There was a cry, a call. And that was all.